CONSPIRACY of KNAVES

CONSPIRACY
of KNAVES

DEE BROWN

WINGS BOOKS
New York • Avenel, New Jersey

No part of this book may be reproduced or transmitted in any form or by
any means electronic or mechanical including photocopying, recording, or
by any information storage and retrieval system, without permission in
writing from the publisher.

This 1996 edition is published by Wings Books,
a division of Random House Value Publishing, Inc.,
40 Engelhard Avenue, Avenel, New Jersey 07001,
by arrangement with Henry Holt and Company, Inc.

Wings Books and colophon are trademarks of
Random House Value Publishing, Inc.

Random House
New York • Toronto • London • Sydney • Auckland
http://www.randomhouse.com/

Printed and bound in the United States of America

Designer: Ann Gold

Library of Congress Cataloging-in-Publication Data
Brown, Dee Alexander.
Conspiracy of knaves / Dee Brown
p.   cm.
ISBN 0-517-14892-7 (hardcover)
1. United States—History—Civil War, 1861-1865—Secret service—
Fiction. I. Title.
PS3503.R7953306   1996   95–46290
813´.54—dc20   CIP

10 9 8 7 6 5 4 3 2

CONSPIRACY
of KNAVES

1

BELLE RUTLEDGE

NOW THAT MOST OF us have been pardoned and released from prison, the newspaper scribblers keep pestering me for personal stories about the Chicago Conspiracy. The Northwest Conspiracy, some call it, but I think of it as a conspiracy of knaves, three sets of deceivers, each attempting to flimflam the others. Some of the ones who were pardoned are now telling what they know, but none of them knows more than two sides of the triangle, so that what the newspapers are printing is never more than two-thirds of the truth.

Perhaps I am the only one who moved through the three sets of knaves and knows the whole truth. If the whole truth is to be told, I do not wish it to be done by the likes of any of these grubby newspaper ink slingers who knock on my door almost daily. I shall tell the story myself. After all, I was a participant in or witness to many of the plans and deeds. For those incidents where I was not present, details were supplied me by both Charles Heywood and John Truscott, who confided in me to their sorrow. If you've followed the newspaper accounts, you know their names well, and must think of Heywood as a ruthless plotter and Truscott as a victim. It was not that way at all. Lord! What did I not learn of Johnny Truscott during those miserable last days in Canada!

My birth name was Jennie Gray, of Louisville, Kentucky, but to those who attended theaters before and during the war, I am

< CONSPIRACY OF KNAVES >

Belle Rutledge. The name was given me by Mr. Alexander Placides, who managed theaters in New Orleans and Charleston. When the Louisville minstrel show I danced with traveled to Charleston for a series of performances, Mr. Placides offered me an opportunity to take speaking parts in some of the skits and entr'actes. It was also he who had me cut my hair very short so that I could play roles of girls impersonating young men. Audiences were delighted when I appeared transformed near the end of the acts in a dress and wig with long golden curls. For these roles Mr. Placides costumed me in white trousers and jackets. You might have seen me in *Black-Eyed Susan* before Maggie Mitchell stole my part away from me, but that is another story.

After the minstrel company left Charleston, we played several weeks in Richmond, Baltimore, Philadelphia, and New York. I liked Richmond especially, because the audiences were so responsive. That was in the old Marshall before it became the Richmond Theater. New York was the best place for ambitious actresses, however, and when our engagement concluded there, I did not return to Louisville with the others. I hoped to join Wallack's New York repertory company because they paid their regulars twenty-five dollars a week and supplied wardrobes. I longed for the independence this would give me, making it unnecessary to seek out "patrons" as I had been forced to do on the ten dollars I'd been receiving from the minstrel show.

Although I was unsuccessful in finding a place with Wallack's, one of the assistants there recommended me to a company that was hiring actors for a tour of the larger theaters around the country. I think it was my ability to play girls disguised as boys, and my short hair and white costume, that obtained for me the role of Rosalind in *As You Like It*. Everywhere we went audiences applauded my speeches with enthusiasm, and I was dreaming of becoming as famous as Maggie Mitchell or Charlotte Cushman or even Laura Keene, when war broke out and spoiled everything.

At the time we happened to be in Washington, playing at the old Washington Theater on C Street—not far from where Mr. John T. Ford was soon to build his famous theater. I was rehearsing every morning for Portia in *The Merchant of Venice*, but it was not to be. Fearful of the upheaval that was bound to affect theaters both north and south during the first weeks of the war, our manager canceled the tour and disbanded the company. For the next year or so I eked out a living by going back to comic skits in minstrels and varieties, the naughty sort of things that the hordes of Union soldiers crowded into Washington especially liked.

I've always regretted never having the chance to play Portia, but it was during this time that I found my grand patrons, two of them, and so became involved with the Copperheads and the Chicago Conspiracy. But I am getting ahead of myself. None of this might have happened if Captain John Truscott had not succeeded in robbing the Farmers Bank of Mount Sterling in Kentucky.

2

BELLE RUTLEDGE

BEFORE RELATING THE details of the bank robbery at Mount Sterling, perhaps I should explain my presence at Richmond early in 1864. As I mentioned, it was while I was acting in those risqué music varieties in Washington during the first months after the war started that I found my two grand patrons. My patron in Washington was a Union officer who arranged for me to slip through the lines in northern Virginia. A military pass took me across the Potomac bridge, and a buggy drawn by a big lazy bay mule along back roads soon brought me into Confederate territory. I was thus spared the indignities of body searches and insolent questioning.

My patron in Richmond was Colonel Richard Fennell of the Confederate Army's intelligence service and, as I was soon to learn, a director of secret operations in the Northern states and Canada. He possessed no knowledge whatsoever of my patron in Washington, who had very cleverly contrived to place me in a position to spy for the Union while acting as a spy for the Confederacy.

I will state candidly here and now that my sympathies for the antagonists in this wretched conflict were terribly torn, I being a Kentuckian with friends on both sides. At that time I was a young woman alone in the world, with both eyes opened to the main chance.

Upon arriving in Richmond I went at once to a small shabby

building on Broad Street, not far from the New Richmond Theater. The weather was unlovely, one of those dripping rainy days that cause my hair to curl outlandishly in dozens of directions, but I was wearing a wig and my appearance must not have been so frightful as to decide Colonel Fennell against the purpose he had in mind for me.

The floor of his office that day was drabbled with mud that had been tracked in from the street and was in varying states from watery to almost dry. Fennell was seated in a slant-backed chair, facing the entrance door, talking with a nondescript man in a wet overcoat. When he saw that I was a woman, he arose from the chair, brusquely dismissed his visitor, and motioned for me to be seated on a haircloth sofa against the wall. He was in his late forties, I judged, but no trace of gray showed in his rich brown hair or beard. For some reason he shaved above and below his thin-lipped mouth, perhaps to exhibit the firmness of his chin, perhaps to please ladies who objected to prickly mustaches when being kissed. He had a habit of half closing his heavy-lidded eyes when studying a visitor, and he was so regarding me.

As soon as the man in the wet coat was out the street door, the colonel asked: "What is the purpose of your visit, miss?"

"My name is Belle Rutledge," I replied.

He nodded and turned to an ancient and dilapidated table that leaned against the wall opposite from the sofa where I sat. Colonel Fennell had no desk, but the table was equipped with a number of large drawers, and its top was a jumble of papers, envelopes, and folders. From this disorganized mass he managed to extract a crumpled sheet and a *carte de visite* photograph which he glanced at for only a few moments. "You're the actress from Kentucky who can dress as a man and delude everyone as to your true sex," he said, his voice rising to a querying tone as if testing me.

"I am told that on a stage I can deceive anyone," I replied. "You see, sir, I have this gift of lowering my voice to that of a tenor." As I spoke, I demonstrated, and at the same time removed the wig I wore over my short hair, which was frizzling out of control in the damp weather.

His eyes opened wide for a moment. "Falsetto," he said then, and smiled like a benevolent father.

< CONSPIRACY OF KNAVES >

"I am not certain," I continued, "whether I could carry off the role of a man without the illusion created by footlights—that is, in the cold light of day."

"I think you might. Certainly by candlelight." He leaned back in his chair and stared at the ceiling. "We had thought of arranging work for you in one of the theaters," he said. "Our interference in the matter would draw attention to you, however, and I think it best no one in Richmond be aware of your connection with Confederate States authority. Do you suppose you could find theatrical employment?"

As I had no knowledge of the Richmond stage at that time, I told him I was uncertain of the prospects. He insisted that I make a firm attempt. He thought it would not be wise for me to circulate through certain levels of Richmond society unless I had a manifest source of honest income.

It was Colonel Fennell's conviction that much of the information about Confederate military plans and strategy that was reaching the enemy in Washington was being gathered by female spies in Richmond, and he suspected that some of them were stage performers. "They may also be in the highest ranks of Richmond society," he added, "and certainly some are in houses of ill repute. Bordellos, if I may speak frankly. No man is more vulnerable, more likely to divulge confidences than one who is enjoying the glow of alcohol in the companionship of a courtesan."

As matters turned out, within a week I was employed as an entr'acte dancer in the New Richmond and was promised parts in a forthcoming minstrel show at the less respectable Metropolitan Hall. These small parts required little rehearsing, leaving me sufficient time for the main enterprise.

My spying assignment in Richmond was a multivaried one. Colonel Fennell expected me to move not only in the drawing rooms of the higher social circles, but also in the gambling halls and bordellos along Cary and Seventeenth streets, amidst the surging crowds at the railroad stations, and in the wards of various military hospitals. At times I was my honest self, Belle Rutledge, actress. At other times I was the wife of an absent Confederate officer, or I was disguised as a male that I modeled after a foppish character I had once played in a melodrama. He was Calvin Blacklock, recuperating from a wound or illness, frequenting the sitting rooms of the better hotels or placing bets in the gambling establishments, conversing briskly, and listening, always listening. Spies and deserters were my quarries. Although I found none of the former, I reported several of the latter. During that last full year of the war, deserters were attracted to Richmond, perhaps because of its constantly changing mass of harried human beings, its turbulence, and growing licentiousness. Several of these fugitives from the Confederate Army were from prominent families of the South, unused to any sort of labor or hardship, and after the glory of the first victories over Union armies, they had been unable to face the realities of battle or camp life, the filth and disease, disfigurement and death.

At other times, quite unknown to Colonel Fennell, I visited a confectionery store known as Pizzini's to all of Richmond. The owners I believe were loyal to the Confederacy, but a little silver-haired man who worked there as a clerk was an agent of the Union's Secret Service. Through him I received instructions from my patron in Washington, and I was supposed to supply him with any useful information I might obtain. Except for very general matters of the sort that often could be read in newspapers, I found little to relay until on one pressing occasion, and then, as we shall see, I was unable to reach the little confectionery clerk.

In my role as a woman of the stage, I was expected to attract suspected deserters and identify them for Colonel Fennell. Like many nontheatrical people, Colonel Fennell held the belief that actors and actresses are of easy virtue, especially actresses who performed in tights as I sometimes did. In his directions to me, he implied that I was to go to any lengths to gain the confidence of men I might suspect of being spies or deserters, even to taking them into my bed. Although during the following months I reported several dozen suspected deserters to Colonel Fennell, I never gave him any indication as to the methods I used to obtain grounds for my suspicions, nor do I see any need for such details to be revealed in this narrative.

One evening after I had finished performing my last entr'acte jig dance at the New Richmond, I went back to the dressing room and was surprised to find the little silver-haired clerk from Pizzini's waiting outside the door. He was carrying a tin box wrapped in scarlet ribbons. At about the same time several of the young vocalists who performed in the last act of the musical show came hurrying out of the dressing room, jostling my friend from the confectionery so that he looked positively unstrung.

He handed me the box and peered into the now empty dressing room. "A present for you, Miss Rutledge," he said. "May I come in?"

"Yes," I replied, certain there was some urgent reason for his presence.

He closed the door behind him. "There's nothing in the box," he said, dropping it on a chair. "I wanted to give the appearance of being a messenger." His voice was soft, barely audible. "The Washington people ordered me to risk coming here. They want a close watch put on all of Colonel Fennell's visitors immediately."

"You know I seldom see Colonel Fennell," I protested. "Only when he summons me to come there."

"They believe Fennell is preparing some sudden action in Chicago. The Copperhead conspiracy, you know. They want names of agents coming and going. Especially any who have been to Chicago."

"The Copperhead conspiracy," I repeated. "What is the Copperhead conspiracy?"

He looked surprised. For one so frail of body, he managed to keep a deliberate balance of energy in his voice: "The Washington people should have informed you. Copperheads are Confederate sympathizers in the North. With aid from Richmond and Canada they are conspiring to take the Northwestern states out of the Union."

I recalled overhearing some talk in the Richmond hotel sitting rooms of a movement in Illinois and Indiana and perhaps some other states to secede from the Union and end the war, but I had paid little attention, considering it to be mere wishful gossip. I said as much to my visitor and assured him that I would do my best to learn all that I could about Colonel Fennell's plans for the Copperheads.

"I'll await your reports," he said.

For the next several days, dressed in my Calvin Blacklock male costume, I hung about the opposite side of the street from Colonel Fennell's office, watching those who were coming and going, and

< **Belle Rutledge** >

sometimes following departing visitors to their places of abode, determined to learn if they had come to Richmond from the North. Also I invented excuses for visiting Colonel Fennell, hoping to overhear something about the Copperheads or perhaps meet an agent from Chicago or some other city beyond the lines. I learned virtually nothing of value, however, and was forced to prepare a spun-out report for my friend in the confectionery store.

Among the places that I frequented in the course of my duties were the railroad depots—the Virginia Central and the Danville. At almost any hour of the day or night we could hear the whistle and rumble of passenger cars bringing fresh troops from the southwest, or Yankee prisoners and Confederate wounded from the north. Among the arrivals was always a sprinkling of deserters, a few spies, no doubt, and human vultures who included double-dealing traitors and blackguard lawyers to prey upon the dying capital of the Confederacy. As railroad trains could no longer maintain any semblance of regular arrival and departure schedules, I simply made it my habit to visit the stations when I was free of other prospects.

Occasionally I dressed in my masculine costume, but more often went as myself, Belle Rutledge the actress, to stare hard-eyed at Union captives bound for Libby Prison, or teary-eyed at the pale and ghastly Confederate wounded, or to wave my handkerchief to some poor youngster fresh in a uniform, departing by the cars for a destination that would surely lead him into bloody battle. Sometimes I glimpsed a furtive wretch who by his very efforts to distract attention from himself would surely attract it. By one ruse or another I would make myself known to him before we were out of the railroad depot, or else I would follow the suspected rogue to his lodging place and then later confront him there.

Early in the month of June I was in the Virginia Central depot, using my handkerchief and tears in good cause, when a remarkable specimen of manhood appeared suddenly out of a crowd of arrivals. He was staring straight ahead, but apparently saw none of the faces before him, not even my tear-stained one. Except for cavalry boots, he wore no uniform, and at first I thought that perhaps he was one of that pack of parasites invading the city—a speculator, a counterfeiter, or worse yet, a lawyer come to join his brethren in profiting more from crime than the criminals.

< CONSPIRACY OF KNAVES >

But when his blue eyes at last caught mine, casually and then sweeping away as he passed, the too brief exchange caused a shiver to run through my whole body, not fear but a deep pleasurable excitement, and I had to force myself to remember the serious purpose that had brought me to the railroad depot. I knew instantly that there was nothing in the way of dross about this man. Insouciant he certainly was; he might have been a spy, but he certainly was not a deserter. He was too stalwart and strapping for that stamp. As I followed along at an angle with the crowd, I had a minute or two to study him further. His dark beard was neatly kept; a long-barreled pistol was holstered at his right hip; his black slouch hat tilted slightly, so that the brim touched the tip of an ear; his civilian shooting jacket was of a soft and expensive velvet; he wore a pair of rough gauntlets, and carried a large valise.

I followed him—unobserved, I thought—to the Spotswood. I was not currently living in that hotel, but often visited its main sitting room in the course of my duties. On this particular day I selected a chair from which I could see both entrances and yet was inconspicuous in my own person. From my handbag I took a small book and pretended to read from it. I had not long to wait. Through the larger entrance I saw him descending the main stairway. He had exchanged his hunting jacket for a black frock coat and matching vest. He no longer wore the slouch hat, and his mane of dark hair had been neatly brushed back from his ears. No actor that I've known ever made a more galvanic entrance upon a stage than he did effortlessly, it seemed, into the Spotswood's sitting room. All eyes including mine were on him instantly, as though drawn by some magnetic force. He surveyed us indifferently for a moment, and then moved on into the men's bar.

Had I been dressed in my male costume, I would have followed, but as it was I swallowed my disappointment and waited patiently. As usual the men's bar was overcrowded, and after a few minutes he returned, a glass in one hand, a newspaper in the other. He found a small table, and soon was comfortably settled, sipping the drink and reading from his folded newspaper. All eyes except mine gradually left him. Over the top of my book I watched him covertly until I saw that the pink-colored drink in his glass was half gone.

Then I arose and started across the room, circling a bit so that I would pass close beside his table, carrying my book loosely in

< **Belle Rutledge** >

my fingers, and pretending that I was unaware of his presence. With the careful timing that I'd learned on the stage, I let the book slip from my hand so that it fell directly upon his nearest booted foot.

"Oh, dear," I cried in the soft tones of a brainless ingenue. "I am so clumsy, sir."

He gave me a look that I read as half pity, half loathing. He waited longer than he should have to lean down and retrieve my book. "Ah," he said then, "Edgar Allan Poe. I should think his tales would frighten a young lady such as you."

"I do prefer George Eliot," I replied in as sweet a tone as I could muster.

"Yes, I expect you would," he said under his breath but loud enough for me to hear.

During this exchange, I'd managed to drop a few things from my handbag upon his table, and while collecting these I sat down in the chair facing him.

"Have we met somewhere before?" he asked abruptly. "You seem somehow familiar."

We exchanged names, I using a fictitious one.

"Are you from Kentucky, sir?" I asked.

He looked surprised. My question had been only a wild guess meant to lead to another. "Yes," he answered. "So must you be. Bluegrass? Lexington?"

"No, sir, Louisville. My husband is with Garrett's Brigade. Somewhere in the Shenandoah. Do you have news of them?"

He shook his head. His blue eyes studied me lazily for a moment, and then he lifted his glass and drained it. "Dreadful drink," he said. "But they tell me there's no bourbon, no whiskey of any sort in Richmond."

"The shortages," I said, "grow worse daily."

"Would you like one of these cherry bounces?" he offered. "Bad as they are, I must have another."

I accepted. He brought out two glasses from the barroom and soon began a flirtation, starting by consoling me for my loneliness, with a husband far from my bed, fighting somewhere in the Valley. I let him burble on until I realized he was cleverly probing for more information about me, but I had become practiced enough at my craft to quickly erect a defensive barrier to further revela-

< CONSPIRACY OF KNAVES >

tions. This man is too well dressed, too well groomed, too well fed, I told myself, to have come from any part of the straitened South. He had come to Richmond from somewhere in the North, I was almost sure of it.

Was he a Union spy, or was he a Confederate agent from the Copperheads? I thought it more likely he was a spy, else he would have gone directly to Colonel Fennell's office. To make certain of my intuitive impressions, I knew that I must find an opportunity to examine him from a different posture. As I sat there sipping the cherry drink he had brought me, a sudden wave of exhilaration almost overwhelmed me because for the first time I was on the very edge of finding a spy for Colonel Fennell. Yet as I thought of the meaning of the word *spy*, I shivered, and wondered if I had the will to jeopardize this gallant's life with such an accusation.

The grandfather's clock striking from a far corner of the sitting room provided me with an excuse to fly, to get my breath as it were, outside the magnetic flow of this fascinating stranger. I muttered something about meeting my "Richmond cousins." He pressed a hand against mine as I arose to leave.

"We must talk again," he said in a low but forceful tone.

"Yes," I replied, "yes, I come here with friends almost every day."

He nodded and gave me a strange smile, cynical perhaps, or was it derisive?

I hurried away, angry because I'd almost let myself become the silly ingenue I was playing. My heart was actually beating like a schoolgirl's after she's received attention from a secret beau ideal. I hurried on toward my room in a house nearby the Ballard that was used for overflow guests of that hotel. So preoccupied was I with my churning emotions, I narrowly escaped being splashed along the way by the Niagara watering machine flushing mud from the paving stones of Franklin Street. At the corner I had to slow my steps for a crowd gathered on the sidewalk. The spectators were watching a carriage pulling rapidly away toward the river bridge. "That was General Lee," an old woman informed me. "I saw into his forlorn eyes," she added. "We are all doomed."

In my room that afternoon I worked with the devotion of an artist at making myself into a jaunty male, a cock of the walk. I had the clothes for it, a recently obtained costume of light gray

< **Belle Rutledge** >

trousers, tight-waisted black lounge jacket, Irish linen shirt with a fancy cravat, and English boots. My mirror told me that without my wig I looked almost too young to be the popinjay I had in mind to play, and so I decided to add a mustache. Onstage, I would simply have attached the whole article, but as I expected to be under close scrutiny I took the time to use clippings from a hair plait, carefully engrafting them to my upper lip with gum arabic.

As luck would have it that evening, however, I saw no evidence of my quarry in the Spotswood and was forced to repeat the tedious preparations the following day. This time he appeared in the main sitting room shortly after dinner. He evidently was waiting with impatience for someone, glancing often toward the entrance, and I was pleased to believe that it was Belle Rutledge he hoped to see enter. As it was, he paid not the slightest attention to me in the role of the unattached young fop who was regarding him from across the room. Eventually, after smoking several small black cheroots, he arose with a gesture of frustration, took his broad-brimmed slouch hat from the rack, and proceeded to leave the Spotswood.

I followed him at a distance along Main Street and was not surprised to see him enter one of the gilt-numbered doorways that indicated a faro bank and other games of chance could be found within. I had visited the place before; it was one of the better class in Richmond, although that categorization is no endorsement of its respectability or the probity of its management.

As usual in such places, the air was a fog of strong tobacco smoke infused with the reek of those foul liquors and wines then prevalent in the city. Even the oil lamps suspended above the tables seemed to have difficulty burning, and occasionally one would smoke itself out, adding its own stench to the malodorous atmosphere.

I found my quarry at a round table where he and two other men were awaiting additional players to broaden their game of poker. They accepted me readily, therefore, and with scarcely a glance at my face, each shook my hand hurriedly and the cards were dealt. When the game began, my suspected spy was wearing a pair of brand-new lemon-colored kid gloves, which he soon removed and placed between us on the table.

At first we played for small stakes, but very soon the limits

< CONSPIRACY OF KNAVES >

were set higher. I had brought along a plentiful supply of Colonel Fennell's Confederate notes and bet recklessly until my reserves fell quite low, and then I had to play cautiously, dropping out early in each round so as to remain at the table as long as possible. A lucky hand or two brought me back into the game, but it gradually became apparent that the contest had settled into a duel between my insouciant neighbor and an obvious professional across the table. At last came the crucial game, the stakes so high that the fourth player and I dropped out to become spectators.

"Let's play for real money this time," said my suspect, and he reached inside his coat to remove a sheaf of United States bank notes. "A hundred to begin?"

The gray-bearded professional sucked in his breath, his voice betraying surprise and disappointment. "I have only Confederate," he said.

"My hundred U.S. against a thousand Confederate?"

The man nodded. "Even odds at that, I suppose," he said wearily. Five minutes later he had lost the thousand, and he and the fourth player excused themselves to visit the bar.

The arrogant winner cast a quizzical blue-eyed glance at me. "You wish to continue?"

Alone in his presence I was having difficulty keeping my voice down to a masculine tenor. I shook my head negatively, and tried to regain my composure by picking up his lemon-colored kid gloves and examining them. On one glove the name of the maker and *Cincinnati, Ohio* were stamped on a tiny leather tag sewed at the edge of the lining. "I haven't seen gloves this fine since the war began," I said, managing a deep tone of voice.

"Plentiful, where those come from," he replied, taking them carelessly from my offered hand, the tips of his long slender fingers brushing my wrist. "Would you care for a drink?"

I walked with him to the bar. After many weeks of practice I'd learned how to take sips of the abominable liquor served in such places and then discreetly dribble them into my handkerchief while pretending to wipe my lips. But my companion was regarding me more closely now, and I had to swallow a bit of the vile stuff. Only my acting experience enabled me to hold steady and not gag in front of his piercing eyes. "Bygod, you have a familiar face," he said suddenly. "Have we met somewhere?"

"I think not," I replied quickly, my voice rising too high as I spoke. "I'm Calvin Blacklock. From down James River."

"Blacklock?" He shook his head. "Don't recall any Blacklocks. I'm Charles Heywood."

I wondered if the name was as false as the one I'd given him. He began berating the quality of the alleged liquor we were drinking and expressed an earnest wish that he might soon venture north of the Ohio River, where the amenities of life were taken for granted.

After I declined to join him in a second drink, he inquired if I might be interested in another game of poker.

"Regretfully I must leave your company, sir," I replied in my deepest tone. "I have a late appointment that I must keep."

His blue eyes turned so flinty that I shifted my gaze away from him, hurriedly saying that I was already late and must leave at once.

"A late appointment, eh?" His voice was as cold as his eyes. "Not with a lady, surely," he asked, and although I did not dare glance back at him as I started for the door, I would have wagered there was a sneer on his lips to match the mockery in his voice.

Outside, the night air of Virginia seemed almost chill after the miasma of the crowded gambling hall. Off to the south toward Petersburg, artillery growled a distant thunder, but above Richmond glittering stars filled a peaceful spring sky. From darkened doorways an occasional prostitute called softly and showed herself briefly in the starlight. I found some satisfaction in beguiling them; I had spent hours on and off the stage perfecting the male strut— prideful swagger of the hips, pelvis slightly advanced, bouncing on the balls of the feet with toes kept straight forward.

Three ammunition wagons rattled past to the clop-clop accompaniment of hooves against pavement. I turned a corner toward Capitol Square and almost collided with two drunken cavalry officers. Beyond them was the Gethsemane Reading Room, its unobtrusive sign barely visible, a faded yellow light in the empty window. The place never closed. During recent winter months it had usually been filled with unkempt ill-smelling beggars seeking refuge from the cold, but on this evening I found only one man resting his head on a table littered with worn newspapers. He was either asleep or in an intoxicated stupor. I took a thin sheet of paper from a box, wrote a message to Colonel Fennell, and folded

< CONSPIRACY OF KNAVES >

it carefully. For a minute or so I stood in silent deliberation, and then with what must have been a gesture of finality, I slipped the note through a slot beneath a lettered sign: OFFERINGS.

Before daylight, Colonel Fennell would have my brief report on Charles Heywood. The Gethsemane Reading Room was not entirely what it appeared to be. Fennell and others in the C.S.A. government used it as a covert message center.

For me, the night that followed was a mixture of insomnia and dreadful nightmares. If this man was a spy, I had betrayed him and my Union patron in Washington. Never before, since I'd begun my work for Colonel Fennell, had my conscience troubled me after sending him reports of suspected offenders. The Confederate authorities seldom executed deserters; the army was too much in need of men, and so those found guilty were merely sent to prison, from which they were soon released. Spies, however, were another matter, and I was well aware that most of those caught were executed by firing squads. All night long I suffered recurring horrors in which the bloody face of Charles Heywood regarded me with stony accusation. Again and again, the hallucination brought me upright from my pillow, and after I'd lain wide awake for long periods of time, I'd fall back into the hideous nightmare. Sometimes I'd awaken with a grinding of teeth, and once brought blood from my tongue during the terrible dream images.

With relief I greeted first break of day, my mind sternly resolved to see Colonel Fennell and withdraw my imputation of Charles Heywood. Fennell's instructions forbade visits to his headquarters except in emergencies, but if there was ever a crucial situation, I considered this to be one, with a man's life hanging in the balance. Once the machinery of arresting and accusing was set in motion in wartime, stopping it was almost impossible even though the accused might be innocent. Although I was far from believing Heywood innocent, I could not bear the notion of his being shot dead through my instrumentality.

Very well, I'll grant that perhaps I was already in love with Charley Heywood. But I don't think so. Under his spell, perhaps, but not in love with him. Charley was not the sort of man a wise woman of the world such as I would easily allow herself to fall in love with.

After concealing the dun-colored pouches under my eyes as

best I could with a powdering of starch, and pinching my pale cheeks into some semblance of living flesh, I was just beginning to dress myself as a modish Belle Rutledge when a loud knock sounded on the door. To my surprise a messenger from Colonel Fennell was there—the young one with wild curly hairs sprouting from his pimply chin, the one who sometimes sniffed like a dog at the sight of me. He moved forward as if to come into my room, his goggly eyes ogling my thin dressing gown, but I closed the door and made him stay in the hallway while I read the message. It was in Fennell's scrawl: "Come to my office at once." Very peremptory indeed, I thought. I opened the door a crack to tell the sniffling messenger to be off to inform the colonel I would be there in a matter of minutes.

On the way to Broad Street I totted up in my mind a plethora of reasons for dismissing all suspicions of espionage against Charles Heywood. You see, I was certain that Colonel Fennell had summoned me because he was in haste to take the suspected spy into custody before he could escape Richmond, and I wished to avoid that consequence.

Colonel Fennell had recently advised me to visit his office through an alley door, and I made my approach by that route, knocking gently and entering at his response. Ready with prepared absolutions for Heywood, I was struck dumb, as they say, when I stepped inside and saw my suspected spy half reclining on the haircloth sofa, his long-fingered hands tipped together across his neat waistcoat. Both men arose, smiling at me with self-satisfied masculine smirks. Heywood made room for me on the sofa.

"I believe you and Major Heywood have met," the colonel said dryly.

"Yes, sir."

"I played poker last evening," Heywood said, "with one Calvin Blacklock from down James River. A high-voiced tidewater Virginian with a mouthful of Kentucky cadences." He was rubbing it in, all right.

"I gulled you for a time," I protested.

"Until I had a close look at that false mustache. There's not even a peach fuzz on your lovely cheeks, Miss Belle Rutledge, and yet wiry hairs were growing off your upper lip. Not natural."

Fennell coughed slightly and interrupted: "Miss Rutledge has

< CONSPIRACY OF KNAVES >

been a first-rate agent since coming to Richmond. She warned me that her male disguise might not be deceptive enough away from an artificially illuminated stage."

Heywood strode across to a dimly lit lamp on the colonel's work table and lighted one of his little cheroots from the wick. "Then she shouldn't try a man's disguise off the stage," he said slowly. He turned to face Fennell. "I suppose I'd better be readying things for the journey. Anything else, colonel?"

"No, it's all your design, now, Major Heywood." Fennell stood up and offered his hand. "We may not see each other for some time. But after you pick up the Mount Sterling goods, we'll expect to hear from you."

"Yes, you should soon be hearing good news—that is, if Johnny Truscott nabbed the whole lot."

"I'd lay a bet the captain got the whole," Fennell said, his voice indicating impatience.

"Yes." Heywood set his slouch hat on at an angle. "Johnny's heart is still in it." His blue eyes fixed briefly on me. "Well, Miss Belle Rutledge. Until later."

For a minute or so after Heywood left by the alleyway door, Colonel Fennell sat silent in his chair. Then he looked up at me. "What do you think of him, Miss Rutledge?"

"A nonpareil, I'd say, sir. I've never known anyone like him."

"Yes, very much his own man. He's what society sometimes calls a 'rantipole,' a pursuer of women and a breaker of hearts, so I'm told. Do you think you could handle him at close quarters?"

My face must have revealed my surprise, but before I could speak, the colonel continued: "Your work is finished here in Richmond. We need you to try for much bigger game in the North."

I took a deep breath; everything seemed to be coming at me too fast. I stammered incoherently: "When—I was not—"

"You will be leaving with Major Heywood early in the morning. Do you think you can deal with him, Miss Rutledge?"

"Oh, but sir," I protested. "To go on such brief notice?"

He reacted with a cutting tone in his voice: "You have no theatrical commitments at present. So no excuses to make there. Pack your necessary things in a single portmanteau. What you must leave will be stored for you. Major Heywood will be around for you at the Ballard House with a carriage about sunrise."

< **Belle Rutledge** >

"That's all? No instructions?" I was piqued at his curtness, his almost rude dismissal of me. "Where are we going?"

"Of course I have instructions for you." Fennell laid down the feathered pen he had just dipped in his inkwell on the table. "And the major can tell you where you're going. The plan is partly his, but I suppose you deserve some explanation of it. You know what Copperheads are?"

"Northerners who sympathize with the South?"

"Or who in any case want the war stopped, yes. Knights of the Golden Circle, Order of American Knights, Sons of Liberty, Peace Democrats, Butternuts. They delight in fancy titles and secret organizations. Major Heywood has worked with them for several months. They've promised to help free our soldiers from prison camps in the North."

"And how do I fit into this, colonel?"

He picked up the pen staff and turned it nervously in his fingers. "I chose you for two reasons. First, the sharp way in which you winnowed Charles Heywood out of the crowd and judged him to be a spy. He is a spy, of course." Fennell hesitated for a moment, studying me with his heavy-lidded eyes. "I have orders for you, Miss Rutledge, that must be kept from him. I don't fully trust Heywood, you see. Oh, not that he's disloyal in any way. It's his grandiose schemes that I don't trust. He wants to stir up a revolt in the Northwest, using the Copperheads. Whereas our main objective is first to free our soldiers—in particular, those hundreds of General John Morgan's cavalrymen confined at Chicago. Turned loose and mounted again, they could disrupt Sherman's supply lines, and perhaps aid in forcing him to withdraw from Atlanta. If Atlanta falls . . . well . . . but I'm talking grand strategy. What I need from you, Miss Rutledge, is that pair of sharp eyes watching Major Heywood. He's to pick up a sizable amount of money that's been captured, and every dollar of it must be spent to free prisoners. No fancy deals to overthrow Northwestern state governments— at least not yet."

"So I'm to spy on Major Heywood?"

"Yes." He began scratching with the pen on a small scrap of paper. When he finished, he blotted the ink and handed the paper to me. He had written names and addresses of two people—one in Cincinnati and the other in Chicago. Through them I could

< CONSPIRACY OF KNAVES >

communicate with him in Richmond. At the slightest indication that Major Heywood was going off track, I was to inform him with all haste.

"You said there were two reasons you chose me," I said. "What was the second?"

"Your experience as an actress. Because of the urgency of this commission there's no time to waste in a tediously furtive crossing through Union lines. You both will assume identities of Northerners whose papers we have. You will go straight through by the rail cars where possible."

He went on to explain that some weeks earlier a Michigan physician, Dr. Campbell, and his wife, a nurse, had been granted permission to come to Richmond for the purpose of attending ailing Union soldiers at Libby Prison. The Campbells' passes were in Colonel Fennell's possession and would be used by Major Heywood and me on our journey north. "To keep in the character of Mrs. Grace Campbell," Fennell added, "you should dress and behave in a most demure manner."

"That should not be too difficult," I replied, but then the colonel gave me another jolt: "There'll be a third party with you," he said. "A six-year-old child, a boy." The boy's father, a Virginian, was killed early in the war. The mother, an Ohioan, had recently died, leaving instructions to send the child to relatives in Cincinnati. Fennell had arranged with Federal authorities for the Campbells to escort the orphan; therefore, the child would now go with us, as we were playing the roles of the Campbells. "The little boy should distract attention from you and Major Heywood," the colonel declared. He may have been correct in his assumption, but I knew nothing of children. In fact, whenever they came into my ken, I was afraid of most of the little savages, with their noses and bottoms to be wiped and their cunning ways of harassing their elders.

The colonel then gave me a small pack of U.S. greenbacks, which I had to sign for. "If you need more," he said offhandedly, "Major Heywood can supply you." He bade me good-bye, thanking me generously for my loyal service to the Confederacy, and warning me again to beware of the profligate major.

"One more thing," he added hastily. "When you reach Chicago—and it is essential that you and Major Heywood proceed as quickly as possible from Cincinnati to Chicago—you are to report immediately to the man whose name I just gave you, Dr. Julian Aylott, on State Street."

I assured him that I would do so.

"I suppose I need not remind you," he shouted after me, "to commit those names and addresses to memory, and then destroy the paper I gave you?"

Before returning to the Ballard annex to pack my indispensables, I still had one urgent errand. Turning off Broad Street I hastened to Pizzini's Confectionery, but to my dismay the place was closed. With sugar and honey and other sweeteners in such short supply, it was surprising that Pizzini's could stay in business at all, but I had never found the confectionery closed in daytime before. Although the family lived above, I did not dare disturb them to inquire as to the whereabouts of the little silver-haired man who worked there as a helper.

In the first place, I had never been told his name, and I did not wish to draw attention to him or to myself by asking about him. After walking back and forth along the sidewalk, hoping that someone would open the confectionery door, I decided that I should leave before arousing any interest in my presence. Somehow I must find another means of sending intelligence of my sudden departure from Richmond to my second patron, the one in Washington. Although I did not know exactly how or where we were to cross through Union Army lines, I was hopeful that once we were in United States territory, I could surely find some means of getting a message to my Washington intermediary.

EXCERPTS FROM A
RICHMOND SCRAPBOOK

MAY–JUNE 1864

GRANT'S ARMY
Reaches North Anna River

Twenty-five Miles from Richmond

NEW RICHMOND THEATER
Corner of 7th and Broad Streets

FIRST NIGHT OF THE NEW FASHIONABLE COMEDY
Now Being Played in the European and Northern Theaters

PURE GOLD

All the company in the cast

Mayor's Court

POCAHONTAS KYPER was charged with assaulting and beating Mildred Bohannon. The latter keeps a house of questionable repute on Main between 23rd and 24th streets. The difficulty, as Kyper alleged, took place only because she (Kyper) was "excited with whiskey." Several girls in flashy attire were brought up as witnesses, and the Mayor determined at one time, to require the whole batch to give security to be

< **Richmond Scrapbook, May–June 1864** >

of good behavior. He, however, reconsidered his purpose, and let all off save Mrs. Bohannon, who was held to bail for keeping a disorderly house, and Kyper required to give security for originating a disturbance therein.

TOM, slave of Mrs. S. Dabney, was ordered to be whipped for throwing stones on First, near Fouchee Street.

Advt.

MADAM SESNAWAKI'S Institute for Young Ladies

Barhamville, 1¹/₂ miles from
Columbia, South Carolina

The annual session of this Institute will commence Oct. 1, 1864 and close June 30, 1865

Advt.

$200 REWARD—Stolen from my lot at Mt. Laurel, on the night of the 25th inst., a SORREL MARE, slightly roan, four years old, of good height.

Advt.

$200 REWARD—Runaway on the 24th of April, 1864, Beverley, a black man about twenty years old, 5 feet 6 or 8 inches high; no marks recollected, only his feet, the next to the big toe rides the big toe and the other.

Advt.

NOW READY—*Southern Literary Messenger* for June, with numerous attractive features . . . $2 per single copy.

Advt.

RECRUIT WANTED—I will pay a liberal price for a recruit. I wish the said recruit to join a Partisan company and then make

an exchange with me. I am a member of the 18th Reg't Va.
Cavalry. State price and address.

R. W. Lewis
Co. D, 18th Va. Cav.,
Chambliss Brigade

Advt.

WANTED TO HIRE—Twenty Negro men, able-bodied, and fifteen Negro women,
without children. Good washers required. Apply to A. G. Lane, Surgeon in
Charge, Winder Hospital.

JERRY, slave of Wm. Ratcliffe, was charged with stealing three chickens
and a lot of crackers from some person unknown. Officer Sand came
across Jerry at an early hour in the morning, near the corner of 6th and
Broad streets, and arrested him on suspicion.

NEW RICHMOND THEATER
Corner of 7th and Broad Streets

MURDER AT THE MOUND

Fancy Dance
by
Miss Belle Rutledge

Next Week—ICI ON PARLE FRANÇAIS

MORGAN'S RAID—Fight at Mt. Sterling—
Cynthiana Burnt—2,000 Strong—
General Burbridge in Pursuit

LATEST FROM THE UNITED STATES

**The Yankees Still Claim to Be
Victorious**

Advances in Gold Price

< **Richmond Scrapbook, May–June 1864** >

CONTRIBUTIONS FROM THE ARMY TO THE POOR OF RICHMOND

The Army Committee acknowledges with pleasure the receipt of one day's rations, contributed by the gallant soldiers of Gen. Lee's army for the benefit of the poor of this city, as follows . . .

DESERTERS—Joshua West, a deserter from one of the batteries, was arrested yesterday by Miss Fanny P. King, and sent to Castle Thunder. John McAnally, a deserter from the 19th Virginia regiment (a triple deserter in fact, having left his regiment three times without leave) was also apprehended yesterday and put in the Castle for trial by court-martial.

DOG HIDES—It has been suggested to us that the skin of dogs makes as good leather as that of any other animal. Last week dogs enough were captured on the streets to make $2500 worth of leather.

RE-NOMINATION OF PRESIDENT LINCOLN

The Baltimore Convention Balloted 484 for Lincoln, 22 for Gen. Grant

Gov. Andy Johnson, of Tennessee, for Vice-President

THE KENTUCKY RAID

A portion of *MORGAN'S* command entered Lexington at 2 o'clock this morning, burned the Kentucky Central Railroad depot, robbed a number of stores, and left at 10 o'clock in the direction of Georgetown and Frankfort. *BURBRIDGE* followed them.

4

CHEER, BOYS, CHEER,
WE'LL MARCH AWAY
TO BATTLE

A N D N O W I C O M E to the robbery of the bank at Mount Sterling, Kentucky. Captain Johnny Truscott's company was riding escort for General John Morgan and his staff on that last night when they came down out of the mountains and found the Kentucky turnpike to Mount Sterling. After I got to know Johnny Truscott during our long exile in Canada, he spoke of that expedition many times. To me it was a foolish endeavor, but to him it was one of the high adventures of his young life.

As they approached Mount Sterling, the horses' hooves beat against the hard gravelly surface, and the drumming, combined with the creak of leather and clink of harness metal, must have awakened sleepers in farmhouses along the way. Even if there had been enough light to see the riders, only the most knowledgeable of observers could have told at first glance whether they were Union or Rebel cavalry. A closer glance, however, would have discovered the tattered uniforms. Some riders were barefoot in their stirrups, and there was a gauntness in the forms of men and mounts that had become symbolic of the Confederate Army in the fourth year of war.

Eleven months had passed since Morgan led more than two thousand mounted raiders across the Ohio River in early summer of 1863 to create panic through Indiana and Ohio, a feat of derring-do that ended with the destruction of his command, and the capture

< **Cheer, Boys, Cheer, We'll March Away to Battle** >

and imprisonment of Morgan and some of his staff in the state penitentiary at Columbus, Ohio. Several hundred other Kentucky cavalrymen, the most seasoned and most audacious of all the Confederacy's horsemen, were locked into Camp Douglas prison at Chicago.

In late November of 1863, Morgan and six of his officers escaped. A brilliant deliverance it was, daringly planned by Charles Heywood, one of the six. With the assistance of Copperhead friends in Ohio, Heywood quickly made his way to Detroit, slipped into Canada at Windsor, and registered at a hotel as John Hunt Morgan. A Federal agent stationed in Windsor took the bait and telegraphed his discovery to superiors in Ohio, throwing them off the real Morgan's trail. Morgan meanwhile managed to cross the Ohio River into Kentucky, and at Newport he surprised a trusted friend who got him started on his way south to rejoin what was left of his shattered command.

Mounted on a wiry Standardbred and armed only with a horsewhip, Morgan passed as a buyer of mules for the Union Army until he was safely through the lines. In southwestern Virginia during that winter and into the spring of 1864, he gradually rebuilt his cavalry force. Missing were the most daring of the Morgan men, however, who were still in that Chicago prisoner-of-war camp.

Only the veteran Morgan units—hard-bitten survivors who had swum the river to safety after the last disastrous battles in Ohio—still believed in the war. They were eager for more action, and cheered mightily when Morgan informed them that they were going on a June raid into Kentucky. Being a Kentuckian myself, I can understand the emotions that impelled them to this mad and all but hopeless undertaking.

The announced military purpose of the raid was to cut supply lines to Sherman's army in Georgia. For the Kentucky boys, however, especially those who had to march on foot across the mountains, the main objective was the capture of cavalry horses, plus a taste of Bluegrass victuals and a visit with wives or sweethearts still waiting at home.

One of the best of the veteran mounted companies was led by Captain Truscott, who had soldiered with Morgan since organization of the first cavalry unit at Lexington in the autumn of 1861.

< CONSPIRACY OF KNAVES >

At that time Truscott was nineteen years old, and now, at twenty-two, after three years of surviving numerous battles, skirmishes, charges, and hand-to-hand saber fights, he still retained a boyish, almost innocent appearance. Most of his surviving contemporaries looked to be ten years older than they were. Like them, Truscott had seen dozens of his comrades shot or slashed to pieces, killed or physically impaired for the remainder of their lives; but if these experiences seriously affected him, he showed no evidence of it.

His hair was light brown, quite curly and bushy above his ears. His eyes also were light brown—hazel, to be more exact—constantly shifting their gaze in a manner that some of his female admirers considered indicative of his whole-souled gentility. He attracted women without meaning to, and at first glance a stranger might be fooled into thinking of him as a frail young man. He was small, but tough as a jack oak, and never showed fear. Possibly he never experienced a truly deep sense of fear. More than once in my presence he claimed that he had not, and his friends said that Johnny Truscott never boasted because he saw no need to do so.

Truscott believed himself to be a reincarnation of Sir Gawain, El Cid, Ivanhoe, and the Scottish chieftains (as delineated by Miss Jane Porter in her book on the subject) combined into one magnificent model of knighthood. Dashing horsemen were they all, out to set the world to rights, and Truscott was happy in the belief that he belonged to so noble a band.

Now, on that soft June night of return to his native ground, Truscott rode with his men just ahead of Morgan's headquarters staff. A few miles east of Mount Sterling, the column turned into a thick woods, following a pathway between towering big-trunked trees, barely wide enough for a wagon to pass. Vegetation was in full leaf, blocking out starlight. "Dark as Erebus," Truscott said half aloud, and remembered the croaky voice of old Professor Moncrief, the classics teacher at Transylvania College in Lexington, reading lines from *The Merchant of Venice*:

> *The motions of his spirit are dull as night,*
> *And his affections dark as Erebus.*

< **Cheer, Boys, Cheer, We'll March Away to Battle** >

According to Professor Moncrief, Erebus was the son of Chaos, and chaos was what had engulfed Morgan's men after the Great Raid. In the months before John Morgan's return, Truscott had suffered doubts for the first time since becoming a Confederate cavalryman. During the last few weeks, however, as the depleted battalions were re-formed in the Virginia hills, his spirits revived and in idle moments he returned to reading his tattered copy of *The Scottish Chiefs*, which had been in his saddlebag since the day he left home to join Morgan's cavalry. On this night, as he was to tell me later, he clearly saw in retrospect that their hard march across the Cumberlands was a test, a proving of their fitness for knighthood.

The darkness of Erebus, as Truscott termed it, began to lighten gradually, the trees thinning until ahead of them was an open field freshly plowed. Another line of Shakespeare's sprang from Truscott's memory: "How sweet the moonlight sleeps upon this bank!" The glow was not moonlight, however, but the first reflection of dawn from the sky behind them. A sudden slight breeze rustled the leathery oak leaves above their heads. They were on the edge of the Bluegrass, and Truscott could smell its springtime perfumes—newly opened earth and dewy grass scents, blossoms wild and domesticated, heavy and rich in the young morning before a hot sun burned fragrances away.

Truscott felt a wave of nostalgic emotion, but as he had learned to do after many months of war-compelled exile, he willed it quickly down into his consciousness. From the edge of the field he could see the buildings of Mount Sterling nestling together, with farmhouses scattered out along the roads. Roosters were beginning to crow in the distance, and the woods behind were filled with twittering birds unmindful of the column of horses snorting and stamping impatiently.

General Morgan was still in his saddle only a few yards to Truscott's right. He was studying the town through a field glass. Off to the left a dozen riders appeared abruptly out of the shadows of the woods. Truscott recognized them immediately as Lieutenant Tom Quirk's legendary trackers. They'd gone ahead at midnight to scout the town. Quirk and his boys were the best in the world, as any Kentuckian will tell you, at that sort of reconnaissance. The scout leader still had a sling on an arm that was winged somewhere

< CONSPIRACY OF KNAVES >

in northern Georgia while Morgan was still in prison. Even in the dull light his cat's eyes found Truscott. Quirk gave him a half salute. "Howya, Johnny."

"What's it like, Tom?" Truscott asked.

"Nothing to it. Greenhorn militia. Maybe three hundred."

Quirk rode on to Morgan, and five minutes later the forward battalion was forming in columns of twos to cross the field. Squads trotted off to right and left, their assignments to block roads around Mount Sterling, sealing exits and entrances. Colonel Howard Smith, Truscott's immediate superior, rode for a minute or two beside the captain.

"Quirk says they're in two tent camps," the colonel explained. "One small, one large. You take your boys in on the right against the smaller. I'll bring the other two columns in behind you to encircle. Colonel Giltner with Bowles' battalion will strike the big camp."

Out of the shadows of a fold in the rolling land, a farmhouse took shape. A figure in white stood beside the yard gate.

"Mack Everett?" Colonel Smith called softly.

Everett was wearing a long-tailed nightshirt over his pants and was barefooted. "What took you so long?" he asked, a hint of irritation in his voice.

"Where're the Federals?" Smith asked.

"Right over that rise." Everett pointed, and began shaking his head. "Their pickets are close enough to hear us."

"Then let's charge 'em," Smith replied. He glanced back at the three columns, still in motion across the field, and shouted the order.

Skilled at responding to commands and signals, Truscott's surviving veterans knew exactly what they were expected to do. As they drove up the grassy slope, the column of horsemen wheeled expertly into a line ready to charge whatever lay on the other side. They found fifty small tents in neat geometrical placement along a crooking stream, a few wagons, a rail-fenced corral of horses and mules. The camp was no more than a hundred yards from the Confederate cavalry line that easily moved into full gallop down the other side of the slope. The Yankees had received some kind of warning only moments earlier, and a frantic bugler was trying to sound an alarm. In front of the tents, a dozen half-clad members of a platoon were forming to the harsh commands of a sergeant. Three or four other men were hastily saddling horses in the corral.

What most struck Truscott was the bountifulness of the camp— the brand-new tents, the wagons filled with sacks and boxes, high stacks of hay, the well-fed animals. A primrose glow from the dawn sky brightened the gray tents and canvas-covered wagons, so that they appeared to be blanketed with snow. Then the firing began.

Even as Truscott shouted the command, his men were halting to begin dismounting, every fourth cavalryman holding four horses while the others took firing positions. For two or three minutes there was an earnest firefight, but as soon as the confused and inexperienced militiamen in the Union camp saw two more mounted companies swing over the rise and gallop right and left to encircle them, they began abandoning their arms. A white flag went up over the command tent.

While the prisoners were being dismissed and separated into easily guarded formations, a spirited firing sounded from the larger camp off to the left. The sun was above the horizon now, and Truscott could clearly see a company of Union infantry streaming in fairly good order toward the town. Another of the militia's units had managed to hold off a force of dismounted Confederates for a few minutes, but they also were now breaking away and racing for cover in the streets of Mount Sterling. The small wounded unit of Morgan's men stationed on the road into town was unable to halt the rush of men on foot.

Truscott rode quickly over to Colonel Smith, who sat straight in his saddle, glaring at the distant action. "Damn," the colonel said. "Giltner's horses didn't have the vigor to get him into position quick enough. Now it's going to be a house-to-house shoot."

"Should I take my company in, sir?"

"No, no!" Smith shook his head, still not looking at Truscott. "Giltner can handle those raw militiamen. If you take your boys into the streets, we'll only suffer more casualties we can't replace." He turned his head, his eyes blinking against a gleam of sunlight that exposed the weariness of his face. "Your men are looting the Federal tents. Give them a few minutes more and then bring them up to the edge of town. General Morgan may be in a hurry to move out for Lexington." He sighed against the thought of another long

< CONSPIRACY OF KNAVES >

day's ride. "I'm going to start some of the captured wagons moving east to pick up our foot cavalry in the rear."

Truscott watched Colonel Smith canter off toward the corral. Within the hour the camp would be picked bare of everything portable—tents, utensils, clothing. The commissary stores came first, of course—flour, hardtack, salt meat. Truscott could already taste the *real* coffee, sweetened with sugar. As he rode closer to the area where his men were busily rolling their collected prizes of war into new blankets, he saw a sergeant smashing an officer's trunk by jumping up and down on it with both feet.

In the first months of war, John Morgan had rigidly forbidden such behavior, but they all had gradually learned to accept it as necessary for the survival of Confederate cavalry. Truscott still hated looting of personal items, and especially frowned upon the opening of captured mail, which often yielded a few greenbacks in letters to the boys in blue.

The sergeant was hurriedly digging shirts and underwear out of the smashed trunk. He held up a pair of black hussar boots, shiny in their newness, and his eyes met Truscott's for a second. Then he set one of the boots alongside his worn footwear and shook his head in disappointment. "Couldn't squeeze my big toes in these, Cap'n Truscott. You want a try?" He brought the boots over and held one against Truscott's stirrup. "Might fit you to a ty-ty," he added cheerfully.

Truscott's boots were hatched with widening brown cracks, but he declined the offer firmly. "Give them to one of the barefooted men. And, sergeant, get your squad mounted. We're moving up to Mount Sterling."

From the town, sounds of firing increased in intensity, but by the time Truscott brought his men to the outskirts, there were only desultory shots as the frightened Union militiamen were flushed out of houses. Truscott halted beneath a wide-limbed oak at roadside and was dismounting when two riders approached at a gallop from the town. He recognized one of them as Lieutenant Parr of Morgan's headquarters staff. The other man was a rather handsome civilian, his face covered with a short sandy beard. He wore a stained gray duster and a countryman's hat, flat-topped with a wide brim. (Had I been there, I would have known this man.)

Lieutenant Parr swung his horse alongside Truscott's and dropped

< **Cheer, Boys, Cheer, We'll March Away to Battle** >

down beside the captain. "Special order for you from General Morgan," he said, drawing a folded piece of paper from an inside pocket and handing it to Truscott.

"In writing?" Truscott asked. His tone must have indicated his surprise.

Parr's lips held only the slightest suggestion of a smile. "I reckon headquarters wants some kind of record of this."

Truscott had already read the short message. "Good God! We don't rob Kentucky banks," he cried.

"We've robbed plenty of other banks," Parr said evenly.

Truscott looked past him to the civilian in the gray duster. "Why did General Morgan pick me for this nasty work?" Without waiting for a reply, he glanced at the written message again. "The general didn't write this. It's Withers' handwriting."

Parr nodded. "But it's General Morgan's order."

Truscott turned and climbed quickly back into his saddle. "I want to see Withers about this." He started his horse into motion, and as soon as Lieutenant Parr came alongside he urged the animal into a brisk enough pace to leave the civilian several yards behind. "Who is he?" he asked Parr.

"I thought you knew him. Says he's working with Charley Heywood. Name's Kendrich." (The man's name was not Kendrich, but I was not there to tell Truscott that, and I would not have done so had I been.)

They were in the main street of Mount Sterling now. On the wooden sidewalk in front of a general store, a surgeon in a blue uniform was attending three wounded men. Two dead Union soldiers lay nearby, their faces covered with a dirty muslin sheet. Truscott turned his head away from the scene; even after three years he could not accept the stark results of battle.

Morgan's staff had established temporary headquarters on the porch of a large rambling house at the end of the business structures. Three or four junior officers and two of Quirk's scouts were lounging on the wide steps. Captain Withers, Morgan's adjutant, was seated in a rocking chair, his booted feet propped on a banister. He had a long black stogie in his mouth, and when he grinned at Truscott he kept his teeth clenched tight on the cigar. The whole relaxed tableau on that porch gave no hint that only a few minutes before a deadly skirmish had transpired nearby.

< CONSPIRACY OF KNAVES >

Truscott responded to Withers's grin with a cold nod. "Is the general inside?"

Withers dropped his boots to the porch flooring and sat upright. "No. He's moved out with Quirk and Company B on the road to Lexington. We're awaiting his orders."

Dismounting, Truscott removed the written message from his gauntlet. "Are you certain General Morgan wants this done?"

Withers shrugged. "I wrote the words as he gave the order, John. He told me to sign his name."

"Why me?"

The adjutant took a long draw from the cigar and blew a cloud of smoke at the porch ceiling. "He said something about Major Charles Heywood—that you were in the scheme with Charley— that you would rob the bank with more zeal than anybody else because Charley wants it done."

Truscott jerked a thumb toward the civilian known as Kendrich, who had halted his horse several yards back down the street. "What's *he* to do with it?"

"Hell, I thought you knew. He's to deliver the bank money to Charley Heywood."

With a gesture of displeasure, Truscott glanced again at Kendrich. "He must be one of Charley's Copperheads," he said softly. "I don't see how Charley can have any confidence in the bastards. They gave us none of their promised help during the Indiana raid."

Withers laughed without humor as he started down the porch steps. "They sure as hell didn't. But General Morgan thinks they might help get our boys out of Camp Douglas in Chicago."

For the first time Truscott was interested in the project. "Yes, I've heard that from Charley. Still, I don't like taking Kentuckians' bank savings to pass on to Copperheads."

Withers was close enough now to speak almost in a whisper. "It's not Kentucky money we're after in that bank, John. Charley Heywood learned somehow that the Union Army keeps its payroll in there. I reckon they figured it would be safer here than in Lexington. They never expected us to come in the back door, over the Cumberlands." He bit the soggy end off his cigar and grinned again.

They began laughing together. "In that case," Truscott said, "I'll rob the bank with pleasure." He turned to mount his horse.

< **Cheer, Boys, Cheer, We'll March Away to Battle** >

"You'll want some help. Lieutenant Parr can give you a hand. It won't be easy."

"Won't be easy?" Truscott was in his saddle. "With our guns controlling this town? They wouldn't resist."

"A woman is in charge. Widow of a Union officer." Withers's voice turned serious. "If you get the plunder, bring it back here for accounting."

"And then you're just going to hand it over to that Copperhead?"

"Why, he's a noble Knight of the Golden Circle, John." Withers lowered his voice. "Don't worry. General Morgan's sending the Fielding brothers along to keep the knight honest."

Truscott's dislike for the man in the gray duster was aggravated. He resented Copperheads using the word *knight* to designate members of their secret brotherhood. Before he turned his horse, he glanced again at the two scouts drowsing on the porch steps, Paul and Andy Fielding. To Truscott they always looked like a pair of woods bumpkins, but he knew them to be among the sharpest of Tom Quirk's boys. With them watching Kendrich, the money should be safe enough. "All right, Lieutenant Parr," he said, "let's go take that Yankee gold away from the Union officer's widow."

The Farmers Bank of Mount Sterling was on a corner of the main street, with a tree growing out of a brick walk in front and towering over the building. Truscott and Lieutenant Parr hitched their mounts to a weathered railing and dismounted before Kendrich caught up with them. Beside the bank a man wearing an unbuttoned vest stepped out of a combination book and jewelry store to stare at them. Through the glass window behind the man, Truscott noted a display of watches, a few books, and copies of *Harper's* and *Leslie's* weekly magazines. The bank's heavy double door was closed. The tall windows on each side of the door were protected by iron bars that looked as if they had recently been installed. Worn window shutters, their paint peeling, hung loosely at the sides of the windows.

The double door was locked, but through the barred windows Truscott could see a woman and an elderly man looking out from behind caging wire over the bank counter. He rapped hard on the oaken door, but neither the man nor the woman responded. He moved

< CONSPIRACY OF KNAVES >

to a window and tapped it gently with his pistol. Their only reactions were quick hostile glances. He then broke one of the four panes and shouted above the tinkle of falling glass: "Unlock the door!"

The elderly man moved as if to comply, but the woman commanded him to stay where he was.

"Ma'am," Truscott called calmly, "I don't fancy to break down your fine oak door, but if you don't unlock it I shall be compelled to smash it into splinters."

Her face contorting with fury, she stormed out of the side of the bank cage, marched angrily to the door, slid back the metal bolts, and opened it. (You know the sort of resolute female she was. The ravages of war have left this country filled with her kind. Widowhood had accentuated her impatient determination.)

"Despicable Rebel thieves!" she cried out as Truscott and Parr pushed past her to the counter.

Two iron safes stood against the wall behind the wire cage. The smaller one was old, with a simple tumbler lock. Across the top of the larger safe, gold lettering spelled out UNITED STATES WAR DEPARTMENT. Truscott was wondering if he should summon a detail of men and simply have them carry the safe down to Withers's porch, or attempt to unlock it where it stood.

The man known as Kendrich had come close to Truscott and was studying the military safe. "Is a new Yale pin tumbler," he said. "We needs must haf a key." The man spoke with a broken accent of some kind, hissing and shortening his words. Truscott remembered General Morgan saying that messengers with foreign accents were less likely to be suspected when crossing enemy lines. He thought that might be why Kendrich had been chosen for the task of delivering the money, but of course he was wrong in that assumption.

The woman reentered the cage, hooking the door behind her. She was about forty, and Truscott guessed she might have been attractive had her face not been constantly twisted with anger.

"I want the safe keys," Truscott said to her, trying to keep a note of courtesy in his voice.

Suddenly she changed her tactics. Instead of screaming out again, she gave him the look of a Sunday School teacher chiding a boy who had failed to learn his Bible verses.

< **Cheer, Boys, Cheer, We'll March Away to Battle** >

"You ought to be ashamed," she said. "You Kentucky boys stealing Kentucky folkses' money. Ever' cent some people have in the world is in this good bank."

"The safe keys, ma'am," he repeated.

She gave him that shaming look again. "Some of the money's mine and I'm a widow woman. My husband was killed at Perryville."

"He must've been on the wrong side, ma'am," Lieutenant Parr said with mock gravity. "Had he been with us, he'd most likely still be in the land of the living."

The woman grimaced, as though the very thought of Parr's remark made her ill.

Truscott tried to speak with forbearance, but the tone of his voice must have indicated he was losing his patience: "We want only the Union Army payroll money, ma'am."

"You'll never get the safe key from me, young man. I took an oath to guard well that money for President Lincoln's army."

Kendrich cleared his throat loudly. "We are wasting our time, captain." He moved around to the wire door. "I know where women usually hide their keys." He winked at Truscott. "In their bosoms, yes? I'll shake the keys out of her if I haf to turn her downside up."

Truscott shook his head firmly and turned his attention to the elderly man, who had not moved from his perch on a high stool. The man wore a loose neckcloth around a high tight collar. His skin was pale, washed out. An indoor man, he could not conceal his disdain for the weather-browned young men, dusty, unwashed, smelling of sweat, who had intruded upon his domain.

"You must have a key, sir," Truscott said to him. "You open the army safe."

What little flesh color showed in the bank clerk's pallid face drained away when Truscott addressed him.

"Suppose I don't open the safe," the man replied in a tremulous voice. "Would you shoot me, young man?"

"My orders are to burn every building in this town if you refuse to turn over the Union Army payroll." With some success Truscott had used that threat of burning during the Great Raid across the Ohio, but he was uncertain of its effect upon this unlikely pair of bankers.

< CONSPIRACY OF KNAVES >

The old man's head doddered on his thin neck. "We took the oath, like Miz Ellicott says, we took the solemn oath."

Truscott reached through the opening in the wire, caught the man's cravat, and loosened the big-knotted tie, so that his shirt opened to reveal a narrow band of black ribbon around his neck. Two keys were at the end of the ribbon, inside the man's shirt.

In the military safe they found a surprising amount of gold and silver, recently minted coins, along with numerous neat stacks of Federal bank notes. A few minutes later Truscott and Lieutenant Parr had the canvas bags fastened to their saddles and were riding back to Captain Withers's temporary headquarters at the end of the street. Like an anticipatory hunting dog, Kendrich followed a few paces behind.

"How much do you figure it?" Parr asked.

"A hundred thousand," Truscott guessed. "Maybe a good deal more. If it gets to Charley Heywood, he should be able to *buy* all our boys out of Camp Douglas."

Captain Withers was back in the rocking chair, waiting for them. He led them inside the house, and they counted out the money on a long dining-room table. The total amount was slightly more than a hundred thousand dollars. From one of the stacks, Withers removed a few of the smaller denomination greenbacks and slipped them into a leather pocket case.

As soon as the adjutant had recorded the exact figures in the headquarters record book, Truscott requested permission to accompany Kendrich to the rendezvous with Heywood. "I need to talk with Charley," he said. "About our boys in that Chicago prison. Where is the delivery place?"

Withers glanced at Kendrich as if hoping he would reply. "A bit uncertain," he said then. "You see, Major Heywood has been in Richmond plotting grand strategy with the Confederate Canada Commission."

"You're not traveling all the way to Richmond, surely?" Truscott asked Kendrich.

"No, no, captain. We are to meet at a previously arranged place."

"Where?"

Kendrich shrugged and spread his hands. "I'm not at liberty—"

"Oh, hell, I saw the messages," Withers interrupted. "Somewhere south of where the Baltimore railroad crosses the Ohio River. Kendrich and the Fielding brothers have a first check at Catlettsburg. That's all you or anybody else need know, Captain Truscott."

The Fielding brothers were bringing their horses around from the rear of the house. The stolen payroll had been transferred to shabby burlap and blanket rolls, and Kendrich was fastening two of them behind his saddle.

"Can't you delay departure," Truscott begged Withers, "until I can get permission from Colonel Smith to go along?"

Withers shook his head. "Don't waste your time, John. While you were robbing the bank, messages came in from General Morgan, one concerning you. You're to meet the general at his Pine Grove bivouac around sundown, with a dozen of your best riders. I've informed Colonel Smith that you're being detached." He handed Truscott the pocket case in which he had put some of the greenbacks. "You'll need these where you're going."

5

TO HORSE! TO HORSE!
THE BUGLE CALLS

JOHNNY TRUSCOTT told me afterward that he had an uneasy feeling about leaving Mount Sterling for the rendezvous at Pine Grove. General Morgan's orders told him to bring "twelve of your best riders" but he chose only eleven. Twelve men and himself would have made thirteen in the detachment and Truscott was a superstitious young man. The eleven he selected were intrepid but not foolhardy. They were survivors, not madcap bravados, and formed as bold-spirited a troop as could be assembled from Truscott's company.

They rode westward out of Mount Sterling only a few minutes after Kendrich the Copperhead and the Fielding brothers started in the opposite direction, carrying most of the money that had been taken from the Farmers Bank. For the next two hours, at every crossroad Truscott passed, pickets recognized him and his men with the usual banter or with silent motions to pass on.

By the time they reached Morgan's headquarters bivouac, the sun was almost down and cooking fires were starting along a small stream. A few tents, captured that morning, formed white rectangles against a background of green undergrowth. As soon as he sighted Morgan's unsaddled black stallion, Truscott dismounted his men and went on alone. The general was resting on folded blankets that also had been captured that morning, his back against

< **To Horse! To Horse! The Bugle Calls** >

a rotting pine log, one arm braced over a saddle. His eyes were closed but he was not asleep. Hearing Truscott's footsteps in the brush and leaves, he became wide awake, eyes open, and he sat erect. Even so, Truscott thought, he looks weary to death, and a sprinkling of gray is beginning to show in his short beard. But after all, he's almost twice my age.

"Captain Truscott," the general acknowledged. "Captain Withers informed me you snared the bank money for Charles Heywood." He tried to put force into his voice, but fatigue burdened his words.

"Yes, sir. The Copperhead took it north."

"Did the Fielding brothers—"

"Yes, they went along."

Morgan nodded, his smile of satisfaction quickly fading. "Now comes a harder duty, John." He struggled to his feet, breathing deeply for a second or two. "I want you to know that I was against putting the task on you. Colonel Smith was also opposed, said he could not spare you, but Charles Heywood insisted it be you."

"I suppose it has to do with freeing our boys in that Chicago prison camp."

"Yes, you know something of it, I'm sure. But new problems have arisen. Horses mainly. When freed they'll need two thousand mounts." A breeze floated a scent of frying bacon up from one of the cooking fires. "You remember Judge Yancey? In Lexington?"

"Yes, sir. I know the Yanceys' big house on Winchester Street."

"It's necessary that you see him. About plans for the horses. You'll be going north somewhere. The judge should have the destination by now. You and your boys are to act as drovers."

Truscott raised his head to look straight into Morgan's bloodshot eyes. "Will Judge Yancey come to us, or do we go to him?"

Morgan laughed softly. "The judge doesn't likely know we're any closer than Mount Sterling. And I doubt if the Union home guards in Lexington know where we are either. Soon after dark, Tom Quirk's scouts are going in to feel out their strength. You and your boys will ride with Quirk as far as Judge Yancey's place. I'll try to hold off the shooting until after midnight. By then you should be on your way."

"Do you mean to take Lexington, sir?"

Morgan nodded. "I'm betting the home guards will have their

< CONSPIRACY OF KNAVES >

best riding horses collected in the old racing stables. We need them to carry us back south. Besides, I want to see how the Yankees are treating my house."

Truscott was trying to remember if this would be the third or fourth time General Morgan had returned to his home town. Usually they captured Lexington with no difficulty; the hitch was they could never hold it for more than a few hours. Yet Truscott did not view these ventures as exercises in futility, but as knightly quests, grand gestures worthy of chivalric sons of the Bluegrass.

As soon as darkness fell, he led his men into the outskirts of Lexington, riding with a squad of Lieutenant Quirk's scouts. When they reached the first big houses on Winchester Street, they slowed their horses to a walk. Quirk fastened a white cloth to the end of his lifted saber and began calling out: "Bearer of flag of truce!" No one responded; there was no evidence of pickets anywhere. Truscott heard movements from the dark houses, doors opening and closing, windows being raised or lowered. Then from one window a woman's voice called clearly in the night: "Are you Morgan's men?"

"Yes," Quirk replied in his cheery voice. "Where are the Yankees, ma'am?"

"Farther down the street. Captain Hawes' command. Be careful, boys." The window slammed shut.

As they moved on toward Limestone Street, Truscott recognized the high gables of the Yancey house. "Here's where I leave you," he called to Quirk. "Take care, Tom."

"Same advice to you," Quirk answered.

Instead of a lieutenant for his second-in-command, Truscott had chosen his best sergeant, Joe Stiles. On several occasions both Truscott and Colonel Smith had recommended that Stiles be commissioned, but the sergeant always declined. He was from somewhere back in the Cumberlands, and frequently joked about how many of his brothers and cousins were riding with the Union Army. Whenever Truscott raised the subject of promotion to lieutenant, he would reply courteously but firmly: "Don't want to keep them paper records." But he would never admit that his sparse schooling in the mountains had left him without the ability to properly read or write. Nevertheless, as a horseman, a shrewd judge of men, and a wizard at outwitting the enemy, Sergeant Stiles was unri-

< **To Horse! To Horse! The Bugle Calls** >

valed. Truscott had come to view this lanky dark-bearded hill man, who was ten years older than he, as his shield bearer, a knight's true squire.

Now, at Truscott's soft-spoken order, the sergeant hastily formed the detachment of mounted men along a broad brick sidewalk outside the iron fence of the Yancey house.

Truscott dismounted and hitched his horse to the fence. "I'm going inside," he said. "If Lieutenant Quirk calls for help, give it to him. If he and his scouts make a quick retreat, go with them. I'll find you later."

The heavy iron gate bore only a latch that lifted easily. Truscott followed a curving brick pathway past full-leaved sycamores that cast deep black shadows. The house's veranda, containing several rocking chairs, enclosed the front and both sides. Knocking softly, then louder, then finally pulling a bell cord, Truscott aroused someone inside. For a moment or so he had a sudden feeling of dread that perhaps a Union officer might have commandeered the stately house. In that case there'd likely be a guard outside, he reassured himself, and then thought: And again maybe not.

He heard an old man's tremulous voice: "Who's there?" and knew it was Judge Yancey.

"Captain John Truscott," he answered. "Of General Morgan's command."

The heavy door opened a few inches, a lifted lantern illuminating Yancey's white hair and beard. "Are you Will Truscott's boy?"

"Yes, sir."

"Come on in, son." He extinguished the lantern and opened the door fully. "I thought I heard cavalry."

The judge led the way into a book-lined study, where a single candle burned feebly. "I've been expecting you for the last week," he said, and motioned impatiently to a chair. "Rest yourself." Truscott could feel a slight warmth from the fireplace, but the coals had died completely. Even in June the old man had to have his fire, Truscott thought, and then wondered why he had been expected.

"You were expecting me, sir?"

"Yes. Charles Heywood stopped here for a day. Last month." His voice faded and then rose to a dry chuckle. "You young fellows

< CONSPIRACY OF KNAVES >

do most of your traveling by night in these parlous times," he observed.

"Yes, sir."

"Charles Heywood's Illinois friend was here day before yesterday. He's arranged a meeting for you at a place called Tamaroa. About the horses, don't you know. He has a plan for you and your boys to personate horse buyers for the Union cavalry."

"General Morgan said we'd need two thousand."

The judge, who was wearing a gray linsey-woolsey dressing gown, left his chair to stand facing Truscott in front of the warm fireplace. "The Copperheads swore to young Heywood they would have plenty of horses ready two weeks before the Fourth of July. That's the day for the breakout." He shook his head to express his doubts. "Since the Union Army discovered the importance of mounted soldiers, good riding horses are scarcer than greenbacks hereabouts. Young Heywood's Illinois friend—name of Hatfield—says most will come from Missouri."

Truscott waited politely for the judge to continue, but the old man was listening to the renewed beat of hooves on the hard-surfaced street. The horses were moving slowly, and Truscott guessed that Morgan had sent another company in to reinforce Quirk's scouts. If there was to be any shooting, it would start soon.

"This man Hatfield, is he a Copperhead?" Truscott asked.

"Yes, he is."

"Not many of that stripe can be trusted, sir. We learned that in the big raid across the Ohio."

Judge Yancey coughed softly. "I might remind you I have a brother-in-law in Chicago who I believe to be an honest Copperhead. And Mr. Hatfield claims to have Kentucky blood kin. However, you may be right as to not trusting the lot of them. But they are our last strong hope. Clement Vallandigham is returning from Canada to stir up thousands of Peace Democrat followers. The Copperheads can build a hot fire in Lincoln's rear, maybe lead the Northwestern states into secession if Lincoln don't stop the war and let the Confederacy be."

"Where and when do I meet Mr. Hatfield?"

"On the Ohio River." The judge crossed to his polished desk, took a key from a pocket, and unlocked one of the drawers. "He drew up a map for you. The route fairly well follows the old

< **To Horse! To Horse! The Bugle Calls** >

Shawnee Trail, and then heads up toward the land-pirate crossing at Cave in Rock. A rendezvous point is marked. Hatfield has a stock farm on the Illinois side of the river."

Truscott took the map closer to the candle. It was a rough but simple drawing. If the scale was fairly exact, three or four nights' travel would be needed to reach the Ohio River crossing, then two or three more to Tamaroa.

Outside on the street, shouts and faster hoofbeats shattered the quietness of the night. From the town came a distant flurry of rifle shots. Truscott folded the map and tucked it far down into an inside pocket. "We'll need citizens' dress to go into Illinois," he said.

"Yes. Enough farmers' trappings have been collected in my pantries to clothe a score of stockmen," the judge assured him. "Just bring your boys around through the side garden."

A minute or so later Truscott found an edgy Sergeant Stiles waiting on the dark sidewalk with the detachment. Rifle firing had stopped in the town, but a line of orange flames brightened the sky where the railroad tracks ran. Truscott guessed that Quirk's scouts had set fire to military storehouses that had been erected there. He unhitched his horse and told Stiles to mount the men and bring them around to a side gate.

Judge Yancey was waiting for them in the dark recess of a rear door, from which a strong moldering odor flowed out to drown the perfumes of the garden. On a table inside was a heap of citizens' clothing, some pieces streaked with powdery mildew. Truscott brushed the powder from a pair of high-topped rawhide brogans that fit fairly well. He found a flat-crowned hat and long-tailed coat, duster, and jeans, and dressed quickly. Two or three at a time the men came into the narrow room to find similar apparel. They undressed and dressed hurriedly, keeping only their carbines, spurs, and personal effects.

Truscott handed the judge his saber and belt and asked that they be guarded well. "You'll burn our uniforms, I suppose, such as they are," he added.

"No, I'll put them in the dry cistern were I kept some of the citizens' clothing," the judge replied. "If our plans succeed, I'll be expecting you boys to ride triumphantly into Lexington later this summer. You'll want uniforms then for a parade." He offered his

< CONSPIRACY OF KNAVES >

frail and bony hand. "Good luck to you, son. It's a risky enterprise."

"It's worth any risk to get our boys out of that prison," Truscott said as he moved toward the rear door.

"Yes, and the Northwestern states out of the Union." Even in the dim light the judge's eyes brightened. The tension that had been growing affected all of them. Fires were still burning down in the town, and brief sharp rifle volleys were beginning again.

"We're taking the road to Versailles," Truscott told Sergeant Stiles. "I'll ride vanguard with you as far as the Kentucky River. Then we'll split up. We don't want to look like cavalry anymore."

As they were leaving Lexington, they were challenged suddenly at an angle in the road. A horseman sprang from the undergrowth, and a dismounted man stepped out to level a rifle at Stiles. "Nobody leaves Lexington till daylight," the horseman said sternly.

"In whose command are you?" Truscott asked.

"That's for me to know," the rider replied. "Now, turn around and go back till daylight."

"I'm Captain Truscott, Colonel Smith's regiment."

"Anybody know a Captain Truscott?" the horseman yelled out.

Sergeant Stiles spoke up: "You're Jim Sands. From Blue Lick town."

"That you, Joe Stiles?"

"Yup. Captain Truscott is our commander."

Sands pulled in closer. "You're riding the wrong way, captain. We're all going up to Cynthiana—soon as General Morgan passes the order."

"Not us. We're heading the opposite direction."

The horseman was still uncertain. "God, you all look like a bunch of rusticans."

"For the present that's what we are," Truscott said, and turned his mount around the blocking horseman. "Lead us out, Sergeant Stiles. At a trot."

By moving at a steady pace, alternately trotting and walking, they reached the Kentucky River bottoms before midnight. As Truscott expected, the Lawrenceburg bridge was protected by home guards. The riders had to detour and swim horses, losing almost an hour before they came out of the woods at Salvisa. There Truscott divided the party, he and five men taking one road, Sergeant Stiles and five men the other. He made certain there were riders

< **To Horse! To Horse! The Bugle Calls** >

in Stiles's detachment who knew the country. "In the event some of us become separated for any reason, we're heading for Heywood's Hundred. Across the Chaplin River ford. When you ride through the stone entranceway to the Hundred you'll see a thick growth of cedars. We'll rendezvous there at daylight or soon afterward."

First dawn caught Truscott's party at Beaver Creek, and he separated his riders into pairs, keeping a mile apart. They met two wagons, and a boy herding sheep, but there was no challenge or any indication of suspicion from any of them. Nevertheless, he was relieved to see that familiar landmark of his youth, the stone archway, shining almost white in the slant of morning sunlight.

From childhood Truscott had been familiar with the Heywoods. To him, the males were like Scottish chiefs, and he knew their pasts as well as he knew his own. When the first Heywood, Charles's grandfather, had come from Virginia, he built a blockhouse on that very spot of ground where the arch now stood. It was his first son, Edmund, known by Truscott's generation as Old Edmund, who built on the site of the blockhouse ruins the horseshoe arch of wedge-shaped limestone blocks. A mile back into the parklike woods Edmund Heywood then constructed the largest house in that part of Kentucky, eighteen rooms fronted with four Doric columns that supported upper and lower piazzas. He had brought in a wood-carver from Virginia to add the lacy balustrade, and then filled the rooms with furniture from Europe.

During his early youth Truscott spent many pleasant weekends there. Later the house became a headquarters for meetings of rival militia companies, with jousting tournaments, and picnics in the groves. But what he remembered with most pleasure were not the visits to what they all called the Big House, but rather to the more modest house known as Little Hundred.

As he waited in the cedar thicket for his men to gather for the first rendezvous, Truscott wondered if Little Hundred was still occupied, indeed if it was still standing after three years of passing armies. Little Hundred had been built by Old Edmund's younger brother, Samuel, a sad-faced aging man when Truscott first knew him. Only a few weeks before outbreak of the war, Samuel Heywood had fought a duel over some inconsequential precept. In proper Heywood fashion, Samuel slew his opponent with a well-

< CONSPIRACY OF KNAVES >

aimed ball, but in return had received a grievous wound in the abdomen. After lingering for several days, Samuel died in agony, leaving a forlorn wife, an inept son, a charming daughter, and several manumitted slaves.

It was the daughter, Marianna Heywood, who had drawn Truscott to Little Hundred in the carefree days of youth. Two years younger than he, she would be twenty now, he thought, married probably to some man unfit for military service. He remembered her quick way of moving, always rushing, running across the lawns, dancing on tiptoes, smiling teasingly, mischievously playing him against her cousin Charles. At the time he'd suspected that Charley was jealous; Charley never allowed Truscott or any other young man to be alone with Marianna if he could help it.

Without incident, the six riders in Truscott's party reached Heywood Hundred during the early morning and took cover in the cedars. Truscott ordered them to unsaddle and await Sergeant Stiles and the others. Then they could forage grain for the horses and food for themselves. All they had to eat was a few hard crackers taken from the home guards' camp at Mount Sterling, and some of the men were already beginning to nibble at them.

After an impatient wait of half an hour, Truscott heard the beat of trotting hooves on the road, and a few minutes later four riders appeared under the stone arch. He hurried to signal them in. Bringing up the rear was Sergeant Stiles. As soon as Stiles was into the cedar cover, he dismounted and approached Truscott, shaking his head. "Jack Nelson," he said, "tried to rob a hen house. The farmer caught him."

"Where's Shannon?" Truscott asked.

"Yes, sir, Alex Shannon was with him. Shannon got away, but I let him go back to see if Jack had talked his way loose, Jack not knowing exactly where Heywood Hundred is. The farmer rang a signal bell for home guards. Shannon wanted to see whether they'd be taking Jack to Bardstown or to Harrodsburg. Thought maybe he'd follow along and guide Jack in here if they turned him loose."

"Damn," Truscott said. "Nelson could've waited for his eggs till we rendezvoused."

Stiles shrugged. "You know Jack's nature, sir. One of the best, but always hungering for food and women."

Truscott smiled wryly. "Keep the men and horses quiet, sergeant, while I ride in search of breakfast for us all. If I'm not back in an hour, bring the men down that little sandy road there, ready for a fight."

A few minutes later, near the end of the sandy road, Truscott saw the two high chimneys of Little Hundred above a screen of trees, and then rode into the clearing. The house was still there, but the lawns that had once been kept so magnificently were overgrown with weeds. At first he saw no sign of life, but as the stables and tobacco sheds came into view he heard a ping of metal against metal and caught a flash of movement through a wide door. That would be the smithy, he remembered. He rode up cautiously, and as he was dismounting, a heavyset black man with a close-cropped gray frizz of hair appeared in the entrance. He was carrying a shotgun at the ready.

"Lijah," Truscott said quietly. "Remember me?"

The black man squinted hard at him, keeping the gun leveled. "Don't recollect," he replied.

"John Truscott. From other side Kentucky River."

The black man nodded, his teeth showing in a smile of relief. "Oh, yessir. Mr. Will Truscott's boy. Young Mr. Johnny." He let the gun down. "Used to come here for the sociables with Mr. Charley Heywood and the others."

"Good old times," Truscott said. "Are any of the Heywoods here now, Lijah?"

"What's left of 'em. Old Miz Heywood and Miss Marianna still here."

"Then I'll pay my respects," he said.

"Yessir. Just go and knock on side door. They keep front of house closed up. Boards rottin' through on front porch, and none to be found to take the'r place."

After hitching his horse to a pole above a water trough, Truscott slipped his carbine from its boot and followed the old moss-grown pathway. Marianna must have seen and recognized him through the window; the door swung open as he approached it, and she just stood there, on tiptoe like a bird preparing to soar, her arms opened wide, saying his name. He leaned the carbine against the doorframe and bowed to her before catching her by the shoulders while she hugged him and then kissed the side of his lips.

"Johnny," she whispered. "I thought I'd never see you again."

He had forgotten how fair and feminine she was, his Lady of Shalott. Her hair was golden in the morning light, and her violet-blue eyes were moist with emotion under her long black lashes. She drew away quickly, blushing, and stammered apologetically: "You think me too forward." Her manner changed abruptly. "It was not you in particular, Johnny. If you'd been any other young man of my acquaintance, I'd have greeted him the same. You have no idea how lonely we are back here."

He laughed. "You know that I think of you as one of my dearest friends, Marianna. And you're still the prettiest girl in Kentucky."

"Now it is you who are being forward," she said. "But Lord, how glad I am to see a familiar face. I've read every book in this house half a dozen times, and knitted hundreds of sweaters and stockings, but passage of time seems to do nothing to end this war and bring the living back home."

"Have the Federals bothered you?" he asked.

"No more than you Rebels," she retorted. "Seems like every time a body of soldiers comes near the Hundred, they stop to take something from us. But you're not wearing a uniform. Are you committing untellable deeds like cousin Charley?"

"Have you seen Charley?" When he asked the question, he felt a twinge of jealousy, and the old resentments of his youth rose up at her reply: "Charley visited one day last month. He was so weary he kept nodding while we talked."

"Yes, we both do most of our moving around by night, and then try to catch a few winks by day. Which brings me to ask you—how safe is Little Hundred? Do the home guards prowl around here?"

She shook her head. "Not unless they're in search of some fugitive. They used to come every day or so, knowing where the Heywood sympathies lie, and hoping to find us concealing escaped prisoners, I suppose."

"Can you hide a dozen mounted men till nightfall?"

Startled at first by the question, she remained silent for some moments, as though deliberating the risks. "In the stables or tobacco sheds, of course. There's hay in some of the stable lofts."

"We're provendered with hard biscuits only. If you're scarce of food that'll have to do."

< **To Horse! To Horse! The Bugle Calls** >

She gave him one of those impish grimaces he remembered from their childhood. "At Little Hundred," she replied teasingly, "we've learned the art of supporting beggars."

The awkwardness between them was now completely dispelled. She led him into the sewing room, where her mother sat in a shaft of warm sunlight that flooded the double window. The garden outside was an overgrown tangle of neglected flowers and shrubs. On the floor between Marianna's mother and the fireplace were several skeins of wool and silk.

Samuel Heywood's widow was one of many aged victims of the war, her spirit broken by painful and rapid changes, her memory bewildered, her body deteriorating rapidly. Truscott would not have known her, and evidently she was not certain who he was. At first she confused him with Charles Heywood, then with Truscott's dead father, and even with her ne'er-do-well son, who supposedly had fled to Missouri.

"Wesley's riding with Quantrill's guerrillas, we've been told," Marianna explained quietly.

The morning was advancing, and Truscott wanted to get his men into more secure cover, where they could rest through the day. Below the smithy was a row of empty stables in which horses and men could be concealed from view of any casual visitor, and he remembered a route of approach to them through woods and across a meadow.

After excusing himself, he returned to the cedar thicket, following the sandy road on which he had come to Little Hundred, leaving tracks to show that a single horseman had visited and departed from the house. Sergeant Stiles reported no sign of the missing Nelson and Shannon, but Truscott decided not to chance posting a man there to bring them in to Little Hundred in case they should appear. If the two men had not found each other, only Shannon knew the area, and he was clever enough to figure they would have sought cover at or near one of the houses.

Explaining why they would not ride to Little Hundred along the same road, Truscott scattered his men out through the woods. From long experience they knew how to pick ground surfaces that horses could tread upon without leaving a trace of their passage. By midmorning they were installed in the stables, guards posted, and Marianna, with Lijah and his wife, Cora, was bringing them

< CONSPIRACY OF KNAVES >

dishes and pans and pitchers filled with food and drink of the sort that none of them had tasted for many months.

Truscott returned to the house with Marianna, apologizing along the way for plundering Little Hundred's food supply. "I know the boys are death on milk," he said. "None of us has had a drop for weeks. I don't believe a cow survives in all of southwestern Virginia."

"Oh, bosh," she answered. "The two crocks of milk would've soured in the springhouse and Lijah would've fed them to his pigs."

He held the side door open for her. "Lijah and Cora, they're still loyal?"

She assured him they were like members of the family. Most of the other black freedmen had crossed into Indiana, a few returning to the Hundred to work tobacco for shares on Old Edmund's tilled acreage. Because almost all the horses had been impressed or stolen, there was little stable work to be done anymore.

When they entered the kitchen, his senses were pleasured by the aroma of smoked meat frying. She made him sit at the rough table while she piled a plate high with slices of ham and buttered muffins, apologizing because the dining hall was nailed shut. Her mother had ordered it done after she heard of soldiers raiding for silver and china in other houses in the county.

"I wouldn't trade this goblet of cool milk and that piggin of preserves for all the silver in Kentucky," he said.

She sat across from him, resting her chin in her hands, watching him silently for two or three minutes. "It's almost over, isn't it, Johnny?" she asked.

A shy, almost boyish look came over his face. "The war, you mean?" He swallowed a sip of the milk. "Charley thinks we have one more chance."

"Uncle Edmund says the South has gone up."

"Perhaps. Perhaps not. Does Old Edmund have any horses at all?"

"They left him one old mare to pull his buggy and a few mules for plowing and wagon work."

Truscott shook his head. "I was hoping I could trade him for fresh mounts before going on."

< **To Horse! To Horse! The Bugle Calls** >

Her violet eyes seemed to be probing his face for some revelation. "You're riding north again, aren't you?"

"You know I can't tell you that, Marianna."

She sighed. "Charles was more talkative than you. Something *is* happening up north in Illinois. I receive letters from the prisoners at Chicago, from some of the Morgan men who came from around here. They drop little hints."

"They should be more careful," Truscott said. "They must know their captors read what they write in their letters." He took a whole spoonful of peach preserves and let the sweet morsels melt slowly in his mouth. "Half of my old company is in that prison. How do you get letters to them?"

"We send knitted things through a Federal organization in Louisville. And the boys write back their thanks."

He finished the goblet of milk with a long audible breath of appreciation, but when she offered to refill it, he refused with thanks. "Noon is coming on, and I must sleep a few hours before nightfall. We have another long ride ahead of us."

He reached for his carbine and started to leave by the kitchen door, but she put a restraining hand on his arm. "Take Wesley's bed, Johnny. It'll be much more comfortable than stable hay."

"You're certain it's all right with Mrs. Heywood?"

She laughed. "Mama's fast asleep herself. You come on upstairs."

He was awakened abruptly by her hand gently touching his damp cheek and an urgency in her voice. "Johnny! One of your lost men has come in." With an effort, he pulled himself from a deep abyss of sleep and dreadful dreams. He had sweated his shirt, and he shivered involuntarily against its clamminess.

"Where?" he asked. "Who—"

"Says his name is Shannon. He's in the kitchen, wolfing food like a starving animal." She was suddenly contrite. "Oh, dear, I should have let you sleep and sent him out to the stables, shouldn't I?"

"No." Forgetting that he was wearing only his underdrawers, he flung his legs over the side of the bed. With no change of expression she handed him his trousers and left the room.

< CONSPIRACY OF KNAVES >

Private Alex Shannon, lanky and red-haired, was still eating when Truscott entered the kitchen, but he got to his feet quickly and began a rueful account of his recent adventures. He had followed the home guards and the captured Jack Nelson into Bardstown, hopeful that Nelson would be released there. Unfortunately, a Union sympathizer in Bardstown had recognized Shannon and was on the point of reporting him to the guards as a Morgan cavalryman when Shannon sensed the danger and beat a hasty retreat.

"They must've used the telegraph, Captain Truscott. No other way the soldiers at Bloomfield could've known I was coming through there. Anyway, they was waiting for me. If my horse wasn't a jumper, they'd've snared me there and then, but Blackie took me over a rail fence like a buck deer with shot in its ass. That gave me enough start to shake their heavy mounts."

"You sure?" Truscott demanded. He still felt muddled from interrupted sleep, and there was a note of exasperation in his voice. "You rode in here on the sand road, didn't you? If they trace you to the Hundred, they'll follow your tracks right down on us."

Shannon's sunburned face turned even redder. "I only did what I thought best, captain."

"All right." Truscott curtly motioned for him to follow out the side door. "Let's get you and your horse out of sight in the nearest stable."

Shannon's horse was lathered, caked with sweated dust, and still breathing hard. "Rub him down before you crawl into the loft," Truscott ordered in the chiding tone of a disappointed parent as he led the way into a stable adjoining the smithy. It was empty. The other men were farther down, a hundred yards from the house, with a double guard posted front and back. No straw was in the loft of the smithy stable, but two or three musty horse blankets hung on a wall. Truscott warned Shannon to stay inside. "And get some sleep. We'll be riding all night."

Marianna was waiting for him in the kitchen. "You look completely tuckered," she said sympathetically.

"Yes." He shook his head. "The boys are losing their sharp edge. Shannon knows better than he's been acting. He's getting careless like the rest of them, as if they don't care anymore."

She was studying his face again. "I wish you would all just

< **To Horse! To Horse! The Bugle Calls** >

come back home so things would be the way they were before the war."

He forced a smile, and then leaned down, wanting to kiss her hard on the mouth, but instead he took her hand and touched it with his lips. To him she was still the Lady of Shalott, robed in snowy white.

(Lord in Heaven, say what you will about Southern womanhood, Dixie belles, you know the sort I mean. If it were not for such romantic male fools as Johnny Truscott, the supply of silly Southern belles pretending helplessness would rapidly diminish. Should I ever return to the stage, I could play her part to perfection and make my audience die of laughter.)

"We'll be back," he promised her. "Maybe sooner than you expect, Marianna. Right now, would you do something for me? Seat yourself where you can see up the sand road, and wake me again if anyone approaches."

She nodded, and he went on up the stairway, his legs heavy with weariness, and fell upon the bed.

He was having difficulty crossing that mysterious threshold between consciousness and sleep when he heard the first sounds— leather and metal sounds, a distant brushing tonality, a cadence that could be nothing else but mounted men moving together across soft earth.

In an instant he was on his feet and into his trousers and boots, and reaching for his carbine. At the same time, he heard Marianna's rapid footsteps on the hall flooring, and when he opened the door he saw the fear and excitement in her eyes. She motioned for him to follow into her room. From the window he sighted a line of blue and brown moving slowly out of the woods, a column of twos.

"Regular Union Cavalry," he said half aloud. "Not home guards." He drew in his breath. "I must warn Shannon." He knew that the big house would screen the smithy and stables from the riders' view until the column was halfway across the open space.

He had about ten minutes to cross to the building where Shannon was. "Where're Lijah and Cora?" he asked quickly.

"Likely in their cottage out back."

"Let's hope they stay there." He caught her by the shoulders.

< CONSPIRACY OF KNAVES >

"Look, will you try to divert the Federals? Wait until they ride up to the smithy, then step outside and act agitated at sight of them."

"I won't have to act," she said.

"Should they ask you if a horseman came in here, tell them you were busy sewing upstairs, or something. Now I must run."

As he hurried across to the smithy stable, he heard the cavalrymen's voices, diffused, from the front of the house. He noted that the guard who had been posted in front of the farther stables had taken cover inside and was probably awakening Sergeant Stiles and the others. The silence from there was complete, but Truscott knew that a nickering horse could give them away in a second.

He found Shannon already half asleep, rolled in a blanket on the boards, and warned him of the approaching enemy. "If they paid any attention to your tracks, they know you're here somewhere. Whatever the reason, they're coming in. We have to distract them from going on to the lower stables."

"How?" Shannon asked.

"You can walk out of here and give yourself up."

"No! They would as soon shoot me for a spy."

"Tell them you deserted from Morgan's command in Lexington. That you're trying to find your way home."

Shannon laughed. "Lexington is where my pa lives."

"You couldn't find him. Thought he'd moved to Shepherdsville or somewhere. Look, here they come."

The column coiled around the elms at the side of the house and moved on toward the smithy. Loud commands echoed between the buildings. Through a narrow slit in the stable loft, Truscott and Shannon watched them; there were about forty men, two platoons, a captain in the lead with a sergeant and guidon bearer, their blue uniforms bright with newness.

"They look untried," Truscott said.

"Unlicked like fresh-born colts," Shannon agreed. "I make out Ohio on that guidon."

"Let's hope their captain is an old hand," Truscott said. "Not so keen on following the book."

Marianna was outside the kitchen door now, one hand on her forehead, the other across her breast. Truscott wondered if she might be overdoing it. The Union captain dismounted, and walked with a pronounced limp that Truscott hoped was an indication he had been seasoned with a battle wound. He was saying something to Marianna, his attitude one of politeness. She was shaking her head, the captain turning half around and shouting back to the sergeant.

"Go out now, Shannon, and surrender," Truscott ordered. "Hurry, before he starts a search all around."

"Here goes my neck," Shannon answered, and dropped down into the stable.

"Remember, you're a Confederate deserter."

"They know Morgan men don't desert," Shannon retorted. He pushed the stable door open, and lifted his hands in surrender.

Through the slit in the loft wall, Truscott watched the Ohio captain's head tilt back in surprise. The officer waited until Shannon was within ten paces, and then called to him to halt. Truscott could not hear what either of them was saying, but the captain motioned to his sergeant, who sent two men hurrying toward the stable with rifles at the ready.

Against such odds Truscott had no intention of resisting, but in hopes of avoiding discovery he lay down and flattened himself into the shadows against the loft wall. "Here's his horse," he heard a nasal voice say matter-of-factly. Neither soldier bothered to climb the loft ladder. They led Shannon's horse outside, and a minute or so later Truscott heard the Union captain speaking courteously to Marianna. Familiar cavalry commands followed, and the column began wheeling back toward the sand road.

Truscott slept fitfully into the late afternoon. Pursued by dragon demons, he fled to a green river and leaped into a flower-bedecked boat. He could not see her, but Marianna's voice was repeating over and over:

> *The knights came riding two and two;*
> *She hath no loyal knight and true,*
> *The Lady of Shalott.*

He heard music of a sort then, so shrill that it woke him. A cardinal was singing sforzando notes on an elm limb not two feet from the open window. When Truscott raised himself out of bed,

< CONSPIRACY OF KNAVES >

the bird flew away. The light outside was turning the color of cinnamon. Darkness was less than an hour away.

As he went down the stairs, he was met by multivaried red-olences of cooking. Steamy soup smells and baking fragrances mingled with spices. The kitchen table was filled with pies, and Marianna was placing dishes around the edges of it. Cora grinned at him from the big stove, where she was stirring something in a huge black pot.

"Glory," he said. "Fit for kings. But you must not deprive yourselves, Marianna. *Pies* for my alligator horses?"

"Hush. We've got a lot of put-up cherries, more than we can use. I want all your boys to come in here and enjoy a sit-down dinner."

"They won't know how to behave."

In spite of the urgency of rushing time, however, the alligator horses comported themselves like gentlemen. Only occasionally did some of them forget and laugh too loudly during the dinner. They had grown unused to dining at table under a roof, with females watching and listening.

At duskfall Truscott had to remind them that they must saddle and ride, and as they filed out the kitchen door, each man thanked Marianna and Cora with phrases ornate and almost forgotten after three years of living in a masculine world of battles and raids and encampments.

He hated the thought of saying good-bye to Marianna and Little Hundred—the lost world of his youth—and he tried to avoid the pain by quickly following the last man out the side door. But she would not have it. "Johnny, wait." She clung to his arm, her upturned face lit by reflections thrown upon the ceiling from a grate of the cooking stove. Her cheeks were crimson from warmth and excitement. The first freckles of summer were beginning to show in her translucent skin, and tiny beads of perspiration had formed on her forehead, a forehead shaped almost exactly like Charley's—the Heywood forehead, they used to say. Truscott re-membered how desperately both of them, Marianna and Charley, hated being freckled, how they were forever wearing scarves and wide-brimmed hats to shut away sunlight; yet no matter the care they took, no sooner did they venture into summer light than freckles would dapple their skins in random polka dots.

The Lady of Shalott took a pair of scissors from an apron
pocket. "I want a lock of your hair," she said. "I don't want one
sent to me from some distant field of battle like poor Isabella. Cut
from her dead husband's head at Vicksburg by her brother. You
remember Isabella Frazier at Fairfield? She'd been wed only three
months." Her fingers touched his ear and he heard the scissors
snip.

"I'm surprised you are still unwed," he said.

"Posh, I'll marry no soldier, nor old man," she replied. "Rather
be a spinster."

(Marianna Heywood was no fool, I'll say that for her; but if Johnny
Truscott's head had not been filled with such romantic notions, he
could have had her then, and not spent all those months in Canada
pining for his lost love.)

He pushed the flat-crowned hat down tight on his head, and then
bowed and kissed her hand exactly the way he had done mockingly
in years past when they were at children's play. But the Lady of
Shalott wanted a lover's kiss, and he gave her one. "Stay, stay,"
she whispered then. "Don't go, Johnny. Stay with me."

He pulled away from her and went out into the darkness,
wondering why it was he always feared rejection from her, had
always felt the presence of "Cousin Charley" between them. And
he was still not free of Charley's intrusion. She had said: *It was
not you in particular, Johnny. If you'd been any other young man
of my acquaintance, I'd have greeted him the same.* Who else
besides Charley? he wondered; yet he could still treasure the im-
perativeness of the lover's kiss.

That night they rode into the brushwood thickets of Muldraugh's
Hill, using one of the same narrow trails that Truscott's company
of cavalry had followed on Morgan's Christmas raid a year and a
half past. They had ridden out of their Tennessee winter camp, a
hard seven days' march, to burn the trestles of the Louisville and
Nashville Railroad and thus cut supplies to the Yankee general,
Rosecrans. For that raid, General Morgan's regiments were at their
glorious peak, four thousand men with plumes in their hats and
mounted on the finest Kentucky horseflesh.

< CONSPIRACY OF KNAVES >

Truscott remembered vividly the icy rain falling incessantly, and how they had driven the bridge defenders out of their cozy stockade with the heavy shells of a captured Parrott gun.

Around daylight Sergeant Stiles, who was riding in advance, came back to report an abandoned farm, so long uninhabited that little remained of it except a rail fence adjoining a coppice thick enough to conceal the presence of men and horses. When Truscott reached the place, he found dew on the grass shining like frost in the slant of morning sun rays. As soon as guards were posted, he unrolled his blanket in an angle of the rail fence and slept so soundly that when the heat and brightness of the early afternoon sun awoke him, he could not believe so many hours had passed.

At dusk they resumed the journey, with Stiles well forward again, and two other riders far out on the flanks. When a bank of clouds moved from the west to obscure the stars, darkness became so intense that Stiles used their old nighthawk signal to rejoin the squad. He'd found a crib filled with corn, provender that was essential to both beasts and men. Truscott brought in the flankers, and Stiles led them to the edge of a clearing. Dim candlelight showed in two windows of a farmhouse.

"We'll wait till they go to bed," Truscott said. Grain fed, the horses should make up most of the lost time. "Are you certain they have no dogs?" he asked Stiles.

"Not outside, I'll wager." Stiles sat down with his back against a tree. "Have you noticed, captain, how few dogs are left in the South? If the war don't finish up, they may all be gone soon."

"The Indiana farms sure had plenty dogs last summer," Truscott said.

"Yeah. Barkin' and bitin' against us Rebs." Stiles raised his head. "You've never said much about where we're headin', sir. The hills around here remind me of the way General Morgan took us to Brandenburg for the big crossing last summer. We goin' to cross the river again?"

"Farther west," Truscott replied. "If we cross at all. Depends on the smell of things."

"Scaredest I ever been was when we had to swim back across at Buffington Island. I come near drownin'. I wasn't scared goin'

< **To Horse! To Horse! The Bugle Calls** >

over at Brandenburg, though. Especially after we captured the two steamboats, smooth as you please—you recall, captain?"

Truscott recalled silently that Brandenburg was the last place he'd seen Major Charles Heywood. In an attitude of acute boredom, Charley was leaning against a wharf boat at the Brandenburg landing. His melancholy face brightened at first sight of Truscott, and then he acted as if he were responsible for the whole invasion, as if he had arranged everything, and perhaps he had. When Morgan rode down the slope and dismounted, the general deferred to Charley, listening without a challenge to Charley's recital of the ease with which Morgan's cavalry regiments could sweep through Indiana and across Ohio, aided along the way by countless Copperheads eager to see an ending to the war. "How many will help us?" Morgan finally had asked. "Hundreds and hundreds," Charley answered. "Thousands."

During the nineteen days of the raid, Truscott had seen only one Copperhead, a man who assisted in the thievery of a horse. And during the disaster at Buffington Island, east of Cincinnati, he had wondered where Charley's hundreds and thousands of Copperheads had disappeared to. He'd not seen Charley since, but he'd heard later from others that Major Heywood offered a justification for the Copperheads' absence: Morgan's cavalry had simply moved too fast. The Copperheads were always left far in the rear, Charley explained, the Confederate columns racing ahead of them while they were attempting to organize their forces.

And now Charley had a new scheme in play with the Copperheads north of the Ohio, in Illinois this time. Whether things would be different was doubtful in Truscott's opinion, yet anything was worth a try at freeing the Morgan men in Camp Douglas. "But how far can you trust a Copperhead?" he muttered aloud.

"What was it you said, sir?" Stiles asked politely.

"Nothing." One of the pale lights in the farmhouse vanished. "Looks as if they're going to bed."

"Yes, sir. There went the other candle."

They waited for a few more minutes, and then Truscott led six men carefully across a freshly plowed field to the corncrib. As silently as possible they loaded saddlebags and tow sacks with corn ears, and then returned to their horses.

< CONSPIRACY OF KNAVES >

Leaving the undulating high ground near the river, they turned straight westward, following lonely roads through thinly settled country. They covered far more miles than on the previous night journeys. Near daylight a brief shower warned them they might need some kind of shelter for the day's rest, and in the sudden darkness under the rain clouds, Truscott came near being thrown from his saddle when a low-hanging wild grapevine caught him across the forehead. He had to dismount to retrieve his hat, and he decided to halt the squad under the thick-foliaged trees and use the rest time to assess conditions of men and horses.

Aside from a few bites from ticks they must have acquired during the day's bivouac, the Kentucky boys were in their usual state of hardiness. Some of their horses were beginning to fail, however, and trades would soon have to be made, by impressment or by stealth.

For another hour they rode slowly onward. The sprinkle of rain ceased; a gray dawnlight matched the coloration of the breaking clouds. The trail they were following narrowed into a seldom used approach to the river. The Ohio had made its big bend northward and back again, and they were in what had been land-pirate country only a generation past—where innocent river travelers bound downstream for the Mississippi frequently became victims of ruthless predators, the worst of whom made their headquarters on the river's bank at Cave in Rock.

In a badland of limestone and rank vegetation, Sergeant Stiles found a half cave, and there they stopped for the day, the location so remote from settlements that Truscott ordered fires built for cooking. They boiled and baked corn ears, mixed hardtack with hot water, and rationed what remained of the "Lincoln coffee" captured from the Federals at Mount Sterling.

Early on the morning of the following day, the map that Hatfield had left with Judge Yancey told Truscott they were nearing the first rendezvous. The dark sky was graying when he sighted the place. Raven's Head was the name Hatfield had lettered on his map. Although there was no road marker, a crude sign above the largest structure spelled out RAVEN'S HEAD STABLES. FARRIER & CHAIN MAKER.

(Months later, when Johnny Truscott told me about this, I recalled Raven's Head from my childhood. My mother had relatives, cousins and aunts, living near there, and one summer she decided to pay them a visit, taking me along. We traveled by steamboat from Louisville. I delighted in the journey, but from the moment we arrived at the river landing at Raven's Head until we departed a week later, I was in a state of unease. There was something sinister about that place. Perhaps I was too young to define the dark mystery that I imagined, but I sensed a derangement in the atmosphere, a strangeness among the people, even among my mother's relatives. The fog and mists that shrouded our bedroom window almost every morning accentuated the threat of evil.)

Truscott had a similar feeling when he approached Raven's Head. As he and his men rode closer, the sounds of boats puffing in the river mingled with early morning bird chatter and the distant braying of a donkey. No dwellings seemed to exist in Raven's Head, only the long livery stable with a two-story grogshop attached. Alongside the grogshop the road angled sharply to the right and dropped precipitately toward the river, vanishing in a layer of thick fog. Somewhere below the rolling gray mist a steamboat whistle hooted uncertainly.

Truscott ordered Sergeant Stiles to get the men off the road and into woods cover, and then he rode slowly on alone. He dismounted and hitched his horse at a watering trough. From a half-opened door came the scent of saged sausages frying, and for the first time since leaving Little Hundred he felt acute hunger pangs.

"Hello, hello," he called out as he rapped on the doorframe.

"Come in," a hoarse voice replied.

Truscott pushed the door open and faced a man with a mass of uncombed graying hair who was regarding him with a querulous stare. The man was seated at a table upon which were the shell remains of half a dozen boiled eggs, and he was in the process of cracking another with a large-bladed hunting knife.

"My name's Truscott. Horse buyer. I'm looking for a stockman who lives across the river, somewhere in these parts. Name of Hatfield."

The gray-haired man hurriedly got to his feet, crossing both arms over his chest as he did so, and turning his head first to the

< CONSPIRACY OF KNAVES >

left and then to the right. "Who cometh?" he then recited in his hoarse voice. "Stranger, advance and declare thy way and purpose."

Believing the man to be at least half mad, Truscott waited patiently for a few moments before trying again to explain his purpose. "I've been told that Mr. Hatfield has horses for sale. Do you know him? Hatfield?"

With his right arm the supposed madman gestured toward the wall behind him. A large five-pointed silver star set in a square frame was the wall's only adornment. "Hath thee a sign?"

When Truscott shook his head, the interrogator continued: "Hath thee a password?"

"No. I was given no password."

"Hath thee the watchword?"

Truscott realized then for the first time that he had fallen into the incantations of a Copperhead secret society, and he was also rapidly losing his patience. "All I have is a map," he retorted, "drawn by Mr. Hatfield." He added forcefully: "If you don't know Hatfield, I'll be on my way."

"Brother, thy way hast been lost. Danger lies at thine every step." He motioned to a frazzled cane-bottomed chair. "Wait there until I return." With the quickness of a young man, the gray-haired Knight of the Golden Circle vanished through a side door, and somewhere beyond it another door opened and closed. Truscott started to sit down, but thought better of it and was considering immediate departure when he heard voices, first from outside the door he had entered and then from the inner rooms. The voices were all masculine, with overtones of excitement. The next sound was a concerted clicking of cocked weapons, and when Truscott whirled around he faced two men with pistols drawn on him, and beyond them, outside the door, were two additional ruffians armed with rifles. Standing in the doorways on either side of him were more armed brigands. The old gray-haired madman advanced unarmed, his yellow-stained teeth showing in a smile of triumph. "Now, stranger, let us have a look at that map you say Phil Hatfield drew for you."

6

BELLE RUTLEDGE

WHILE CAPTAIN TRUSCOTT and his little band of knights were scrambling around somewhere along the lower Ohio River, I was making my departure from Richmond down the James River. Just about sunrise, Major Heywood called for me at the Ballard House and carried my portmanteau out to a dilapidated one-horse carriage driven by an aged black coachman. Seated beside the driver was a six-year-old imp with a mop of hair like yellow wheat. He was very sleepy and was muttering crossly to the world.

After helping me into the ragged seat, Heywood, with a whoop, lifted the little boy into his lap and tried to bounce him into a more cheerful mood, but the youngster responded with a single word so profane it is never used in proper society. Heywood laughed loudly and I pretended I had not heard. "This is Master Winslow Barber," Heywood shouted, and then as the carriage began rolling away he added softly: "And I am Dr. Campbell of Detroit, Michigan, and you are my wife, Grace."

I think I managed a smile at the major's high spirits, but I must have been as sleepy as the child. During the previous evening I'd visited Pizzini's Confectionery twice more, hoping to see my little silver-haired friend, but was unsuccessful in finding him. These efforts put me to bed quite late, and then during the remainder of the night I'd slept fitfully. Naturally, I was on edge about our journey and destination, wondering whether our course would take us to or near Washington, and what dangers might lie ahead of me.

"Where are we going, Dr. Campbell?" I asked the major, using a bold manner of speaking that I had perfected after long practice on the stage.

"Home to Michigan, of course, dear Grace," he replied, with a teasing note in his voice that aroused my ire.

"I have the right to know by what means," I insisted.

He patted my hand, the way an affectionate husband would. "Yes, of course. Downriver on a truce boat to City Point. There we'll transfer to a Union vessel that will take us to Baltimore. From Baltimore—"

The imp interrupted with a loud yowl from its unusually wide mouth, complaining of hunger.

"Good Lord," Heywood said. "I forgot to feed the little creature."

"From Baltimore," I reminded him, "where to? Direct to Cincinnati and Chicago?"

His blue eyes showed his annoyance, either at my question or the wailing child, or perhaps both. "Heaven knows," he said impatiently.

Whether or not he meant to tell me our route and ultimate destination before the child's interruption, or whether he truly did not know, I could only guess. "To Washington?" I dared to ask.

"Washington? Why to Washington?" There was a sudden wariness in his voice and attitude.

I pretended that my feelings were hurt. "If I'm to work with you," I said with forced petulance, "I need to know what to expect."

By this time the carriage was rolling noisily upon the wooden boards of the James River landing. A boat carrying three masts and a slanted smokestack was docked with its loading plank in place. From the forward mast a large white truce flag flapped idly in the slight morning breeze.

"You take the little elf," Heywood said, handing the squalling child over to me.

"Stop the carriage," I replied. "Over there is a boat-supply store. They must have something the boy can eat."

After we stopped, I led Master Winslow Barber into the store, hoping to find sweetmeats of some sort, but the best they could

< **Belle Rutledge** >

offer was an assortment of stale tea cakes. Using the last of my Confederate money, I bought the lot of them, as well as a loaf of dark bread that must have acquired its color from age rather than its ingredients.

The boat we boarded was called the *Chantilly*, and everything about it bore an atmosphere of weariness and decay. At our approach, a lanky gentleman wearing a captain's cap arose from his deck stool and, with an air of deep melancholy, waited for Major Heywood to present our passage papers. For a minute or so, the captain puzzled over the boy's transfer. "You are going to Michigan but the child only to Cincinnati?" he asked, somewhat puzzled. Heywood explained that we were acting only as temporary guardians for an orphan. The captain nodded vaguely and handed the papers back.

"Do you have a cabin?" Heywood asked him. "For my wife and the little boy?"

The captain gave the major a surly glance. "I have only two fit cabins. One is mine. The other, poorly furnished, is sometimes used for wounded." He turned his head at the sound of wagon wheels on the rough planking. "There come the ambulances now."

The ambulances were bringing about a dozen Yankee prisoners who were to be exchanged for wounded Confederates at City Point. At that stage of the war, only the most severely disabled prisoners could be exchanged, General Grant having instituted a policy of no exchanges early in the year, believing this would shorten the war. The Confederacy suffered not only from a shortage of manpower; many more of its soldiers had been captured than it had Union captives to exchange for them.

This situation should offer my readers some rational grounds for Captain Truscott's and Major Heywood's willingness to risk their lives in a conspiracy with Copperheads to free their former comrades from Camp Douglas in Chicago. As anyone who has been reading the newspapers must know, Heywood wanted to go even further and seize Chicago and establish a Confederacy of Northwestern States.

I felt a profound pity for the Yankee prisoners leaving the ambulances. Certainly none of them would ever be uniformed for battle again. Those who had not lost arms or legs, or their eyesight, had been so debilitated by wounds and imprisonment that they

< CONSPIRACY OF KNAVES >

were little more than walking skeletons. One man had to be carried upon a litter. He had lost both legs, but his young teen-aged face brightened with cheerful smiles as he was brought aboard the *Chantilly*. "I'm going home," he announced joyfully to all within sound of his voice. "At last, I'm going home."

While I was observing this tragic show, Major Heywood vanished with little Winslow down the nearest companionway. I followed and found the major silently fuming inside a poorly furnished stateroom. "Damn," he said. "I had no warning from Colonel Fennell about this exchange of hospitalized prisoners. Some of them may've been patients of the real Dr. Campbell."

I confessed that I had not thought of this possibility, but tried to reassure the major by telling him that all the exchange prisoners were being made comfortable in the morning sunshine on deck, and none appeared likely to descend the steps to the cabin quarters.

"Nonetheless," he growled, "I am made a prisoner down here. You go up and inform the captain that I'm indisposed with a severe malarial attack. I don't want anyone calling on 'Dr. Campbell' to give aid to some suddenly ailing exchange prisoner who might expose me as a fraud."

I reminded him that Grace Campbell had served as a nurse in the Richmond prison hospitals.

"Fennell said she was only an *occasional* nurse," the major replied. "Go on up and give the good captain a convincing account of my chills and fever. And take the papoose with you."

Winslow was jumping up and down upon a brown-stained mattress, trying to reach enough height to see out the square of window above the bunk. When I took his hand he resisted vigorously, and as I lifted him down he kicked me sharply in the abdomen with his rawhide shoes.

"Lord!" I cried, "what a handful you are!" and set him down with such force on the cabin flooring that he burst into tears, melting my heart, as perhaps he well meant to do. I was simply not accustomed to younglings and their devious tricks and stratagems.

On deck again, and with a good grip on Winslow's hand, I found the exchange prisoners arrayed in chairs, except for the one on the litter. A chaplain in Confederate uniform and a sad-faced sergeant with a carbine slung carelessly over his shoulder were the

< **Belle Rutledge** >

sole guards, and they both nodded politely to me as I appeared from the companionway with my charge.

Although I was wearing the plainest of dresses, black alpaca, and had left my face free of any false colors, I was immediately aware that the eyes of almost every male on that deck were directed toward me. Had I been upon a lighted stage, this rapt attention would have pleased me, but under the particular circumstances of the occasion I felt embarrassed, being quite certain that the same gaping stares would have been fixed upon almost any other female on earth had she been in my situation.

Noting the captain standing on the bow, I went directly to him and related the little falsehood about my husband's sudden attack of malarial fever that kept him confined to the cabin below. The profession of spying, as you may have guessed, requires the telling of many untruths, and because it has always been painful for me to lie, if I had not been an actress I am certain I could never have convinced a single listener to my webs of deceit.

The captain may or may not have believed my story. He expressed his sympathies, but he was probably only dissembling. In a sour tone of voice he muttered something about my husband being fortunate that he would be able to obtain plenty of quinine when he reached the North, and then he turned his attention from me as the *Chantilly* pulled away from the wharf and moved easily into the current of the James. From his first meeting with us, the captain had made no effort to conceal his disdain for Yankees, whom he believed us to be.

My bugbear Winslow was struggling to free himself from my grip and clamber upon the boat's railing for a perilous view of the passing scene of Richmond's waterfront. Keeping a firm hold on his squirming body, I held him up so that he could see the curving splash of water made by the boat's prow. He was a heavy little demon, and I was immensely pleased when the graybeard chaplain approached us and offered to relieve me of my burden.

"Ma'am," he added, "the lad on the litter asked if I thought you might be willing to speak with him." I glanced toward the poor wretch who lay flat on the deck with one blanket drawn over his mutilated body, another folded beneath his head.

I agreed to visit with him, of course. To be shed of Winslow for a few minutes, I would have been willing to talk with the devil.

< CONSPIRACY OF KNAVES >

As it turned out, the legless young man was of a cheerful and charming disposition. His home was somewhere in Massachusetts, and he had the true Yankee pattern of speech. He said that I reminded him of his older sister, and asked for my name and where I was from.

"I am Mrs. Campbell," I replied cautiously, "returning home to Michigan."

"Campbell, Campbell," he repeated, squinting his eyes against the sun. "Oh, yes, the surgeon who attended me in that church hospital while my stumps were healing, he was a Dr. Campbell. A Union man, too. Is he your husband by any chance?"

I knew at once that I must lie one way or the other, and no matter which course I took, it would place Major Heywood and me in jeopardy. I decided to continue with the elaborate fabrication we were traveling under.

"My husband is a physician," I said calmly. "Perhaps he attended you." Before the young man could continue his unintentional exposure of our deception, I added quickly: "Excuse me, but I must see to my little boy."

"Thank you, ma'am," he said. "Just talking with you and holding your hand has done me a world of good."

I hurried away toward the chaplain and Winslow, and found each enjoying the company of the other. "Please excuse me for a moment," I repeated to the chaplain, "while I look after my ailing husband." As hastily as I could, I descended the companionway to find Major Heywood reclining on the old mattress and smoking one of his long cheroots. "Sick men don't smoke cigars," I whispered angrily, and then told him of my conversation with the legless exchange prisoner.

He tossed his cigar through the open window into the river and swore under his breath. "Damnation. I daren't let that fellow see me as Dr. Campbell. I was afraid of something like this. Colonel Fennell should've been more careful."

"He can't foresee everything," I said.

"No. But this mission of all missions. My reaching Ohio safely and speedily is absolutely essential."

I spent the next two or three hours leading Winslow around and around the deck, going up and down the companionway, occasionally calling a greeting to the old chaplain or to the legless

< **Belle Rutledge** >

young man, and then descending again to listen to the subdued grumbling of the frustrated Major Heywood. At midday the *Chantilly*'s cook provided the prisoners and us with plain fare—a bowl of gruel, a bit of fried fish, and some overcooked squash. I carried the major's portion down to him. He dutifully left most of it on his plate, as a sick man would, but he took generous bites from my plate. Luckily I had that loaf of dark bread for dipping into the gruel.

In the afternoon, as we neared City Point, activity increased considerably along the river. We saw many small boats loaded with blue-clad soldiers crossing to the Petersburg side of the James— reinforcements for General Grant's army. The river had numerous bends in it now, and here and there the banks were clad in vines, some with yellow blossoms that filled the air with a sweetish perfume. Just after we rounded the last big bend in the river, a monstrous ironclad with slanting sides came into view. Its whistle sounded an imperative hoot, and our pilot turned the *Chantilly* toward the right bank. There, under a shelter beside a crude landing made of logs, stood a boat's crew in Union Navy uniforms. As soon as a plank was put out, the Confederate crew disembarked and the Union crew came smartly aboard.

The reason for this, as I learned later, was that the Confederate Army no longer held City Point. Earlier in the war the Rebels had used the little river port as a busy prisoner-exchange station, but after the Federals seized the place in the spring it was converted into an ordnance depot. A few days before Major Heywood and I began our journey down the river, Confederate saboteurs blew up one of the Union ordnance barges at City Point. After that incident, crews of truce boats from Richmond were forbidden to come within sight of the port. When Major Heywood explained all this to me afterward, he claimed that the explosion plot was hatched in Colonel Fennell's office and that the man who made the bomb was a friend of his from Kentucky. The facts of this incident I cannot vouch for. Heywood was generally a truthful man, but given to boasting, and as I have said before, spies habitually tell many untruths.

The Union naval officer who took command of the *Chantilly* was much more thorough in checking our travel papers than the Con-

< CONSPIRACY OF KNAVES >

federate captain had been. After questioning me at length about my reasons for being in Richmond, why I was returning to Michigan, and my tenuous relationship to Master Winslow Barber, the officer started to descend to the cabin deck. When I moved as if to follow him, he politely ordered me to remain where I was. I guessed that he would try to lead Major Heywood into some discrepancy from the story I had told, but apparently the major convinced him that we were Dr. Campbell and wife, as our false papers described us. At any rate, the Union commander was friendly enough to me and little Winslow during the short time that passed before we reached City Point.

Here the river widened considerably, and except for the cedar-clad bluff above the wharves, earth and water formed a flat landscape. A breeze brought faint scents of salt sea and fish. Sailing ships, steamships, ironclads, a vast assemblage of vessels—some in motion, some anchored or lashed to the docks—filled the curve of harbor. Like spokes of a wheel, long piers built of new yellow lumber jutted from the high ground across mud flats to the deeper water of the river. With a clanging of bells, the *Chantilly* was guided expertly alongside one of these wooden platforms.

In a few minutes ambulances appeared, and the Union exchange prisoners prepared to disembark. Winslow was quite curious about all the hustle and bustle ashore, and we were standing at the railing watching a freight train puffing slowly in and out of sight behind warehouses that, like the piers, had been very recently built of freshly sawn boards.

"Mrs. Campbell," a low masculine voice called behind me, and then repeated the name before I remembered he was speaking to me. I turned quickly to face the Union officer in command. "Yes," I replied as calmly as I could.

"The young man on the litter," he said, "has asked if you would be kind enough to accompany him to the hospital. It is only a short distance up the rise." He pointed to a row of tents and brushwood arbors along the top of a low bluff.

Although my suspicions were immediately aroused—all spies are wary of the unexpected—my first thought was that if I bluntly refused, I would most certainly cause him to distrust me. "Yes, I would do so gladly," I told him, "but my husband and I are to board a boat here for Baltimore."

< **Belle Rutledge** >

He smiled and motioned to an adjoining pier, where a gang of workmen was unloading crates and bags from a large side-wheeler. "We're putting you and Dr. Campbell aboard that fast commissary steamer. But it won't be leaving for at least two hours. If you'll help us with that legless young man—he's terribly disheartened that he must spend more time here until he's assigned to a hospital ship going north. Poor fellow had tears in his eyes talking with me just now. Says you remind him of his sister."

"I'll inform my husband," I said hesitantly. "And take the little boy down to him."

"Allow me to make the explanations to Dr. Campbell," the commander replied with a nod of thanks. "The ambulances are almost ready to go." He reached for Winslow's hand. "I'll look after the laddie," he promised.

Something did not seem quite right about this sudden development that would separate me from Major Heywood. Yet the Union naval officer's voice and manner were forthright enough. Perhaps I had been around actors and spies so long I was beginning to distrust everyone's outward display of identity and motives.

Humidity was heavy in the June afternoon, and the canvas sides of the ambulance wagons were rolled up to allow air to flow upon the convalescents. I took a seat beside the young man and tried to cool his face with my ivory fan. His fingers gripped my free hand tightly, and he smiled his gratitude.

We rode through a commotion of vehicles, soldiers, and workmen, past tents, new buildings, heaps of wooden boxes, and parks of cannon. The profusion was in sharp contrast to the shortages of Richmond, and I saw little hope for the Confederacy's future here.

When we reached the top of the bluff, a sudden breeze set the ribbons of my bonnet to flying. Refreshing though it was, the moving air was weighted with those hospital odors I'd never grown accustomed to in Richmond—strong antiseptics barely cloaking the stench of mortifying flesh. Suddenly I hated it all—the unceasing months of mutilation and death, the corruption of human spirits, the roles in which I had allowed myself to be cast in this too real macabre drama.

Our sudden arrival at the hospital area drove those unwelcome thoughts from my mind. They were replaced by a realization that

< CONSPIRACY OF KNAVES >

I was on soil held by the United States and that my absence from the *Chantilly* and Major Heywood offered an opportunity to attempt communication with Washington. I think it may have been a glimpse, beneath an open tent, of a battered field desk piled high with medical forms and other papers that brought this awareness to mind.

Orderlies, many of whom appeared to be convalescents themselves, surrounded the ambulances to assist new arrivals. One of them shyly held me by the arm as I stepped down. He assumed that I was a relative of the legless young man. I asked him if letters could be sent directly to Washington, and he assured me that a military mail boat departed every morning. Consequently, I wasted no time in requesting permission from one of the surgeons to pen a short note, which I sealed into one of his small official envelopes and addressed to my patron in Washington. The note was composed with care so as to reveal little or nothing to anyone who might read it either by chance or purposely. You see, I was still suspicious of the casual yet almost contrived way in which I was given an opportunity to be separated from Major Heywood.

An hour or so later we were aboard the army commissary boat bound for the estuary of the James, the entrance to Chesapeake Bay, and then Baltimore. Apparently we were the only passengers aboard. Little Winslow and I were put into one cabin, and Major Heywood shared with one of the boat's minor officers, a Portuguese who spoke only a few words of English.

I saw very little of anyone on the voyage. The waters of the lower bay were rolling quite vigorously and the boat was running light without cargo, so that the constant pitching put me into a very queasy state. Like so many clever younglings, Winslow sensed my temporary weakness and took advantage of it, using his vocal cords and mobility to irritate my nerves and provoke my temper. Every time Major Heywood looked in on us, the little demon would utter one of those vile oaths he'd learned somewhere, causing the major to break into explosive laughter.

"Don't speak so," I shouted at Winslow more than once, "at least not in the presence of your elders!"

My warnings, however, had no effect, until eventually I forbade the major ever to laugh again at any scabrous outburst from the incorrigible imp. Being an actress, I knew that Winslow re-

quired an appreciative audience for his peccadilloes. The major
saw my point and agreed to cooperate, but he could not always
restrain himself.

Because I was unable to join the other diners, I knew nothing
firsthand about the quality of the meals served aboard the commissary boat. Major Heywood said the food was only tolerable,
but Winslow, who in his recent life must have been unused to
anything other than the commonest of fare, recited to me the dishes
he had enjoyed, describing them in childish detail until my poor
stomach heaved and my head throbbed in agony.

Never was I so happy as at that moment when I stepped upon
a cobbled quay in Baltimore and felt the steadiness of solid land
beneath me. The major had his papers ready and our luggage
assembled for inspection, but after a few minutes' wait, we realized
that no one was interested in our arrival. We did form a rather
drab trio. Heywood was still wearing his plain black physician's
suit, which had rumpled badly, and even his wide-brimmed hat
lacked its usual flair. Winslow possessed only two changes of shirts
and pantaloons, and both sets were streaked and spotted with that
grubby mixture of grit and stickiness that children have a natural
gift for accumulating even in the most immaculate surroundings.
As for me, I had dressed that morning in my flabby-dabby alpaca,
adding a cheap cameo breast pin and a crepe veil for good measure.

Eventually Major Heywood managed to find a dray cart on an
adjoining street, and into it went our portmanteaus and cases and
"Dr. Campbell's" physician's bag. Winslow and the major rode
with the luggage while I joined the fat Irish drayman on the seat.
He knew the arrival and departure times of passenger trains and
informed us that the next Baltimore and Ohio train for the west
would leave at five o'clock, barring some unforeseen delay. Most
unforeseen delays, the drayman added, were caused by Rebel raids
around Harpers Ferry, which sometimes held up arrivals from the
west for several hours, or perhaps a day or two.

"Outrageous. Shameful acts, indeed," Major Heywood declared in a tone that struck my actress's ear as a bit too unctuous,
but the Irishman responded with a loud grunt of accord.

Once before I had visited Baltimore, in those days when I was
but a fledgling stage performer, and I recognized the towers of the
railroad station when they came into view. We were soon inside,

< CONSPIRACY OF KNAVES >

and at the ticket window I caught my first glimpse of the thick packet of greenbacks that Heywood carried in a leather holder strapped inside his coat. He had been much better funded than I, but isn't that the way it usually is with men and women in this world? When he requested two tickets to Cincinnati, I breathed a bit easier, believing that at least we would not be engaged in anything aberrant or perilous until we had disposed of Master Winslow Barber. I had not yet learned, however, that when one travels with Charley Heywood, one must always expect the un-expected.

The train left promptly at five o'clock that afternoon, but the condition of the cars had deteriorated dreadfully during three years of wartime service. Soldiers, many of them convalescents, filled most of the seats, and they did not seem to mind the discomfort, the cinders and acrid smoke pouring through broken windows, but my eyes were soon burning, and after the sun went down, cold air set my body to shivering. I wrapped Winslow in a shawl, and he slept most of the way to Harpers Ferry. There the train jerked and creaked its way across bridges and rough track until he was shaken awake, but I managed to keep him fairly quiet by calling his attention to flares that illuminated the figures of workmen and armed guards who formed continuous lines alongside the slowly moving train.

At last we came to a jarring halt, and shortly afterward two military officers entered our car, demanding that soldiers display their passes and that everyone else give their destination and rea-sons for travel. Major Heywood pretended to be asleep, but one of the officers shook him roughly by the shoulder, and I must say the major gave a splendid performance of an indignant physician awakened from well-deserved repose. Although anyone with half a brain should have recognized the impossibility of sleep upon that train, Heywood soon had the blustering official apologizing to both of us. All would have gone quite smoothly had not Winslow chosen that moment to utter one of his odious expletives in his sweet childish voice, the sound keen enough to be heard from one end of the car to the other, and causing a ripple of astonishment and nervous laughter. One of the officers turned the color of a beet; the other just shook his head and clucked his tongue to shame us

< **Belle Rutledge** >

for being the parents of so foul-mouthed an innocent, if Winslow could be so described.

Soon after the officers left the car, a young girl came through selling meat pies and apple tarts from a basket. She had not the cleanest of faces or hands, but we'd eaten only a tidbit of lunch in the Baltimore depot, and Major Heywood decided to buy a pie and a tart for each of us. I found both to be quite delicious, the buttery pastry melting in my mouth, but Winslow spat out his first bite of meat pie with the blackest of oaths and refused to touch it again. The tart he made no comment upon, but consumed it entire, and after the train resumed its motion he soon fell asleep again.

From time to time I dozed off briefly, but the constantly swaying car kept me in a state of suspension halfway between sleep and wakefulness. During a quick stop that brought my eyes wide open, I read the name Cumberland on the front of a small depot, and then we were off again. I'm not sure how far we'd traveled after that when the train stopped with such suddenness that it almost threw me from my seat. Scattered gunfire sounded somewhere outside in a world of utter blackness. Several passengers began opening windows cautiously, peering out, trying to determine what was happening.

"Rebel raiders, likely," a voice growled behind us, and shortly afterward one of the military officers who had come through the car at Harpers Ferry entered the forward door and strode quickly along the aisle to stop beside Major Heywood. The officer leaned down so that his mouth almost touched the major's ear, and spoke a few words so softly that all I could hear above the hubbub in the car were the words "Dr. Campbell." Heywood arose, his face quite calm, and reached for the medical bag on the rack above. With no explanation to me, he followed the officer rapidly through the forward door.

Soon after that the cars began rolling again, very slowly at first, the wheels making repeated sharp clanking sounds followed by pronounced thuds as though we were passing over badly connected rails. Eventually, however, we resumed a steady speed. I had no way of knowing whether Major Heywood was still aboard the train. Each time the forward door opened with a swirl of sulphurous smoke and showering cinders, I glanced up hoping to

< CONSPIRACY OF KNAVES >

see his stalwart form framed there. Had his real identity been discovered? Why had he taken the physician's bag with him? Had he used this opportunity to escape from me and the child? A hundred questions went though my mind, until gradually the pale light of dawn began showing against the windows, and then the sun rose to reveal the summer green of fields and forests.

The morning lengthened. Winslow awakened, fretful and hungry. But still there was no sign of Major Heywood. Occasionally the locomotive came into view on a curve of rails ahead, white steam and black smoke pouring from its cabbage-shaped stack. The whistle sounded, and then I saw a broad river and a town. Our speed began to slacken, the car shook and rattled, and with a squeal of metal against metal we lurched to a halt beside a graveled platform. "Breakfast stop! Breakfast stop!" a hoarse voice called from somewhere, and the passengers stood up to stretch, some taking their bags, others leaving them on the racks.

In the midst of all this turmoil, Major Heywood suddenly appeared. "We'll take our bags," he said brusquely, and after lifting them down he led the way for Winslow and me.

Outside, the morning was quite cool, with wisps of mist floating from the river. A dining hall the size of a barn stood near the track, and we joined the other sleepy-eyed passengers in a herdlike press for food. When at last the three of us were seated at the end of a slab table, well supplied with Yankee viands, I asked Major Heywood where he had been during the night.

"A party of mounted Confederates struck a B. & O. bridge somewhere near Piedmont," he explained in a matter-of-fact tone. "Gilmor's raiders, most likely. Wounded a Union defender. He was put on the train. The military officers aboard think I'm a doctor." He stopped and took a long appreciative swallow of real coffee.

"You don't mean you—"

"Yes. 'Dr. Campbell' attended the poor devil." Heywood's blue eyes brightened at the humor of it, but I suppose my face revealed unspoken rebuke.

"Oh, confound it, Belle. I only removed a Rebel bullet from a Yankee's butt. Many a Yankee bullet I dug out of my boys when I was raiding with John Morgan. Nothing to it. A clean sharp knife and a dash of whiskey in the wound—anyway, the Federal

< **Belle Rutledge** >

officers were grateful enough to serve me with some good old Kentucky bourbon."

Winslow was noisily spooning porridge partly into his wide mouth and partly down his already bedraggled shirtfront. "Don't eat so fast," I said with quiet firmness.

"Let him eat as fast as he can," the major said. "We're short of time."

"But they gave us an hour," I protested.

He took another swallow of coffee, relishing it. "We're ske-daddling," he said almost in a whisper. "Finish your johnnycake and then we go."

"We're leaving the train here?" I asked. "Before Cincinnati?"

He nodded. "Just keep quiet and follow me out of here."

Neither Winslow nor I was quite ready to go, but with the grubby urchin clasped to one shoulder and my portmanteau grasped in my free hand, I followed the major out the side of the building facing the town. Here Heywood stopped abruptly. Two uniformed men, the same military officers who were traveling on the train as inspectors, looked at us in surprise.

"My wife and the child," Heywood lied instantly, "are so fatigued I thought it best to stop here for a day before continuing our journey."

"Allow me to find a carriage for you," the younger officer said, and went off at a fast dogtrot. The other officer smiled and tried to relieve me of Winslow, who protested violently with his favorite oath, and tightened his sticky fingers around my neck.

With an air of embarrassment, the officer turned to Heywood. "I suppose you are happy to have traveled this far from Rebeldom, eh, Dr. Campbell?"

"Ah, yes," Heywood replied. To the right of the dining hall, a Union flag flapped in the morning breeze. The major faced it. "You cannot imagine, sir, how good it is to see the old flag again," he declared in a tone so sanctimonious that I almost winced at the hypocrisy of it.

In a few minutes we were being bundled into a carriage, but as soon as we were out of earshot of the two solicitous officers, Heywood ordered the driver to take us to a landing on the Ohio River. The distance was short. We might easily have walked there downhill, and I could see that the major was annoyed, no doubt by the fact that the military men had seen us leave the train.

After depositing Winslow and me and the luggage at the foot of a slant of brick steps that led up from the river, Heywood hurried toward a bridge, passed under it, and disappeared for what seemed an eternity. Actually he was probably gone no more than an hour or two, but for a simple actress inexperienced with maternity, who was burdened with a wide-awake, uncontrollable, and profane small boy, even the minutes seemed like hours. Winslow was in constant motion except during those moments when I managed to capture and hold him forcefully. His ultimate goal appeared to be the waters of the Ohio. More than once I was of a mind to allow him to achieve his desire, but I always relented, letting tender mercies prevail, and snatched him from a watery demise.

Occasionally a boat would pass, and he would remain quiet and immobile, uttering a gleeful cry whenever one sounded its whistle. At last a small craft, old and unpainted, floated in alongside the landing. Except that it was powered by a coughing steam engine, it resembled those one-man fishing boats that thronged the Louisville riverbanks when I was a young girl there.

I was surprised to see Major Heywood jump ashore and come striding toward us. Winslow pulled loose from me and ran charging toward him, arms outflung as if he were trying to fly. Heywood scooped him up without missing a step. The major's manner had changed completely. He was no longer the staid physician beset by domestic burdens. He was the insouciant gallant I had first seen in the Richmond railway depot. Although he had not changed his clothing, he had stuffed his trouser legs into his cavalry boots, and again wore his slouch hat tilted so that the brim touched the tip of one ear. It is remarkable how the attitude of a man's hat can change his entire appearance. Charley Heywood was a born actor, no doubt of that. When I caught the exuberant gleam in his blue eyes, I felt that same sense of excitement, that little skip of the heart, I'd felt more than once before in his presence. Oh, how I wanted to let my feelings run free, but I knew my duty and also I kept hearing the warning of Colonel Fennell: *a pursuer of women and a breaker of hearts*.

In a single motion, Charley set Winslow down and reached for his large valise. Opening it, he removed his holstered pistol and strapped it to his side. "We're going aboard that little boat," he said, lifting the bags and leading the way across the landing. The closer we came to the boat, the less river-worthy it appeared. Old boards had been nailed over older boards, and although the small steam engine was housed under a ramshackle roof, passengers had to ride in the open, seated on planks across a bottom covered with at least an inch of grease-flecked water that had leaked through the seams.

Getting aboard was not easy. A short stocky man with bulging eyes took Winslow from me, causing the little boy to cry out in terror until he saw that I was following him into the boat. The man was quite unsettling in his general appearance, with smears of black grease on his hands and clothing and across his grizzled face. Heywood introduced me as Mrs. Campbell, and I believe he called the man Captain Robinson, but it was all done so curtly that I can't be certain of the name. Anyway, as soon as Heywood had stowed our luggage on one of the dry seats and I had found a similar place for Winslow and me, we were off with a loud pounding of the little engine, riding swiftly on a down current of the Ohio. At first, the fresh smells of the river, the changing scenery, the passing boats all combined to please the three of us after the discomforts of the train. But before the day was over, I would gladly have changed back to the cars.

By early afternoon the summer sun was like a fire. Gnats, mosquitoes, and heaven knows what other flying pests frequently assailed us, and there was no way of keeping our feet dry with the scummy water sloshing in the boat's bottom. Heywood complained even more bitterly than I. He fastened handkerchiefs inside his hat, letting them hang over his neck and forehead, but his face reddened perceptibly. "My fair skin burns," he shouted more than once to the boatman. "Can't you keep to the shady bank of the river!" Until late in that long afternoon, however, there was no shady side, only broiling sun the width of the Ohio. From time to time we stopped at woodyards to take on fuel for the boiler, but if we went ashore to stretch our legs, we were attacked by biting flies or swarms of gnats.

At one of these stops was a river inn, and Major Heywood purchased some cheese and greasy cakes and slices of meat. Only the cheese was edible, the meat being so gamy that it must have

< CONSPIRACY OF KNAVES >

been venison slaughtered weeks before. Winslow's reaction was predictable—a summation of almost his entire repertory of profane invective. Nevertheless, on the advice of Major Heywood, I stowed the uneaten food into my canvas handbag.

Sundown came, and then twilight and darkness, yet on we went, the thumping of the steam engine never ceasing. It was like the beating of a monstrous heart, and I could feel its counterpart at the temples of my throbbing head. At last Heywood arose from his seat, a shadow against the starry sky, and moved to the prow. He leaned there for several minutes, studying the left bank, and then turned back to the engine shed. He said something to the boatman, who reached to his engine and shut it off. The silence that followed was intense, relieved only by a chirr of insects from the wilderness and the occasional clamor of frogs in the distance.

Soon we were floating almost motionless. "A hundred yards or so farther down," Heywood said, so quietly that I barely heard him. Both men began using oars, making light splashes in the river. Again I heard the major's urgent voice, and moments later we were turning into a small inlet overhung with vine-covered tree limbs. We were in the mouth of a creek barely flowing out of thick woods so dark that I did not see the square of logs that formed a raft landing until we nosed into the bank alongside it.

Heywood got our luggage ashore and then helped me and Winslow from the boat. The child was so sleepy it made no outcry. Heywood turned back to the boat and affected some kind of body sign, raising his right arm and intoning with the utmost seriousness: "Sons of Liberty shall be thy watchword."

The stocky boatman stood erect in the prow, making the same odd motions. He repeated the words and added: "Onward!" He then faded into the shadows of the boat and Heywood gave it a hard shove away from the bank. When the silhouette of the boat showed against the starlit water of the river and then disappeared, we picked up our bags and began climbing a narrow pathway.

"He was a Copperhead," I said.

"Yes. A loyal old Ohio Butternut." A touch of sarcasm was in his voice, I thought, but he had nothing more to say about "Captain Robinson."

We came out upon a sandy road, and in less than a quarter mile reached a steepled church, dark and hushed in the warm

< **Belle Rutledge** >

night. Heywood opened the door, and there was just enough light inside to see the pews.

After making little Winslow as comfortable as possible on one of the benches, the major and I placed pallets of clothing on two others. I stretched out for the first time since leaving the commissary boat at Baltimore.

"Where are we, Major Heywood?" I asked.

"You don't recognize the soil of your own native state?" he replied.

"Kentucky? How far to Louisville? And Cincinnati?"

"Miles and miles. And you'd better doze, Miss Rutledge. In these parts they start church early."

Tomorrow is Sunday, I remembered, and as hard as the bench was, I slept until Charley awakened me in a chilly gray dawn. By the time we'd got everything back into our bags, the sun was up, and while he was leading us down a parklike slope to a spring, I could feel the beginnings of a hot day.

The gush of water flowing from the spring was too cold for bathing or washing clothes, but the shallow creek was fairly tepid above the inflow. I stripped Winslow of every stitch of clothing he wore and washed them with his filthy extra set in the creek. The only way that I could entice the imp into the water to scrub him was to remove my shoes and stockings, roll up my skirt to my waist, and wade in with him. While we were so engaged, Charley built a fire and warmed the left-over greasy bread and venison. We were hungry enough to eat all of it, yet not with any savor.

Although the sun was hot and there was a downslope breeze, I had to hold Winslow's clothing and some parts of my undergarments near the fire in order to dry them completely. Charley then gathered all our bags and, to my surprise, concealed them in a nearby holly thicket.

"We're going to Sunday meeting," he explained as we started back up the slope toward the church. "Pray that the preacher today is a young man."

"Why so?"

"The old reverend is Lincoln loyal. The young one is a Knight of the Golden Circle."

"Copperheads must be thick around here," I said. "If the younger one comes, are we in for another long boat ride?"

< CONSPIRACY OF KNAVES >

"If he does not come, we sleep on a hard bench again tonight."

I hoped the preacher would be young. When we topped the last rise, we saw buggies and farm wagons and riding horses hitched to trees around the church. Hymn singing had already begun inside. They were singing "Rescue the Perishing," and I felt as though it were meant for us.

As the congregation was finishing the hymn, we slipped quietly into the church and seated ourselves on the last unoccupied bench. In his usual loud treble, little Winslow protested indignantly that he had no desire to lie down and go to sleep on a bench again, and every head in the church turned to look at us. Fortunately the bratling was standing upright on the seat, his face freshly scrubbed, his clothes clean for the first time since we'd left Richmond, and with his golden hair he may have given the impression of being an innocent angel to those who knew him not.

Anyway, these simple rural folk smiled as I took him into my lap, necessarily using force, which I tried to conceal. I attempted to keep one hand free to clap over his mouth and at the same time prayed silently to heaven that he would not utter one of those awful oaths that dominated his small vocabulary.

The major frowned at him, shook a finger, and made a stern shushing sound. Gradually the congregation stopped whispering and tittering, and rustled itself back into silence as the preacher arose behind the plain pineboard pulpit. He was a young man, about Charley's age, I judged.

"This morning," he began, "let us turn to Jeremiah the prophet, who tells us that in time of troubles why shouldst thou be as a stranger in the land, and as a wayfaring man that turneth aside to tarry for a night." I heard Charley suppress a slight chuckle. He was smiling beatifically at the preacher, who glanced for an instant at us, and continued in his Ohio Valley accent: "The psalmist tells us that blessed is the man that walketh not in the council of the ungodly. And he shall be like a *tree* planted *by the river* of water that bringeth forth his fruit in his season."

The preacher paused to look out the nearest window, seeming to listen to birdsong coming from the trees. Below the woods a steamboat hooted on the river. "On this summer day," he resumed slowly, "let us look *westward* toward the setting of the sun. Let us hearken to the Song of Solomon. The fig tree putteth forth her green figs and the vines with the tender grapes give a good smell." He paused and added slowly: "Those who have studied the Scriptures tell us that Solomon's figs may have been similar to our persimmons."

After a tin plate was passed along the rows to collect offerings of coins, the preacher launched into a eulogy of the summer season, gradually working around to calling on the sinners in the congregation to repent. "And be not forgetful to entertain strangers," he said in a strong voice, "for thereby some have entertained angels unawares." His rich voice became so soft at the close that I could barely understand the last words. "Let us sing," he said then with force.

I was surprised to hear the voices join in a wartime hymn I'd heard many times in Richmond:

> We shall meet but we shall miss him
> There will be one vacant chair
> We shall linger to caress him
> While we breathe our evening prayer.

It occurred to me then that the people in this little country church in Kentucky must have kith and kin on both sides of the war. What did it matter who sang the sad song, or where? So wrapped was I in reverie, only the frantic squirming of little Winslow gave me notice that the services were ended and the people were rising to leave the church.

Charley nudged me into the aisle, and we moved out with the others, pausing to shake the hand of the young preacher, who thanked us for coming. "By chance are you from Philo? Did I not see you at Lyons Hotel?" he asked politely, and without waiting for reply he bent down to pat the top of Winslow's head. "Go *westward*, young man," the preacher murmured; but at the first pat, the yellow-haired imp dodged as though expecting a blow. He kicked the preacher in the shin, jerked his fingers free of my grasp, and bounded away on his short legs. Charley quickly went in pursuit, and with a hasty word of apology to the preacher, I set out after Charley.

Beneath a full-leafed coffee tree where a churchgoer was helping his long-faced wife into a buggy, I overtook the pair. Charley

< CONSPIRACY OF KNAVES >

had picked Winslow up in his arms and was tickling him. The boy's laughter covered the epithets he was trying to utter. The long-faced woman on the buggy seat called out nasally: "You folk live hereabouts?"

"Passing through," Charley replied. "We just felt the need of some preaching and prayer."

The man unfastened his horse and turned to climb into the buggy. "You river people?"

Charley nodded, and the man asked: "Boat nearby?"

"Friends coming by to pick us up soon," Charley replied easily.

The long-faced woman pursed her lips suspiciously, but when Winslow called out a cherubic good-bye to her and waved his hand at the turning buggy, a smile formed briefly on her sour lips.

"Nosy old hen," I said softly.

"Yeah." Charley waited until the buggy fell into line with the other departing worshipers, and added: "This little tadpole has been a big help to us today."

"All that prattling and fidgeting in church?" I replied tartly. "A big help to us?"

"Diversion," he said. "They'll remember towheaded Winslow for a while, but they'll soon forget us." As the last of the vehicles and saddle horses vanished through the trees, he turned and started us both down toward the spring. There we retrieved our bags from the holly thicket, and then, without a word of explanation, the major led the way into a thicket of underbrush and vines.

After a struggle to break our way through the tangle, we reached ground that was soft beneath our feet, and the fetid odor of decaying vegetation filled me with a dread of snakes. I had to carry Winslow on my shoulders while Major Heywood floundered with our baggage. At last we came upon a round knob of dry ground, and Heywood slowly scanned the line of trees between us and the river.

"Do you know where you're taking us?" I demanded.

"Yes. The preacher told us where. Westward, he said."

"Westward? And all that rigmarole about a tree planted by a river?" I pulled a handful of dry grass and used it to clean my shoes. "Fig trees and grapevines?"

The major laughed and stepped close enough to grasp my arm and lift it. "Sight across there, Belle Rutledge. Remember the

< **Belle Rutledge** >

preacher told us that Solomon's figs may have been persimmons. He likely invented that little story. But if I'm not mistaken, the dark green trees you see are persimmons."

They were persimmon trees, the tallest standing close to a dank backwater, with wild grapevines festooning its limbs. Beneath it in the brown liquid of the slough, and half concealed by a leafy branch, was a sun-bleached rowboat half filled with water.

Heywood removed his boots, rolled up his trouser legs, and began bailing with a wooden pail that someone, the Copperhead preacher probably, had left in the boat. Then he stepped into the muddy water and pulled the boat loose from the bank.

We were soon inside, Winslow and I seated on our bags, watching with some trepidation an inflow of seepage through the bottom seams. Heywood handed me the pail and took up a sturdy pole, which providentially had been left with the oars. Half crouching to avoid overturning the dilapidated craft, he pushed us slowly through a morass of muck and vegetation. Although I was not surprised, I could not suppress a cry of fear when a shiny water snake suddenly appeared no more than a foot from where I splashed water from the bailing pail. Both the major and little Winslow laughed at my shrill outcry. Somehow I managed to steady my nerves by recalling a few lines of Mr. Coleridge's ancient mariner: "Blue, glossy green and velvet black, they coiled and swam; and every track was a flash of golden fire."

These words took me back to more tranquil times, my happy days with the Louisville minstrel troupe at Charleston, where Mr. Alexander Placides himself sometimes entertained audiences by reciting verses on the proscenium during scene changes. Among his favorites were "The Raven" and "Rime of the Ancient Mariner." With the sun boiling down upon my back, the stench of rotting vegetation in my nostrils, the fear of snakes making my skin to crawl, oh, how I wished I was back on the stage and had never heard of spies and counterspies and Rebels and Yankees and Copperheads.

"Well, we're free of it at last," I heard Major Heywood say. Shaking myself out of the brief daydream, I looked up to see the clear green waters of the Ohio before us.

"Now where to?" I asked somewhat caustically. "Do we float in this leaky tub all the way to Cincinnati?"

< CONSPIRACY OF KNAVES >

Heywood was stowing the pole in the bottom of the boat and taking up the oars. "You heard the preacher ask if we were from Philo, didn't you? That's where we're going, if we can find the place, to rendezvous with friends, and then on to Cincinnati."

I felt like shouting one of little Winslow's favorite profanities. "Why must these people be so devious, so hokey-pokey? Why could we not have escaped all this misery by simply journeying on the cars to Cincinnati to meet your Copperhead friends there?"

Heywood shook his head in the manner some men use when they wish to indicate that members of their opposite sex are too dense to understand even the most minor complexities of life.

Without moving my lips I whispered one of Winslow's expletives. Truth was, as I had come to understand, Charley Heywood loved all the rigmarole, the contrived hugger-muggery of the Copperheads. He may have believed himself an outsider, but at heart he was one of them.

"The people we're meeting," he explained impatiently, "are from General Morgan's command, and as for the local Copperheads, you must remember, Belle, they're taking great risks. They can be arrested and imprisoned without trial, or court-martialed by a Federal military commission and sentenced for treason, hanged, or shot by a firing squad." He swung the boat farther out from shore, and we went sweeping along in the current.

"What about us?" I asked.

"The same fate awaits us if we're caught. Except Master Winslow, of course."

At the first widening of the river, where the currents ran slower, we crossed to the Ohio side, I bailing continuously, Major Heywood rowing steadily. Winslow gave us no trouble. He was not yet sleepy or hungry and pleasured himself by trailing one hand in the water in a pretense of catching fish.

The time was late afternoon when we sighted the little town of Philo, set cozily into a long slope of riverbank. Major Heywood nosed the boat in beside a landing float, and we disembarked as casually as though we belonged there. Up the partially cobbled street was the Lyons Hotel, a crudely drawn head of a lion above the entrance.

When we entered the establishment's small foyer, fragrances of afternoon baking struggled to prevail over a mustiness of leather and stale tobacco smoke. Two elderly men sat at a round table, regarding us with sleepy indifference. I held a fretful Winslow in a sagging chair while Major Heywood approached the registry desk, where a bald-headed man awaited.

After a quick glance around, Heywood made a covert gesture, turning his coat lapel to reveal the copper penny fastened there. He then crossed his arms and offered a thumb in a Copperhead handshake. The bald-headed man gave him a pen, waited until he had signed, and then came around the desk to help with the luggage. He led the way upstairs to a fairly clean room with a single bed. Closing the door behind us, he looked expectantly at the major. "The rooms on each side are empty, Dr. Campbell," he said. "We can talk freely."

"Yes." Heywood walked slowly to the window and looked down into the street. "A man, two men perhaps, should be staying here, waiting for me."

"Three men," the bald-headed hotel clerk said.

Heywood swung around to face him. "Three? Yes, perhaps. Where are they?"

"We had to spirit them out of town last night, sir."

"Spirit them out? Why?"

The hotel man rubbed a hand across his bare skull. "The Grand Seigneur of our temple suspects an informer, sir, a leakage of some kind. Too many strangers were about, watching—you know how the authorities have been in Ohio since Vallandigham returned from Canada. They suspect everybody."

Shaking his head in disgust, Heywood walked back to the window. I picked Winslow up and set him squirming upon the bed.

"How far away were they taken?" the major asked.

"I'm not certain, sir. The Deputy Grand Commander was in charge. Perhaps only a few miles into the country. I'll make inquiries."

"Yes, do that. Meanwhile, my family and I would like dinner."

The obsequious hotel man bowed slightly. "The dining room should be open in a few minutes."

As I expected, the food served by the Hotel Lyons was not of the best, but Major Heywood and I did enjoy the real coffee, and Winslow gulped down enough cherry pie and milk to gorge an

< CONSPIRACY OF KNAVES >

adult. The major leaned back luxuriously in his chair and was starting a cigar when the hotel man appeared, an expression of satisfied accomplishment upon his face.

"Your friends," he said quietly, "are in the country. With the Grand Seigneur. A ride of an hour and a half, perhaps. If you wish, I'll have a horse saddled for you."

"By all means," Heywood replied.

A few minutes later he departed, leaving me in the hotel room at the mercy of Winslow. The little rogue insisted upon going outside, and he ran wildly up and down the sidewalks until he fell and got a nasty bruise on his chin. The accident set him to howling like a banshee, disturbing the drowsy town, until I finally carried him back inside the hotel. Of course, I knew nothing then of children's humbugs, and how the little beasts can exaggerate wounds and make the world believe they are near expiring in order to receive earthly rewards before they become angels in heaven. Luckily for me there was a good-natured old Negro woman who worked in the hotel kitchen. She came to my rescue with a bowl of cream and honey, and while I spooned the mixture into Winslow's cavernous mouth, she applied a malodorous poultice to his chin.

Shortly afterward the young monster fell fast asleep in one of the fusty chairs in the deserted foyer, and rather than risk awakening him I let him lie.

While I was waiting, the hotel clerk lent me his Cincinnati newspaper. On the first page was an account of the notorious Copperhead leader Clement Vallandigham, who had returned defiantly from exile in Canada to the town of Hamilton, Ohio. There he had made a speech challenging the Federal government to arrest him again for treason, and the Democrats of his congressional district soon afterward chose him as a delegate to the Chicago convention that was meeting later in the summer to nominate a presidential candidate to oppose Abraham Lincoln.

Suddenly I recalled my last meeting with Colonel Fennell in Richmond and how he had stressed the importance of our traveling promptly on to Chicago after we reached Cincinnati. Did this journey have some connection with the Democratic convention, I wondered, and perhaps with Clement Vallandigham, chief mogul of the Sons of Liberty and other Copperhead legions?

In another column of the newspaper was a report of a speech

made by President Lincoln at the Sanitary Fair in Philadelphia. Wars are terrible, he declared, and the one we were fighting was more terrible than most, but the object was worthy and the war would end when the object was obtained.

The depressing battlefield news was mostly from Virginia. Another assault by Grant's army against Petersburg had brought enormous casualties but no ground gained. The long columns of names of Ohioans, the dead and wounded, revealed how furious this fighting had been. Petersburg and Richmond seemed so far away to me, sitting there in that quiet village on the river, waiting for Major Heywood to return from wherever he had gone.

He did not return until after dark, his face revealing anger and frustration, his voice filled with repressed rage. The Copperheads had passed the three men and the money stolen from the Kentucky bank on toward Cincinnati, and we would have to wait until morning to board a train to join them in that city.

After a late supper, Heywood's choler subsided. When he came up to the hotel room, where I was luxuriating on the bed—with Winslow chattering away at sights he saw from the open window—he brought a small folding cot he'd borrowed from the hotel clerk.

"You can't sleep on that little bed," I said.

"I don't mean to," he replied. "It's for Master Winslow."

"He could sleep on this bed with me."

"I'm sharing that bed," he said, and went over to join Winslow at the window.

I don't recollect how long the silence was before I spoke: "If you were a gentleman, you would take another room."

"And further arouse their distrust of us? Some of these Copperheads are as skittery of strangers as wild ponies. So far as they know, we're man and wife, and we should be occupying the same room and bed."

In the end I yielded, but I placed a long bolster down the middle of the bed. Charley laughed about it at first, but as we lay there in the darkening June evening with a cool breeze flowing across us from the river, and the sound of summer insects singing a soft melodious chorus, I felt myself drawn to him as metal to a magnet.

"I did not lie down here to bundle," Charley said in a half whisper.

< CONSPIRACY OF KNAVES >

I raised an arm to point at the child's bed. Winslow was lying on his belly, his chin bandage askew, watching us with eyes as big as silver dollars. I had allowed him to sleep too long that afternoon.

"Damn the little rascal," Charley muttered.

Of course, the youngling could not stay awake all night. Eventually his eyelids grew leaden, but what occurred after he fell asleep has no bearing on these momentous events that I am attempting to narrate, and therefore should be of no concern to my readers.

7

TRAMP, TRAMP, TRAMP, THE BOYS ARE MARCHING

LOOKING BACK ON that eerie morning at Raven's Head, where he found himself surrounded by a band of armed and suspicious natives, Johnny Truscott often remarked on the importance of timing in the affairs of mere mortals. Complying with the demands of the old gray-haired American Knight, he withdrew Hatfield's map from his coat pocket. Two or three other Copperheads had just moved closer to examine it when Truscott heard the drawling mountaineer voice of Sergeant Joe Stiles. With his usual aplomb, the sergeant informed the Copperheads that every man of them was in the sights of a gun, and if they did not drop their weapons instantly he would give the order to fire.

If Sergeant Stiles and his alligator horses had arrived a few minutes earlier or a few minutes later, Truscott believed, a bloody gunfight might have resulted. That is what he meant by the importance of timing, an element that any actor will tell you is as vital upon the stage as it is in life.

At any rate, the Copperheads obeyed Sergeant Stiles's order to abandon their weapons, one of them shouting an obscenity and crying out: "The Federals! The Federals! I warned you all of a trap!"

"We're not Federals," Truscott said. "Show me the way to Hatfield's place and we'll leave in peace."

One of the younger Copperheads, a pale-faced youth with dirty

< CONSPIRACY OF KNAVES >

ashen hair, snorted with relief. "You're Forrest's or Morgan's men, ain't you? Looking for horses, ain't you?"

"Morgan's men," Truscott replied. "Where's Hatfield's place?"

"Across the river," the old man said, his voice almost contrite. "Likely you'll find him on the ferryboat. He runs that, too."

With tensions removed, the attitude of the Copperheads changed completely. The pale-faced youth offered to go in search of Phil Hatfield, and the old man banged on the ceiling with a long pole and called to his womenfolk upstairs to come down and cook up a mess of victuals for John Morgan's boys. As homely a woman as Truscott had ever seen quickly appeared with a crookbacked daughter in tow, and they were soon rattling pots and pans over a wood stove.

The pork they served was too greasy for Truscott's taste, but the biscuits and eggs were edible. He and his men were just finishing their hasty breakfasts when the pale-faced youth returned in company with an older man. He was Phil Hatfield, weather-beaten in appearance, his reddish side-whiskers splaying untidily from his cheeks. After introductions around, Truscott complained mildly to Hatfield about the rough treatment given him upon first arriving at Raven's Head.

"They were testing you, captain," Hatfield explained in a firm tone. "They acted properly. Had you known the secret signs of the Knights, you would have been welcomed as a brother."

Truscott winced at Hatfield's use of the word *knight*. To his mind there was nothing chivalrous in the manner or appearance of any of these Raven's Head ruffians; quite the opposite, in fact.

As for Hatfield, Truscott quickly classified him as humorless but efficient, a man who set his mind in one direction and held it there no matter what.

"My ferryboat is almost constantly under surveillance," he explained to Truscott. "Sometimes they stop me to inspect passengers. Ten saddled horses and you and your nine men would attract their attention."

"Can't we wait until after dark?"

Hatfield's response was more of a grimace than a smile. "The Federals allow no ferry passage here between sundown and sunrise. But we have a way. The fog will help us. Let's go before it lifts."

As they made their way down the winding passage to the river, the fog thinned, but the flatboat used as a ferry was moored in a slight cove that offered some concealment from boats moving up and down the Ohio. Two muscular young boys, Hatfield's sons, were waiting with the boat, and at a signal from him they began lifting loose boards from the flooring. Saddles and other gear from the horses were stored in a hidden compartment beneath the boards.

"We'll have to make two crossings," Hatfield told Truscott. "Bring five of your animals aboard. Three of your men will crawl in the hold and lie down with the saddles. Two can help me and my boys with the sweeps." Truscott decided to go with the first crossing, leaving Sergeant Stiles with the second group.

In a few minutes the loose boards were back in place, and five horses were led aboard and fastened inside a rickety pen. As Hatfield was untying the mooring rope, one of the Raven's Head Knights who had accompanied them to the river landing called out to Truscott: "When can we expect the invading army, captain?"

"Soon," Truscott replied, although he was not certain what the man meant.

"Will it be John Morgan or Bedford Forrest?"

The question startled Truscott. This was the first intimation he'd had that the Copperheads were expecting another invasion similar to the disastrous one led by Morgan a year earlier. The notion was contrary to everything he'd been told. In his mind the movement of armies was designed to be in the opposite direction— freed Confederate soldiers storming out of prison camps in Illinois and Indiana and, accompanied by a host of armed Copperhead allies, riding southward to sever Sherman's supply lines to Georgia. The main objective of Morgan's raid into Kentucky had been to acquire enough horses to drive southward against those lines, not to cross the Ohio River northward again. As for Bedford Forrest, the last report Truscott had heard of that audacious cavalry leader, he was as desperate for men and mounts as Morgan, and was somewhere far below Memphis struggling to keep the Union Army out of Mississippi and Alabama.

All these thoughts ran through Truscott's mind before he shouted back a reply to the Copperhead's query: "Likely be Forrest. This far west."

The flatboat slipped slowly into a sluggish current, and he went to assist with one of the massive side oars that propelled the craft.

< CONSPIRACY OF KNAVES >

Hatfield was handling the big tiller sweep, sometimes letting it drift loosely, sometimes struggling desperately against an erratic swirl of water.

They were about halfway across when a small gunboat came steaming around the first bend in the upper river and sounded its hoarse whistle. Truscott heard Hatfield's loud "goddamn" and then the ferryman called to him: "They want to inspect us, Captain Truscott. Better let me do the talking."

Hatfield and his sons worked their long oars hard in an effort to hold the ferry in position until the gunboat, its paddle wheel splashing vigorously, moved close enough for a boarding. At such proximity, Truscott could see that the craft was not really a gunboat but was only a small steamboat boxed up with boards painted the color of black metal. Even the portholes were faked.

"Where'd you get them horses and where you takin' 'em?" a deep voice sounded from the pilothouse.

"They're used-up cavalry mounts," Hatfield shouted back. "We're taking them over to my farm to feed and restore."

"Who're them two men there with your boys?"

"Drovers. They brought the horses up from General Woolford's remount station. We'll be crossing again to pick up another load."

After a minute or so of what was probably deliberate delay, the bass voice sounded again: "Pass on."

"Hey!" Hatfield shouted at the interrogator. "I've drifted below my course waiting for you. Could you oblige us with a roll from your wake?"

The sham gunboat chugged into motion, swinging around the ferry, and sent a strong swell rolling against the flatboat, rocking it so that the horses reared and almost broke loose from their pen. Yet the Hatfields still failed to bring the ferry ashore until it was a quarter of a mile below their farm, and it had to be poled back upstream along the bank shallows.

The second river crossing was uneventful, and soon after dark Truscott and his men—with Phil Hatfield accompanying as guide— resumed their journey northward into Illinois. Although Hatfield supplied them with fresh mounts, the Kentuckians knew horseflesh. well enough to perceive that in the long run the Copperhead had the better of the swap. His animals were decidedly inferior to the temporarily exhausted Bluegrass mounts.

< **Tramp, Tramp, Tramp** >

Sure enough, at first daylight after their all-night journey, two horses showed signs of faltering. When Truscott pointed this out to Hatfield, the stockman led them to a farmhouse near the Wabash River. The farmer was not at home, but his wife, a corpulent woman who Truscott guessed must weigh at least 250 pounds, gave them permission to feed their mounts at a corncrib.

"Where's Henry?" Hatfield asked her.

"You could guess that easy enough, I reckon, Mr. Hatfield," she replied somewhat testily. "He's gone down to Shawneetown to a special important meeting of the Sons of Liberty."

More Copperhead palavering and folderol, Truscott thought, and wondered if these people ever did anything except hold meetings and talk, talk, talk. When he approached the formidable woman about trading a couple of horses, she asked so high a price for a pair of heavy road ponies that he objected. Not even Hatfield's intercession could bring her to reduce the amount. And after she prepared breakfasts for them, she demanded what Truscott described as "Richmond hotel rates for Frog Hollow fare." Added to that was a goodly sum for the corn from her crib. A considerable portion of his allotment of greenbacks from the Mount Sterling bank robbery was thus rapidly transferred to the placket of the female Copperhead.

After they turned westward, Hatfield suggested that they travel half by day and half by night; he believed they could cover more miles that way. Horse traders, farmers, and stockmen frequented the southern Illinois roads, and by separating into twos and threes and keeping a quarter of a mile apart, they attracted little notice.

On the second day, however, Truscott was startled when he and one of his men met head-on with a party of mounted home guards. They numbered about a dozen and were escorting a prisoner in a dust-covered frock coat; the man was bareheaded, red-faced, and appeared very agitated. Truscott gave the home-guard leader a smile and half salute, but after the short column passed over a ridge and out of sight he halted and waited anxiously for Hatfield to come up.

Hatfield was angry, declaring that the perfidy of Abraham Lincoln in abolishing the writ of *habeas corpus* gave home guards a license to go into anyone's house, to arrest whomever they pleased without a specific charge, and to try them by military court on any trumped-up accusation that came to mind. "You saw that prisoner. He may or may not be a Knight," Hatfield said. "He may merely be of Southern birth, or a Yankee who spoke out against Lincoln."

On the morning of the third day Sergeant Stiles, who was riding in advance, sighted a detail of militia guarding a railroad bridge. After a few minutes of cautious scouting, he counted eight men. Four of them were playing cards at one end of the bridge; the other four appeared to be asleep under the trestlework. They had no pickets out, and their eight unsaddled horses were rope-corralled beneath a cluster of oaks, well out of sight of the bridge.

Stiles convinced Truscott that he and three men could capture the horses and be miles away before the careless bridge guards missed their mounts. The feat was accomplished, and the Kentuckians trotted away without being discovered. The captured horses were fresh, and strong enough to maintain far steadier gaits than the ones they had been riding. The only difficulty was trying to stifle laughter until they were well out of hearing of the bridge guards. In his earthy way, Stiles kept describing the forthcoming bewilderment of the green militiamen when they discovered eight inferior animals left by the Kentuckians in place of the splendid government steeds. He regretted mightily that he could not be present to witness the consternation.

For a noon rest stop, Hatfield led them across a broad field of wheat stubble to a tree-screened creek. As soon as all the pairs rode in, they unsaddled and napped fitfully in the heat and humidity until late in the long June day.

Afternoon shadows were lengthening when they started northward, following the straight track of the Illinois Central Railroad. The air remained sultry and windless. Clouds gathered and hung low in the sky. Sweat dripped from Truscott's forehead; he felt moisture collecting in his armpits and beneath his belt.

After an hour or more, they crossed the railroad and turned away from it, following a trail with deep gullies along either side. Eventually they reached a grove of trees and rode up to a dark unpainted building. Even in the dusky light Truscott could see from the shape that it was a small church, a chapel.

"Abandoned," Hatfield said. "After the railroad came through." He motioned to the right. "Tamaroa and the railroad are over there."

"Where's the horse farm and the man I'm to meet?"

"Couple of miles maybe. I've been here only once before. The place is called Barton Farm."

The other pairs of riders were arriving, gathering near the chapel. "Dismount them," Hatfield said. "If it rains, they can take shelter here. You and I will go to Barton Farm."

After instructing Stiles to unsaddle the horses and post pickets, Truscott turned his horse in beside Hatfield's and they rode down a narrow lane pockmarked with many hoofprints.

"Who is this Barton?" he asked Hatfield.

"Not Barton. He's dead. The man's name is Colquett. Brigadier Alonzo Colquett."

"Livestock raiser?"

"Trader mainly, out of Missouri. He bought Barton's Farm after the war broke out and uses it as a place to hold mules he brings over from Missouri. Folks say he's made a fortune selling mules to the Union Army."

Daylight was failing fast under the canopy of trees and the darkening sky. From somewhere ahead of them, a low rumbling shook the heavy air. Truscott shivered involuntarily. "Sounded like artillery," he said with a slight laugh.

"Going to rain for sure," Hatfield said.

"This man Colquett. Does he have any sympathy for the Confederacy?"

Hatfield pulled his horse aside to avoid a limb drooping with green half-formed walnuts. "He founded the Circle of Honor in St. Louis. They're now part of O.A.K., the Order of American Knights, in which he ranks as brigadier."

"Can he truly supply us with two thousand horses?"

Hatfield turned to look at Truscott. "That's a large order, is it not? Well, he convinced Major Heywood that he could."

They reached Barton Farm just as the first spray of warm rain swept into their faces. Hatfield dismounted hurriedly, opened a wide gate, and waved Truscott on toward a long row of stables. A stableboy waited inside an open shed until both men led their horses under the roof. "Mr. Colquett expectin' you?" he asked.

"Yes," Hatfield said.

The boy did not move until he was told their names, and then he ran off through the drumming shower toward a large house that

< CONSPIRACY OF KNAVES >

was slowly fading into the grayness of rain and light. In less than five minutes the boy was back, obsequious in his manner now, offering to unsaddle and rub down their mounts.

A huge man was waiting for them in the candle-lit doorway of the big house. He greeted them heartily, his voice booming as he led them into a high-ceilinged room, the walls of which were of barked brown-stained logs. After Truscott and Hatfield were seated, Alonzo Colquett lighted a large candle, placing it on a table between his guests, and then he sat in a rocking chair facing them so that he himself was in much dimmer light.

"I was expecting Charley Heywood," Colquett said, his voice rumbling oratorically as though he were addressing an outdoor throng.

"I am here at Major Heywood's request," Truscott explained.

"And you are . . ."

"Captain John Truscott, General Morgan's Second Kentucky Cavalry Regiment." He could barely see Colquett's eyes searching him from head to foot.

"About the right size to jockey a horse, eh?" Colquett teased, his words dying off just before the explosive boom of his laughter.

Truscott let the remark pass. He had lived long enough to expect occasional comments about his slightness of body; he was too tall and too heavy to ride as a jockey, yet he knew from past trials that he could outride the majority of racetrack professionals.

"Is the organization going well over in Indiana, Mr. Hatfield?" Colquett asked abruptly.

"Extremely well, brigadier," Hatfield replied. "At last report, membership in the combined orders reached a grand total of eighty thousand."

"Splendid. I note you said 'combined orders.' I suppose you've heard that since Clement Vallandigham's return he's advocating that we all unite into the Order of Sons of Liberty. He fears the Federal authorities have penetrated the Knights of the Golden Circle, Order of American Knights, and even some of the smaller circles."

Hatfield nodded. "Yes, the rituals are being revised. New passwords and secret body signs will be passed from the Supreme Commander down orally through the Grand Seigneurs."

"Excellent, excellent." Colquett rose and moved bearlike over to a sideboard, where he poured three full glasses of whiskey, bringing two of them in his huge ham of a hand to his guests. In the light of the bright candle, Truscott saw for the first time that Colquett's long beard was streaked with gray. The lower part of his high forehead had been darkened by the sun, but above the line of his hatband to the roots of his tightly combed and receding hair, the flesh was as pale as a fish's belly. He had a great bony nose, and his eyes were large and constantly roving. He smelled of horses and stale sweat, wore Wellington boots, and boasted that the Missouri pinetop whiskey they were drinking was the strongest distilled spirits on earth.

After he had lowered his bulky frame back into the rocking chair, Colquett said: "Missouri can raise thirty to forty thousand men on a day's notice."

"They're to aid us in freeing our prisoners at Chicago?" Truscott asked.

"Hell, Illinois's got three times our force. If we cross the river it'll be at Rock Island, to help free the prisoners there." He took a long swallow of the strong whiskey, and chuckled. "Some of the St. Louis brothers went up to the town of Louisiana a few weeks past and practiced crossing the Mississippi near there. They used pieces of oilcloth shaped so that all you need do is cut four willow poles, fix them in place, and you have a one-man skiff. After you cross, you fold up the oilcloth and hide it until you're ready to return. Hundreds of men could cross that way in a single night. Most of our men, though, especially around St. Louis, are preparing to join General Sterling Price when he invades Missouri later this summer." Colquett paused to lick the whiskey-soaked hairs around his mouth. "St. Louis is like a ripe peach ready to drop back into our hands."

Truscott did not like the fiery rawness of his host's liquor, but he sipped it until he felt it burning the lining of his throat. Weary from the long day's ride, he wanted nothing more than to lie down and sleep. Colquett's reverberating voice was beginning to irritate him, rambling on with grandiose schemes of conquest, rebellion, and creation of a Northwestern Confederacy. It all suddenly seemed bizarre to Truscott, who had come so recently from the heart of the Confederacy, where Richmond and Atlanta were both besieged, where shortages of food, weapons, and men to fill depleted

< CONSPIRACY OF KNAVES >

ranks were stark realities. He had traveled to Tamaroa to receive information about horses, two thousand horses for the Morgan men in that military prison at Chicago, but Colquett had yet to mention horses.

At last the big man paused to take another long swallow of whiskey, and Truscott spoke: "My duty in coming here, sir, is to see that horses are driven into Chicago before a certain date. On General Morgan's orders I've brought nine good men with me. We lost two in Kentucky."

"You brought cavalrymen here with you?" Colquett's voice and eyes indicated astonishment.

"Dressed as stockmen," Hatfield explained hurriedly. "We left them at the empty church."

"Very imprudent. I don't like to have too many Southern-talking men around Barton Farm." Colquett stared at Truscott as if willing him to explain his actions.

Truscott ignored Colquett's admonishing tone. "Where are the horses at present, sir?" he asked.

"In Missouri. Scattered, but they can be brought quickly into St. Louis for ferry crossings. When I give the word."

"Would not two thousand horses attract the attention of the authorities?"

Colquett laughed. "The authorities will aid me, give me the fastest passage, because they'll believe they're for the Union Army. I've spent two years establishing credibility here as a loyal trader in mules and horses to the Union."

Truscott wondered how much wealth Colquett had amassed as a trader to the enemy, but he held his tongue and said instead: "It was General Morgan's understanding that the horses would be ready."

Rising from the rocking chair, Colquett took three or four steps toward Truscott, towering over him, jabbing at him with a pointed finger: "If you have funds with you, Captain Truscott, deliver the money to me now and I will set the gears in motion before next daylight."

"I was provided with only enough greenbacks to support me and my men for this venture."

Colquett shook his head. "Money makes the mare go, as they say. Charley Heywood assured me that he'd have it here by this

< **Tramp, Tramp, Tramp** >

day, and I can tell you, captain, that no horses will move out of Missouri until there is gold or good greenbacks to pay for them. Bills of sale I'll need for the Federal inspectors. Prices are rising for good horseflesh. We're talking of thirty thousand dollars at bottom."

Truscott thought of the hundred thousand taken from the bank in Mount Sterling, the bags of it he'd last seen in possession of the Copperhead named Kendrich and the two Fielding brothers. "I'm confident the money is on its way. But time is vital. A date has been set for the breakout."

"I know the date," Colquett said curtly. "July the fourth."

"Doesn't give us much time."

Colquett turned toward a curtain doorway. "Time enough. If Charley Heywood shows with the money." He turned to look back at Truscott.

"Meanwhile, where do my men and I keep ourselves?" Truscott asked.

Colquett smiled. "I'll figure on that. You could help me and my boys on this side the river at St. Louis." He parted the heavy curtains. "Right now I want you and Mr. Hatfield to meet a pair of visitors who are going to be of great benefit to us. If I can pry them from their card game."

Hatfield stood up to follow Colquett, muttering something about a need to relieve himself. A minute or so later Truscott heard voices rumbling within the farther rooms of the house.

One of Colquett's visitors startled Truscott when he stepped through the curtains. He was Wesley Heywood, Marianna's brother, who, he had been told, was riding with Quantrill's raiders in Missouri. Wesley had been drinking heavily, a habit that always accentuated the flaws in his behavior and appearance. Truscott had never liked Wesley Heywood, considering him to be a lazy weakling, and tolerated him solely because he was Marianna's brother. When Wesley entered the room, he wore his usual half grin on his twisted mouth. The fact that when he smiled he never raised more than one side of his lips had somehow become symbolic to Truscott, indicative of the young man's halfheartedness, his unwillingness to participate in the harder quests of knighthood. Wesley Heywood loved ease and luxury, and from boyhood had treated horses badly.

After they exchanged greetings, Truscott told Wesley of his

< CONSPIRACY OF KNAVES >

recent visit to Little Hundred. "Your mother is not well, but Marianna keeps her high spirits, and her courage is admirable." The partially inebriated Wesley nodded uncertainly, his pale blue eyes moistening as he muttered a few words about his war duties keeping him from paying a visit to his family.

"They believe you are riding with Captain Quantrill," Truscott said.

"Oh, I was, I was," Wesley declared. "Until I met Brigadier Colquett. The brigadier is showing me how—ah, ah—" He fumbled for words. "How to line my pockets from the war." He laughed feebly. "Quantrill was much more fun, Johnny, but a man has to think of his future, don't you know."

The second visitor was from Chicago, a man only slightly taller than Truscott, but rather heavy of chest and belly. He was Joseph Milligan, sometimes addressed as "colonel" by Colquett. Milligan wore a drooping mustache, his hair smelled of pomade, his eyes were filled with a frustration approaching madness. His face alternately expressed elation and dejection.

Milligan had come down on the cars from Chicago to meet Charley Heywood. "Major Heywood promised to provide me with ten thousand dollars for purchase of rifles and ammunition," Milligan said in a loud whisper after drawing Truscott aside. "To be used in storming the Camp Douglas military prison in Chicago." Truscott wondered why the man was whispering. Probably a matter of habit, he guessed.

In the same conspiratorial undertone, Milligan told the group about Greek fire. "An ancient weapon recently rediscovered and improved by one of our brother knights, a Mr. Bockling." He drew a small glass vial from an inside pocket. "Filled with Mr. Bockling's secret formula, this vial can be quietly thrown down and broken against a government warehouse, a wooden railroad car, a freight vessel, an ordnance depot. Hours later—after the saboteur is safely away from the scene—a hot fire will break out. We plan to start such fires all around Chicago to draw attention from the Camp Douglas assault. The beauty of Greek fire is that water will not extinguish it, but only makes the flames burn with greater force."

They talked and drank until after midnight, and when at last the seemingly indefatigable Alonzo Colquett began yawning and

< **Tramp, Tramp, Tramp** >

pleaded an overpowering desire for sleep, Truscott rose from his chair with relief.

"I suppose you'll be rejoining your men, captain," Colquett said.

"Yes," Truscott replied.

"I'd prefer a bed here, brigadier," Hatfield said, "if you can put me up."

Colquett nodded to Hatfield, and then he moved unsteadily toward the front door. He slurred his words as he bade Truscott good night and invited him to return for breakfast.

"What about my men?" Truscott asked. "They've almost no rations left."

Colquett's big hand pressed against Truscott's back, as though giving him a reassuring pat but almost propelling him out upon the veranda. "We'll have something fixed up for your boys, don't worry, captain. Until tomorrow."

The summer rain had stopped, and strong upper winds were sweeping the darker clouds eastward. Truscott had to awaken the stableboy to find his horse and saddle.

Before he reached the chapel, sleep almost overtook him, but he remembered to sound a whippoorwill call to let the pickets know he was approaching. He was surprised that there was no response. Weariness and overconfidence were no excuses for carelessness, he thought. Yet it was a peaceful place, secure and silent except for an irregular dripping from the rain-washed trees and an occasional whir from a tree toad.

Under tall elms near the small rectangle of open ground in front of the chapel, the horses were rope-corralled, and Truscott rode in beside them, dismounting and unsaddling hurriedly, eager for sleep. First, though, he must find Sergeant Stiles and report the pickets' lack of vigilance.

As he walked across the soft wet earth to the chapel entrance, he expected a challenge, but none came. He knew then that something was wrong. With all the men sleeping inside, Joe Stiles would have put guards at the entrance. Truscott's first reaction was anger that any one of them had grown careless enough to let fatigue overcome the sharp alertness that had kept them alive through three years of danger.

The chapel door was half open on rusty hinges. Inside was

< CONSPIRACY OF KNAVES >

nothing but blackness, no sound of sleeping men. Truscott was just about to back away from the entrance when he heard Sergeant Stiles's voice call out a warning, and then his carbine was snatched from his hands and something struck the back of his neck. Strong arms encircled him, pinning his own arms to his sides. He saw the shape of a man against the chapel wall, spinning a rope that tightened his limbs to his body.

After being half dragged and half carried into the chapel, Truscott was shoved down upon the flooring. A light flared and someone held a box lantern close to his face.

"That'll teach you to come in here and wake us up," a nasal voice complained. "I take it you're the top sawyer of this ring of horse thieves."

In the lantern's glow Truscott could see that the man was wearing some kind of Union home-guard uniform. Several other vague shadows stood behind him. And on the floor, bound with ropes as was he, lay his nine Kentuckians.

"I'm a horse buyer," Truscott said calmly, "and I'll thank you to release me."

The man with the lantern snorted. "Horse thief, more likely. For now, you just lay there with your fellow poachers. Think about a hanging. No talking, no noise, so me and my company can get our sleep." He blew out the lantern. Boots tramped on the flooring, followed by a metallic clicking of released gunlocks, and a murmuring of voices. For several minutes Truscott lay quietly; then he edged closer to the nearest of his men. "How did it happen?" he whispered.

"They come down on us like ghosts, Captain Truscott. Captured our pickets without a sound, then slipped inside the church, seized our weapons, and had us trussed up like hogs ready for slaughter before we knew what was happening."

"You Sam Baird?"

"Yes, sir."

"What did they accuse us of, Sam?"

"Horse stealing."

"That's all?"

"Yes, sir."

A voice called from the chapel entrance. "Shut up that talk, or I'll blast y' in there."

< **Tramp, Tramp, Tramp** >

Truscott spent the remaining hours of that night fighting sleep and attempting to loose the tight ropes around his body. He managed to free one arm and was making progress on the other when daylight came with the suddenness that is usual on a cloudless June morning. A few minutes later, several home guards tramped into the chapel and on an order from their leader they began untying the halter ropes they had used to bind the Kentuckians.

As soon as this was done, the prisoners were marched out in front of the chapel and formed into a single rank. Facing them was a company of about thirty dismounted home guards, weapons at the ready, obviously well pleased with themselves. Some of them were old men, others very young. The officer in command had lost an arm somewhere; he wore his empty sleeve pinned across his chest. Like most of his men, he appeared to be a farmer or stockman. From somewhere behind the chapel, the guards' horses were being led into the open ground by young boys, some of them Negroes, who appeared to be no more than ten or twelve years old. After a series of ineptly executed commands, the guards mounted and then the captives were ordered to march ahead of them on foot.

"We'd prefer to ride our horses," Truscott called to the commander.

"Per-fer all you like," the one-armed man replied. "You can just say good-bye to yo'r stolen horses."

Although the distance to Tamaroa was no more than two miles, all cavalrymen detest foot marching, and Truscott and his Kentuckians grumbled audibly as they were hurried along a road by the mounted horse guards. Their own horses, under care of the young boys, were moving along at the rear.

When they reached a small railroad station at Tamaroa, they were ordered to halt alongside the tracks. The one-armed officer dismounted and went inside the station. A few moments later Truscott heard the steady clacking of a telegraph key, interrupted by short periods of silence. Eventually the one-armed man reappeared. He called his company to attention, ordered them to dismount, and then addressed himself to Truscott. "First thing you rascallions do is unfasten yo'r spurs and toss 'em over here. My company ain't so well ac-cootered as yo'rs."

"We'll keep our spurs and demand our horses be returned to us," Truscott said.

< CONSPIRACY OF KNAVES >

"Obey my order," the guard commander shouted angrily, "or my men will fire on you."

For the first time since his capture, Truscott realized that he was in a deeper predicament than he had first imagined. The home-guard leader had made up his mind that they were horse thieves and was going to treat them as such.

"Unfasten yo'r spurs and put 'em in a pile there," the one-armed man shouted.

"I want to speak to your superior officer," Truscott replied coolly, but the last word was scarcely said before the home-guard leader drew his pistol and fired over Truscott's head.

"Next shot will be lower down," the man said. "Obey my order!"

Truscott motioned to his men to obey, and he bent to unbuckle his own spurs, tossing them in front of the line of guards.

"Now, sir," he said as he raised up, "I request the right to be taken to your commander or to the county courthouse. I'm a law-abiding citizen—"

"Shee-it!" the one-armed man shouted. "You think I don't know who you bastards are? I been telegraphin' up and down the line." He raised his chin and pointed with his single arm to a line of railroad freight cars on a switch track a few yards across the main line. "You Kentucky horse thieves step right over there and climb in one of them common stockcars. Yo're Rebel spies and we could hang you for that, but the high command in Chicago wants to hear talk from you before they put ropes around yo'r necks."

They were marched across the tracks and ordered to climb into a boxcar that had been converted to a livestock carrier by cutting a row of small squares along the upper part of each side. Obviously the car had not been cleaned since last being used for shipping animals. The manure on the floor was shoe-top deep and only par-tially dried. By the time Truscott had climbed in behind his men and taken a position at one of the square apertures, the home guards were closing the door. He heard a chain rattling in the fastening and then laughter as the guards walked away toward the station.

Truscott turned to look at his men. He wondered why Sergeant Stiles kept avoiding him. He wanted to offer a word of encour-agement, give some hope of escape from their plight. Most of their faces showed concern, but only Stiles looked beaten, utterly dispirited. His head was bent forward, and his unkempt beard and the deep lines in his weathered forehead gave him the appearance of an old man.

"We're not defeated yet, Joe Stiles," Truscott said quietly. "Remember last summer when we slipped away from Buffington Island and swam the Ohio?"

"This whole doin' is my fault, Captain Truscott," Stiles replied bitterly, his gaze fixed on the filthy floor of the stockcar.

One of the men spoke up, defending Stiles. "The home guards had us pegged, captain."

"No doubt of that," Truscott said. "They know everything about us."

Stiles's tortured face at last turned toward his captain. "If I had not made a big brag and captured them militia horses, back at that bridge, they'd never bothered us," he said.

"That was miles from here, Joe," Truscott replied. "They couldn't've tracked us to that little church. Not along the roads we followed. No, someone around here betrayed us."

They spent the next hour searching every square foot of the stockcar's interior. The flooring was solid oaken beams, the walls almost as strong, and the ventilation squares cut into them were too small for a man's shoulders to squeeze through. In the ceiling at one end of the car was a closed hatch about two feet square. Climbing upon the shoulders of two of the men, Truscott examined it hopefully, but it was soon apparent that the hatch had been spiked shut. That left only the entrance door, and they had all heard the heavy chain rattling in the latch.

All through the late morning and into the afternoon, cattle and horses and sheep were loaded into empty cars along the side track. Eventually a locomotive arrived to begin moving cars back and forth on the two tracks. A work crew's car was hooked to one end of the prisoners' car. From a ventilation square Truscott watched the one-armed officer march a squad of home guards aboard the work car. Shortly afterward, footsteps sounded on the roof above them, and then the freight train began slowly moving, gathering speed as it drove toward the Illinois prairies, heading north for Chicago.

8

BELLE RUTLEDGE

•────────•

IF CAPTAIN JOHN TRUSCOTT could have seen the dispatch from Chicago that was telegraphed to newspapers across the Union while he and his men were still traveling northward in that filthy livestock car, his worries might indeed have been magnified. Charley Heywood and I read about the capture in a Cincinnati newspaper. We were on our way to that city from the river town of Philo. Our train had stopped for connection with the Little Miami Railroad at Loveland, and there a hawker came aboard with a tray full of sweetmeats and a bag of newspapers. While I chose a piece of candied fruit for that voracious little monster, Winslow Barber, Charley purchased a newspaper.

In his skeptical but jocund tone, Charley read the headlines aloud as the train began rolling again. "SHERMAN'S ASSAULT UPON GEORGIA MOUNTAIN. REBELS SUFFER HEAVY CASUALTIES. HEROISM OF OUR WESTERN ARMY." He sniffed. "The Northern papers lie as freely as the ones in Richmond. Heavy casualties are suffered by the attackers of mountains, not the defenders." He turned the page and a moment later cried out: "Aha! They snared good old Johnny Truscott." He shifted the paper closer to me so that I could read the single paragraph under a small blackface heading:

CAPTURE OF REBEL SPIES

Chicago, Saturday

A telegraphic dispatch from southern Illinois reports the capture of ten suspicious horsemen by the Perry County home guard. At first believed to be only horse thieves from Kentucky, the captives are now suspected of being spies from John Morgan's bushwhackers allied with the Copperheads. They were under the command of the notorious Captain Truscott. Military authorities at Camp Douglas in Chicago are awaiting arrival of the captives on the Illinois Central Railroad sometime tomorrow.

"This Captain Truscott," I asked, "is he the man who robbed the bank at Mount Sterling?"

"The one and only. But honestly I've never considered Johnny as being notorious." Charley laughed. He did not appear to be the least bit concerned that his friend and fellow officer was in danger of losing his life if convicted of spying.

My thoughts on this strangely callous attitude of Major Heywood were rudely interrupted by a sudden outburst from Winslow, who had devoured the last of his candied fruit and wanted more. When he eventually understood that there were no more sweetmeats to be had, he changed his demand to a drink of water, and so he and I had to wander through the jolting cars until we found a water jug that had not been emptied. During this venture the little imp picked at the scab forming on his chin and set the blood to running again. I had to use one of the major's handkerchiefs to stanch and bind it up again.

The hour's ride into Cincinnati therefore passed rapidly, and we were soon running along the crowded riverfront, slowing gradually as we neared an enormous station. The locomotive, in fact, pulled the passenger cars through a cast-iron arch right inside a vaulted enclosure. Although the ceiling was very high, with tall generous windows on either side, the presence of two idling locomotives filled the interior with black smoke of varying densities. We were soon out into a maelstrom of hurrying human beings, struggling with our baggage and trying to calm Winslow, who one moment was trembling with terror at the sights and sounds, and the next shrieking in a state of uncontrolled glee. I took some comfort from the knowledge that at last we were in Cincinnati,

< CONSPIRACY OF KNAVES >

where the youngster's relatives would relieve us of our burden.

Charley led us past a women's parlor, which I would have dearly loved to enter to clean the soot and cinders from my face and hair, but he was determined to hurry on to a hotel. Once outside the station we were free of the coal smoke, yet the air was burdened with a most unpleasant pungency, a malodor that I was soon to learn came from the numerous slaughterhouses of this meat-packing center of the Union. Indeed, soon after Charley put us into one of the hacks lined up outside the station, we crossed an open stream running red with the blood of butchered animals as it flowed toward the Ohio River. The repulsive sight turned my stomach, but Charley ignored it and began extolling the wonders of Cincinnati.

"The Queen City of the West," he cried. "Order, thrift, and plenty!" He raised up in the seat to survey the solid buildings we were passing. When the hack made a turn, he pointed to an array of packets along the riverfront, with smoke curling from their stacks. Long lines of workmen were loading enormous quantities of goods in barrels, crates, and bags. The only indication of war in the busy scene was a small squad of uniformed guards posted at the end of the suspension bridge.

"And over yonder," I said, "lies poor Kentucky."

"Ah, yes, but we poor Kentuckians came near to capturing this city last summer." He lowered his voice so the hack driver could not hear him. "We had her encircled from the north, Belle. We rode right into the outer ring of homesteads, but General Morgan feared the place too strongly fortified. I swear we could have taken her."

Winslow squirmed from my grip, but Charley caught him before he could fall beneath the gritting wheels. "You little black-guard," Charley shouted. "We're taking you to your Yankee kin before this day ends. God help 'em!" Winslow thrust his lips into a pout, and an adult expression of disbelief came into his eyes.

We stopped at the Packet House, a rather ornate establishment. When Charley signed the register, he was told that a gentleman was awaiting his arrival. That sudden look of wariness that I'd grown accustomed to see in Major Heywood's manner showed itself, replacing the ebullience he had been luxuriating in since our arrival in Cincinnati. The man in question had been seated so that

< **Belle Rutledge** >

he faced the registry desk, and as he approached us, he casually put his right hand over his heart and with his left hand touched the elbow of his right arm. Charley's solemn face immediately broke into a boyish smile, and they shook hands in that absurd fashion I'd noticed before when he was dealing with Copperheads, linking their thumbs like a pair of silly schoolboys.

When Charley introduced him as a "Mr. Woodbridge," he identified me as Miss Belle Rutledge, and I knew we were no longer traveling as Dr. Campbell and wife. I wondered what difference that was going to make in the relationship we had formed in that little hotel in the river town of Philo.

Mr. Woodbridge accompanied us to our rooms on the second story of the Packet House, and they were *rooms*—a magnificent parlor furnished with a dozen fine chairs and sofas, a large bedroom with two beds, and a bathing room. I desperately wanted to fill the round tub with water as hot as I could stand it and seat myself in it for an hour, but the major kept pressing me to get Winslow's clothes together. He left Mr. Woodbridge in the parlor and followed Winslow and me into the bedroom.

"I can't go with you to take the boy to his relatives, Belle," he said. "You'll have to do it alone. The Copperheads are trying to find my three men, who should have arrived from Philo by now."

"Winslow and I both need baths and a change of clothing. His kinfolk will think we're vagabonds."

"No time for that." He lowered his voice. "I need you back here as soon as possible. Mr. Woodbridge is a Grand Seigneur, and he and some other high muck-mucks of the Sons of Liberty will be meeting here in a short while. I want you to keep a record of what is said."

Well, as it turned out, it did not matter in the least that Winslow and I resembled vagabonds. We rode in a horse cab to the address on the papers that Colonel Fennell had given Charley in Richmond, a house on Fourth Street west of Vine. Half the residences along that section of the street had either been demolished or were in the process of being torn down to make room for commercial buildings, some of which were already being erected. The cab stopped in front of a dilapidated wooden house. The yard gate lay on a brick sidewalk, and the yard itself was filled with litter. On the rickety porch, four children clad in unwashed and ragged clothing, the

< CONSPIRACY OF KNAVES >

younger ones wearing only long gray shirts, had stopped their mindless play to stare at us. I told the driver to wait for me, and led Winslow up on the porch. He eyed the dirty younglings nervously and clung tightly to my wrist with both hands.

Before I could knock on the frame of the open doorway, a woman materialized inside. She reminded me of the drawings of slatterns I'd seen in Mr. Charles Dickens's illustrated novels—sad but resentful eyes, defeat all over her face, her body in the attitude of a last stand. I told her who I was, that I had brought her little orphaned nephew from faraway Virginia to be placed in the bosom of his family.

Wiping her hands on a dirty apron, she forced herself out upon the porch as though with a final summoning of flagging energies. Two more bratlings followed, clinging to her skirts. Somewhere inside the house a baby was crying. She began talking, her voice rising and falling in an unsteady whimpering, a recitation of woes. Her husband worked on a steamboat and was gone most of the time. He had sent no money home for weeks, and they were living off the charity of their church, which wasn't much. Yes, they had received two letters telling that her dead sister's child was being sent to Cincinnati. Her husband had gone to the orphanage and the manager there had agreed to take the boy. She had a letter to prove it, and would I deliver the child to the orphanage? It was way out on Poplar Street, and she could not leave her brood to make the journey.

I waited until she went inside and returned with a folded letter, and then I fairly fled with Winslow to the waiting horse cab. All the way to Poplar Street and the forbidding smoke-stained brick structure of the orphanage, Winslow sat as close to me as he could, his hands folded in his lap, silent as death. For the first time since our meeting in Richmond, I felt sorry for the little creature.

Inside the orphanage we met with one of those mealymouthed types of males who connect themselves with such institutions, flabby of mind and body and about as sincere as a weasel. When he patted Winslow's head, he of course received a hard kick in the shins. The man winced, reached for a flat stick, caught Winslow's hand, and gave the palm a stinging blow. I knew then that it was time for me to leave. "Good-bye, Winslow," I said. "You must be a good boy now."

A string of profane words erupted, his entire vocabulary of body functions and blasphemy. The orphanage manager gasped for breath, and he tried to shame me with a glare and a clucking tongue. "That calls for a washing-out with soap," he cried. "We'll soon have this wicked child put right."

At the door I could not resist one glance back. Winslow's accusing eyes were moist, but he was too indignant to cry. His wide mouth formed silent invectives, but what touched me most deeply was the way he turned his head slowly from side to side, his grieving eyes urging me not to betray him, not to leave him there. I turned my back on him for what I thought was a final good-bye. I felt like a female Judas Iscariot.

The fates and my zodiacal stars conspired to make that day a succession of lacerated emotions, bitter disappointments, and thunderbolt surprises. A wholly unexpected shock occurred upon my return to the sumptuous suite in the Packet House. Try to imagine how I felt when I walked up the carpeted stairs, found the entrance door wide open, and saw standing inside, instructing a hotel domestic to clean and dry his muddy boots, a handsome gentleman whom I had last seen in Washington. No wonder I suffered a sudden wave of faintness and palpitations. This was the man to whom I had written that hasty letter on stationery of the Union Army's Medical Corps at City Point, Virginia, which I had then given to a hospital orderly for posting on the military mail boat to Washington. In the man's gray eyes was recognition but no surprise; he had been expecting my arrival.

Major Heywood's clear voice called from the door of the bedroom: "Mr. Kendrich, this is Belle Rutledge. Belle, meet Mr. Kendrich, our liaison courier from the Order of American Knights in New York."

I was quite aware that Kendrich was not this man's name, and from what I knew of him I thought it most unlikely that he was a genuine courier from the New York Copperheads. In the course of this narrative, however, I shall refer to him as Kendrich because surviving members of his family believe that he died bravely in the service of his country, and to reveal his real name would add nothing to the events in which he participated.

He bowed, clicked his heels together, reached for my hand,

< CONSPIRACY OF KNAVES >

kissed it, and muttered something complimentary in a thick accent. Only an experienced actress could have kept her aplomb in such a situation, and I pride myself in not having given way and revealing that I was a past associate of Kendrich, in fact had acted in naughty skits with him in the lower-grade theaters of Washington. Kendrich was a natural mimic. He could imitate a Scotsman, a Dutchman, a Frenchman, a Southern Negro—almost any pronouncing of the voice he could perform to perfection. As had happened to me, the upheavals of the war had lost him opportunities to play in real dramas. He was trapped in Washington, where he had established a reputation among theater managers as an actor who could be depended upon to speak a variety of comic accents, and had become especially popular with German and Irish soldiers, who laughed wildly at his imitations of their speech and behavior.

"Mr. Kendrich is Bavarian by birth," Major Heywood was saying as he came walking across the carpeted room, "but he has spent much of his life in New York." Only the second part of that remark was true, I knew, but I could see that Kendrich had charmed the major in the way he could charm theater audiences when he put his mind to it.

"He came here to arrange a shipment of Garibaldi rifles to the Ohio temples," Heywood continued. "Because of his foreign manner, the Grand Commander drafted him as an ideal courier to bring the Mount Sterling bank money into Ohio. He proved to be an excellent choice."

I could almost smell that money. Excusing myself, I went into the bedroom, and there the booty was, in small bags of burlap and blanket cloth, piled helter-skelter on one of the beds. Charley followed me into the bedroom, and I noticed that he had taken time during my absence to acquire a new waistcoat and a fancy shirt and cravat. There I was in a wrinkled old dress, needing a bath, no doubt resembling a harridan, and there was Charley Heywood disporting himself like a dandy. My ire rose to a boil.

"It would be hard on any man," I said tartly, "to live up to those clothes you're wearing."

"Ah, Belle," he responded with that disarming smile of his, "you know it is necessary in my duties here."

"And what about me and my duties?"

"Of course, of course. You shall have what you need." He

< **Belle Rutledge** >

gestured toward the heaped bed. "We have plenty of real green-backs now."

"You're so wrapped up in your schemes," I said, "you haven't even asked about Winslow."

"Winslow was given a welcome reception, I trust."

I told him about the slattern and her collection of whelps, about the orphanage, about the look in Winslow's eyes when I abandoned him there.

"Good God, Belle, you could have offered the woman some money." That was always Charley's solution, money. He believed money could make any wretched thing all right, yet no matter how much of it came into his possession, he could seldom keep any, and was always hustling for more. He muttered something about taking care of Winslow's situation himself just as soon as matters settled down, but at that moment we were interrupted by a loud yell, raucous laughter, and an outburst of barnyard profanity. While I had been talking with Charley, I thought I heard splashing from the bathing room, and now suddenly the door was flung open and out rushed a pair of young black-haired sunburned boys, look-ing like wet Newfoundland dogs but as merry as grigs, laughing and buttoning up their new brown jeans and shirts. They were the Fielding brothers, Paul and Andy, who had accompanied Ken-drich from Mount Sterling. In past years I'd seen their counterparts in Louisville, innocents from the hill country awed by the city sights, grinning to cover their ignorance. For some reason my mother always called them "woods colts."

They both blushed at the sight of me, and were obviously eager to escape from the bedroom so they might fasten up their loose buttons unobserved. Charley gave them some greenbacks, told them to go downstairs and eat but to avoid talking with anyone unnecessarily. As they were departing, I heard one of them ask: "What's this about Captain Truscott and some of his boys gettin' captured?"

"It's true. They should be prisoners in Camp Douglas by now."

"Bad luck."

Charley's answer to that natural response startled me. "Tem-porarily, perhaps, for them. But for us, Captain Truscott can be most useful in Camp Douglas—the night we seize Chicago."

< CONSPIRACY OF KNAVES >

For the next several weeks, particularly after I met Johnny Truscott, I was to hear much about why it was that he was so easily trapped with all of his men to become a prisoner in Camp Douglas. Indeed, I was to hear about it many times during our exile in Canada, and even now I cannot escape occasional conjectures about the incident.

The bathing room was an unholy mess, with water all over the flooring and not a dry towel left anywhere. Yet somehow I managed to make myself presentable and get downstairs in the overelegant dining salon of the Packet House for my first real food since leaving the Lyons Hotel in Philo. Major Heywood, with Grand Seigneur Woodbridge and the spurious Mr. Kendrich had dined during my absence with Winslow, and so there I was, a put-upon woman, forced to dine alone. Charley's hurried instruction as I started downstairs was to hasten back upstairs so that I might record statements and promises made during the Copperhead meeting. I was beginning to get a bit sick and tired of the imperious side of Major Heywood. Deliberately I lingered over my coffee and sweet biscuits, and stared boldly back at the half dozen males in the dining room who kept gaping at me, the lone woman.

Through an arched doorway I saw the Fielding brothers pass along a corridor, still awed by the splendor of the hotel, moving warily as though stalking a deer, their eyes wide with wonder. Seconds later I sensed the presence of someone behind me, and before I could turn my head Kendrich was standing at my side.

"I have but a few moments," he said without his stage accent. "You must travel as quickly as possible to Chicago."

"Major Heywood and I are under instructions to journey there next," I interrupted.

"Yes, but he may delay, or go elsewhere first," Kendrich said impatiently. "Whatever he may do, you are to use any pretext you can muster to reach Chicago. We can no longer trust the telegraph or mails into that city." He glanced cautiously around the dining room. "When you arrive there, go immediately to Camp Douglas, ask for the commandant, Colonel Wright—Bartholomew Wright— and tell him you have a message from K. Tell him the rising is now set for July the fourth. That he should be prepared for attacks upon essential buildings in the city of Chicago as well as an armed assault at the camp. Tell him that names and places will be sent him as they become known."

We were both surprised by the sudden appearance of the Fielding brothers in the arched doorway at our right. How much they heard of what Kendrich was saying, I do not know. They both grinned at us and then moved on along the corridor, still stalking wild game.

"I must go," Kendrich whispered. "I came downstairs on a pretext of obtaining a bottle of Stoughton's bitters for my stomach. If those wily mountain boys heard anything, I'll need more than bitters."

"I sent you a letter from Virginia," I said quickly.

"Yes. It reached me only this morning. That's how I knew you must be here with Heywood." He moved away, covering his nervousness with a bow, a click of heels, a stage smile, and a thickly accented phrase of farewell.

I wondered what had happened to the real Mr. Kendrich.

Fortunately, I still have some of the notes I wrote down for Major Heywood during the long blustery meeting in the hotel suite, else I probably should not be able to give the numbers and statements put forward by various officers of the Sons of Liberty and Order of American Knights. At first, Major Heywood thought it might be advisable for me to listen from the bedroom, but after introducing me to the gentlemen and praising my work with Colonel Fennell, a name they all seemed to recognize and approve of, he placed me in a chair in one corner of the parlor room, and I sat there quite unobtrusively, recording whatever seemed important to me. I don't believe I have mentioned that during the precarious months when I was performing in those risqué comic turns in Washington, I spent some of my free time learning the Pitman system of stenography in hopes of obtaining employment in the Treasury Department, which had opened its offices to large numbers of young women. Therefore, I was able to get a considerable amount of information down quickly in a small space, and in such form that only a few could interpret it.

About a dozen Copperheads had assembled for this meeting, at least one high representative from each of the Northwestern

< CONSPIRACY OF KNAVES >

states, and they reported on the numbers, activities, plans, and urgent monetary needs of their temples.

Before this official meeting began, however, Grand Seigneur Woodbridge brought in two men, one of whom was not a member of the Knights. He was a Mr. Gatling, who had invented a gun with revolving rifle barrels, mounted on wheels. He said that he had exhibited his weapon many times to artillery officers of the Union Army, but the government had not seen fit to advance any money for manufacturing Gatling guns.

"The Lincoln government is a tyrannical usurpation," Grand Seigneur Woodbridge declared in his clipped manner of speaking.

Major Heywood interrupted, and from the tone of his voice I could tell he was annoyed by Woodbridge's inane remark. "How rapidly does your gun fire, Mr. Gatling?"

"As many as three hundred and fifty shots a minute," Gatling replied. "Depends upon how fast the hand crank is turned."

Heywood whistled. "I've heard of your gun. Could you give us a demonstration?"

Gatling replied that it could be arranged, but he wanted assurances that if the Copperheads were satisfied with the gun's performance, they would immediately advance several thousand dollars in orders. A heated discussion followed, the crucial point seeming to hang upon the expected arrival of a man from Canada whom they called "J.T." Most of the Grand Commanders argued in favor of all moneys for purchase of weapons being issued directly to them. They would then decide what weapons to buy. Major Heywood wanted the Gatling guns commissioned all together and then distributed to strategic places in the forthcoming Northwest Confederacy. Eventually they agreed to leave the decision to "J.T." when he arrived in Cincinnati. After all, as I was to learn later, he controlled the Confederate States funds that had been amassed in Canada.

Grand Seigneur Woodbridge escorted Mr. Gatling from the room, returning a few minutes later with a Mr. Bockling, who proceeded to empty a satchel filled with hand grenades, glass tubes, brass shells, and something he called an "infernal machine" with a small clock attached. Mr. Bockling was a shortish man, about five feet six, wore spectacles, had dark hair and whiskers. He had just arrived that morning from Louisville.

He addressed the Copperheads somewhat in the manner of an auctioneer or street vendor, describing himself as the inventor of Greek fire, a concoction that could not be extinguished by water; in fact, it would burn under water. Like Mr. Gatling he had once demonstrated the uses of his invention to high officers of the Union Army. They appeared to be interested in obtaining large quantities of Greek fire, but not one cent had been advanced to Mr. Bockling to begin manufacturing.

"I am a member of the Order of American Knights," Bockling said, "and my sympathies, of course, lie with your organization's aims. If you can advance the necessary funds to me, I will begin manufacturing at once. I believe the gentleman from Indiana has seen demonstrations of my Greek fire, has he not?" He gestured toward a tall long-necked man with a mop of pure white hair who nodded and spoke approvingly of Greek fire as an excellent compound with which to sabotage the enemy.

"Are the materials easily obtained?" Major Heywood asked.

"Obtainable, but very dear. I based my patent upon the original secret mixture used by the Greeks against Arab ships that attacked Constantinople in the seventh century."

"Ancient," the major said. "Could you tell us what the mixture consists of?"

Mr. Bockling shrugged and spread his hands. "A petroleum base. The difficulty—and the expense—comes in the addition of phosphorus and bisulphate of carbon."

Charley was keenly interested now, and so were most of the others. "Suppose we wanted to set fire to the principal office buildings in a large city," he said. "How much Greek fire would be required?"

"Please name a city," Bockling replied.

"This one. Cincinnati."

The inventor leaned back in his chair. "Get me fifty thousand in gold or greenbacks," he said slowly. "And you shall have your Greek fire in a week. And enough to spare to burn all the gunboats along the riverfront."

For several minutes the Grand Commanders discussed the matter of Greek fire, eventually deciding to refer a strong request for fifty thousand dollars to the mysterious "J.T."

After the departure of Mr. Bockling, they took a short interlude

< CONSPIRACY OF KNAVES >

from these weighty matters, bringing out flasks and cigars, and Major Heywood asked me to withdraw to the bedroom, close the door, and wait until I was summoned for duty again. Next on the program was a temple meeting of the Knights from which non-members were barred. Although I was confined to the closed bedroom, I could hear occasional recitations and declamations as they went through the ridiculous schoolboy antics of their rituals. No woman that I have ever known could have been able to endure such repetitious nonsense of who cometh, worthy brothers, onwards, most excellent knights, holy signs, and watchwords.

While waiting, I relaxed on the empty bed, stared at the heaps of moneybags on the opposite bed, and pondered the possibilities for me if I simply took one of the bags and walked out of the lives of Charley Heywood and the man called Kendrich. Before I could reach a conclusion, Charley opened the door and asked me to return to my recording duties.

What was said during the final hour was a revelation to me, although even then I was growing a bit skeptical of what the Knights put into words and numbers. They were not reluctant at all to estimate the amounts of money they required in order to carry on their work of recruiting and arming, but were reluctant to reveal how many active Copperheads were enrolled in the temples of their states. Major Heywood at last persuaded Mr. Woodbridge to provide him with the total for Ohio. "One hundred and eight thousand," he said. The representative from Illinois then boasted that his state could raise as many as one hundred and forty thousand. "Forty thousand are well armed," he added, "and if the Confederate Commission will issue us more money, say a hundred thousand dollars, we can put an armed force of eighty thousand men into the streets of Chicago."

The man from Missouri was slightly apologetic. His state could raise only twenty thousand Knights around St. Louis, but there were at least twenty thousand more out in the state awaiting the arrival of a Confederate army under General Price, an army that they would join and lead into St. Louis for a speedy capture of that city. They also needed thousands of dollars for procurement of arms and ammunition.

Kentucky's numbers admittedly were rough estimates, that state's representative said, but he believed there were at least forty thou-

< **Belle Rutledge** >

sand members, perhaps seventy thousand. The Knights of the
Golden Circle were forced to be very cautious about listing names
and numbers in Kentucky.

That left only Indiana. The state's spokesman was the thin
long-necked gentleman with the shock of cottony hair. He had
been introduced as "Colonel Smith," but judging from the titters
and knowing winks of the others, I guessed that was not his real
name. During the latter part of the meeting, he had placed his
chair so that, with a slight turn of his head, he would face me
directly. He had been giving me the eye as if measuring my read-
iness to be agreeable to him, but I would sooner have been agreeable to a fish. That is what he reminded me of, a cold fish with a
pursed mouth and eyes so pale blue they were almost colorless.

"The Indiana Sons of Liberty pride themselves on the exacti-
tude of their records," he said in a voice like cracked glass. "A
total of a hundred and twenty-four thousand eight hundred and
fifty-two members in all temples. Self-armed, with six thousand
rifles and sixty thousand pistols. At a meeting in Indianapolis last
week, four thousand dollars was subscribed for arms. The Grand
Seigneur of Indiana is asking the Confederate commissioners for
forty thousand dollars. With that amount, Indiana can put seventy-
five thousand armed men into the field. Another twenty thousand
dollars is needed to start manufacture of grenades and rockets in
a secret location near Indianapolis."

During the discussion that followed, Kendrich was asked a
number of questions about Garibaldi rifles. He was quite glib in
his replies, speaking in that stage accent of his, stating that with
enough money in hand to bribe functionaries between New Jersey
and Buffalo on Lake Erie, and still more greenbacks to hire a
Canadian fishing vessel on the lake, he was confident that as many
as twenty thousand of these imported weapons could be delivered
across from Windsor, Ontario, without interruption.

"By July fourth?" Heywood asked.

"The money for the rifles and their transport would need to be
in my hands," Kendrich replied easily, "within the next forty-eight
hours."

"How much money?"

"Eighty thousand at the least."

I doubt if any of these noble knights had given any thought to

< CONSPIRACY OF KNAVES >

the total amount of wealth their demands were adding up to. Each one was interested solely in his own craving for the gold and greenbacks that "J.T." was supposedly bringing them from Canada. I wondered to what use Major Heywood was going to put those bags of lucre that had earlier appeared so grand piled on the bed, but that now, after comparing them with the collective requisitions of the Grand Commanders, seemed quite paltry. All that money taken from the Mount Sterling bank by Johnny Truscott would satisfy only a very small part of the desires of the Sons of Liberty.

Suddenly the talk switched from numbers of dollars and Copperheads to numbers of Confederate soldiers, and where and how the two forces were to be brought together. It soon became apparent that this was a subject dear to Major Heywood's heart. He unfolded a map of the Ohio Valley and Northwestern states, and with Kendrich's assistance held it against the wall. Three simultaneous invasions were planned from Kentucky across the Ohio River, he explained, indicating entry points on the map. General Longstreet would lead the right wing into Ohio, General Morgan the center into Indiana, and General Forrest the left into Illinois. At the same time generals Price and Marmaduke would drive into Missouri from Arkansas to capture the St. Louis flank.

Considerable applause followed Heywood's brief presentation, but some of his listeners expressed doubts that the Confederates could bring three armies into Kentucky in time to strike simultaneously with the uprising of July fourth.

"The men are already there," Heywood declared with his usual insouciance. "Weeks ago some of them returned home to Kentucky and swore allegiance to the Union and are living there openly. Others are hiding with friends and relatives. On signal from us, Longstreet, Morgan, and Forrest will be there to lead them north to join the Sons of Liberty."

Grand Seigneur Woodbridge leaped to his feet, pounded a fist into his palm, and yelped like a hunting dog sighting his prey in a tree. "Hurrah for the Northwestern Confederacy," he shouted so loudly that the others warned him to keep his voice down.

I must admit the scheme did have an aura of excitement and glamour about it, and those two or three Grand Commanders who expressed fears of bloody fighting and damages to property in their

< **Belle Rutledge** >

home cities were quickly reassured. The thousands of armed Sons of Liberty in the streets backed by thousands of Confederate soldiers streaming northward in four great columns would make resistance futile. The Northwest Confederacy would become a *fait accompli*.

They boiled over with talk, talk, talk—talk of a proper signal to start the uprising, talk of whether a certain hour of the day on July fourth should be set for all to act in concert, talk of leaving the decision to Supreme Commander Vallandigham. But they could agree on nothing, except the need for thousands of dollars in gold or greenbacks.

Abruptly, Major Heywood brought the meeting to a close, announcing that he would send a coded message to each of them the instant that "J.T." arrived. They drifted out of the suite, singly or in pairs so as to attract no attention. The last to leave was "Colonel Smith," who kept edging closer to my chair until I felt the pressure of one of his bony knees against my leg.

"You are a handsome woman, Miss Rutledge," he said in that strange cracked voice of his. "Major Heywood tells me you have been an actress." I did not like the suggestive look in his powder-blue eyes when he pronounced the word *actress*.

"Excuse me, sir," I said, rising from the chair. "The heavy cigar smoke in this room is making me ill, and I have many things to attend." I went right on into the bedroom, and would have stretched my weary limbs on the empty bed had not the major followed as soon as he was rid of "Colonel Smith."

"God, Belle, they are a tiresome bunch. Did you get down all the numbers?"

"Yes, but how much of it is bona fide, Charley Heywood?"

He gave me a strange, almost hostile glance. "What do you mean?"

"The three Confederate armies, for one thing, marching northward out of Kentucky. I know, as well as you do, how critically short of men—"

"But you don't know how thoroughly Colonel Fennell and I have planned it," he interrupted angrily. "Only a handful of high officers in the Confederacy have been informed, and not until this afternoon did the Grand Commanders of the Sons of Liberty hear

< CONSPIRACY OF KNAVES >

of it. They *needed* to know that when they swarm into the streets on July fourth they'll not be alone."

As I commented before, the last hour of that Copperhead meeting was a revelation to me. President Lincoln had said something about a fire in the rear, but until then I'd not realized the enormity of that fire. I also felt a sense of unease because all the while I was in Richmond I had learned nothing of Colonel Fennell's and Major Heywood's scheme for those underground armies in Kentucky. The design seemed directly contradictory to Fennell's instruction to me. *It's Heywood's grandiose schemes that I don't trust*, the colonel had said. *Our main objective is first to free our soldiers in Camp Douglas. No fancy deals to overthrow Northwestern state governments, not yet.*

I knew that it was time for me to find the Cincinnati man whose name had been given me by Colonel Fennell. Not once during that afternoon of talk had any mention been made of freeing the Camp Douglas prisoners. How much I would tell this man about Major Heywood "going off track" I was not certain, but I had to see him before journeying to Chicago. Else Colonel Fennell might become suspicious of my loyalty to him. First thing tomorrow, I told myself, I would find a way to meet with Fennell's agent, unknown to Major Heywood.

I had been looking forward to an evening with the major, an evening of pleasure, perhaps a visit to a Cincinnati theater, a leisurely dinner with the sort of wines no longer obtainable in Richmond, and a long night together in the suite without Winslow's presence, lovers away from war and scheming and constant dissembling. But it was not to be.

From the hotel windows Charley and I were watching evening shadows fall over the Ohio River when a messenger rapped on the door, summoning him to some mysterious assignation. At least it was mysterious to me. Charley simply announced that he would be returning very late, and that I must fend for myself. And so again I was forced to dine alone with the usual predatory males in the hotel's *salle à manger* watching me consume a bottle of wine entire, almost literally licking their chops in anticipation of some signal of wantonness from me.

Truth was, I developed a fearful headache before leaving the

< **Belle Rutledge** >

table. Following the example of my friend Kendrich, I obtained a
bottle of Dr. Stoughton's bitters from the pharmacy and returned
to the suite.

To my surprise I found the two Fielding brothers propped on
cane chairs outside the door. Major Heywood, they explained, had
ordered them to guard the rooms during his absence. I invited them
to come into the parlor room, where they'd be more comfortable,
but they refused. "You'll be quite safe, ma'am," one of them said,
"with us out here." I had not the heart to tell them it was not me,
a romantic lady, they were guarding, but the bags of gold and
greenbacks inside.

Those bags were the last things I saw from the opposite bed
as my eyes closed. I swallowed a double dose of Dr. Stoughton's
bitters, which must have had a very high content of laudanum
since I dreamed wild dreams in color, dreams of joy in which
Charley and I performed as lovers upon a stage, dreams of sadness
in which little Winslow drew away from me until he vanished with
mournful shakes of his head, dreams of terror in which the long-
necked Colonel Smith pursued me across a snake-filled bog.

When I awoke, the moneybags on the opposite bed were gone,
replaced by Charley Heywood, who lay naked with a sheet covering
the lower half of his splendid body. On the floor beside the bed
were two new leather valises and a little heap of empty canvas
and blanket bags. Charley was breathing in that soft sibilant way
of his, not a snore but a murmur of confident contentment, which
I'd so quickly grown accustomed to.

We had breakfast together that morning, and afterward Charley gave me a packet of greenbacks as thick as my coin purse and
told me to go out to a ladies' emporium and buy what I needed.

He was gone almost before I could thank him, or make inquiries
as to when we would be leaving for Chicago. "Not until we hear
from J.T.," he replied hurriedly, closing the door behind him.

I decided to dress in my best for the visit to Colonel Fennell's
Cincinnati agent. I had memorized his name and address, Mr.
Lester Marmot on West Fifth Street. A rather unusual name, I
thought, possibly a quite handsome young gentleman. For him I
wore my black velvet and point lace, and rode to Fifth Street in
a two-wheeled covered carriage, most fancy.

The address on Fifth Street was not imposing, but the June morning was delightful, with birdsong right there in the busy city and the scent of honeysuckle on a gentle breeze.

Cincinnati begins its sharp rise from the river at Fifth Street, and I stood on the brick sidewalk for a minute or two, just enjoying being alive and looking up at the hilltop houses surrounded by fresh summer greenery.

Two different signs, on opposite sides of the doorway, left me wondering about Mr. Marmot's occupation. HOT-AIR FURNACES, announced one, in large block letters. The other was more discreet, handwritten in broad pen strokes: *Wanted: Handsome Women to Pose for Photographs*. The unlocked door let me into a hallway, and there was Lester Marmot's name in gilt with a pointing finger directing me into an open area of sheet-iron stoves, chandeliers, and rows of *carte de visite* photos displayed along the nearest wall.

"Mr. Lester Marmot," I called out in my deepest tenor, and regretted too late that I had not dressed in my masculine attire for this visit.

From somewhere behind a collection of stoves, I heard a stirring noise like that made by a large rat surprised in a cellar. A voice sounded then: "Who's there?"

The timbre of it was too familiar, alas, like a rasp of breaking crockery, and in that particularly solitary place making my skin to crawl.

He materialized then, white hair and long neck rising from behind a packing box like Mephistopheles ascending from a trap-door in a stage floor to buy the soul of Dr. Faust.

"Ah, Miss Rutledge, I've been expecting you."

I had the sinking sensation that overwhelms any actress when she forgets an important response to a cue from another player. Stammering would not do, I told myself; that's the mark of an amateur. As coolly as I could, but in a higher pitch than I wanted, I said: "Good morning, Colonel Smith, but I came here to see Mr. Lester Marmot."

He grinned like a tight-mouthed fish. The shade of the oil lamp hanging from the ceiling gave his skin a sallow cast, his face the look of a cadaver's. "Lester Marmot at your service, miss," he said, obviously enjoying my astonishment.

< **Belle Rutledge** >

"Yesterday you were Colonel Smith from Indiana," I objected.

"In these days we must play many parts."

He came so close to me that I stepped back. He took my arm, squeezing it, and almost forced me into a maroon plush chair.

"Indiana's Grand Commanders are under too close surveillance to come to Cincinnati," he explained. His eyes were red and swollen as if he had slept badly.

"Why were you expecting me?" I asked.

Mr. Marmot sat down in a chair facing me, so close our knees touched.

"I communicate freely with Colonel Fennell in Richmond," he said. "In spite of that ghoulish hyena, General Sherman, telegraphed messages can, with a little delay, arrive in Richmond." He reached out and patted my knee, letting his hand linger there.

"You were coming to ask me to report on Major Heywood, were you not?"

I removed his hand from my knee.

"Perhaps. Colonel Fennell wants the prisoners freed at Camp Douglas before anything else."

His fish mouth worked silently for a moment as if searching for the proper words.

"And our good major is putting the Northwest Confederacy ahead of freeing the prisoners. You want me to inform Colonel Fennell of his dereliction? Perhaps advise that Major Heywood be sent back to Richmond?"

"No!"

I had not meant to speak so strongly, and the fact that I almost shouted the word made me realize that I was losing my objectivity, that I was protecting Charley, that I did not want to break our association. At the same time, I suspected that I was under some kind of trial arranged by Colonel Fennell to test my loyalty to him and the Confederacy.

Lester Marmot was grinning his Mephistophelian grin, the tip of his tongue moving along his wet lips.

"What shall I telegraph?" he asked.

"Tell Colonel Fennell that Major Heywood is going off track. He'll know what is meant by that. He used the words himself."

Lester Marmot slapped the arm of his chair. "It shall be done as you say, Miss Rutledge."

He turned his head from side to side on his long neck, as though measuring me from different angles.

"I would like to make a photograph of you," he said abruptly. He motioned to the rows of *cartes de visite* along the nearer wall. "I am a professional. Your perfect oval face, your full lips, large eyes set wide apart, the direct stare with which you try to frighten men but which serves only to draw them to you, I could capture these rare qualities with my camera."

"I have some *cartes de visite*, thank you." I started to rise, but he reached for my shoulders and pushed me roughly back into the chair.

"That was not what I had in mind, Miss Rutledge. We could make a great amount of money, you and I." He took an envelope from the narrow table beside his chair, slipped out a small photograph, and dropped it into my lap. A woman wearing white tights smiled at me from between her own legs. I had seen many actresses in tights, and had worn them myself onstage, but I had never seen any female in so lewd a pose. Turning the picture over, I handed it back to Lester Marmot.

"Do you know how much money soldiers are paying for photographs like this?" he shouted. "Sutlers sell them by the hundreds for five dollars in army camps and in the field." He stared hard at me as if forbidding me to leave him. "I have observed that you do not wear corsets, yet you have an exceptionally fine figure. Your face and your figure would bring twice five dollars. If you would pose for me *au naturel*, as they say, we could sell thousands."

"Mr. Marmot," I said, rising and forcing my way past him, "I do not pose for artists."

His face reddened with a furious anger. "You've no call to be so sanctimonious!" he shouted after me. "You who show your limbs upon the stage and who cohabit openly with Major Heywood."

Not until I was out of the building and into the brightness of the June morning did the gathering quiver of dread leave the back of my neck. I walked briskly on to a large emporium and set about obtaining new clothing for my journey to Chicago. With dismay I examined the latest hoopskirts. Each month, north and south, the

< **Belle Rutledge** >

hoops seemed to expand farther in circumference. Fashionable though they were, I foresaw difficulties they would surely cause me in my duties. Getting on and off railway trains, entering and leaving horse cabs, dining in public places—all would be time-consuming with a ballooning hoopskirt to manage. The only advantage I could see in hoopskirts was the possibility they offered for concealment, for smuggling contraband of considerable bulk. And so I settled for a Zouave jacket and an ordinary gray bombazine dress with a splendid ruffle. I also selected some new shifts and pantalets and other undergarments. The sales clerk eagerly showed the latest corsets, but as the beastly Mr. Marmot so correctly observed, I do not wear corsets. Up to that time I'd owned only the one that my mother presented me when I came of age. I wore it a few times to please her, but because I am slim-waisted I have no need for that instrument of torture, that pillory of a habiliment for women.

Having plenty of greenbacks in my possession, I went over to the men's side of the emporium and, as spies must, I spoke falsely to a clerk, telling him that I wanted to buy a frock coat for a brother who was exactly my size. I chose one of plain black broadcloth that would attract no notice, but I could not resist adding a mouse-colored waistcoat ornamented with silk facing and buttons of pearl.

Fairly well laden with bundles, I hailed a horse cab. I felt quite happy with my purchases, and completely free of the wretched cloud that the odious Mr. Marmot had temporarily cast over my spirits.

On the way back to the Packet House, we passed three or four theaters, and each time I asked the driver to slow his horse so that I might read the playbills. To my surprise, Melodeon Hall, at the corner of Fourth and Walnut, was offering Newcomb's Minstrels. This was not the company I had performed with before the war, but I knew that several of my old friends from those days had joined Newcomb's troupe. For a moment I felt a keen desire to leave the cab and seek out dear comrades of both sexes for a joyous reunion and reminiscences of happier times. I quickly realized, however, that I would be faced with the dilemma of explaining my presence and purpose in the city of Cincinnati and therefore deprived myself of a pleasant hour or so of companionship.

< CONSPIRACY OF KNAVES >

Passing Wood's Theater, I noticed that Miss Alice Placides was playing there in *Peep O'Day*, no doubt taking the part of Kathleen Kavanaugh. I would have dearly loved to call upon Alice, but I could not recall whether she was daughter or niece of Mr. Alexander Placides, who gave me my first real opportunity as an actress. All I remembered was Alice's strong disapproval, perhaps jealousy, of me when she discovered that Mr. Placides was my patron during the time I was performing in Charleston. And so I decided not to renew acquaintanceship with Alice.

That night was to be the last I would spend with Charley Heywood in Cincinatti. Perhaps I sensed his unspoken intentions before we fell asleep in each other's arms, yet I asked no questions about his plans, wishing to keep espionage and war as far away from *l'amour* as I could.

When I awoke at first dawn, he was gone. The two leather valises into which he had transferred the Mount Sterling booty had also vanished, along with his portmanteau and clothing. On the top of the bedroom dresser was a note in Charley's peculiar slanted handwriting:

> My dear Belle,
> Sudden developments require my presence in distant parts. I trust you will understand. Perhaps we'll meet again in Chicago. If you see Master Winslow before you leave Cincinn. give the little devil a sound thrashing for me.

Wrapped inside the note was a large roll of greenbacks.

How singular, I thought, that the busy major would take the time to remember Winslow before decamping from Cincinnati. I would gladly have gone to see the young imp myself, but I had bade good-bye to him too recently to cause both of us to suffer the wrench of another parting so soon.

For about half an hour I felt quite low in spirits because of Charley Heywood's unannounced departure, but I am not one to repine over matters that can't be helped. Besides, I was looking forward to my first visit to Chicago.

Before leaving the Packet House, I attempted to find Kendrich, but the registry clerk informed me that Mr. Kendrich also

< **Belle Rutledge** >

had departed very early that morning. I was certain that he had either accompanied Major Heywood or had gone in pursuit of him.

With a full budget of baggage, I returned to the smoke-filled railroad station and made arrangements to ship most of my things to Chicago by Adams Express. After purchasing a ticket, I waited in the women's parlor until the announcer called my train.

When I walked out into that vaulted enclosure filled with re-verberating sounds of panting locomotives and shouting voices, and with swirling odors of steam and sulphur and unwashed humanity, I remembered little Winslow's mingled terror and exultation there. A wave of remorse swept over me at the thought that I'd left him in the hands of that coldhearted orphanage master. These regrets were swept away a moment later, however, as I moved closer to the entry of the nearest passenger car.

Standing between me and the car steps was Lester Marmot, a narrow-brimmed black hat resting atop his white hair, his long arms held outward like those of a scarecrow.

"How did you—" I started to cry out, but stopped the question, knowing that he had probably been watching every Chicago-bound train that morning.

"Change of plans, Miss Rutledge," he whined out of his round mouth. "You are to stay in Cincinnati and work with me."

I tried to step around him, but one of his arms blocked my passage.

"By whose orders?" I demanded.

"I can't tell you here," he said, his fingers clutching at one of my sleeves.

Two soldiers—sunburned, clear-eyed, wearing fresh-issue blue uniforms—were standing on the car steps, watching me. Two others were smiling at me from an open window of the car.

I raised my free arm, waved my hand at the young soldiers on the steps, and called at the top of my voice: "Soldiers! Please help me! I must go to Chicago to nurse my wounded husband!"

Almost instantly they were at my side, brushing Lester Marmot away and assisting me up the steps and into the car.

"Who was that gentleman?" one of them asked as he led me to a seat and took the one beside me.

< CONSPIRACY OF KNAVES >

"A relative," I replied in modulated tones of shyness, "who did not wish me to go."

Both soldiers murmured sympathetically. "Your wounded husband, ma'am," one asked, "how bad off is he?"

As spies must, I began playing a character I was forced to invent as I went along, desperately trying to remember names, places, regiments, and battles so that I would not contradict myself in my own hastily contrived playbook. At Indianapolis, to my great relief, my gallant escorts left the car to transfer to another railroad.

EXCERPTS FROM
A CINCINNATI
SCRAPBOOK

JUNE 1864

From SHERMAN'S ARMY

—

Movements Slow But Certain

—

Heavy and Constant Skirmishing

—

TREMENDOUS ARTILLERY FIRING

—

Our Troops Carry Lost Mountain

—

THE CITY OF ATLANTA IN SIGHT

—

Arrivals of Sick and Wounded at
Nashville

WANTED. Correspondence—By as gay and festive a cuss as ever signed a muster roll. Ladies, write me a kind letter to cheer the lonely hours of camp life. Object fun, love, and pastime. Address U.Z., Company F, 88th O.V.I., Camp Chase, Ohio

< CONSPIRACY OF KNAVES >

WANTED. SUBSTITUTE! $2,000 will be paid for four acceptable substitutes for draft of men today. Call at Room No. 6 upstairs, No. 57 Third Street.

THE GREAT CAMPAIGN
Military Review of Situation Before Petersburg
The Strategy of a Week
Movement from the Chickahominy to the James

For Memphis, Vicksburg and New Orleans
Leaves THIS DAY, 25th at 4 P.M.
The Fine Side-Wheel Passenger Steamer

EMPEROR

Captain Kelsey
For freight or passage apply on board or
to W. M. Hawn & Co., Cunningham and Bennett, or
E. S. Butler & Co.

Robert Clarke & Co.'s
WEEKLY BULLETIN OF NEW BOOKS

The Bridal Eve, by Mrs. Emma D.E.N. Southworth
clo. 1.50

Faith Gartney's Girlhood is the best story for
young ladies ever written

MILITARY OUTFITS

India Rubber Blankets
India Rubber Ponchos
India Rubber Coats
India Rubber Havelocks

BART J. HICKOX
No. 49 West Fourth Street

< **Cincinnati Scrapbook, June 1864** >

SMITH AND DITSON'S HALL
The Four Smallest Human Beings
of Mature Age
Ever Known on the Face of the Globe!

In Cincinnati Saturday Evening
Three Levees Each Day
GENERAL TOM THUMB
And His Beautiful Little Wife—
the late
MISS LAVINIA WARREN
—
COMMODORE NUTT
—
Elfin Minnie Warren

THE HEROES OF FIFTEEN PITCHED BATTLES COMING HOME

Among the many returning braves who have been received at the hands of a grateful Cincinnati public, none should attract or enlist more attention than the return of the remnant of the gallant 5th Ohio Volunteer Infantry which is expected to reach the city this morning at 9 A.M.

 Thomas Everitt, the keeper of a low house of prostitution on Front Street, was yesterday before the Police Court on three charges, viz: Keeping disorderly house, harboring lewd women, and malicious shooting.

PIKE'S OPERA HOUSE
The last night of the Martinetti Troupe and the last night of the amusement season is at hand. With the performance this afternoon and evening, the doors of the opera-house will close until September.

< CONSPIRACY OF KNAVES >

U.S. GUNBOAT SERVICE
Mississippi Squadron
500 Men Wanted Immediately

A.S. Bowen, U.S. Navy
Commanding Rendezvous
No. 5 East Front Street

JOLLY CLUB OF FIVE
will give a
GRAND PICNIC at
Parlor Grove, Wednesday

PHOTOGRAPHS

Rich, Rare and Racy!

A very beautiful picture of the handsomest woman in the world, a peculiar rich-colored photograph in oil, taken from life. She is a bewitching beauty, a perfect gem.

Sent free by mail. Price fifty cents.

DAVIS & Bro. 1232 Post-office
Cincinnati, Ohio

NATIONAL THEATER—The new champion clog-dancer, Tim Hayes, and new minstrels are creating a sensation at this establishment.

HANG OUT YOUR BANNERS
July 4, 1864
Freedom Reigns
FLAGS!
Of Best English Bunting from 7 to 9 feet Long
Longley and Bro., 143 Walnut St.

< **Cincinnati Scrapbook, June 1864** >

COPPERHEADS PREPARE
FOR CHICAGO CONVENTION
Vallandigham to Speak
The WAR Democrats and the PEACE Democrats
at Variance

Advt.

Havana Cigars
Opera-House Building
Cincinnati

10

IN THE
PRISON CELL I SIT

NEITHER CAPTAIN JOHN Truscott nor any of his nine men slept very much in the jolting livestock car that carried them northward through the chilly June night. When exhaustion overwhelmed him, he would remove his coat and use it as a pillow over the odorous manure emitting a vaporous pungency that seemed to envelop his whole being.

During the times that he was awake, he could think of nothing but the entrapment at the abandoned chapel near Tamaroa. It had all happened too smoothly to have been a simple blundering encounter between his men and the Illinois home guards. Someone had betrayed them. Was it the Copperhead Phil Hatfield, who had guided them there from the crossing at Raven's Head on the Ohio? Hatfield could have given a message to the farmer's greedy wife when they stopped near the Wabash River to trade for horses. Certainly Hatfield had been quick and eager to ask Colquett's permission to stay the night at Barton Farm rather than return to the chapel with Truscott. Or perhaps it was the doing of Colquett himself, another act to ingratiate the horse trader with the local Unionists. And what of Wesley Heywood, who was as avaricious as the rest of them? Or the stranger from Chicago, Joseph Milligan, who had come there to obtain money from Charles Heywood, and talked incessantly of Greek fire? Or was the whole crazy scheme one of Charley Heywood's elaborate machinations?

< **In the Prison Cell I Sit** >

When daylight came, to reveal from the stockcar the flat un-
fenced prairie land of northern Illinois, and then the sandy shoreline
of Lake Michigan, he guessed that Chicago was truly their destination. To him, Chicago meant the Camp Douglas prison camp.
The entire affair was all too apt, as though it had been arranged
by someone who was very clever, someone like Charley Heywood.

After passing a row of beach houses that were nearly covered
with sand blown around them by lake storms, the train began to
slow. Remembering the greenbacks he had hidden in an inner lining
of his coat, Truscott decided to distribute the money among his
men. By the time he had done this, warning them to conceal the
bills as best they could, the cars shuddered to a sudden stop.

From a venthole, Truscott could see a few sailing boats on the
lake, mostly fishing craft, moving lazily in the early morning breeze.
He crossed to the opposite side of the car.

Several yards up the curve of track, a captain and a sergeant
were herding a squad of awkward convalescents in Union infantry
uniforms toward the livestock car, the sergeant's loud commands
interspersed with profanity.

A few minutes later the chain rattled violently on the car door,
followed by several resounding blows, and then the door was pushed
open. A beefy pockmarked face frowned fiercely at the prisoners
inside.

"Here the spies are, captain," the big sergeant growled, and
an officer stepped into view.

His face was half covered with muttonchop whiskers and he
wore spectacles. His eyes blinked rapidly behind the lenses. "Get
them out of there, sergeant," he said coldly.

"All right, boys," the sergeant shouted at his squad. "Rifles at
the ready!" He turned back to face Truscott. "On the ground, you
Rebs!"

Truscott jumped out first, the sergeant motioning him to move
along between the two lines of infantrymen who were holding their
rifles level. If these makeshift troops facing each other should panic,
or are suddenly ordered to fire at us, Truscott thought, they'll shoot
as many Yankees as Rebels.

He saw no sign of the one-armed home-guard commander or
his men in the railroad work car, but far off to the north he caught

< CONSPIRACY OF KNAVES >

a glimpse of the smoke-hazy outline of Chicago, broken by church spires and the tops of square buildings several stories high.

Somehow the fleshy sergeant got his squad of two dozen men and their ten prisoners into marching formation, and ordered them to turn away from the railroad. As they swung into a sandy street, Truscott saw another party of prisoners in Confederate gray marching from a passenger car that had been attached to the train sometime during the night. What impressed him was the contrast between the two different groups. Only four Union soldiers were guarding an entire company of uniformed prisoners, while six times that number were escorting Truscott and his few men in their soiled stockmen's clothing. The Kentuckians evidently were believed to be either invaluable or very dangerous.

Less than a quarter of a mile ahead were long rows of barracks behind high board fences. They passed a horse-drawn streetcar waiting at the end of a narrow rail track. On the left was a large two-story building bearing a sign: COTTAGE GROVE HOTEL. From the windows and a side veranda, well-dressed and well-fed hotel guests stared with idle curiosity at the prisoners in mufti. Although he had no knowledge of who these people were, Truscott felt a surge of loathing for them, envying their freedom and obvious prosperity.

The sergeant ordered a halt. They waited until another streetcar passed them and turned into a short side track. With his barking commands, the sergeant marched them across the street, ordered a quick left turn, and there before them was a castlelike portal, the arch above spelling out C-A-M-P D-O-U-G-L-A-S. Guards quickly swung the gate open and the prisoners entered a triangular enclosure.

This part of the prison resembled a small town, with its post office, barbershop, sutlers' stores, chapel, and photographer's gallery. Here most of the infantry guard was dismissed. Only the captain, the sergeant, and two men escorted the prisoners into a rectangular compound of barracks that housed the several hundred soldiers assigned to guard Camp Douglas's prisoners of war. A large United States flag stirred at the top of a high flagpole at one end of a parade ground where two squads of men were drilling.

After passing a water hydrant and a wooden trough, Truscott and his Kentuckians were led into a room that was empty except

< **In the Prison Cell I Sit** >

for a crude bench along one wall. "All clothes off but under-drawers," the sergeant ordered.

The sergeant and his two men began a methodical search of the divested pants and coats. "God, you Rebs stink," the sergeant said. "You smell like a stable." He glanced at his captain, who had been standing silently at the entranceway.

"When you've finished the searches, sergeant, have them take their clothes out to the water trough and wash them," the captain ordered.

"Yes, sir."

"Then report to me at headquarters." The captain turned and left with a disdainful sigh, as though offended by the affair in which he was forced to be involved.

Fortunately for Truscott and his men, the sun was hot and a drying land breeze soon took much of the dampness from their hastily washed clothing. During the searching and laundering, most of their concealed greenbacks were discovered and taken by the sergeant, who placed the bills—along with their knives, coins, and keepsakes—in a large leather box.

"When do we get our properties back?" Truscott asked.

"If you're hanged for spies, never," the sergeant replied with a hoarse laugh.

They were then marched through a succession of narrow maze-like passages between high board fences into the open, where they passed a hospital and a cemetery filled with many fresh graves, and entered a tightly guarded fenced area of compact barracks. There, with a loud whistle, the sergeant summoned another non-commissioned officer and told him to collect a rations issue for ten new prisoners.

The sergeant then led them into an empty building that was equipped with shelflike sleeping stalls around the walls. At one end was a stove for cooking and heating.

After a commissary corporal brought in what he declared to be a seven-day supply of hardtack, bacon, pickled pork, coffee, sugar, potatoes, hominy, salt, soap, and candles, the sergeant shrugged and departed, leaving the two infantrymen to guard the only doorway.

Truscott's first act was to inform Joe Stiles that he was now official mess sergeant and that his duties were to assign a rotation

< CONSPIRACY OF KNAVES >

of cooks, water carriers, and dishwashers, and to make certain the supplies issued to them lasted for a full week.

As they'd had nothing to eat for a day and a half, the sight of the unprepared food made all of them ravenous. Nowhere in the barracks, however, could they find a single cooking utensil. Nor would the guards allow anyone to leave the building in search of pots or pans among the other barracks.

Finally Truscott persuaded one of the guards to summon a prisoner from a nearby barracks. When this was done, the neighboring prisoner readily agreed to lend them a coffee pot, skillet, and tin cup, and to bring them a pail of water. This man said that he and his barracks mates were mostly Tennesseans, some of whom had been cavalrymen with General Forrest. After he brought the utensils and water to the door, Truscott asked him if he knew where the Morgan men were.

"Oh, they're over in the main stockade. This here is White Oak Square. They keep new prisoners here until enough Morgan men break out to make room for us in the big stockade."

"Have many escaped?" Truscott asked.

"So we hear. The Yankees capture some, though, and put them in the dungeon."

At this point one of the guards decided to end the conversation by raising his bayonet and ordering the Tennessean to move away from the barracks door.

Although the bacon was old and rancid, the "Lincoln coffee" was so savory they voted to use their next day's ration for an immediate second round. While they were preparing another pot, a sharp command sounded outside and a few moments later the bespectacled Union captain stepped inside the doorway frame and stood there.

"Which of you is Captain Truscott?" he asked in the same remote manner in which he had ordered them out of the livestock car.

Truscott arose, holding himself at attention. "I am Captain Truscott."

"My name is Spooner, Captain Spooner, acting as liaison officer between you and Colonel Bartholomew Wright, commander of the prison camp. Whatever questions you have about quarters, rations,

< **In the Prison Cell I Sit** >

sickness, anything else, will be directed to me." He took a folded slip of paper from his pocket and squinted at it.

"We have strict rules in this camp," he continued in his monotonous voice. "You will rise at the sound of the reveille bugle. One hour later, roll call. Because of your peculiar station, roll call will be taken in here instead of on the parade ground. Not until after roll call will you prepare your breakfasts. Fatigue duties in your case will be done inside this building. Thirty minutes recall at noon, but no cooking until five-thirty P.M. At seven P.M. all your outer clothing must be removed, and no candles are to be lit after that time. You will sleep in the cubicles along the walls. At Camp Douglas we do not issue bedding. Some prisoners have obtained blankets and pillows from family or friends in the South by writing for them. In Chicago there are Butternut sympathizers who may bring you blankets if Commandant Wright decides to let them resume visits here." In that last remark, Captain Spooner's voice turned from monotonous to sarcastic.

He rapped on the wall, summoning the big sergeant, who had been waiting outside the door.

"Sergeant Beadle will now enter your names, ranks, regiment, and state on an official prisoners-of-war roster." He paused briefly. "If you expect to receive any letters or gifts from relatives, I'd advise you to give your true names."

In spite of the hard boards of the cubicle floor on which he slept—leaving him feeling as if he had been beaten all over with a stick—and the chill air that crept into the building late in the night, Truscott felt refreshed enough the next morning to be angry again at whoever had "arranged" his capture at Tamaroa.

Someone had brought buckets of water, placing them inside the entrance, and he dipped a tin cup into one of them and washed the sleep from his eyes. At first he thought rain was falling outside, but the sound was only a heavy dew dripping from the eaves.

Shortly after breakfast Sergeant Beadle appeared to inform Truscott that he was wanted at camp headquarters. "Just follow me, Reb," Beadle said, and led the way back through the passages to the parade ground and the headquarters building.

Inside, the sergeant motioned Truscott to a bench in a small

< CONSPIRACY OF KNAVES >

anteroom that had wooden cases built around the walls. Sheets of paper the size of muster rolls lay helter-skelter atop the cases.

Sergeant Beadle disappeared through a door at the end of the anteroom, and Truscott could hear his rasping voice conversing with someone inside. Although the door was closed, the partition was so thin that he heard his own name mentioned more than once. Truscott moved closer to the wall. The sergeant and the man inside were going through the list of captured Kentuckians.

"All right," the other voice said in a tone that was almost Bluegrass in its softness. "Send this Captain Truscott in here and wait outside."

The man inside was Colonel Bartholomew Wright, commandant of Camp Douglas prison. He wore his bush of brown hair in an uneven part on the right; his eyes were deep-set like those of some hunting hounds. His thick mustache curved down on each side of his mouth to the line of his chinbone. He would have been fairly handsome except for a buttonlike nose that was too small for his face. His military blouse, with its double row of brass buttons, was open to a dark blue collarless shirt.

As there was no other chair in the small office except the one in which Colonel Wright sat, Truscott remained standing, his eyes meeting those of the commander. After a studied delay, the colonel broke the silence.

"You are Captain John Truscott?"

"Yes, sir."

Colonel Wright kept a stern face. "The greenbacks taken from you and your men were stolen from an army paymaster's safe in Mount Sterling, Kentucky, by John Morgan's bushwhackers. Yet you had them in your possession a few days later in southern Illinois. What was this money to be used for?"

"To buy horses," Truscott replied.

Wright's lips tightened before he spoke again. "Why would Morgan's bushwhackers buy horses when they could as easily steal them?"

"Stealing horses is not easy in Union territory. Buying is safer and quicker."

"You and your men will be charged with spying," Wright said hoarsely. "You were dressed as citizens, not soldiers."

"Horse thieves we might be, colonel," Truscott said. "But spies never."

"You brought greenbacks to Copperheads," Wright persisted. "Aiding traitors to the Union is worse than spying. You and your men will hang for it."

Truscott shook his head. "What money left our hands, sir, and it *was* spoils of war, went only for our sustenance."

Colonel Wright stared down at his desk top for a full minute, his hands clasped tightly together. "I knew your father," he said quietly.

Truscott was startled, but before he could speak the colonel continued: "Some years ago, before I moved north of the Ohio, I knew Will Truscott quite well. If your father had lived, you would have fought for the Union."

"For me the choice was a matter of honor," Truscott said quickly. "I think my father would have agreed."

The commandant made no reply to that. He kept tightening and untightening his clasped fingers, and when he turned to face the opalescent panes of the single window at his left, his nose was almost flat in his silhouetted profile.

"This war is bleeding the country," he said in his slow Bluegrass accent. "It should have ended months ago. But it's too profitable for too many. Sometimes I think we may never see the ending of it." His gaze was still fixed on the window. "What a pity if you and your boys end your lives upon a gallows."

He turned back to face Truscott. "There may be a way out. If you will stand together with us."

"What do you mean?" Truscott asked.

"I'll inform you later," the colonel said, adding almost as an afterthought: "If you're not hanged first."

Three days later Sergeant Beadle came again for Truscott, and this time when he entered Colonel Wright's office, a man in citizen's clothing was waiting there with the commandant. The man's face was vaguely familiar, but not until he stepped forward into the full light of the window and spoke did Truscott remember him with a jolt of surprise.

"Otis Jordan," the man said. "Remember me, Captain Truscott?"

< CONSPIRACY OF KNAVES >

"Yes, but I've never seen you before out of Confederate gray."

"I was captured on the Indiana-Ohio raid," Jordan explained. "At Buffington Island. I heard that you and some of your men escaped."

Colonel Wright interrupted: "I wanted you to meet Jordan before they set the date of your military trial, Captain Truscott. I want Jordan to explain to you a means by which you and your men may escape sentences of death for spying."

In the anteroom, Jordan disclosed that a plan was under way at Camp Douglas to recruit prisoners into special volunteer regiments for service on the Western frontier. "All that you and your men need do," Jordan said, "is to renounce your oaths to the Confederate Army and take oaths of allegiance and join the Union Army. None of you will be sent against Confederate soldiers. You will go into the Far West to man forts and guard telegraph lines to California. If there is any fighting, it will be against hostile Indians."

While Otis Jordan was explaining this proposal, Truscott recalled the distrust with which he and other veteran Morgan cavalrymen had viewed the black-haired shifty-eyed Texan.

It was Lucius Eberhart, a doughty British colonel, who had brought Jordan into Morgan's winter camp at Murfreesboro, Tennessee. Jordan claimed that he had been a captain with a Texas company that was virtually destroyed at Stone's River, and on the Englishman's recommendation General Morgan had given him a temporary commission.

Not long after that, Eberhart accused Jordan of trying to steal some of the colonel's prized horses to sell to another cavalry command in the area. Although Eberhart made no formal accusation, he refused to have anything more to do with Jordan, referring to him as "a lowborn loafer," and advised General Morgan not to give the acting captain a command.

Even under this cloud, however, Jordan was permitted to remain with the Kentuckians, and at the beginning of the Indiana-Ohio raid, he talked Charley Heywood into letting him ride with the forward scouts. Perhaps Charley thought Jordan's guile might have been of some use on that venture.

"I have already taken an oath of allegiance to the Union," Jordan was saying, "and I can tell you truthfully, Captain Truscott,

< **In the Prison Cell I Sit** >

as a result my life in this prison has changed from hellhole to more than tolerable. I have the freedom of the entire camp, and once a week, in company with an officer, I am permitted to go into Chicago. Furthermore, I am paid one hundred dollars a month for my duties with the commissary and as clerk for a surgeon in the hospital. As soon as enough prisoners are converted to form a regiment, off we go to the West. Colonel Wright has assured me that I'll have command of a company, a responsibility that General John Morgan would never trust me with."

Although Truscott had little use for Otis Jordan, the man later proved helpful on two or three occasions. After Truscott told Colonel Wright that he could not stain his honor by renouncing his oath to the Confederate States (and doubted that any of his men would do so either), the prison commandant summoned him back to his headquarters a day or so later and tried to persuade him to reveal all that he knew about the Knights of the Golden Circle and other Copperhead organizations in the North. Truscott's response was to remind the colonel that as his prisoner of war, he was required to tell only his name, rank, regiment, and state, whereupon Wright shook his head sadly and expressed astonishment that Truscott would not tell what he knew in order to save his neck from the noose.

Soon after that encounter, Otis Jordan paid a visit to the Kentuckians' barracks in an effort to convince all of them that they should change allegiances and become galvanized Yankees. He gained no recruits, but as he was leaving he swore Truscott to secrecy and in conspiratorial whispers informed him that he and his men need no longer fear being tried for spying. Somewhere in Virginia a squad of Union soldiers had been captured and accused of spying. The Confederate government had notified the Union commissary general of prisons that should the ten Confederates being held in Camp Douglas be tried and executed, the same fate awaited the Union prisoners in Virginia.

Truscott was aware that such maneuvers—swaps, bargains, games as elaborate as chess—had been going on throughout the war, yet he was skeptical of Jordan's volunteered information until the following day, when Colonel Wright summoned him once again to headquarters. With no explanation of his reasons for doing so,

< CONSPIRACY OF KNAVES >

the colonel quietly offered to transfer Truscott and his men to a barracks in the main prisoners' stockade, where they would no longer be confined to a building under guard, but would be treated as ordinary prisoners of war.

"There is one condition," the colonel said. "I want you to help me with the Morgan captives. They are the most troublesome of all the prisoners. Admittedly my predecessor was very hard on them, singling them out for harassment, goading them into fool-hardy attempts to escape."

"Escape is the first duty of a prisoner of war," Truscott said.

"Yes. But escape from Camp Douglas is almost impossible, and when it is accomplished the escapees are quickly recaptured in Chicago. One of the reasons I was brought here was to introduce more humane treatment of the prisoners—to see if such treatment might lessen difficulties on both sides."

"How can I help you with the Morgan captives?"

"You're an officer from Morgan's command. Most Confederate officers are imprisoned at Camp Chase in Ohio, or elsewhere. The few officers here are kept together in a special barracks. But I want you to accompany your little detachment into the main stockade. Because you are one of Morgan's officers, the Morgan men should be inclined to listen to you. Also it is my wish that you assist me in compiling more accurate rosters of the prisoners. My predecessor and his staff were rather negligent in recording physical descriptions, deaths, names of escapees, and so on. The records are quite disorganized—do you know there are eighty-four men unaccounted for?—and Commissary General Hoffman is insistent that the rolls be set to rights. I believe this can be better done from the inside."

Colonel Wright's soft voice flowed on, as though the pronouncing of words relieved him of some terrible strain. Truscott suspected that the commander had no confidant with whom he could converse with ease, and perhaps was beginning to find in his fellow Kentuckian a receptacle for his doubts and fears and half-formed theories of rewards and punishments.

Life in the main prisoners' stockade was by no means pleasant, but in contrast to total confinement in White Oak Square, it offered considerably more freedom of movement. During the first day or two, Truscott and his men spent most of their time in reunions with comrades of Kentucky regiments. Most of the veteran prisoners had been there almost a year, having been captured during the Indiana-Ohio raid of 1863, but a dozen or more were recent arrivals, cavalrymen who had been outflanked and trapped during Morgan's recent withdrawal from Cynthiana and Lexington.

As for Truscott, he found that by agreeing to cooperate with Colonel Wright in rectifying rosters of prisoners, he gained even more freedom. With a pass that was given him by the colonel, he could visit the sutlers' stores en route to the headquarters building, where he worked a few hours each day. Prisoners were permitted to make purchases of tobacco, candy, writing paper, pens, inks, newspapers, books, and other small items by using sutlers' checks. The checks were issued against money received by prisoners in letters sent them by relatives and friends. Although Colonel Wright refused to allow any credit for the stolen Mount Sterling greenbacks that had been taken from them, the Kentuckians quickly wrote supplicating letters to their home folks, and against the expectation of money to come, they were able to borrow sutlers' checks from former comrades who had been in Camp Douglas for several months.

As a part of Colonel Wright's program to keep the prisoners more content with their lot, he reinstated the practice of permitting weekly visits from representatives of churches and charitable organizations in Chicago. Truscott first learned of this from Captain Spooner, and it was evident from that officer's attitude and tone of voice that he thoroughly disapproved of his colonel's decision. Spooner even went so far as to mutter dire predictions of trouble that was sure to be brought on by allowing Rebel sympathizers and Copperheads to come inside the prison camp.

On the first visitors' day, Otis Jordan came to Truscott's barracks, bringing him a pass.

"An opportunity to obtain bedding for you and your men," Jordan declared, and then volunteered to introduce Truscott to a certain Mrs. Evelyn Ward, a Kentucky native who lived in Chicago. Mrs. Ward, he said, had a wide acquaintance among former Southerners in the city, and seemed to possess some magical ability to scrounge or otherwise obtain innumerable small comforts for the prisoners. Furthermore, in the past she had never failed to appear on visiting days at Camp Douglas. Colonel Wright's predecessor had taken a violent dislike to Mrs. Ward and some of her

< CONSPIRACY OF KNAVES >

companions, and had discontinued visitors' day shortly before he was replaced by Wright.

The first visitors' day under Colonel Wright's command was held in the sutlers' area, and Truscott was waiting there with Otis Jordan when the entrance gate was opened to admit about thirty women and men. Assembled under the watchful eyes of Captain Spooner and his squad of convalescents was a group of representatives from the prisoners' stockade, most of them being commissary or mess sergeants from each barracks. Several of them carried lists of desiderata.

Most of the visitors were women, predominantly of that age known as the "meridian of life," although there were occasional damsels who kept close to the skirts of their elders. The few men were well along in years, their dress and bearing indicating that they were of some branch of the clergy. They carried baskets of religious tracts and Bibles. The women's baskets were filled with cakes, pies, fried chicken, roast beef, and other delicacies. As the visitors came through the gate in single file, everything they carried was carefully examined by a pair of alert young lieutenants.

Once they were passed through, the visitors were quickly surrounded by prisoners waving their lists. Truscott had no list; he had not thought to ask any of his men what luxuries they might wish to request. Blankets for all of them was foremost in his mind. When winds blew off Lake Michigan, even on nights late in June, the men shivered and cursed the hard board bunks.

"Aha!" Otis Jordan cried. "There's the old girl, Mrs. Ward."

Several other veteran prisoners had also seen Mrs. Ward and began rushing toward her with loud and enthusiastic greetings. Jordan, however, managed to catch her eye, and with a rude lunge that Truscott considered decidedly ungracious, forced his way to her side.

"Dear Mrs. Ward," Jordan began in his most unctuous tone, "how pleased we are to see you come again to brighten our enforced stay in these unhappy surroundings. My good friend here, Captain John Truscott, is most eager to meet you and plead the needs of his little company of Kentuckians."

"John Truscott," she responded in a declamatory voice, "we have made many inquiries about you and your poor boys. All unanswered, of course, by the coldhearted authorities."

"They need blankets, ma'am," Jordan interrupted.

"And blankets they shall have," Mrs. Ward declared firmly.

She was a woman of considerable height and girth, perhaps two or three inches taller than Truscott, with an enormous bosom that seemed about to burst loose from its crinoline bindings. Her dark eyes were warm and filled with curiosity, like those of an artless little girl eager to please everyone, yet hinting at something secretive, something hidden in that head beneath the black silk bonnet with its bright red ribbon tied in a bow.

"I have a present for you, Johnny Truscott," she announced, and began rummaging in her basket. "A pair of socks knitted by Miss Marianna Heywood." Her tightly bound bosom brushed his shoulder as she handed him the socks.

"She sent no letter?" He pushed the socks into a coat pocket. "I wrote her a letter."

"Only a note to me, dear boy, asking me to see that you received her gift. If she had sent the socks to this prison!" Her eyes crinkled as she lowered her voice. "The Unionists would have taken them." She winked at Otis Jordan. "If Miss Heywood sent John Truscott a letter, the commandant may be reading it in search of hidden meanings."

Truscott started to step back to allow some of the others to talk with her, but she caught his arm and whispered almost without moving her lips: "What are the plans," she asked, "for July fourth?"

He shook his head. "We've heard nothing in here," he replied.

"You will," she said aloud. Handing him a broken cake wrapped in thick paper, she pushed him gently aside to make room for the others.

A few minutes later, a shrill whistle sounded the close of visitors' day, and while one squad of soldiers shepherded the civilian attenders outside, another squad turned the prisoners back into the passageway to the main stockade.

Using his pass to headquarters, Truscott entered the parade ground and crossed to the building behind the large flag, which was flapping in a refreshing lake breeze. When he walked into the anteroom to the commandant's office, he was surprised to find Colonel Wright seated at one of the work tables examining the prison rosters that Truscott had been preparing.

The colonel smiled benevolently at him. "Had you not come,

< CONSPIRACY OF KNAVES >

Captain Truscott," he said, "I would have sent for you." He clasped his hands, interlocking his fingers tightly.

"What do you know about a plot to break out on the Fourth of July, Independence Day?"

Truscott almost dropped the cake that Mrs. Ward had given him, but managed to place it carefully on the table. For some reason he thought of the knights and ladies of *Ivanhoe*, the betrayals, the unexpected surprises.

Even if he had wished to do so, he could have told the colonel nothing because he had heard nothing since arriving at Camp Douglas. Every passing day he had thought of the entrapment at the Tamaroa chapel. And he had thought of Alonzo Colquett, smelling of horses and talking of two thousand horses, his voice booming with absolute authority. Had Charley Heywood arrived yet at Barton Farm with the greenbacks stolen from the Mount Sterling bank? And were the horses already en route to Chicago to be ready for whatever was going to happen on the Fourth of July? Was Charley somewhere in Illinois, preparing in his light-hearted way a rescue of the prisoners in Camp Douglas?

"Well, Captain Truscott," the commandant persisted, "for your own sake, tell me what you know of this foolheaded plot."

"I know nothing, sir," Truscott replied.

11

WE ARE A
BAND OF BROTHERS

ON THAT DAY Charley Heywood was hundreds of miles from Illinois and Chicago and Camp Douglas. Just as I'd surmised, he was in Canada, across from Detroit in the little town of Windsor, living the life of a happy cavalier. Like a plant that flourishes on water, Charley was animated by a flow of money, his revived energies driving him through day and night.

At the Hirons House, he found a little band of Morgan men who had been eking out an existence while awaiting his promised arrival. Eventually I was to meet some of these young centaurs—George Stubblefield, Ben Drake, George Ellsworth the telegrapher, and Bennett Young who later would startle all of New England with his raid into Vermont to rob the St. Albans banks. And Henry Stone, hardly out of his teens, carrying a sorrowful burden of knighthood: his older brother had joined the Union Army.

My favorite was a foreign gentleman, Colonel Lucius Eberhart, a soldier of fortune who had joined General Morgan's staff in 1862 and served for several months. He was a Britisher, old enough to be the father of any of these boys, or me, and he was also as tall and wiry and sun-bronzed as any of them. Colonel Eberhart was a great flirt, and I must confess there were times when I allowed myself to dream of journeying to England with him to become Lady Belle Eberhart. But more of Lucius Eberhart at the proper time in this narrative.

< CONSPIRACY OF KNAVES >

Charley Heywood's first action upon joining his comrades was to distribute an abundance of greenbacks among them, making them all as jolly as larks. He then took the two valises, still packed with what remained of the Mount Sterling booty, to the Bank of Upper Canada for storage in one of its safes.

Accompanying Charley to Windsor was the man known as Kendrich. Clever as Charley was, he failed to see through Kendrich until the very end, and I'm not certain that he ever did learn who Kendrich really was. Anyway, when the two arrived together in Windsor, Charley introduced Kendrich as a courier from the Order of American Knights in New York. "And don't get the idea," he would warn, "that because he's from the East, he's some kind of dandy Miss Nancy. Mr. Kendrich brought the Kentucky bank money across the Ohio River through the snares of Federal detectives and assorted blackguards. And he's going to deliver twenty thousand Garibaldi rifles to us just as soon as we can persuade J.T. to issue the necessary money."

In a matter of hours after his arrival, Charley arranged a meeting with J.T., virtually ordering the Confederate commissioner by telegraph to come down on the cars from Toronto. They met in one of the larger rooms of the Hirons House, with Kendrich and about a dozen of the Morgan men present. Almost every one of the Morgan men was eager for the raid upon Camp Douglas on July fourth, which was then less than a week away.

Soon after the meeting began, however, Charley dashed cold water upon that enterprise. Because the Copperheads were determined to seize the governments of the Northwestern states, and because they were not fully prepared to act in unison by July fourth, the uprising was being delayed until July sixteenth, a Saturday, the day of the week when soldiers guarding official buildings, camps, and prisons were known to be at lowest strength and least vigilant.

Although I was not in Windsor at that time, I later learned from Ben Drake and Colonel Eberhart that a bitter debate arose between the few who wanted to delay and those who wanted to journey to Chicago immediately, join forces with the armed Copperheads there, and raid Camp Douglas on July the fourth as originally planned.

Colonel Eberhart was one of those who wanted to strike Camp Douglas at once, before the plot leaked to Union authorities.

"While the iron is hot," he said. "You know, gentlemen, I came to Canada to go hunting up on Georgian Bay with friends from Toronto. Alas, they are so enfettered by the marts of commerce, they could not tear themselves away. And now that iron is cold. When I chanced upon Ben Drake at the Queen's Hotel in Toronto and he revealed great plans afoot to free our imprisoned *camarades*, my heart leapt with anticipation. I will gladly lead a cavalry charge against that infamous prison camp."

Charley remained obstinate. "The attack upon Camp Douglas is only a part of a grander plan," he said. "The main object is to force the Northwestern states out of the Union. Our particular task is to seize the city of Chicago. Our comrades, freed from Camp Douglas, will assist in this, of course."

George Ellsworth, who in his work as a telegrapher had traveled widely through the Northwestern states before the war, expressed doubts that such a coup could be accomplished. The original plan, he said, appealed to him: break the Confederate prisoners out of Camp Douglas and head southward into Kentucky and Tennessee to destroy General Sherman's supply lines.

Both Charley and the Confederate commissioner, J.T., pointed out the difficulties of moving several thousand freed prisoners of war from Chicago to the Ohio River and across it. Only close cooperation with the Copperheads would make this possible. And the price for their cooperation was a general uprising from Missouri to Ohio.

Had I been present, I suppose I would have taken pride in how well Charley had memorized the figures I recorded during that earlier meeting in the Packet House at Cincinnati. Ben Drake later told me that Charley rattled off the enormous numbers of Copperheads in each state, the money required to purchase arms for their various temples, the amounts needed for purchase of horses and to start the manufacture of Gatling guns and Greek fire.

At the end of his peroration, Commissioner J.T. shook his head and declared that only a large infusion of funds from Europe, or robberies of many more United States banks, would bring his exchequer to a level sufficient to meet the demands of the Copperheads. He promised, however, to bend all his efforts to that end.

< CONSPIRACY OF KNAVES >

And so as June dwindled away into July, the restless Morgan men waited in Windsor, Canada, for a final signal to travel to Chicago for the Copperhead rising and the postponed assault upon Camp Douglas. As though meant to break the tedium of waiting, that pair of rustic woods colts, Paul and Andy Fielding, put in a sudden and unexpected appearance in Windsor with an unintentionally comical tale of their adventures.

On the morning that Heywood and Kendrich had left Cincinnati, Charley gave the Fielding brothers a sufficient quantity of greenbacks to take them to General Morgan's headquarters in southwestern Virginia. Somewhere on the outskirts of Cincinnati, however, the brothers had come upon a disguised bordello. In their bucolic imaginations, the place appeared to be a theater of some kind, but the entertainment they found therein was not what they had expected. In a very brief time they were not only fleeced of every greenback they possessed, but were roughly cast out upon the road.

Somewhat humiliated, the Fieldings turned back into the city, hoping to find Major Heywood and request a replenishment of their lost traveling money, but he had already departed. While wandering along the waterfront, they noticed a sign outside a public hall announcing a meeting that evening for the hiring of substitutes to take the places of men who had been drafted into the Union Army.

Now, Paul and Andy Fielding may have been country boys, but they had heard about the large sums of money sometimes paid by well-to-do Yankees for men who were willing to take their places in the army. As soon as the hall opened, they walked in and took seats on the first row. By the time the meeting started, about seventy-five men were crowded on the stage eager to bid for substitutes, and as the audience was not much larger than the number of draftees, the Fielding brothers figured the bids would run high.

Most of the draftees started bidding at one hundred dollars, but none of the men in the hall responded until the amounts reached about five hundred. By waiting patiently, the Fieldings won bids of around eight hundred dollars apiece, several times as much money as they had lost in the bawdy house. When their acceptances were recorded, they were presented with cards bearing the address

< **We Are a Band of Brothers** >

of a law office where they were to call next morning to receive the bounty and be inducted into the Union Army.

Because they had no money at all in their pockets, they went without their suppers and spent the night in an old shed near the river. At first dawn they hurried cheerfully to the law office to collect their money. The stacks of greenbacks they received delighted the brothers, and they did not especially mind being inducted into the Union Army, but they were dismayed by the large number of soldiers waiting to escort them to the nearest army camp.

They were marched for miles out into the countryside, past the very same bordello where they had lost their traveling money, until they reached a stockade with a high board fence. Having had no food since the previous day, the Fieldings devoured the plain army rations offered them, and then watched the sun go down in a bank of clouds that promised rain. When a bugle sounded tattoo, they were ordered into a tent with eight other men, and a sergeant informed them that they would receive their uniforms on the following morning.

Why wait around for Union blue, they asked themselves, when we have enough money to buy suits of any color we choose? As soon as they heard raindrops spattering on the canvas above them, the sound mingling with the snores of their eight companions, the Fieldings quietly left the tent. Under cover of darkness and rain, they sneaked down into a little ravine and followed a stream they had noted before sundown. At the point where the stream flowed out of the stockade, boards had been nailed level with the surface of the water. To escape, they had only to submerge themselves and swim underwater until they were past the fence and outside the camp.

Three days later the Fielding brothers were in Windsor, dressed like prosperous merchants, their pockets filled with greenbacks, and entertaining the Morgan men with embroidered tales of their adventures.

Before the yarns grew stale, Charley Heywood advanced another addition to his Grand Design.

"We need an armed vessel," he announced one morning at breakfast in the Hirons House. "With a gunboat on Lake Michigan

< CONSPIRACY OF KNAVES >

we could hold Chicago at bay. We could shell the artillery protecting Camp Douglas."

The boys smiled at Charley's remarks, but they knew him too well to laugh aloud at any of his conceits. When Charley Heywood got an idea into his head, he usually kept it there until it came to fruition or was proved impossible.

12

BELLE RUTLEDGE

FIRST IMPRESSIONS OF a place are usually enduring, and I still think of Chicago as the most exciting and energetic and captivating city of all those I have known. My first sight of Chicago was on a beautiful summer's day, with elongated white clouds hurrying across a deep blue sky that was mirrored in the even deeper blue of Lake Michigan, where sailboats and steamers moved as though under some mysterious urgency. Along the sidewalks men, women, and children were scurrying, apparently driven toward their destinations by matters of life and death. Everything in the city, it seemed to me, was rushing somewhere—clouds, boats, people, and the horse cab in which I was riding.

I had told the coachman at the railroad station that I wanted to go to the Tremont House. Charley Heywood had mentioned the Tremont as the place where we would stay in Chicago because it was the city's tallest building. Perhaps he would find me there, I thought, if he was of a mind to look for me.

The coachman agreed that the Tremont was indeed a tall building, five stories, but the Sherman House had surpassed it with an additional floor. "Eighty-four feet high," he declared proudly in a German accent much stronger than my friend Kendrich's stage pronunciations. "Chicago never stands still."

We crossed two or three bridges, sometimes being forced to halt while long spans opened for the passage of a procession of

< CONSPIRACY OF KNAVES >

boats with smoking funnels and screeching steam whistles. Railroad trains dashed back and forth from every direction, adding to the constant din of men and machines in perpetual motion. Along the banks of a river named for the city, tall grain elevators stood in rows broken by occasional slant-roofed warehouses.

We passed solid blocks of buildings of cream-colored brick and limestone that had been carved and fluted into gingerbread shapes, sometimes fronted with ornate ironwork. The streets were wide and straight and clear of mud or dust. The only perverse sights were the enormous numbers of legless, armless, and sometimes eyeless men on the sidewalks, open evidence amidst the city's dizzy prosperity that a malignant war was in progress a few hundred miles in the distance.

The Tremont House was more elegant by far than Cincinnati's Packet House, with window curtains of damask lined with silk, marble mantels, rosewood chairs, speaking tubes in every room, and door transoms to aid the ventilation. These luxuries were all reflected in the rates, unfortunately, and I realized that not even my generous supply of greenbacks would keep me for long in the Tremont waiting for Charley Heywood to appear.

Early the next morning while still in bed, I suddenly recalled the last order given me by Colonel Fennell in Richmond. *When you reach Chicago*, he had said, *report immediately to Dr. Julian Aylott on State Street.*

From the hotel's registry clerk I learned that the address on State Street was only a few blocks away. I decided to walk, joining the army of Chicagoans who, under the force of a strong wind, moved with still greater celerity than on the previous day.

Most of the pedestrians were males, tall and short, slender and heavy, their faces varied as pebbles along a shore. On the Tremont House's bulletin board that morning I had noted, amidst the sheaf of fresh telegraphic war dispatches, a city information card. Total numbers of Chicago inhabitants, it announced, was 109,000, far more than lived in Richmond. Half of these would be males, I guessed, more than fifty thousand, including infants and boys. How many of these pink-cheeked, gray-bearded, blue-jowled, handsome and plain and hard-visaged males were members of the Sons of Liberty, Knights of the Golden Circle, and other secret orders

< **Belle Rutledge** >

designed to overthrow the Union? One of every six, one of three, or one of two that I met or who passed me by on those windy streets—how many of them were Copperheads? At the meeting in Cincinnati, the Grand Seigneur from Illinois had boasted that he could put eighty thousand armed men into the streets of Chicago, provided, of course, that the Confederate commissioners allotted him many more thousands of dollars. Where would this armed horde come from? Were its members already here, on these crowded sidewalks?

At street corners windy blasts lifted the ruffles of my dress, ballooning my skirt to my knees, and I had to keep one hand constantly atop my little black bonnet or else it would have blown skyward. The fitful gusts from the lake were almost too chill, and I was relieved to come upon the address I was seeking, the large numerals embossed in an imposing rectangle of copper with the name Dr. Julian Aylott below.

There was something authoritative about the building and its sign; they told me that those who resided within were personages of consequence in the city of Chicago. I pulled the bell cord, and after a minute or two the door was opened by a dark-complexioned young woman wearing a sort of maid's uniform, with the usual apron and white lace cap. Remembering the boorishness of Colonel Fennell's agent in Cincinnati, the abominable Lester Marmot, I was gratified to know that I would not be closeted alone with the as yet unknown Dr. Julian Aylott.

When I told the maid that I wished to see Dr. Aylott in order to bring him greetings from a mutual friend named Fennell, she curtsied politely, and repeated my name and Fennell's in what was assuredly a New England Yankee pattern of speech. After seating me in a cozy little foyer, she vanished through a glassed door curtained in cretonne.

A very odd odor surrounded me, remindful of incense and musk, balsam and antiseptics, and then I realized the mixture of scents was that of an apothecary's shop. Odors have colors, you know, and that which permeated Dr. Aylott's house from cellar to attic was brownish, snuff-colored, almost bronze. I was soon to learn that it penetrated everything—furniture, curtains, carpets, the very clothing that one wore.

< CONSPIRACY OF KNAVES >

Instead of sending the maid back alone for me, Dr. Aylott came with her, greeting me quite seriously in that same New England accent used by the young woman. In fact, there was some resemblance between the two of them, their chins and noses being longer than usual. Indeed, his profile—nose, mouth, and jaw—was the shape of a nutcracker, and his bushy wild-haired eyebrows gave him a fierce mien, but there was nothing fierce at all about Dr. Julian Aylott's nature. Or so I believed after our first meeting. His skin was rather pale, while that of his maid was swarthy; her lips were full while his formed a thin line below a shaggy yellow mustache. Not then, but later, I pondered upon the curiousness of a doctor obviously from New England, the heart of abolitionism, acting as an agent for a Confederate spy master. And whose female servant, niece or daughter, appeared to be the partial product of a dusky race. Politics, like religion, creates strange alliances, and I came to know for certain that Dr. Aylott was an earnest member of the Democratic party.

He led me into an alcove of his study, where library shelves were filled with volumes that had begun to smell of the very drug formulas they contained. The maid brought us coffee, and in a soft voice informed the doctor that his first patient of the day was waiting.

"Excuse me," I said, "I shall leave and call upon you later."

"No, no," he replied in the cultured tone he affected. "I see only a few patients these days. My time is taken up with the manufacture and distribution of patented medicines. And, of course, my work with the Sons of Liberty." He went on to say that he had no communication from Colonel Fennell for me, but that on the previous day a message had been delivered by hand from Canada. Reaching to a nearby escritoire, he opened a drawer and withdrew a letter upon which was my name in the slanted handwriting of Major Charles Heywood. "You may wish to read it immediately," he said politely. "Perhaps it is urgent."

I was not so unobservant as to overlook the fact that the wax seal on the envelope had been broken and resealed, but I made no comment, simply separating the wax again, and wondering if Dr. Aylott had put aside his decorum long enough to read my letter. It was only one page, and I was disheartened because the salu-

< **Belle Rutledge** >

tation, text, and complimentary close were all devoid of any am-
orous expressions toward me.

"Major Heywood wishes me to visit Camp Douglas," I said,
"and furnish a prisoner there with details of the July rising."

"Do you know any details?" he asked with sudden eagerness.

"Nothing whatsoever," I replied. "I was hoping you could tell
me what the Copperheads' plans are."

His face revealed his disappointment. "For several days I have
been expecting an officer of the Sons of Liberty to report to me
with the details. I believe he is somewhere in southern Illinois
attempting to raise money for purchase of arms. All I know is the
date. July fourth."

At that time I had not yet heard the name or met Joseph
Milligan, the Greek-fire enthusiast, who had been to Barton Farm
near Tamaroa for a failed rendezvous with Major Heywood; he
was the man that Dr. Aylott had been expecting.

"Is it possible," I asked, "for me to pay a visit to a prisoner in
Camp Douglas?"

"Possible, yes," Dr. Aylott said gravely, "but not so easy to
accomplish. Who is the prisoner that Major Heywood wishes you
to visit?"

"A Captain Truscott. One of the major's fellow officers in General Morgan's cavalry."

"I see." If the doctor had read the sealed letter, he most certainly
knew the name already, but he rocked his head back and shifted
his hairy eyebrows up and down as though pondering the most
arduous of tasks.

"I think you will need help from someone more familiar with
Camp Douglas than I. Perhaps a Mrs. Ward, yes, Mrs. Evelyn
Ward. She is a fine Christian lady who represents various church
societies in missionary endeavors among the prisoners."

He went to the writing desk, dipped a pen in ink, and wrote
out her name and address on a sheet of notepaper. When he handed
it to me, his nose and chin moved closer together as though he
were crushing a trapped nut beneath his yellow mustache.

Major Heywood's letter and Dr. Aylott's recommendation to visit
Mrs. Evelyn Ward placed me in a fine dilemma. My original

< CONSPIRACY OF KNAVES >

plan for that afternoon was to follow the instructions that Kendrich had hastily passed to me in the dining room of the Packet House in Cincinnati: *Go to Camp Douglas*, he had said, *and ask for the commandant, Colonel Bartholomew Wright. Tell him you have a message from K. Tell him the rising is now set for July the fourth.*

While I was returning to my room in the Tremont House, the solution to my dilemma came suddenly to mind. I would visit Colonel Wright dressed as a man, using my old Virginia *nom de guerre*, Calvin Blacklock. Later, if I was able to visit Captain Truscott, I would dress as a woman, my own true self, Belle Rutledge.

Back in the Tremont House, I removed the auburn wig I'd been wearing since leaving Cincinnati and scissored my real hair a fraction of an inch around so that it was of a length I'd seen worn by dandified young men on the streets of Chicago. Dressed in gray trousers, and the dark frock coat and mouse-colored waistcoat I'd purchased in Cincinnati, I set out by horse trolley for Camp Douglas.

The ride was quite pleasant, with frequent views of the lake, and the car stopped almost directly in front of the prison entrance. I was astonished by the enormity of the place, and feared that because of this I would have great difficulty in obtaining an audience with the officer in command of so formidable a stronghold.

Experience in stage acting is always helpful in such situations, and I soon convinced the two guards at the gate that I was an admirable young man on an important errand. One of them trotted away like an obedient spaniel, in search of the commandant's adjutant, a lieutenant, who escorted me to the headquarters building. There I waited only a few minutes in an anteroom, where a handsome but rather slight young man was copying something from one foolscap sheet to another. He was dressed in shabby clothing, and I wondered if he were a prisoner or a citizen employed by the War Department at such low wages that he could not afford to buy decent clothes.

From time to time, he stopped what he was doing to glance at me, his hazel eyes wavering shyly, so that I imagined him to be as sensitive as a romantic poet. Had I not been dressed as a male, I might have played a little game of eye flirtation, but as it was I

< **Belle Rutledge** >

nodded and spoke politely in my deepest voice: "Sir, you appear to be quite absorbed in whatever task you are engaged upon."

"I'm compiling a book of the dead," he replied coldly. "But I suppose it would not concern a young man of your stamp that one of every eight captives who has entered this prison has died here."

He had hardly finished this somber statement when a colonel, resplendent in a brass-buttoned blouse, appeared at the inner door. Somewhat impatiently, and decidedly not with cordiality, he motioned for me to enter, and as soon as I had done so he closed the door behind me.

"What is the nature of this compelling business you refused to reveal to my adjutant?" he demanded. Obviously he did not care for my foppish appearance, and I could not blame him for that, in wartime.

"I have a message from K.," I replied.

His manner changed instantly. Instead of sitting in the only chair in the office, he remained standing beside his desk.

Colonel Bartholomew Wright has already been described, as Captain John Truscott saw him at first meeting. Physically the prison commandant appeared virtually the same to me, the long drooping mustache, unkempt bush of hair, his almost comical button nose. But I sensed none of the yielding kindness that he had shown to Captain Truscott. Instead I saw a craftiness in his deep-set hound-dog eyes, a latent cruelty that one finds in petty men who suddenly find themselves in positions of power.

"Who are you?" he asked in a harsh voice.

"My name is Calvin Blacklock," I lied, as spies must. "From Washington City."

He looked me up and down, derisively, and smiled without humor. "You are young to be what you say you are."

"For that very reason, sir, because of my youthful appearance," I replied, "I was chosen to work with K."

Colonel Wright moved around the desk and sat down heavily. "I need some proof of who and what you are."

For the first time since acquiring it in Washington, I removed a card from my pocket purse and laid it on the desk in front of Colonel Wright. He bent forward to study the simple signature that had been inscribed neatly at the bottom of the card.

When he glanced up, his eyes met mine directly.

"Signed by the President," he said. "K. told me that Mr. Lincoln himself presented the card he carries. Did you also meet the President?"

"Yes, sir."

"Ah. Now, what message did K. send me?"

"He said I should warn you that the uprising is set for July fourth."

The colonel shrugged impatiently. "Young man, we've known that for days now. What more?"

"That you should be prepared for incendiary attacks upon essential buildings in the city as well as an armed assault upon this camp."

"Yes?"

"That names and places will be sent to you as they become known."

"Ah, yes, names and places certainly will be useful to us. I have been informed that fifty thousand armed Copperheads are preparing to seize Chicago on the Fourth of July. And that thousands more will rise up in adjoining states. But I have very few names of these traitors, or places they may be planning to strike."

I told him of the Copperhead meeting in Cincinnati where both Kendrich and I had been present, and that I could give him descriptions of the leaders and the membership numbers they had reported by states. At once, he reached for a sheet of official gray paper, and with his eyes showing more respect for me, began writing down the descriptions and numbers that I had put to memory.

When I finished, he asked: "Do you know where K. is at present? In the past two weeks I've received only one cryptic telegram from somewhere in Ohio."

"I believe he is in Canada."

"Into the nest of the Rebel traitors, eh? What are your next duties, Mr. Blacklock?"

I shook my head. "I'm awaiting further instructions from him, sir."

"Very good." He smiled that humorless smile again. "Perhaps you could undertake a task for me?"

"Of course."

< **Belle Rutledge** >

"There's a woman in Chicago who I suspect may be working with the Copperheads. I permit her to enter Camp Douglas on visiting days so that we can observe what prisoners she may single out for attention, possibly to pass messages back and forth. My suspicions of her have increased because on her recent visits she sought out a young Rebel who I believe may be a leader among the worst of the prisoners, the Morgan men, cavalrymen who rode with the bushwhacker, John Morgan." He paused and turned his flat-nosed profile to the window beside his desk.

"The young Rebel should have been hanged, but if we had put him on the gallows, the Jeff Davis outlaws would have retaliated by hanging good Union men in doubles. So I've cozened him, made prison life easy for him, and watched him carefully. What I would like you to do for me, Mr. Blacklock, is gain the confidence of the Chicago woman, try to discover who her associates are, what her part in the uprising may be on the outside, and see if she will reveal what my Rebel suspect may be planning on the inside. His name, by the way, is John Truscott."

He lifted his pen and scratched across the bottom of his gray sheet of paper, tore it off, and handed it to me.

At that moment, I can tell you, every particle of my acting experience had to be summoned up to keep my face from revealing astonishment. First, the name John Truscott, whom I had heard much about from Major Heywood. And then the name on the piece of paper that Colonel Wright handed me. It was the same name that Dr. Aylott had written on his notepaper that I was carrying in my pocket purse—Mrs. Evelyn Ward.

As excellent a spy as I thought myself to be, however, I completely failed to identify the wiry young man in shabby clothing at work in the anteroom as Major Heywood's friend, John Truscott. When I left Colonel Wright's office, Truscott was still there, but I was unaware of the hostile glare he directed at my retreating backside. He was to tell me about that later, along with many other particulars that form a considerable part of this narrative.

Next morning, in one of my plainest feminine costumes, I visited Mrs. Evelyn Ward at her home on Randolph Street. Having learned that she was a former Kentuckian, I decided to tell her straightaway

< CONSPIRACY OF KNAVES >

that I was Belle Rutledge of Louisville and that her name and address had been given me by Dr. Julian Aylott. To gain her complete confidence, I added falsely that I had heard of her good works from a dear friend of mine, Major Heywood.

She responded almost ecstatically by asking if I was acquainted with the major's cousin, Miss Marianna Heywood, who frequently sent clothing and other articles to be given to the Camp Douglas prisoners. I replied that I did not know Miss Marianna but had heard of her good works from the major. It was true that the major had told me enough about his cousin so that I was able to create a plausible playbook for the benefit of Mrs. Ward, and my little plot worked marvelously well. She was an admirer of all the Heywoods, she said, and led me into an inner part of the house to meet her husband, a lawyer whom she referred to as "the Judge."

He was a bantam rooster type of a man, full of contentious energy that kept him bouncing about. His graying reddish hair was cut short like a brush. When he stood erect, the top of his head barely reached the bottom of my chin. He had a habit of echoing the last three or four words of any remark spoken to him, and more often than not would challenge whatever was said. I soon learned to avoid any conversation with Judge Ward, but his full-bosomed wife simply ignored his comments by talking over them in her declamatory manner.

I found Evelyn Ward to be a quite jolly woman, childlike at times, constantly hinting at dark secrets that must not be told. She was proud of her husband's rank in the Sons of Liberty, boasting that he always acted as Grand Seigneur of the Chicago temple when Dr. Aylott was unable to be present for meetings. "We are going to elect a Democrat president in November," she declared more than once during my visit, and her husband would echo: "Lincoln the Republican is a tyrannical usurper." I had the oddest feeling that if there had been no war or presidential campaign in progress the Wards would have invented some elaborate intrigue in which to become involved.

We finally left the judge's cluttered little law office and went into the sitting room, where there was an array of gaily painted rocking chairs. I admired them, and she was as pleased as a little girl to tell me that painted chairs were all the rage in Chicago. She

served tea and some deliciously light tea cakes. By this time I felt
that I had gained her confidence sufficiently to broach the subject
of a possible visit to Camp Douglas.

"I've received an urgent message from Major Heywood," I said
boldly. "He wants me to visit Captain John Truscott in Camp
Douglas and give him the details of what is to happen on July
fourth."

Evelyn Ward's eyes brightened with the joy of a secret sharer.
"Fiddlesticks!" she cried. "Don't you know the date's been changed
to July sixteenth?"

"Dr. Aylott told me it was the fourth."

"Dear me! The message came from the Supreme Commander,
Mr. Vallandigham, just last night."

"I have not seen Dr. Aylott since yesterday," I explained.

She rocked joyfully in one of her painted chairs, lifting her
slippered feet rhythmically off the floor. "Do you know the details
of the uprising, Miss Belle?" she asked slyly.

"No, I do not. I think Charley—Major Heywood—expected
Dr. Aylott to furnish such information to me. But the doctor says
he knows nothing. Do you suppose Judge Ward could help me?"

She placed one of her plump hands in front of her mouth and
whispered: "He knows where the guns are hidden." She hesitated
a moment, suppressing a giggle. "But he won't tell even me, his
wife."

"Do you suppose Captain Truscott knows of the delayed date?"

She shook her head. "Not yet, most likely. Shall we go together
to tell him?"

"That would please me," I said.

"Next visiting day is July the seventh. I'm a regular visitor, so
they don't notice how I dress anymore, except hoopskirts are forbidden. But you'd better wear a black dress that buttons tightly
at the collar, sanctimonious, don't you know, and a black hat. No
hoops, or they'll stop you at the gate. Meet me here just after
noontime of the seventh."

Later that afternoon I called upon Dr. Aylott, mainly to learn
if he had heard from Charley Heywood again, but also to report
that Mrs. Ward had offered to assist me in communicating with
Captain Truscott. Before I could ask the doctor if he had heard

< CONSPIRACY OF KNAVES >

of the change in dates from July fourth to July sixteenth, he offered me that very intelligence in the lofty manner of an oracle delivering a revelation. He apparently was so pleasured by his font of inside information that I did not have the heart to tell him that Mrs. Ward had scored a beat on him.

When I asked if he could provide me with additional funds should my supply of greenbacks become exhausted, he appeared to be offended. He replied that since I was working for Major Heywood, I should apply to him for my subsistence.

"I have no way of communicating with Major Heywood," I said, "and the Tremont House is very expensive. Perhaps I should seek a cheaper hotel or a boardinghouse."

"My dear Miss Rutledge," he replied in a fatherly manner, "there is no need for you to do either. My house has bedchambers for visitors, and you're welcome to stay until you hear from Major Heywood."

He called the young woman who I had assumed on the previous day was his maid, and asked her to show me an available room. Again I was struck by the slight resemblance between the two. Her name was Ilena, but whether she was daughter, niece, or whatever was not explained to me by either of them.

Ilena led me down a short flight of steps and along a hallway, the walls of which consisted of shelves filled with bottles bearing a variety of labels. The odor of drugs was very heavy, almost overpowering to me, but it did not seem to bother Ilena. At the end of the hall we ascended another flight of steps to a row of three bedrooms, the doors open so that breezes flowed through to diminish the brownish odor of the house.

"Choose the bedchamber you like," Ilena said in a rather indifferent tone.

Stacked in the corners of all three rooms were wooden boxes stamped with the names of medicines and distributors.

"Dr. Aylott must have a thriving business," I said.

"Yes, we are both kept busy," she answered in the same disinterested way.

I chose the largest room, so that I would have more space to move about among the boxes, and informed Ilena that I would gladly accept the doctor's hospitality.

< **Belle Rutledge** >

Later that afternoon I left the Tremont House and moved my
baggage into Dr. Aylott's place on State Street. He insisted that I
be his guest for dinner. Ilena served the meal and then joined us
as an equal for coffee in the library. For the evening the doctor
had dressed in a wide-lapeled alpaca coat and striped trousers. He
wore a large white tie outside his shirt collar, and a gold oak-leaf
pin on his coat. Charley Heywood owned a pin exactly like it, and
had told me that the oak leaf stood for O.A.K., or Order of American Knights.

Although the doctor and Ilena offered little information about
themselves, they obviously wanted to know all about me. Avoiding
any references to my life as a spy, I talked freely about my adventures as a dancer and actress, and was just about to excuse
myself to retire to the bedroom when the front doorbell sounded.
Ilena responded instantly as though on command, closing the library door behind her. A few moments later, I heard voices in the
corridor outside. Dr. Aylott's wild eyebrows moved up and down.
He fingered a round silver box from a waistcoat pocket, took a
brown pill from it, and popped it into his nutcracker mouth.

Three knocks sounded then upon the library door. Dr. Aylott
arose, went over to the closed door, and stood facing it. "Who
cometh without?" he demanded solemnly.

"Oak-oun, oak-oun, oak-oun," a muffled voice replied. "An
Ancient Brother seeks admittance to the temple."

"State your name and residence," Dr. Aylott replied mechanically.

"Joseph Milligan, residence on Cottage Grove."

Opening the door, the doctor stepped aside to admit a heavyset
man wearing a gold sash around an ample belly. The visitor offered
his hand in that silly Copperhead grip of thumb locking. With his
left hand, Dr. Aylott then squeezed the man's right elbow, this
being followed by clumsy heel-and-toe placements that always reminded me of two bull cows pawing the ground before butting
heads.

As soon as these ridiculous rituals were completed, Dr. Aylott
nodded in my direction and spoke my name, explaining briefly who
I was, and then introduced the visitor as Mr. Joseph Milligan.

"So you are the young lady who works with Major Heywood,"

< CONSPIRACY OF KNAVES >

Milligan said to me in a sour tone that I found offensive. "Do you know I've wasted a week in southern Illinois waiting for Heywood to show himself with money for horses and arms?"

I assured Mr. Milligan that I had nothing to do with the Confederate commissioners' distribution of funds and advised him rather curtly to take his complaints directly to Major Heywood.

"I shall certainly do so, if he can be found. The major's failure to supply money for purchases of horses and arms has forced us to delay action for two weeks."

Milligan sat down in a plush chair, the cushions sinking slowly under the weight of his broad buttocks. A scent of apple pomade mingled with his stale sweat.

Dr. Aylott was nodding his head slowly. "We can use the added time to complete arrangements," he said. "How many of your men are without arms at present, Joseph?"

Milligan hummed to himself as he counted on his fingers. "Fifteen hundred, plus a few, less a few. Ten thousand dollars I'll need for rifles and ammunition, and some bribe money for the boys at the arsenals."

"Your figures may be low, Joseph," the doctor said. "I shall ask Major Heywood that amount for Greek fire—"

"Greek fire, oh, yes!" Milligan's eyes brightened. "Have you seen it tried, Dr. Aylott?"

"No, I have not. But my informers tell me that Chicago can be reduced to ashes in a night."

Milligan winced as though he'd been painfully struck. "That is not what— After all, doctor, my draying business, and your drug manufactory—we want only *control* of Chicago, not its destruction."

Dr. Aylott's nutcracker profile broke into a fearsome grin. "I was only jesting, Joseph. But we must call a meeting of the grand council to select carefully the sites that are to be destroyed."

"Indeed, sir, indeed. And places must be found around the city's outskirts for stabling and pasturing horses for prisoners who are freed from Camp Douglas, the horses that Brigadier Colquett is supplying us."

"The horses are on their way here, Joseph? How many?"

Milligan shook his head so hard that the ends of his drooping mustache quivered, and he replied in a conspiratorial whisper: "Another delay caused by Major Heywood's dillydallying. The horses are still in Missouri. Colquett can't move them until he has thirty thousand dollars, some of it in gold, he says."

Dr. Aylott's bushy eyebrows moved rhythmically up and down as he scribbled in a tiny notebook. When he completed the entry, he took a pill from his silver box and snapped it into the back of his mouth, downing it with one swallow.

For another hour the two Copperheads talked, talked, talked— of money, of Greek fire and rifles and pistols in thousands, of Sons of Liberty meetings and drilling and recruitment, of the relative presidential virtues of George McClellan and Clement Vallandigham, but mostly about money in the hundreds of thousands, how much of it and how soon it could be obtained from Major Heywood and the Confederate Commission in Canada. Although I was weary and sleepy from my long day, I listened closely to their bubbling dreams of glory, to their illusions of grandeur, and expectations of wealth and power.

My impressions of Joseph Milligan were similar to those observed by Johnny Truscott when he met the Chicagoan at Barton Farm near Tamaroa—a man oppressed by lifelong frustrations who was hopeful that at last he had found a way out of the abyss, yet did not dare allow himself to become too elated for fear of ultimate rejection.

Later I discovered that he was dominated by females, by his empty-headed wife, his aging mother-in-law, and his three daughters. His father was no longer living; he had no brothers and but one son. He had been an officer in the Union Army for three months, having organized a company of Irish in his neighborhood only to lose his captaincy to a more popular man in the very command he had put together. Before he could see any military action, his volunteer term expired and he was sent home; he had spent most of his service time in Washington City, and may have seen me doing a naughty song and dance in one of the Ninth Street theaters. He was of the type who would pay good money to see me perform in tights and the scruffy sort of sketches that Kendrich and I were reduced to presenting.

Next morning I awoke in a deep feather bed with sunshine

< CONSPIRACY OF KNAVES >

slanting like a limelight beam through the window upon a stack of Dr. Aylott's boxes. Atop them was a sheaf of broadsides printed in the blackest of inks:

Dr. Aylott's
CONSUMPTION REMEDY
Compounded from Roots, Barks and Leaves
Imported from
INDIAN TERRITORY
Formula known only to the Cherokees
Who
Disclosed the Secret to
Dr. Aylott
Not for Money or Friendship
But Solely for the Benefit of
SUFFERING MANKIND

—

Positive Cure Guaranteed of All Diseases of
the Lungs and Related Organs
Relieves Constant Imaginings of Evil and
Great Depression of Spirits

Beneath the broadsides, the wooden boards of the top box had been removed. An array of bottles labeled DR. AYLOTT'S CONSUMPTION REMEDY rested there, and I could not resist removing one for a sampling of the contents.

Although the liquid bore the now familiar brownish odor, the taste was seductive, perhaps a bit sweetish but warm to the tongue and throat. I took a second generous swallow, and then put the bottle into my handbag.

From somewhere in the direction of the lake a cannon thundered, the reverberations being followed by a distant fanfare of trumpets, and I remembered that it was July fourth, the day we celebrate. From all directions of the city, church bells began ringing, the sounds mingling with popping firecrackers and the occasional whiz and bang of a rocket.

On the previous evening Dr. Aylott had invited me to attend a review at Camp Douglas with him and Ilena. The newspapers announced that the prison camp would be open to the public on Independence Day from two to six P.M. for a grand review and

< **Belle Rutledge** >

dress parade, and the doctor was hopeful that some way might be found for me to meet Captain John Truscott earlier than I had hoped.

I dressed hastily in my grass-green dress, with its gold belt and revealing lacy bodice. Already I was feeling the sublime effects of that secret formula of the Cherokees, and when I tripped along the narrow hallway between the shelves of pills and tonics, I had a sensation of dancing upon clouds.

Dr. Aylott and Ilena were already at breakfast, but they greeted me with hearty good cheer, both asking if I'd slept well. She hurried off to bring me coffee and a warm plate. I noticed that the doctor's silver pillbox was resting on the white tablecloth halfway between his place and hers, and I wondered if the same secret roots, leaves, and barks used in his consumption remedy were also compounded into his pills. Anyway, for so early in the morning, the three of us certainly were in high spirits that could not have been caused by a mere holiday.

Shortly after noon Mr. Joseph Milligan arrived with two large carriages drawn by pairs of heavy-footed horses, animals used ordinarily in his draying business. One carriage was filled with members of his family, all females; the other was for the doctor, Ilena, and me. I had expected we might be traveling to Camp Douglas by streetcar, but after we had gone a few blocks along State Street I was certainly grateful for the more comfortable carriage. Every streetcar that we passed was jammed inside and outside; even the tops were covered with passengers, and the poor horses pulling the cars were straining at their burdens. The intense activity in the city had created a thin cloud of mingled dust and smoke, and the wretched creatures on the cars were covered with it. Perspiration oozed from every fiber of their garments, and they were literally panting like dogs from the heat.

By contrast our ride was quite pleasant. Mr. Milligan took us to the shade of a grove of trees where other carriages, some driven by men in livery, were drawn up in a long line. This parklike haven was halfway between the prison camp and an observatory tower that Dr. Aylott said was used by a local university.

The Milligans had brought along two large baskets of food for a picnic lunch, and while Ilena, Mrs. Milligan, and the oldest daughter were laying out the meats and breads and cakes and pies,

< CONSPIRACY OF KNAVES >

the two younger Milligan girls prevailed upon me to join them in climbing the steps of the observatory tower, from which we could look down inside Camp Douglas.

The Milligan girls were true Irish beauties, as alike as daisies in a meadow, with their bright black eyes, golden hair, and ruddy complexions. They had been atop the tower once before, and the older of the two pointed out various sections of the camp's interior. The parade ground was packed with soldiers in blue, busily practicing for the afternoon review.

"My heavens," cried the older Milligan girl, "not a prisoner to be seen. Oh, but yes, there're three standing in a roof window. Oh, those pitiful fellows, they are so meanly treated. Not allowed even to celebrate Independence Day."

The prisoners' stockade, with its dozen rows of barracks, comprised about a third of the camp's area, but except for the three men on the roof, none of the several thousand prisoners was in view. Obviously they were restricted to barracks for July fourth, and I could well understand the reason why.

The Milligan daughters, I soon learned, had wanted to attend a balloon ascension at Washington Skating Park instead of the Camp Douglas celebration, and they were piqued at their father, who, I gathered, had been more unyielding than was his usual way when they begged him to accede to their wishes.

"I can't understand," the older daughter said, "why Pa would want to come to this awful place for Independence Day. He's a Democrat and detests President Lincoln." She cast a quick glance at me and added: "Pa was a captain in the Union Army, did you know that, Miss Belle? And he blames old Lincoln for taking his company away from him. He's loyal to the Union, but he's a Democrat, don't you know, and wants a Democrat for President. Mr. Vallandigham or General McClellan, he can't make up his mind."

I suspected that some pressure had been put upon Mr. Milligan by Dr. Aylott, mainly for my benefit, so that I might possibly meet Captain John Truscott. No hint of this did I indicate to the Milligan girls, of course, and after looking down from the tower into the desolate stockade, I knew I was not going to meet the imprisoned captain on that day.

Actually I was in no mood to see the prisoner Truscott. I cared

not a fig whether I met him or not. The man I wanted to see was
Charley Heywood. All through the picnic, with its familial atmosphere, particularly the fresh-faced young daughters suppressing giggles and girlish chatter, I kept seeing Charley's mocking
eyes, and found myself listening for his laughter. Thinking of those
few brief days with him and little Winslow almost brought tears.

Bittersweet days they were, and I felt that old sense of guilt
again for leaving Winslow at the orphanage in Cincinnati. And
oh, how my body and soul did ache for a sight of Charley, oh,
how I wanted to cleave to him with all my might.

A cannon boomed from within the high-walled camp, shaking
me from my moody reverie. The noisy salute was repeated again
and again, one for each of the thirty-two states of the Union,
including the eleven wayward members of the Confederacy.

"The gates are opening," Dr. Aylott announced, and we soon
joined a line of citizens moving toward the entrance. On my previous visit in the guise of a male, I had been forced to use my
cleverest wiles to gain admittance; today I was welcomed as a
patriotic lady honoring the defenders of the Republic.

Dr. Aylott, who was leading the way, stepped aside to converse
briefly with a Union officer just inside the gate, a whiskered captain
wearing thick spectacles. The captain shook his head haughtily
and motioned the doctor back into line. When he came alongside
me, Dr. Aylott whispered above the sounds of the brassy military
band: "Prisoners are locked in their barracks today." His eyes
narrowed. "Somebody must have passed the word about the Fourth
of July plot."

As we were directed to our seats by uniformed guards, we
skirted a wooden platform heavily decorated with flags and banners. Seated not ten feet above me was the commandant, Colonel
Bartholomew Wright, his boots freshly blackened, his new uniform
resplendent. He was still watching me when I turned my head
away. I think he admired my saucy hat and the low cut of the
bodice that exposed the rise of my breasts. I doubt very much if
I reminded him of Calvin Blacklock, youthful male spy, or if he
had given any thought that day to Blacklock's promised report on
Mrs. Evelyn Ward.

For an hour and a half the bands played, the soldiers marched,
the spectators waved their flags and cheered. The Camp Douglas

< CONSPIRACY OF KNAVES >

troops were exceptionally skillful at patterns of drill, at forming files and columns and ranks, at deploying as skirmishers, at slinging and unslinging their rifles. Not having to fight in the field, they'd had considerable time, I suppose, to practice playing at war. Escape from reality, that is what the Independence Day celebration was in Chicago in that bloody year of 1864, a glorious day of forgetting the odious war. Horse races, boating on the lake, balloon ascensions, vocal and instrumental concerts in the parks, a European circus, picnics galore—after three years of obscene death, who wanted to remember men still dying in the redoubts of Petersburg and Atlanta?

And there was I, seated amidst Copperheads and their kith and kin, men plotting to bring the real war to the very ground where we enjoyed comfort and security. Two mad men perhaps: Joseph Milligan, collecting arms for an uprising, yet watching with admiration the very troops those arms would be used against, his eyes moistening as he applauded the intricate evolutions of his intended victims. Dr. Julian Aylott, seated so close beside me that I could feel the warmth of his pale aging body, his freakish profile showing no emotion, his cavernous mouth opening only once or twice, not to cheer but to receive a brown tablet from his round silver pillbox. I did not value him a button; he took enough opiates to kill an army. And there was I, perhaps as mad as my male companions, playing both ends against the middle. The countenance of every handsome soldier who passed in review metamorphosed into the face of Charles Heywood. I wanted to place my hands over my eyes and weep.

The July sun broiled us like young chickens on a spit. To my great relief, when the dress parade ended and the greased-pig races began for competing soldiers, Dr. Aylott announced that the time had come for our departure. Only Mr. Milligan appeared reluctant, but he offered no vocal objection.

On our way back into Chicago, I was still reflecting upon the illusions of the day. How unreal everything had seemed! Ahead of our carriage the summer air was heavy with dust, and the sun's slanting rays created fragmented rainbows, a hundred colors dancing so frantically that my head began to throb with pain.

From the carriage in front came shrill cries from the Milligan girls: "The balloon! The balloon!" one of them screamed.

< **Belle Rutledge** >

Against the paling blue of the dingy sky floated a giant lozenge.

Dr. Aylott leaned forward to obtain a better view, his elbow thrusting rudely into my side.

"Ah, a great achievement," he declared in his best pontifical voice. "Properly named the *New World*."

"No, father." Ilena spoke boldly for what may have been her first articulated observation of the day. "I can read the lettering upon the balloon. It is the *General Grant*."

Dr. Aylott sank back in the carriage seat as if his spirits had been crushed. So Ilena was his daughter, I thought, the product perhaps of some mésalliance. Ilena, the three Milligan girls, and I, celebrating the holiday with two stodgy cockadoodledoos and two old hens. We should have been frolicking with five young cockerels. But on Independence Day of 1864 all the desirable males were far away, dying on some gory Southern battlefield or madly conspiring in Canada to create havoc in a Northwest Conspiracy. How my head did ache! I needed at least ten drops of laudanum. Perhaps there was that much left in the bottle of Dr. Aylott's Cherokee consumption remedy still stowed in my handbag.

Three days later I made my third visit inside Camp Douglas, this time dressed not as a fop or a young woman in gaily colored and revealing holiday garb, but as a gentlewoman missionary wearing subdued gray, my wig that of a prim matron, my face untouched by powder, and carrying a small Testament in one hand.

Mrs. Evelyn Ward, who guided me, was in her element, declaiming noisily in her childlike yet almost flirtatious manner to the young prisoners gathered in a triangular enclosure that was confined by little shops and galleries, a post office, and a chapel. These Confederate captives were certainly a variegated lot, some very young, some looking older than their years, some in badly worn uniforms, some in coarse gray osnaburg. Most of them were moving about among us with want lists in their hands, begging permission to examine the contents of the baskets carried by most of the visitors.

I had brought a basket of tea cakes and religious tracts given me by Mrs. Ward; these, she assured me, would create the least bother from the guards at the gate and facilitate my entrance as a newcomer among the regular visitors. Mrs. Ward had brought

< C O N S P I R A C Y   O F   K N A V E S >

muslin towels and underdrawers, and we had to wait while a guard unfolded and shook them out to make certain she was not smuggling messages or some kind of contraband into the camp.

As we moved into the midst of the prisoners, they swarmed around Mrs. Ward, greeting her as an old friend and taking most of the things we carried in our baskets, stowing them into their burlap bags. From time to time Mrs. Ward lifted herself on her tiptoes, craning her neck and peering across the yard. "Ah," she finally cried, "there he is, over by the tintype gallery, our Captain Truscott!"

I did not recognize him, until we were almost upon him, as the slight restless young man in shabby civilian's clothing who only a few days before had spoken briefly with me in the anteroom outside Commandant Wright's office. My throat tightened with sudden dismay. If he recognized me as the foppish Calvin Blacklock, the game I was playing would abruptly turn dangerous for me, if not come to a sudden end. How I wished I had worn a crepe veil, as most gentlewomen missionaries do when they venture into the wicked world! With a silent prayer I summoned all the talents of actress Belle Rutledge. I had brought a folding fan to use against the heat; with a careless gesture I put it into play so that it partially concealed my face while stirring the air.

"Captain Truscott," Mrs. Ward was saying, "my friend Miss Belle Rutledge."

His sensitive hazel-brown eyes searched my face as best he could through my fluttering fan. If he expected me to offer my hand, he showed no sign of disappointment when I did not. He made a slight nodding bow.

"Have we not met before, Miss Rutledge?" he asked politely.

"No, I think not," I lied.

"Do you live in the city of Chicago?"

"No," I whispered and tried not to move my lips when I added: "Charles Heywood sent me to see you."

He stood absolutely still for a few seconds, looking casually about the enclosure as though disinterested in my presence.

"Miss Rutledge," he said then, with what must have been forced affability, "would you do me the honor of posing for a tintype with me?"

Mrs. Ward had already withdrawn, her voice chattering from

the little knot of prisoners surrounding her. Truscott took my arm and led me past a sign that read FERROTYPES, 50 CENTS, and through a canvas entrance. A pretty girl wearing a purple banner, Sabbath School Union, slanting across her bosom was taking turns posing with three young prisoners, each of them with similar banners over their chests.

Truscott motioned for me to sit on a pineboard box while we waited our turn.

"We can talk with more ease in here," he said. "Away from the chicken hawks." A smile flashed for an instant across his classic face.

I kept the fan going between us; the canvas studio *was* quite hot and stuffy.

"Where is Charley?" he asked, keeping his head down.

I told him as quickly as I could that I had received Charley's message from Canada but I was not certain of his present whereabouts. "Major Heywood asked me to inform you of the July uprising in Chicago, but I have been unable to obtain any details."

"You're working with Charley?"

"We came from Richmond to Cincinnati. He went on to Canada from there."

"We heard it was to be on July fourth," he whispered, his head still bent over as if he were studying the loose boards that formed the floor.

"The new date is July sixteenth," I said from behind the fan.

"What will happen then?"

I shook my head. "I don't know."

"My men and most of the other prisoners won't wait many days longer without a desperate try for escape. Their hopes were up, and then got dashed. They're angry." His low voice was edged with the bitterness of frustration. "You tell Charley to quit dallying. We want out of here."

The pretty girl and her retinue of Sabbath School recruits were departing. The photographer gave me a broad smile, took the fifty-cent sutlers' check from Truscott, and posed us against a solid black backdrop. Remembering a bit of stage business I'd seen Miss Madge Turner, an English actress, use in a play at the New Richmond, I held the fan so that it shielded half my face while the tintype was being made.

We had just stepped down and were waiting for the photographer to complete his procedure when a prisoner in a neat gray uniform appeared suddenly at the canvas entrance.

"There you are, Truscott. I was wondering where you'd got to."

He spoke in a nasal Southwestern drawl. His hair was coal-black and combed tight against his skull. Although he turned to face me, his eyes seemed never to meet mine but to be directed slightly to one side or the other.

Truscott made no response to the intruder's greeting, and I sensed that he disliked him. After a moment's silence the man stepped directly in front of me and said: "If Captain Truscott is so rude as to want to keep you all to himself, then I must introduce myself. I am Otis Jordan. Truscott and I are old comrades from our days with Morgan's raiders."

His smile was as artificial as his manner of speaking, but I told him my name.

"Will you pose with me also, Miss Rutledge?"

Truscott interrupted quickly: "Don't annoy the lady, Jordan."

Jordan's face darkened. "I was asking for her permission, Truscott. Not yours."

"Very well," I said, still keeping my fan moving. Once again I held the fan coyly against my forehead in the manner of Miss Madge Turner. But just as the photographer commanded us to draw in a deep breath, hold perfectly still, and count silently to twenty, Otis Jordan abruptly took the fan from my hand.

I should have protested but I did not. Vanity, perhaps? Or the avoidance of a scene between the two men that might have drawn attention to my presence in the camp? I don't know. Anyway, for the first time since we'd met, Captain Truscott, waiting glumly on the pineboard box, could see my face clearly from a few yards' distance. And Otis Jordan would possess a tintype of Belle Rutledge, whose features bore considerable resemblance to those of Calvin Blacklock the popinjay spy.

Outside the canvas gallery a jarring military voice was announcing that the time had come for visitors to leave Camp Douglas. With Johnny Truscott walking silently on my right and Otis Jordan plying me with questions on my left, I was escorted to the prisoners' line, beyond which neither could go. Jordan got no information from me other than that while I was engaged in mission work I had met Mrs. Evelyn Ward, who had invited me to accompany her to Camp Douglas—a spy's lie, of course.

"I hope you will come back again, Miss Rutledge," Truscott said. "And tell us of the news outside."

"Yes, yes, you must return next visitors' day," Jordan added hastily, his eyes fixed in those strange angles that made me decidedly uneasy.

Remembering that I was playing the part of a gentlewoman missionary, I touched Truscott's hand lightly.

"God be with you," I said, with some sincerity.

His eyes were pleasant to look into, but there was puzzlement in them. I knew that he knew he had seen me somewhere, but I hoped he was not clever enough to associate the dandified male character with the gentle female missionary.

Oh, well, I thought, as an actress in similar roles I had succeeded in hoodwinking audiences through at least four acts of most five-act plays. My predicament was that I had not the faintest notion which act of the very real drama was then in progress.

Only a few hours later matters took a most excitedly pleasant turn. There I was, floating in a soft feather mattress with the cool air from Lake Michigan flowing over me, dreaming of that last night with Charley Heywood in Cincinnati. Only this was no dream, as I suddenly realized, coming wide awake in the gray light of dawn to see Charley's sky-blue eyes no farther than an inch from mine and to feel his soft beard against my cheek.

Anger and relief were combined in me, I suppose. I caught his mane of hair in both hands and pulled his head back.

"You ran away and abandoned me," I accused.

"Not for long," he retorted.

"Your forehead is all freckles," I said.

When Charley Heywood laughs, the sound is like Niagara cascading. I tried to stop him by pressing one hand against his mouth. "You'll wake the Aylotts," I whispered.

"Nonsense. I had the devil of a time waking them when I came in after midnight. Most likely they're both dead to the world on the good doctor's opiates."

Charley and I were lovers. That is all my readers need to know, because this narrative is concerned mainly with the Northwest Conspiracy and not with matters of the heart. Admittedly I was very foolish, an experienced woman of the stage and world, supposedly his relentless opponent, allowing herself to become romantically entangled with the likes of Charley Heywood, but that's the way it was, and we'll leave it there with no regrets.

The sun was well up when he left me to get dressed. Sure enough, as he had predicted, when we went down to the dining room there was no sign of Dr. Aylott or Ilena. Fortunately, Charley knew how to light the coal-oil burner, and we soon had water boiling for tea.

Outside on State Street a newsboy was shouting something about Maryland and the Rebs.

"If that's what I think it is," Charley said, "we have some fast work before us here in Chicago."

He hurried out to buy a paper, and before he returned Dr. Aylott and Ilena appeared. Both looked laved and laundered, with a freshness that was marred by the dark pouches beneath their eyes.

"What's happened?" the doctor asked Charley when he came hurrying in with the newspaper.

"Invasion of Maryland," Charley replied, holding the front page so that we could read the banners at the top of the columns: REBELS OCCUPY HAGERSTOWN AND LEVY TRIBUTE. THEY ADVANCE ON FREDERICK AND DRIVE IN OUR FORCES.

"That could end the war," Dr. Aylott said solemnly.

"Not unless we do our part," Charley replied. "If we can seize Chicago on the sixteenth and take the Northwestern states out of the Union, old Abe Lincoln will have to throw up the white flag." He buttered a tea roll with deliberate strokes of his knife.

"How many men can you and Joe Milligan put into the streets on one day's notice?" he asked Dr. Aylott.

The doctor's eyebrows lifted higher. "It's not a question of total numbers, major," he answered. "Fifty thousand, perhaps eighty thousand men on two days' notice, but only a few are properly armed. We need at least twenty thousand dollars for rifles and ammunition. And to seize the city, another ten thousand for Greek fire."

"It's not a question of total money, either," Charley retorted.

"It's a question of time. I passed enough greenbacks to Joe Milligan last spring to arm four or five thousand men. We can take Chicago with that size force."

"Milligan says he has to spend a great deal to bribe the armory guards." The doctor stirred sugar into his tea. "Because of the government's interdiction of weapons sales, the armories are the only places he can obtain good small arms."

"By using Greek fire we can seize all the armories," Charley said with obvious impatience. "They'll be our first targets on the night of the sixteenth."

"What of the prisoners in Camp Douglas?" the doctor asked. "Six thousand men, all ready to be armed."

Charley spread his hands. "Very simple. They'll get the weapons that Joe Milligan's Copperheads take from the armories. Two thousand of the best cavalrymen will be mounted to drive south for Louisville."

"Horses?" the doctor asked skeptically.

"I have a man on the way to southern Illinois with thirty thousand in gold and greenbacks."

"Ah, yes. That would be for Alonzo Colquett, I suppose. Who are you trusting to deliver so considerable an amount?"

"One of our best couriers. Has the air of a foreigner. He brought thousands in gold and greenbacks through the lines from Kentucky."

Kendrich, I thought. My former acting partner was truly burrowing into the conspiracy of knaves.

Charley laughed softly. "Of course, I sent along a couple of my alligator horses to keep the courier honest."

I could guess their names, too. The Fielding brothers.

"That prison camp is well defended by disciplined soldiers," Dr. Aylott warned. "We saw them drill on July fourth."

Charley turned to face me, his blue eyes full of the excitement of the heady talk. "You've seen Johnny Truscott?" he asked.

I told him what Truscott had said about the prisoners being desperate for a breakout, especially since the failed promises for July fourth, and if they were not soon freed they'd do something violent, imperiling their lives and the entire uprising.

"The more desperate they are," he responded bluntly, "the better their chances to escape when the time comes."

< CONSPIRACY OF KNAVES >

"Captain Truscott asked me to tell you to quit dallying," I said.

Charley leaned his head back and laughed. "That's little John for certain. We couldn't have a better man on the inside. I want you to visit him again. Tell him to hold the fort, we'll get him out of there sooner than he expects. You see, the way I envision it, the prisoners will create a mass disturbance inside just before our men attack outside. That way we'll have the guards confused as a stirred-up anthill, running in all directions while the prisoners pour out and help us seize Chicago. Johnny can put a crown on this scheme, I'll bet high stakes on it."

In this world no two things are more intoxicating than love and money, especially when they are compounded. During the week after Charley Heywood's arrival in Chicago, we lived like a pair of Sybarites, dining in the best restaurants, drinking the most expensive wines, and buying fine clothing that neither of us needed. Charley moved us out of Dr. Aylott's medicine factory and back to the Tremont House, where we posed as well-to-do husband and wife thriving on the buying and selling of land throughout the Northwest. For the while, we were gathering roses without being pricked by the thorns.

Sometimes after Charley returned from his numerous meetings with Mr. Milligan and the Copperheads, he showed signs of low spirits. Not always, however.

One day Mr. Bockling, the Greek-fire inventor who was present at the meeting in Cincinnati, came to the Tremont House. He had brought a few samples of his product, and Charley went off with him and Mr. Milligan and Dr. Aylott to witness trials of the fire somewhere up the north lake shore.

I wanted to go along, but Charley would not hear of it.

"You go out to Camp Douglas and tell Johnny Truscott to stand steady, try nothing rash, that he'll soon get his orders for the breakout."

As that day was not an open visitors' day, I knew there was little chance I could see Truscott, but I said nothing of that to Charley. Instead, soon after he departed, I dressed in the masculine clothing of Calvin Blacklock and went out to the prison by horse car to pay a call on Colonel Bartholomew Wright.

His anteroom was empty—for which I was thankful, since I

had feared another meeting in my fop's costume with the sharp-eyed Captain Truscott. Commandant Wright was in a blustery red-faced temper.

"Are you staying at the Tremont House?" he demanded the instant I entered his office.

As I had not given him any address, my face must have revealed my surprise. He chuckled, rather malevolently, it seemed to my ears.

"I had a government detective follow you the day you were here," he explained with a peacockish air. "He reported that you entered the Tremont and did not leave again, so I assumed you were staying there. Yesterday I sent a messenger to the Tremont, but the hotel has no record of a Calvin Blacklock."

His rebuke gave me enough time to invent a spy's lie. "I can be reached there under the name of Christopher Hull," I said as easily as I delivered almost that same line twice daily in a comedy sketch called "The Gallant and the Lady." He did not appear to be entirely convinced, but when I quickly added that I had come to report news from Kendrich, he nodded vigorously.

"Yes, that was why I sent the messenger for you. When K. passed through Chicago, he posted a letter to me from a railway station. Did you see him?"

"No, but he should return to Chicago within a week." This was conjecture, of course, arrived at merely from Charley Hey-wood's remark to Dr. Aylott that Kendrich was on his way to southern Illinois to buy horses. I wondered if Kendrich had informed Colonel Wright of his mission, but Wright gave no hint of what was in the letter, and as I did not desire to become more closely involved with so crafty a man as the Camp Douglas commandant, I shifted the subject.

"I need to see K. very urgently," I said. "I have received no funds from him for some weeks and have almost no money left to continue with my investigation of Mrs. Evelyn Ward."

Colonel Wright's deep-set hound-dog eyes showed no sympathy for Calvin Blacklock, the young popinjay spy, but I suppose he believed I must be of some use as an aide to Kendrich. Besides, I had that card signed by President Lincoln.

"You could move to a less expensive hotel," he said. "I understand the Tremont's rates are quite fancy."

< CONSPIRACY OF KNAVES >

"Yes, sir, I would have moved, but I feared losing connections with K. Now I have too much credit against me to move."

He shook his head, then leaned down to unlock a drawer in his desk. Withdrawing a tin box, he opened it, counted out several greenbacks, and handed me a government voucher to sign.

Spying can sometimes be quite remunerative if one goes about it the right way.

Lord, but I was getting dizzy with all the roles I was playing, and no playbook to guide me. Riding on the streetcar back to the Tremont, I kept casting covert glances over my shoulder, suspecting that Colonel Wright might have put another government detective on my trail. I was wary of everybody in sight, but as far as I could determine, no one followed me into the Tremont. I had gained considerable respect for the shrewdness of the button-nosed commandant of Camp Douglas, and made up my mind to clear out of the Tremont as soon as possible.

Back in the luxurious hotel room, I'd barely gotten Calvin Blacklock packed away when Charley returned full of high spirits and big talk about the wonders of Greek fire. He described it as devilishly magical, a "divine essence" that would soon change the course of the war. He went into a lengthy description of how Dr. Bockling had set a harmless-looking portmanteau beside a water-soaked log washed ashore from Lake Michigan. A clock inside the bag sprung the lock of a pistol, the hammer exploded with a cap that sparked a tube of gunpowder that ignited a bottle of Greek fire that, with the aid of turpentine-soaked cotton, soon spread to the log. Most marvelous of all, he said, water would not extinguish the blaze.

That horrible fire-jinni sounded most fearsome to me, but Charley was so delighted by the possibilities of Greek fire that he asked no questions when I said I wanted to move to another hotel, and he only shrugged when I told him I would not be able to see Captain Truscott until next visitors' day.

He was not always so jubilant, however, when he returned from these meetings with Copperheads. One day he asked Mr. Milligan to assemble the military commanders of the fifty thousand men who were supposedly prepared for action in the streets of Chicago. Only about a dozen appeared, Milligan explaining that

< **Belle Rutledge** >

he had summoned only those officers whose men were armed, and then boldly demanded several thousand more dollars for purchase of arms and ammunition.

A day or so later Charley boarded a train for a rendezvous a few miles out of the city. Milligan had promised to demonstrate the drilling skills of his Copperhead militia. Fully expecting to see at least two or three hundred men executing maneuvers across the stubble of a wheat field, Charley found only a small platoon of indifferent recruits, few of whom apparently had ever shouldered rifles in a military manner or marched to the commands of a drill-master. By accident he discovered that almost all of the men were employees of Milligan, draymen who had been given the day off. He was furious, but Milligan explained that members of the Sons of Liberty were working men and could not leave their jobs without fear of losing them or at least having their wages withheld. Hundreds would come to drill on Sunday afternoons, he was certain, or if Major Heywood saw fit to supply funds to pay railroad fares and lost wages, he might see thousands march on a weekday.

About the only cheer for Charley in those tense days came from the daily headlines that told of a Confederate army marching on Washington and Baltimore, of railroads and telegraph lines being cut to those cities, and the rout of a Union army at the Monocacy River.

On the day following the Greek-fire demonstration, Charley purchased a small ledger book and asked me to set down in it a record of his various expenditures and allotments of funds.

"Make the columns of figures neat," he said. "J.T. is very strict about accounting. I suppose he's obligated to report his debits and credits to the grand panjandrums in Richmond."

I was astounded by the amounts of gold and greenbacks that passed through his hands in less than a week. It all added up to far more than the money stolen from the Mount Sterling bank by Captain Truscott. Thousands for horses, thousands for arms and ammunition, thousands for Greek fire, thousands for miscellaneous Copperhead expenses.

In that last category was a generous wad of bank notes assigned to me "for espionage," and a thousand assigned to none other than Mrs. Evelyn Ward. Alongside this entry Charley told me to note that the money was to be used for purchase of clothing for escaped

< CONSPIRACY OF KNAVES >

prisoners. I wondered to myself what Colonel Bartholomew Wright would pay for that information, but I resolved to withhold it unless a contretemps occurred to push me into a very tight corner. Ally or not, there was something about the colonel that gave me the blue johnnies.

Looking back, I know now that what I was fearful of was losing Charley Heywood. I was torn between love and loyalty, a dilemma that is likely to bring calamity, especially to a young woman such as I, who was attempting to make her way in a world controlled by men. That was my weakness.

Charley's weakness was a willingness to deal out funds to anyone who made a good case—that is, as long as there was money in the valise that he carelessly kept beneath our bed. Occasionally, when he went to those interminable Copperhead meetings, I would take a peek inside that remarkable fount of money. Sometimes its leathery cavity would be packed with U.S. legal tender; sometimes there would be only a few dollars there.

From time to time Charley replenished it at a nearby bank, where they believed him to be a buyer and seller of land. When he returned with the bulging valise, leaving it with me while he went off for an evening with the Copperheads, I admit that I thought more than once of carrying it downstairs and taking a cab to a railroad station, with my ultimate destination being New York. And then perhaps England. But I could not bear the thought of leaving Charley. Money without love, you see, meant nothing to me at that particular time. What a silly fool was I!

After one of our long mornings of what Charley called "unmitigated spooniness," he suddenly grew serious, picked up the almost empty valise, and announced that he would be going to the bank. When he returned, he asked me to make two new entries in the ledger, one a transfer of funds to a man in Rock Island, the other a similar transfer to Indianapolis. Simultaneous uprisings were being planned for prison camps in both those places. For a moment I remembered that Colonel Fennell in Richmond had warned me about Charley going off the track, but I rejected the idea of asking Dr. Aylott to make a telegraphic report through the lines. If Charley Heywood wanted to stir up the whole Northwest, then so be it.

"Dear Charley," I said to him, "you and your moneybag remind

< **Belle Rutledge** >

me of the pitcher that refilled itself as fast as the wine was poured out. Where does it all come from?"

He shrugged. For the first time since I had known him, lines of weariness were beginning to show at the corners of his mouth and around the outer edges of his eyes.

"That's the last of my pitcher of wine, right there in that bag," he said.

I walked over to him and tried to erase the lines from his face by caressing his skin and beard with my fingers.

"But there'll be more gold, more greenbacks," he continued. "A good lot of that came from across the ocean." He reached for one of the little cheroots he carried in a waistcoat pocket.

"Don't breathe a word to anybody about what I just said, about money coming from England. J.T. says we must never talk about that even among ourselves."

He eased himself into one of the big chairs and began blowing tiny rings of smoke from his odoriferous cheroot.

"Thank God, the worst of this will be over after the sixteenth. Maybe a few days of rough trouble, but after that, the old war should be finished."

"What will you do then?" I asked.

"Back home to Kentucky. I could use a spell of peace and quiet." His bantering tone turned serious.

"Will you go with me, Belle? On our way home we'll stop by Cincinnati and rescue that little imp Winslow from the orphanage."

"I would like that," I said.

As everybody should know, nothing of significance happened in Chicago on July sixteenth. The Copperheads asked for a four-day delay to better prepare themselves, and about the same time a messenger arrived from southern Illinois with a report from Kendrich that the first shipment of horses to arrive at Barton Farm had been seized by government agents for use by Union Cavalry. Alonzo Colquett no doubt had been well paid for the animals and was still holding the thousands of dollars that Kendrich had brought him. It was an advantageous arrangement for Colquett, and perhaps for Kendrich.

After the date of the Chicago uprising was delayed from July sixteenth to the twentieth, Charley and I moved to the Richmond

< CONSPIRACY OF KNAVES >

House at Michigan Avenue and Lake Street. I do not know to this day whether the Confederates favored this hotel because of its name, or whether it was operated by Southern sympathizers, but shortly after we arrived there, the Richmond began to fill with guests of a distinctly Rebel stamp.

During the short time we were there, I met only a few of the Morgan men who had come down from Canada. Charley was so circumspect about our relationship that he had me register into quarters of my own, and we rarely met except in the dining room. There I formed a warm friendship with George Stubblefield, who had been one of General Morgan's favorite scouts, and George Ellsworth the telegrapher, whom they all called "Lightning." Ellsworth was a Canadian who had no strong feelings about the war but joined the Kentuckians for the adventure of being a horse soldier with John Morgan.

When these two young men learned that I was going to visit their former comrade, Captain Truscott, in Camp Douglas, both were eager to dress as preachers and accompany me, but Charley would not permit it.

And so I went out there twice more with Mrs. Evelyn Ward, but on neither occasion was I able to see Captain Truscott.

On my second visit, that dislikable man Otis Jordan was in the visitors' compound and he told me, with considerable relish, I thought, that Truscott had been locked in the camp dungeon by the commandant. He said Truscott was suspected of instigating the digging of an escape tunnel. My main purpose on that second visit was to inform Truscott that action to free the prisoners had been delayed from the sixteenth to the twentieth of July.

It was just as well, however, that I did not see him. Anyone who has read accounts of the conspiracy knows that nothing concerned with that inglorious scheme occurred on July twentieth. In fact, later that month, Charley asked me to note in the ledger book the expenditure of several hundred dollars for purchase of railroad tickets to Windsor, Canada. The plot to seize Chicago was delayed indefinitely, and the Morgan men inconspicuously departed the city, singly or by twos and threes.

Among them were Charley and I, traveling in the best drawing-room accommodation of the Michigan Central. I think it was the failure of the Confederate Army to drive from Maryland into Washington that brought the July designs to an end.

On the ferry crossing from Detroit, I was surprised to see Kendrich standing idly beside the boat's wheelhouse.

"You remember Mr. Kendrich, the courier from New York," Charley said, picking up his money valise and taking my arm as we moved toward him. "An important officer in the Order of American Knights."

Kendrich affected his Bavarian accent, nodding and gesticulating as if he were on a stage. He was clever enough to talk about Barton Farm without mentioning names or even horses. Charley told him to find accommodations at the Hirons House in Windsor and then added: "There'll be a meeting in my rooms there tonight."

As the ferry approached the Canadian landing, Charley excused himself to attend our baggage, and asked Kendrich to escort me ashore.

"Thank God," Kendrich said as soon as Charley was out of ear-reach. "I thought I'd never get a chance to speak with you. I could not find you in Chicago. You should have stayed there, Belle, to act as my link with Colonel Wright."

"I had no way of knowing that."

"No. I sent the colonel a letter, but I dared not mention names and places. Prepare yourself to return to Chicago very soon."

I told him quickly that I had visited Colonel Wright in the guise of Calvin Blacklock. When he looked puzzled, I said: "Informers have infiltrated Camp Douglas. I believe that Belle Rutledge should not be seen visiting the prison commandant."

He nodded. "You acted wisely."

"What will these conspirators do now?" I asked.

"They'll wait for the Democrats' convention in late August. We have enough time to prepare."

13

EXCERPTS FROM A CHICAGO SCRAPBOOK

JULY 1864

LEE'S COUNTER RAID NORTHWARD

Latest from the Upper Potomac

THE REBELS 20,000 STRONG

Sigel Defending Maryland Heights

**THE PRESIDENT CALLS ON NEW YORK
AND PENNSYLVANIA
FOR 100-DAY TROOPS**

A Scare in Maryland and Pennsylvania

POLICE COURT

Dr. Fellbrich carrying on business at No. 206 South Clark St., complained of a pandemonium which existed in the building over his store. Hattie Jones, Delia Maley, Susan Bloss and Caroline White, were accused of being the annoyance to the doctor. He said that drunken soldiers and other admirers of the ladies were passing up and down the stairs at all hours of the night, making the darkness hideous with their

< **Chicago Scrapbook, July 1864** >

revelry and dissipation. During the day they sat at the windows smoking cigars and inviting guests to their apartments. He objected to the conduct of the defendants upon moral grounds, but besides this it materially interfered with his business, and many respectable persons were prevented from visiting his store, in consequence of the outrages upon decency which were perpetuated by the females. The justice imposed a fine of ten dollars in each case, with a caution as to their future.

STRAWBERRY & ICE CREAM FESTIVAL

The lovers of dainties—the sweets and luxuries of the season—will improve their opportunity this evening to lay in a good supply at Wollanchee Hall, corner of State Street and Ringold Pl. The South Congregational Church hold a Strawberry and Ice Cream Festival there & invite all their friends and the public generally to meet them on this occasion.

Proclamation of the President:
MARTIAL LAW DECLARED IN KENTUCKY

The Habeas Corpus Suspended

A SEVERE KISS

James Hussey was yesterday complained of by his wife—an ugly looking female—for being drunk and disorderly. The testimony elicited quite a different state of facts than set forth in the complaint. Johanna Hussey is a well known character, and has figured extensively in the police records of the city. A day or two ago she got into a fight with her husband and rather got the worse of it. After the difficulty had abated she approached her injured lord and put her arms about his neck, as she said to kiss him. He innocently turned his face up to hers to receive the token of reconciliation, when she suddenly opened her ugly mouth and seized him by the nose with her teeth and bit a large portion of that organ entirely off. She then ran away and exhibited the greatest delight at the success of her strategy, declaring it the sweetest morsel she ever tasted. After a full investigation her husband was discharged and Johanna was then put on trial for the severity of her kissing. She was fined $40 and costs.

McVicker's Theatre
Madison Street, between State and Dearborn

CAMILLE

Benefit of Matilda Heron
When She Will Appear for the Last Time in
Her Great Production of

CAMILLE

Armand Duval—Mr. B. Macauley
Grand Dance by
M'lle Augusta

To Clear the House of Flies

Use Dutcher's Celebrated
LIGHTNING FLY KILLER

A Neat Cheap Article, Easy to Use

—

Every Sheet Will Kill a Quart

—

Sold Everywhere

OUR ARMY IN GEORGIA

—

Advance Toward Atlanta

—

2,000 Prisoners Captured by General Sherman

EYE AND EAR
Cross Eyes Straightened in One Minute

Deafness and Discharges of the Ear Cured

Dr. Underwood, 124 Randolph St.

< **Chicago Scrapbook, July 1864** >

Colonel Wood's Museum:

UNCLE TOM'S CABIN

POLICE COURT

The Police Court yesterday morning was crowded with vagrants, vagabonds, virtue at a discount, veritable whiskey drinkers, and some few thieves. Justice Miller occupied the bench and in his usual style knocked the parties down as they came up.

Mary Green's case was the first presented to his Honor. She was a goodlooking young woman, about twenty years of age; had lived as a hired girl with Elizabeth Murphy of Lamont. She had a lover, and about a week since took it into her head to elope with the object of her affections. Mrs. Murphy missed $200 and sought Mary out in the city, where she was found and arrested. Pleas of guilty was entertained, and the accused was held to bail in the sum of $500, to answer the charge of larceny in the circuit court.

Exciting from Maryland

GENERAL WALLACE DEFEATED AND DRIVEN BACK

The Rebels Marching on Washington and Baltimore

Intense Excitement in Both Cities.

Stolen from My Shed
in Rear of Wigwam Bldg., on Lake Street
a BLACK MARE, medium size
with a little white hair in part of
her mane, short gaited.

Also, Open Buggy, nearly new.

F. W. Robinson, Agent
Chicago Union Lime Works
Nos. 1 and 2 Wigwam Bldg. Lake St.

< CONSPIRACY OF KNAVES >

VARIETY THEATRE
115 and 117 Dearborn Street
10   NEW STARS   10
Are Engaged and Will Appear
Prior to July 4

First Appearance of Miss Fanny Thompson
the Beautiful Danseuse

Engagement of Mons. Martini Chiriski
Wire Performer, Juggler and Ventriloquist
THE CHAMPION OF THE WORLD

First Appearance of Miss Louise Roulette,
the Charming Danseuse

ANOTHER REBEL RAID INTO PENNSYLVANIA

Chambersburg Captured
and Burned

THE PRESIDENCY in 1864
Acceptance of Mr. Lincoln

N.Y., June 14, 1864
Hon. Abraham Lincoln—*Sir*: The National Union Convention, which assembled in Baltimore on Jun 7, 1864, has instructed us to inform you that you were nominated for the Presidency of the United States for four years from the 4th of March next.

REBEL ENDORSEMENT OF LITTLE MAC

McClellan & Seymour the Principal Candidates
of Democrats

< **Chicago Scrapbook, July 1864** >

NEWS BY TELEGRAPH

The War for the Union

LATEST FROM OUR ARMY BEFORE RICHMOND

—

Details of Comparative Losses—Late Operations

—

The War in Georgia—Lists of Casualties to North-Western Troops

BRYAN HALL
Triumphant Success of

SAM SHARPLEY'S MINSTRELS

Pronounced the Best Company That Has Ever Appeared
in This City

MOBBING NEGROES

A day or two ago a mob of four or five hundred Irish shoremen made an assault on a party of a dozen negro laborers working on a lumber dock, compelling them to flee for their lives. The blacks had committed no offense whatsoever, except wanting to support themselves by honest labor. For this they were mobbed . . .

It is a little singular that no class of people in Chicago fear the competition of the handful of blacks here, except the Irish. The Germans never mob colored men for working for whoever may employ them. The English, the Scotch, the French, the Scandinavians never molest peaceable black people. Americans never think of doing such a thing. No other nationality consider themselves "degraded" by seeing blacks earning their own way by labor.

WASHINGTON IS SAFE!

———

The Rebel Raid Fading Out
Railroad and Telegraphic Communication With
the Capital Restored

14

BELLE RUTLEDGE

AFTER THE SPLENDID hostelries that had been homes for me since leaving Richmond, the Hirons House in the frontierlike town of Windsor, Ontario, seemed gimcracky indeed. Charley Heywood arranged to obtain rooms for us connected by a door that could be locked on either side, but neither of them was much larger than the clothes closets in Chicago's Tremont House. The hallways and stairs were also exceedingly narrow. Several of the young men who came from Chicago, including Kendrich, were unable to obtain rooms there, and had to share beds in a boardinghouse across a grassy alleyway from the hotel.

According to Charley, the reason for overcrowding was an influx of Union spies and deserters. He casually pointed out two or three of the known spies. To my eyes they were very coarse specimens of the breed. I wondered if Kendrich knew them, and later on during the summer I considered approaching one of them myself, but I feared that doing so might jeopardize my entire commission.

Upon first arriving at this bucolic destination, a wave of disappointment swept over me. I am one of those mortals who must always be up and doing; the very thought of idle days sends me into jingling fits, and Windsor and the Hirons House held every sign of a dull show to me. I could not have been more mistaken.

The place was a seething nest of antagonistic conspirators that was bound to result in violence and death.

For me it began when Charley took me into the Hirons sitting room, the only charming part of the hotel. It was clean and sunny, with wide windows overlooking a little garden, and spacious enough for tables and comfortable chairs. At first I thought there was only one person in the room, a man with a ruddy weather-beaten face surrounded by white side-whiskers and a full head of graying hair. He was seated in a red velvet chair, one hand resting on the back of a sad-faced hound at repose beside him. He has been mentioned once or twice before in this narrative as a man to inspire romantic fancies, Colonel Lucius Eberhart, the Britisher who had soldiered for a time with General John Morgan's Confederate cavalrymen.

When Colonel Eberhart heard our footsteps and turned to glance at us, the fierce directness of his dark eyes reminded me of a bird of prey. Immediately upon recognizing Charley, however, his features softened into a smile of pleasure followed by a loud greeting and an explosive laugh.

"Major Charles Heywood," he cried. "So you are with us poor exiles again!"

Charley introduced him to me as "Sir Lucius," a salutation that he acknowledged with a deprecating shake of his head, insisting to me that the rank of colonel was the only title he possessed.

At this moment a well-dressed young man who had been re-clining on a sofa sat up suddenly and greeted Charley in those arrogant tones that so many of the Kentucky Bluegrass gentility affect, with an attitude of superiority that always infuriates me. Charley responded with a mild oath, demanded to know what the young man was doing in Canada, and named him as his cousin, Wesley Heywood.

"I've been waiting for you for two days, Charley," Wesley Heywood said, covering a yawn with one hand. "I must talk with you immediately."

"Talk about what?" Charley asked, his manner quite cool.

Young Heywood glanced from me to Colonel Eberhart and back again. He was, as Johnny Truscott described him in a previous chapter, an insipid sort of dolt, reminding me of my own Calvin Blacklock creation.

< CONSPIRACY OF KNAVES >

"These are trusted friends," Charley said sharply.

"I'm here as an emissary," Wesley Heywood said, "from Amos Ferree."

Charley, as I could see, was suddenly much more concerned with what his cousin had to say to him.

"Yes, I heard General Morgan left Colonel Ferree to recruit, after the withdrawal from Lexington."

"He's collecting an army along the Kentucky River east of Louisville," Wesley said. "When you give him a signal, he'll invade Indiana or Illinois. But he needs money to outfit his recruits."

The same old story, I said to myself. Everybody wants money from Charley.

"How did you meet up with Amos Ferree?" Charley asked. "I thought you were in Missouri—with Quantrill, or was it Colquett the horse and mule dealer?"

"You haven't heard?" The twisted smile on Wesley Heywood's weak face vanished and for the moment genuine grief showed there. "My mother passed away. Marianna sent for me, but I arrived at Little Hundred too late."

"I'm sorry. I didn't know." Charley was uneasy now. "Marianna?" he asked. "How is Marianna? There now alone?"

"I left her grieving. And restless."

Wesley raised his head. "She asked after you. And Johnny Truscott, who was there a few weeks ago. Anyway, while I was back home I met Amos Ferree. He tried to recruit me." The crooked smile reappeared.

"Let's go up to my room and talk," Charley said. He left me with Colonel Lucius Eberhart and his spotted hound for what was to be the first of a series of tête-à-têtes and flirtations during that long summer of 1864.

Later in the afternoon, a one-eyed man of piratical appearance and manner arrived at the double rooms occupied by Charley and me. He rapped roughly upon my door, disturbing my reading of *The Woman in White* by Mr. Wilkie Collins. (Oh, how I longed many times for a trusted female helpmate like Marian Halcombe in that novel!)

The piratical messenger at my door was standing beside a large

< **Belle Rutledge** >

bag made of russet-striped carpet cloth with intricate leather fastenings. When he demanded to see Major Charles Heywood, I pointed to the next door. I knew that Charley was still in there with his cousin Wesley, their Bluegrass voices murmuring beyond my thin walls.

Judging from the lifting effort made by the one-eyed man, the carpet-cloth bag was very heavy, and moments later I was not surprised to learn—from the voices through the wall—that its contents consisted of gold bars. Charley must have sent Wesley downstairs to summon Colonel Eberhart, for soon the Englishman's hearty tones were booming through the wall.

"British bullion," he declared, "with the seal of the Queen upon it to ensure its purity." He estimated the gold's value in dollars and reckoned it could be exchanged for a considerable number of Garibaldi rifles.

"The Garibaldi rifles," I heard Charley say, "must wait. This gold will buy a Kentucky guerrilla force to link with the Copperheads in Chicago. Or it will outfit a raiding party to seize a warship on the lakes."

Colonel Eberhart clucked his tongue in disapproval, but the arguments continued into the evening, with Kendrich, George Stubblefield, Bennett Young, and others joining in. Although there were discussions about choosing a day for the uprising in Chicago during the Democratic convention, most of the argument was between those who wanted to expend the gold for Garibaldi rifles and those who wanted to present it to Amos Ferree to recruit and support a force of invading Confederate guerrillas. Kendrich and Eberhart argued strongly for the rifles, but the Heywood cousins and most of the Morgan men were swept up in the romance of a guerrilla army being raised right under the noses of Union forces in Louisville and other parts of Kentucky.

I could hear and understand all but the softest of the voices in the adjoining room. When it became apparent that the gold was to be used to recruit and supply Kentucky guerrillas, Kendrich volunteered to deliver it to Louisville or wherever Amos Ferree wanted to rendezvous. Wesley Heywood then quickly put in his bid to be the courier, saying that urgent duties required him to travel in that direction anyway. Charley declined both offers, how-

< CONSPIRACY OF KNAVES >

ever, by announcing that as soon as the gold could be converted to greenbacks he would be leaving for Kentucky himself to meet with Colonel Ferree.

I slept alone that night. In the adjoining room, murmuring voices of conspirators lulled me to sleep. Some time before daylight, the piratical messenger sought rest in Charley's bed; presumably Charley occupied the other half of the bed.

Upon rising late the next morning, I called one of the maids from downstairs and asked her to bring pails of hot water so that I might bathe in the barrel-shaped oaken tub in my room. I had just settled myself up to my breasts in the warm soapy water when I heard a terror-ridden scream from the same maid, a cry that began somewhere out in the narrow hallway and continued in an unending wail downstairs to the lower floor. The maid had knocked on Charley's door, and, receiving no response, had opened it to see a sight so horrifying she had fled in shrieking panic.

At the sound of heavy footsteps pounding up the stairway, I reached for a towel, and just as I was stepping from the tub, Charley rushed into my room through the connecting door, carrying the russet-striped bag of gold. The first thing I noticed was the streamer of blood that stained the sleeve and laced cuff of his white shirt and dripped in clots upon the carpet cloth of the bag.

Torn between modesty and fear, I was barely able to stifle a scream and fold the towel about me. "Please compose yourself," Charley commanded hoarsely. "Dress as quickly as you can."

"Are you badly injured?" I gasped.

"I'm not hurt at all," he replied in a low quivering voice. He bent to slide the bag under my bed. "I want this out of my room," he whispered. Others had reached the adjoining room, their voices mingled and high with excitement.

"What's happened?" I asked, shivering involuntarily, feeling very vulnerable with only the towel around me.

"Murder, I think." He went to the door that led into the hall. "Somebody was after the gold in that bag, I'll wager." He took a deep breath. "Dress and stay in here. By now the hotel owner will have sent for a constable."

As matters turned out, the hotelkeeper and the Windsor officer of the law were as eager as Charley and his friends to keep the violent death as quiet as possible. No one questioned the maid's story that when she knocked on Charley's door, she heard a loud thump and the sound of shutters rattling. Upon opening the door, she caught a brief glimpse of a man silhouetted through the window and then disappearing down the slanted roof. The sight of the victim on the bed, his throat slashed, with blood still flowing over the sheets, temporarily drove the fleeing man from her mind. She did not recognize the fugitive as one of the Hirons House guests, but then she saw only his back, a medium-sized man wearing a coat but no hat.

Nor did anyone challenge Charley's story that the one-eyed messenger—if I ever heard his name I've forgotten it—had brought information about farmland that Charley was interested in buying near Toronto. Because all hotel rooms were occupied, Charley had generously offered to share his quarters with the visitor, who was still sleeping soundly when Charley went downstairs to breakfast.

During the morning, the law officer questioned the guests individually, seeking to establish everyone's whereabouts at the time of the murder. While the interrogations were progressing downstairs in the sitting room, several of us waited upstairs in my room. Charley and George Stubblefield were there, and the two Fielding brothers, grinning to themselves as though celebrating a wedding instead of a murder. Kendrich and Colonel Eberhart drifted in separately, the colonel informing us that Wesley Heywood had just gone in to be questioned. Charley worried aloud about how his cousin would withstand the examination.

"It's a rather elemental inquiry," the colonel assured him. "The local official is not practiced in these matters."

Then Charley began to worry about the bag of gold under my bed, suspecting that after the questioning there might be a search of rooms. He reached down and pulled the striped bag out upon the floor.

"I stupidly let blood drip on one side of it," he said.

"Bad luck," Colonel Eberhart said, and clucked his tongue.

Charley looked at Kendrich, who was sitting quietly on a windowsill. "Have you been questioned yet, Kendrich?" he asked.

Kendrich shook his head. "The constable is not interrogating those of us who live in the boardinghouse."

Lifting the heavy bag, Charley turned and handed it to Kendrich. "Take it across to your room."

Kendrich looked down at the open alleyway between the hotel and the boardinghouse. "You think it's safe to cross there with this bag?" He was so surprised at Charley's brusque command that he almost forgot his Bavarian stage accent.

Charley laughed. "Do you want an escort?"

"This place is astir. Suspicious people watching everything out of the ordinary."

"There's a back stairs," Charley said. "You can walk across to the boardinghouse in less than a minute."

Kendrich shrugged and started to leave.

"Wait," Charley called after him. "Are you sharing a room?"

"With Bennett Young," Kendrich replied.

"Tell Bennett that I want him to spell you. One of you stay in that room at all times. Somebody wants that gold bad enough to cut a man's throat. As soon as the dust settles around here we'll take it to the Bank of Upper Canada for exchange."

Very late that afternoon, after the questioning ended and the law officer departed in a hearse with the body of the one-eyed man wrapped in the sheets in which he had died, I went down to the sitting room to finish reading *The Woman in White*. What I wanted most of all was human companionship, but Charley and several of the others had fled to a neighboring saloon. I could have used a bit of strong brandy myself, but the saloon was an entirely male establishment.

In the sitting room, two of the Morgan men were playing dominoes, and the Union spies and deserters were at the poker table. An atmosphere of melancholy hung over the smoky room. When the men laughed, it was forced. Most of them had seen violent death on the battlefields of our beastly war, but in the tumult of combat death was expected. To have it invade with such viciousness the walls of a peaceful hostelry was demoralizing, a grim reminder of the precariousness of life.

I could not keep my mind on the sentences I read in my book. My eyes kept lifting to the pleasant garden outside, where the last slant of the sun's rays lighted the blossoms. To escape the gloom

< **Belle Rutledge** >

and the cigar smoke, I went out and sat on a narrow stone seat. Birds were twittering beyond the hedge, and the clop-clop of dray horses sounded from around the corner of the hotel.

A voice interrupted the serenity: "Belle, I'm going to pretend to be talking about the roses in the bed here. You respond in kind."

Kendrich's boots scrunched on the graveled pathway; he stopped, made a little European bow to me, then gestured toward the roses, holding his head at such an angle that anyone watching his face from the Hirons sitting room could not see his lips moving. I was seated with my back to the windows.

"How far gone are you with Charles Heywood?" he asked, making another slight gesture toward one of the rose bushes.

"What do you mean?" My whole body must have bristled with hostility at his prying question.

"Don't play an innocent Desdemona for me, please. I know you too well, Belle. It has happened before when enemies become intimates."

"I would not want him caught and hanged," I said calmly.

"Look toward the roses." Always the actor, Kendrich leaned to sniff one of the blossoms. "He must be stopped. We can't let that gold go to Kentucky guerrillas, or for whatever mad scheme comes into his head next." He took another step away from me. "I'll try once more to persuade Heywood to let me travel with him. I could stop him in Detroit or Chicago."

"Stop him how?" I asked.

"For old times' sake, for you I mean, Belle, I would not kill him as that man was killed in his bed this morning. Have him arrested for theft, charge him with stealing the gold he'll be carrying."

"Do you know who killed that man in Charley Heywood's room?"

Kendrich stood quite still, his back to me. "Heywood himself, most likely."

"Charley is not a murderer," I said.

"Look toward the roses." He crossed in profile at the end of the rose bed. "You know as well as I that the barbarities of this war have made all of us potential murderers. Survival, that's the thing now, Belle. The fighting should have ended a year ago, after

< CONSPIRACY OF KNAVES >

Gettysburg and Vicksburg, but these Southern lunatics would sooner bring the whole world down upon themselves—and us—before admitting defeat."

"For them it's a game, a tournament to be won or lost with one last desperate throw," I said. "Against all odds. While you and I think only of survival."

"They are the most dangerous set of men this war has turned loose on the world." He pretended to concentrate his attention upon a bush of white roses. "They threaten the survival of the Union."

"Survival again," I said. "Speaking of which, since leaving Washington City last winter, I've received not one penny of the generous payments promised me that day in the White House. I've survived entirely upon the generosity of the Confederacy."

"And quite well, too," he replied sarcastically. "A testimony to your artfulness, Miss Rutledge."

"If you succeed in 'stopping' Charley Heywood, as you put it," I said, "I'll be returning to Washington, and I'll want the money I've earned risking my life."

His back was toward me again and I could hardly hear his scoffing laugh.

"That's why you're in this, isn't it? The money. Will it atone for what the war has made of us?" He clenched and unclenched his fingers, the way I'd seen him do many times on the stage when he was trying to remember his lines.

"A man named Baker in the Treasury Department deposits payments for you and me in the District of Columbia Bank. It will be waiting for us—if we survive to return there."

Footsteps grated on the pathway beyond the hedge. Kendrich began moving slowly away from the stone bench, where I still sat. One of the Morgan men, a very young officer, appeared and called out to him: "There you are, Mr. Kendrich. Bennett Young asked me to tell you to bring him a cigar when you return." The teen-aged cavalryman bowed politely to me and strode on toward the entrance to the Hirons House.

When he was out of earshot, Kendrich said: "Do you know what my temporary roommate, the deranged Lieutenant Bennett Young, is planning? Yes, another bank robbery to bag more funds

< **Belle Rutledge** >

for guerrillas and Copperheads. This time across the Canadian border into New England."

Kendrich made an exaggerated theatrical gesture and realized immediately that such playacting would draw attention from any casual observer.

"We've talked too long, I think, but please come out in the garden again sometime tomorrow. If Major Heywood postpones his return to the States, I'll pass you a letter to take across the ferry to Detroit for mailing. I don't dare mail it in Windsor. Do you know these Rebels have bribed every official in town?"

Without even a farewell glance in my direction, he began strolling away, turning into the street and heading in the direction of a tobacconist's shop. That was the last time I saw Kendrich.

The next morning, just about first light, I was awakened by someone rapping on a door in the hallway. Charley was oblivious to the noise, breathing in that soft hissing sound that was as much a special part of him asleep as was his spirited laughter awake. As soon as I aroused him, he knew that the urgent caller was outside his room, and he wasted no time in hastening through the connecting door.

A moment later I heard an excited voice followed by an angry oath from Charley. Although I had to strain my ears to recognize the Bluegrass accent, I guessed that the early morning caller was Bennett Young. When he spoke Kendrich's name I was certain of it. They departed down the stairs in a great hurry.

By the time I was dressed, the two men had returned to Charley's room with several of their freshly awakened comrades, and without waiting for an invitation I boldly joined the group in order to discover what the commotion was about.

Kendrich had disappeared, sometime between midnight, when Bennett Young fell asleep, and five o'clock, when he awakened. Gone with Kendrich was the striped carpetbag and its many pounds of gold bars.

Charley's first thought was that Kendrich might have taken the ferry to Detroit, but the earliest crossing was at six o'clock, and Bennett Young had reached the landing in time to examine every person who went aboard. Paul and Andy Fielding had al-

< CONSPIRACY OF KNAVES >

ready been sent to the boathouses to inquire if anyone had hired a boat, or if any boats were missing.

I had never seen Charley in such a state of fury. His ordinarily merry blue eyes had turned positively stony. "Betrayal," he kept repeating. "Betrayal. And I trusted the bastard like a brother." He declared his certainty that Kendrich had killed the one-eyed messenger and that if the hotel maid had not surprised him in the act, he would have made off with the gold the previous morning. Charley confirmed Kendrich's guilt in his own mind when he asked the others if any could remember seeing him in the dining room at breakfast time. None of them had seen Kendrich before the discovery of the murder.

"What did he talk about yesterday, to any of you?" Charley asked. "Did he give any hint of decamping? He seemed damn reluctant to take that bag across yesterday morning."

"The last time I saw him," Ben Drake said, "he was in that little garden with Miss Belle."

Charley stared hard at me, and for the first time I saw distrust in his eyes. "What did he say to you, Belle?"

"I went out there to read," I replied. "He came walking along the path, greeted me quite civilly, and stopped to admire the roses."

"What did he say to you?"

"He talked about nothing but the roses," I lied, as spies must.

I knew Kendrich better than any of them, of course, and earlier I had thought of him as the possible murderer because the maid had said the fleeing man was hatless. Kendrich hated hats. In Washington he told me more than once that hats gave him headaches, and he wore them only against the weather. But I had come to accept the general theory of the others that the murderer must have been one of the Union deserters living in the hotel.

While Charley and Bennett Young were still devising a plan of pursuit, Colonel Eberhart burst into the room, redfaced and breathing hard. He had been to the Great Western railway station and was certain that Kendrich had boarded the 4:30 A.M. eastbound train. The station agent had sold five tickets. A man and woman traveling with two children took passage to Toronto. A man traveling alone bought a ticket to St. Catharines. The agent could not recall much about the second man. The lantern light in

< **Belle Rutledge** >

the station was dim and he had noticed no distinguishing features except that he wore no hat and his hair was damp and combed tight against his skull. The bag he carried away from the ticket window appeared to be unusually heavy.

Why Kendrich had bought a ticket to St. Catharines and not to Niagara Falls puzzled all of us. From St. Catharines the distance to the Niagara suspension bridge and passage into a haven in the States was only a few miles. Perhaps he had arranged a rendezvous with an accomplice at St. Catharines. Whatever the reason for his stopping there, Charley prepared to pursue him. Every one of us wanted to join the party, especially Colonel Eberhart, but Charley chose only the two Fielding brothers, ordering them to bring their handarms and be prepared to board the next train east at 8:30. "The rest of you are needed here in the event Kendrich is taking me on a bootless errand," he added. "Colonel Eberhart must deal with the Windsor constable; they speak the same language." His cousin Wesley was to travel at once to Kentucky to assure the guerrilla leader, Amos Ferree, that money would soon be sent to arm his followers.

After the men left the room, I told Charley I was going with him.

"Too dangerous," he said, folding a spare shirt into his valise. "You stay here. The boys need you more than I. Just your mere presence here keeps them from being morose, at least that's what old Sir Lucius tells me."

I made no reply to that. I said good-bye, returned to my room, packed a change of clothing into my smaller portmanteau, and waited until I heard Charley leave his room. After two or three minutes I went down the back stairs, turned into the alleyway, and walked the hundred or so steps to the Great Western station. Charley and the Fielding brothers were sitting on an iron bench facing the tracks. They all gave me amused stares when they saw that I was carrying a portmanteau.

"Are you going to buy my ticket to St. Catharines?" I asked. "Or must I?"

"Almighty God, Belle," Charley said, in feigned disgust. "You're more trouble than a wife."

< CONSPIRACY OF KNAVES >

The cars on that Great Western train were of the old-fashioned sort, with uncomfortable low-backed wooden seats. We stopped at every little town, with loud tootlings of the locomotive whistle and a great ringing of bells. Peddlers came aboard to sell melons and strawberries. Charley resented every stop, every slowing of the wheels. He worried aloud about Kendrich. The scoundrel was only four hours ahead of us, he said, but might he not leave his train before reaching St. Catharines? Or would he continue to his ticket's destination?

At London the train stopped for passengers' lunch, and although Charley grumbled about the delay, he enjoyed drinking the ale that was served up in huge mugs. As the cars rattled on across Ontario, his mood grew mellower and he began to talk of life after the war.

"If the Northwestern states break away from the Union," he said, "Kentucky may go with them, but I would prefer that it become a part of the Southern Confederacy."

"Suppose everything fails," I suggested. "Suppose the South collapses, and the Union prevails."

He shook his head. "If I believed that will happen, I'd board the nearest ship for Europe."

I was looking out the car window, watching the countryside roll past. His face, reflected indistinctly in the glass, held a haunted expression.

"D'you know," he went on, "I've actually thought of that. Especially when I have large amounts of greenbacks or gold in my possession. Let's say we catch up to Kendrich and the stolen bag. You and I could live well on that in England or France. Simply snatch it all and fly—the way Kendrich did. Would you skedaddle with me across the ocean, Belle?" He put his arm around my waist and squeezed. "Treasonable talk, eh?"

Late in the afternoon, with a hissing of steam and a series of jolts, we stopped at the St. Catharines station. The nearest inn catered to ailing folk who had come to be healed by mineral waters. In a small sitting room, I had just settled myself among a few of the convalescents when Andy Fielding came hurrying back from the registry desk to escort me to a room upstairs. As soon as he'd got

< **Belle Rutledge** >

me and my portmanteau inside, he was off again, muttering something about meeting his brother and Major Heywood at the stables.

For what must have been two full hours I waited for them to return. The shabby little room was oppressive with its mingled odors of dust, carbolic acid, and peppermint. Finally, as twilight was descending outside, I went downstairs and asked the registry clerk if he had seen any of my three male companions. Yes, indeed, the handsome gentleman who wore the black slouch hat had left a message for me. On a folded sheet of notepaper was Charley's slanted scrawl: "Going hunting. Advise you take mineral baths to drive dull care away until our return." I did not curse aloud, but I muttered several of little Winslow Barber's choicest oaths.

A few minutes later I found my way to the inn's stables, made inquiries in the manner of a skillful spy, and learned that Charley and the Fielding brothers had hired three horses and departed in the direction of Niagara Falls. Yes, the gentleman wearing the large-brimmed black hat had asked about friends of his who had hired a buggy shortly before noon.

"There was more than one 'friend'?" I asked.

"Yes, two. A gray-bearded but energetic gentleman who carried a rather heavy carpetbag was accompanied by a young woman."

Kendrich could have been either of the two. He was far better at masquerade than I. If one of the pair was Kendrich, then he must have had a confederate waiting with theatrical trappings either at St. Catharines or somewhere along the route of the Great Western railway.

Night had fallen by this time, and as I had no desire to journey alone on horseback over the hazardous road to Niagara Falls, I resigned myself to an evening with the dyspeptics and rheumatics at the inn. We played euchre, consequences, and whist. During the course of the games, I learned from one of the players that a Concord coach departed each morning from St. Catharines, carrying guests for a day's excursion to the Clifton House, where the falls could be viewed in comfort from the Canadian side. Consequently, next morning, dressed in shawl and bonnet, I was one of the first passengers aboard the six-horse coach.

As we bounced along the rough and rocky road to the Canadian town of Niagara, I kept a watchful eye out for horseback riders,

< CONSPIRACY OF KNAVES >

but saw no one resembling Charley or the Fielding brothers. Soon we could hear the fury of the falls and see through the woods sheets of spray flung high above the river. By the time we reached the Clifton House, the sky had clouded and a sprinkle of rain was falling.

The hotel was filled with summer sight-seers crowding the covered balcony, which trembled from the ceaseless thunder of the falls. No one had told me there were two cataracts, the green silklike American Falls to the left and Horseshoe Fall, almost consumed in its own clouds, to the right. They were awesome spectacles indeed, but the churning abyss below, where mists boiled like smoke, reminded me of drawings of Hell I had seen in old books when I was a child. I shuddered and drew away, overhearing a lecturer reciting to a group of excursionists the legend of Hawenio.

"Every spring," he said, "the natives sent a virgin in a canoe over the falls as a sacrifice to Hawenio, the Mighty Voice."

"Ah, yes," remarked an elderly gentleman who had come on the Concord from St. Catharines and had been following me about and giving me the eye all morning, "yes, the falls still take their toll. If you would care to descend with me, miss, I will show you eddies filled with the bodies of foxes, squirrels, even birds of prey. And who knows, perhaps an unfortunate mortal."

Needless to say, I declined the gentleman's invitation. Having seen enough of the sublime phenomenon of Niagara, I returned to my pursuit of Charley Heywood and his two companions. They had stabled their horses and spent the night at the Clifton House, I easily learned, but not even my very best detective crafts could trace their paths after they left the hotel that morning. I was still subtly questioning various attendants around the establishment when my elderly trifler from St. Catharines interrupted to inform me that the excursion coach was ready to return.

I would have liked to continue my search across the border, where I suspected Charley had gone, but fearing he might have doubled back to St. Catharines, I reluctantly boarded the coach.

Finding no message at the St. Catharines inn, I became apprehensive and that evening only the persistent attentions of the aging libertine (he was old enough to be my grandfather) kept me from suffering a bad case of the blue johnnies.

Next morning, while I was moving restlessly around and about

< **Belle Rutledge** >

the inn, Charley and the Fielding brothers came riding up to the stables on horses that were badly in need of currying and rest. The brothers looked the same as ever, sly woods colts too roughhewn ever to acquire a polish, but Charley's black hat had been replaced by a frowzy straw roundtop, and he was wearing green goggles. His face below them was that of a stranger; his usually composed lips were twisted into bitterness, with deep lines running above his unkempt beard. He was carrying the striped carpetbag easily in one hand; I knew it was the same because there were still brown stains on one side. It appeared to be empty.

"We're leaving on the noontime train," he said without otherwise greeting me, and walked on toward the inn, leaving the Fielding brothers to take care of the horses.

Although a bath and a change of clothing improved his outer appearance, Charley was still spiritless when we boarded the train, acknowledging my remarks only in monosyllables. When he removed his green goggles, I tried to make light of the tormented expression in his bloodshot eyes by commenting pertly that his eyes had changed from green to red.

"It was horrible," he said, almost as though he were talking to himself.

"What happened?" That was the first question I had asked him about the pursuit of Kendrich.

"I'm preparing a report to be sent to Richmond by way of the West Indies," he replied coldly, and then turned silent and sullen again.

At Hamilton he reached for our bags and informed me abruptly that we were changing trains for Toronto. He leaned across the seat to whisper something to one of the Fielding brothers; they were to stay aboard until they reached Windsor.

Toronto was cool and windy, with wide streets bordered by trees. We stopped at the Queen's, which was somewhat smaller than the hotels I'd grown accustomed to in Chicago, but was even more luxurious. We were there only two nights and a day. Although I had a magnificent view of Lake Ontario from a latticed balcony covered with climbing plants, I was virtually a prisoner above the blue and shining waters. To this day I am not certain what Charley was doing in Toronto, or who he was seeing. I would have been immensely pleased to attend one of the Toronto theaters, but he said he could not accompany me and forbade my going alone. Had he been in a less distraught state of mind, I think I would have rudely disregarded his wishes, but I had grown too fond of him to disturb him further.

On our second and last evening in Toronto, we dined together in the hotel's grand *salle à manger*. By this time Charley's spirits had improved remarkably; he was beginning to laugh occasionally, and the merry glint had returned to his eyes. During the dinner he whispered to me to look toward one of the tables on our right. "The bald-headed man is J.T.," he said, "the fount of all our fortunes."

I stole two or three glances at the square-jawed J.T., whom I had come to think of as a mythical Croesus dispensing riches to his myrmidons. He was only a hard-featured little man with leathery yellow skin and a ruthless mouth. "Methinks, yond Cassius has a lean and hungry look," I said in my lowest register and imitated Mr. Edwin Booth's manner of playing Julius Caesar.

Charley almost choked on his wine as he tried desperately to stifle his laughter, and I knew he was his better self again.

Next morning at the railway station, however, while I was casually scanning a Toronto newspaper, a small headline drew my horrified attention: VICTIM OF NIAGARA. MAN'S BODY FOUND BELOW FALLS. According to the brief account, American and Canadian officers were cooperating in efforts to determine the identity of the dead man, who may or may not have been killed by being swept over the falls. His body was coatless, the height and weight average, the bruised face nondescript. I slid the newspaper into Charley's lap and said quietly: "I can think of no better word to characterize Kendrich than 'nondescript.' "

Charley's eyes fixed on the lines I indicated; he sucked in his breath, and the misery that had been in his face before suddenly returned. "He could be anybody," he said.

"I must know," I persisted. "Did you and the Fielding brothers take Kendrich's life?"

"The foolhardy bring calamities upon themselves," he retorted, his tone almost hostile.

"I know he left St. Catharines with a companion," I continued. "Were there two accidents?"

"Leave it be, Belle," he said, with angry impatience. "I've made an official report to Richmond. I can tell you nothing more."

The hollow sound of the train announcer's voice broke the tension between us. We both arose and began moving, almost mechanically, toward the tracks, Charley carrying our three bags. One of them was new; the old striped carpetbag had been replaced by a sleek case of black cowhide.

On the train, Charley held that case between his legs, and in my imagination it took on the qualities of a life force, perhaps a fire warming a bloodless victim of a vampire. I thought I knew Major Charles Heywood down to the ground, but I was beginning to realize that I did not. We were both silent almost all the way to Hamilton, where we changed to the Windsor train.

By this time Charley appeared to have forgotten the strain between us. At Hamilton he bought a box of chocolates for me and some expensive Spanish cheroots for himself. When the train pulled out for Windsor, he put an arm around my waist and fondled my thigh until I made him stop.

"You are too bold, sir," I said, using a line from one of the skits I'd played many times in Washington.

In response to that, he told *sotto voce* a very naughty joke at which I could not keep from laughing, he joining in with that ringing burst of joy that made everyone in the car stare at him in amusement and admiration. Charley Heywood was a very handsome man, especially when he was in high spirits.

He left the seat once to go back to the gentlemen's smoking car. Before leaving he propped the cowhide case against my leg and told me not to move until he returned. No more than Pandora could I resist a peek inside that bag. The hooked catch required considerable force to loosen, but then the leather spread open like a yawning mouth to reveal bundles of U.S. greenbacks of various denominations.

Once before in this narrative I have hinted at how possession of money acted like a tonic in restoring the spirits of Charley Heywood whenever they were depressed. Not until that moment on the train, as I closed the clasp on the case, did I realize the enormity of its effect upon him. His despondency at St. Catharines was not a reaction to whatever terrible thing had happened to Kendrich; his despair was caused by loss of the gold. Without the

< CONSPIRACY OF KNAVES >

money he had obtained in Toronto, he would have been desolate, a festering soul, remote and irascible, a bad companion. I should have let the revelation be a warning to me, but in those heart-stirring days I was too much in love with Charley Heywood to acknowledge any weakness in him.

For the remainder of that summer of 1864, I lived like an exile in Windsor, unable to come to terms with my thoughts or emotions. During the times that Charley was with me, I was content, but he came and went restlessly, on short visits to Detroit and Chicago, and a long ten-day journey to Kentucky to deliver greenbacks to Colonel Ferree, who had become for me almost as mythical a character as J.T. in Toronto.

While Charley was absent, my main pillar of strength was the charming Englishman, Colonel Lucius Eberhart, who divided his time between the hotel and daylong journeys into the countryside with his spotted hound and hunting gun to shoot wild game. He seemed to sense my dolor when Charley was away, and would then defer his hunting to remain at the Hirons House in order to play card games with me in the sitting room or accompany me on walks around the town, his dog always sitting or walking by his side.

Sir Lucius, as we all called him, was a consummate flirt and raconteur, skillfully combining both arts when he was with me. We had long talks about the Rebellion, as well as all wars in general. To me war is evil, but the colonel professed to see a certain grandeur in contests between bands of brave and reckless men. In the clash of arms, with life the prize for victory, death the payment for defeat. Yes, to him war was an Ivanhoe tournament, as it was for Charley Heywood and Johnny Truscott and most of the Morgan men I knew in Windsor. Colonel Eberhart admitted that the war between the states had become a blemished struggle because so many noncombatants had been drawn into it to suffer and die. "Wars of the future," he said, "may kill more noncombatants than combatants. If so, all the sport will have gone out of the greatest game on earth."

As a substitute for war, he would say solemnly, let us have a go at a game of chess. No matter how hard he tried to lose to me, he would always win at that intricate game, which I have never fully understood. He more than made up for this by his comforting

< **Belle Rutledge** >

presence when I was undergoing the terror of loneliness. I know of no curse more dreadful than isolation of the human soul and body, and for me the burden was accentuated because out of my obsession for Charles Heywood I had betrayed a fealty to which I had solemnly sworn months before when Kendrich and I went to the White House in Washington. On some days I came very near approaching one of the supposed Union spies who still came and went in the Hirons House, but they appeared to be such oafs, when compared to the young Morgan men, that I always suppressed the urge. And besides, no one could be certain that they were spies instead of the deserters they claimed to be. As for writing a letter or sending a telegram, or journeying to Chicago to communicate with my last Union connection, Colonel Bartholomew Wright at Camp Douglas, I had heard too many boasts from Charley about the Copperheads' control of telegraph, post offices, and express. And so, like a cowardly chicken, I let the terror of loneliness and frustration beget dreadful headaches.

As there appeared to be absolutely no laudanum in all of Windsor, I suffered acutely until one day Colonel Eberhart told me that when he was soldiering in Arabia he had learned a method of exorcising headaches.

The treatment must be done in private, he said, unless I was willing to forego modesty altogether, and so we would go up to my room, accompanied by the spotted hound serving as a kind of chaperon. I did not mind baring my back and shoulders to that kindly man of war. His massive hands moved expertly over my muscles and bones until I felt myself floating painlessly in space, all aches draining away. While at his healing work he would sometimes say: "Think of yourself as a ruffled dove, Miss Belle. I am simply smoothing down your feathers." At other times, when I was particularly low with the fidgets, he would recite a bit of doggerel he had learned while soldiering with Jeb Stuart in Virginia:

> *Let the wide world wag as it will*
> *We'll be gay and happy still.*

To this day the very remembrance of those lines brings moisture to my eyes, for slight as they are, they always restored my spirits when Colonel Eberhart recited them in his resonant baritone.

< CONSPIRACY OF KNAVES >

He and I could have reached a deeper intimacy, I am certain, had not that hound always been present. There was something quite human about the animal. If it possessed a name, I never heard the colonel use it, although he often addressed the dog as an equal. When it was pleased by some remark or action, its mouth opened slightly and, with yellow eyes beaming, would appear to be smiling approvingly. More often than not, however, the hound's face was solemn, even sorrowful, and in those times when the colonel made love to me with his hands, I could have sworn the beast was about to burst into tears.

One rainy afternoon in my room, Sir Lucius gave me quite a start when he removed his always neat Wellington boots. Would his trousers be next, I wondered, but then he explained prosaically that old war wounds troubled his lower limbs on stormy days.

With Charley away much of the time, I confess that I allowed my romantic fancies to roam, and as I have previously noted, I sometimes dreamed of accompanying Sir Lucius to England to live as his Lady in one of those Devonshire seaside towns he was always describing with such passionate nostalgia.

Not that I seriously believed that this hard-bitten old knight would ever settle down anywhere. He had tasted too much of adventurous freedom, cut loose from the cares and joys of ordinary men and women, to return to routines of the common throng. Was not I the same, I would ask myself. Were not Charley Heywood and his comrades caught in the same war-quickened stream that was taking all of us to the edge of some Niagara?

On Sunday mornings most of us went to the nearby Methodist church. The Morgan men sat together, forming a deep-voiced chorus that made the walls of the little structure reverberate from the vocal force they gave to the old hymns. The minister was quite awed by these outlanders, and he was puzzled by my presence among the all-male company. I'm certain he never quite understood my situation among the group.

We often devoted Sunday afternoons in the hotel sitting room to what my mother sometimes called "the finer things of life." Someone would recite or read a poem; another would sing a familiar song ("Annie Laurie" or "The Last Rose of Summer"), and because most of us had read or were reading *Les Misérables,* we would discuss the characters and the plot. Sunday afternoons also grad-

< **Belle Rutledge** >

ually became the only time during the week when the war that had brought us to that exile was seriously debated. On returning from his hurried expeditions, Charley always carried a pack of newspapers, with their usual contradictory accounts of military actions. I recall the excitement created by the explosion of a mine under the Confederate defenses at Petersburg. Union troops tried to break through toward Richmond but were trapped in and around the huge craters created by the explosion. They lost about three times as many soldiers as the Confederate defenders.

The Morgan men were interested in the increasing criticism of General Grant and President Lincoln in the Northern newspapers. Casualties were growing so high as a result of Grant's continuing assaults upon the Petersburg siege lines that on some days the lists of dead and wounded almost filled a page of the larger city dailies. As the casualty lists had grown longer, Lincoln had called for half a million volunteers to fill the depleted ranks of the Union Army.

"If old Abe Lincoln asks for another draft," one of the men said, "there'll be riots worse than last summer's." Almost all of them believed that published rebukes of Union leaders augured well for the plot to seize Chicago and the secession of the Northwest states from the Union.

On one Sunday a three-line notice in a Detroit paper aroused the men to an afternoon celebration. The item stated simply that Confederate General Sterling Price had assumed command of a new Trans-Mississippi army in northern Arkansas. When Charley called attention to the report, they quickly recognized its signifi-cance.

"Old 'Pap' Price will invade Missouri on August twenty-ninth," Charley declared. "Colonel Ferree will cross the Ohio River before sundown that same day, while the Copperheads are taking St. Louis, Indianapolis, Columbus, Louisville, and Chicago. We'll be in Chicago on the twenty-ninth for the Democrats' presidential convention. It may be the most important day of our lives."

What I missed most in that little Canadian town was theatrical entertainment, and to relieve the tedium in the evenings I began to organize charades and tableaux. With permission of the hotel's owner, the Morgan men built a narrow raised platform, like the proscenium of a stage, at one end of the sitting room, and there I

< CONSPIRACY OF KNAVES >

could sing and dance before what was undoubtedly the most adoring audience of my performing career. Colonel Eberhart was a
more than willing partner in the pantomimes. He taught me a
Scottish dance and two or three comic skits that he remembered
from English music halls. I practiced them faithfully with the
intention of adding them to my permanent repertoire should fate
permit me to return someday to the stage.

Because I no longer possessed dancing tights, I was unable to
dazzle the Morgan men with my most spectacular twirls and high
kicks. In my large portmanteau, however, was my Calvin Blacklock costume. I shook the wrinkles out of the clothing, cut my hair
short, and startled everyone except Charley when I appeared on
the narrow platform as a male speaking in a deep tenor. Encouraged by loud applause and shouted bravos, I tried one of the bawdy
dialogues I had done so many times with Kendrich in Washington,
taking both parts with voice changes, but I almost muffed the skit
when the cold realization of my former partner's recent violent
ending suddenly struck me. And so I went quickly into a dance,
lifting my trousered legs as high as I pleased, ending the turn with
a monologue so filled with pathos that I almost wept myself, and
then led my homesick audience in singing "Lorena." Perhaps I
made a goose of myself, but there was not a dry eye in that room,
and I say without boasting that every man jack of them was in
love with Belle Rutledge.

That night in bed Charley told me he did not care for Calvin
Blacklock, whom he could not help but regard as a rival. He begged
that I rid myself of the foppish costume. A time would come when
I would remember his half-serious command, and regret that I had
not followed his wishes.

In the last weeks of August, each day seemed to pass more swiftly
than the preceding one. Meeting after meeting was held in various
rooms of the Hirons House. Several more Confederate refugees
arrived from Toronto until Charley announced proudly that he had
an elite force of seventy-four ready to lead the uprising in Chicago
on August twenty-ninth.

Returning from a hasty trip a few days before that portentous
date, Charley quietly began distributing paper slips bearing a date

< **Belle Rutledge** >

and the number of a room reserved in the Richmond House, with small packets of greenbacks for expenses.

"Chicago will be swarming with incomers," he said. "War Democrats, Peace Democrats, Copperheads from all over the Northwest. We'll be four to a room to start, maybe six or eight by the twenty-ninth. The date written beside your room number is the day you leave Windsor. No more than eight men on each train, and keep apart. Government detectives are thick as fleas at the Detroit ferry landing, and around the Chicago railroad stations."

"How much help can we expect from the Copperheads this time?" Ben Drake asked.

"The promised force of fifty thousand men has dropped to twenty thousand," Charley replied, "but they tell me the twenty thousand are the prime of Illinois, well armed, equipped with Greek fire, and ready to join us in storming the armories, the banks, and government warehouses. More than enough to seize the city."

"And Camp Douglas?"

"One of our first aims. A special company led by Colonel Eberhart will charge the weakest side. Our men imprisoned there have been informed of the hour of assault, and John Truscott is organizing squads to strike from the inside."

With an enthusiasm I had never seen in him before, Charley went on to explain some signals that had been arranged by the Sons of Liberty.

Early on the twenty-ninth, the Copperheads would display at the windows of their houses small flags of white cloth with red ribbons running along the tops and carried down the sides to end in narrow streamers. These flagged houses would be places of refuge in cases of necessity.

Charley then gave each man a Butternut badge and a Mc-Clellan-for-President badge. The Butternut badge was to be worn out of sight under a lapel or inside the coat, ready to be shown as proof of allegiance to the Sons of Liberty. The McClellan badges were to be worn on the right side of the breast instead of the left, where the real McClellan supporters would be wearing theirs. "Vallandigham has no badges," Charley explained, "so that these right-side McClellans will signify that we are for Vallandigham."

What valuable pieces of information these are, I thought, had

< CONSPIRACY OF KNAVES >

I the inclination and opportunity to pass them on to Commandant Wright at Camp Douglas. What a feather in my cap to report them! Being a Kentuckian, however, in love with a Kentuckian, and surrounded by Kentuckians whom I had come to regard as my family, I no longer had the will to try to stop the conspiracy if it meant endangering the lives of dear friends and my lover.

Next morning Colonel Eberhart, who was assigned to one of the first groups to depart, came to my room to bid me good-bye. He found me in a drizzly mood, still torn between my two loyalties.

"Let the wide world wag as it will," he recited, "we'll be gay and happy still."

I kissed his grizzled cheek. "When we rejoin in Chicago," I asked, "will you accompany me to a theater where we can see some genuinely talented performers?"

"There are no better actresses than yourself, Miss Belle," he replied with an exaggerated bow. "But indeed I shall be honored to serve as your escort."

He was wearing a beautifully cut gray uniform that was very much like those I had seen worn by high-ranking Confederate officers in Richmond.

"Colonel Eberhart," I said, "if you wear those clothes into Chicago they will arrest you in five minutes."

"No, no," he laughed. "This is my lancers uniform that I've been carrying about in my trunk for many weeks. I have my British papers, my hunting gun, and my dog, and if they ask me what I am doing, I will say I'm going hunting."

He was at that moment the very model of one of those doughty knights created by Miss Jane Porter and Sir Walter Scott. If only I had used my good sense, put my arms around his neck, and seduced him into flying with me on the Great Western Railway all the way to New York to board an ocean steamer bound for Liverpool and the seaside towns of Devonshire or Cornwall—how different my life might have been!

15

LET THE WIDE WORLD
WAG AS IT WILL

PAIN OCCUPIED the senses and thoughts of Colonel Lucius
Eberhart during the first hours after the train left Detroit. His
bones ached, his muscles ached, and he recognized the onset of
the debilitating fever that had lurked in his blood since Morocco.
Or was it during the Crimean War, or with Garibaldi in Sicily,
perhaps later in Uruguay? Memories were fading with the wasting
flesh around his battered skeleton. He waked at nights from pain
gnawing at the border between sleep and consciousness, uncertain
in the darkness where he was, on which of the world's continents,
or to which lost cause he had bound his military fortunes.

He had spent too many nights on the cold hard earth of too
many battlefield camps, taken too many blows and wounds and
falls from saddles in contests with men he had not seen until the
moment they clashed to draw blood. Soon, he knew, he must die,
but he wanted one more dashing mounted charge, one more rushing
of his sluggish blood to a high peak of exhilaration that for him
came only from a test of mortal flesh against mortal flesh. Major
Heywood had promised him command of the assault upon that
prison camp—what did they call it, Camp Douglas?

He felt like that mad old Spaniard, Don Quixote, except he
had no Sancho Panza to bring him back to reality. Those Confederates, the wild boys of John Morgan the Kentuckian, they were
all madder than he. None of them could comprehend that their

< CONSPIRACY OF KNAVES >

lost cause was ended, had died at Gettysburg and Vicksburg more than a year past. They could not stop charging and dying or being captured, to escape and scheme and try again. Now it was this dream of an Empire of Northwestern States. He counted on his fingers—four more days to the showdown. If he did not die there with them at the prison camp, he would pack his scarred trunk for the last time, and accompanied by his only true friend, his nameless spotted hound, go home to die on a rocky coast somewhere in Cornwall.

The dog was sleeping on the floor of the swaying car, its head resting on the toe of one of the colonel's polished boots. Eberhart had bought a ticket for the animal, but the conductor refused to allow it to occupy the adjoining seat, which remained empty until the train reached Kalamazoo.

At that station a pale-faced middle-aged man, long of nose and chin, with a yellowish mustache, took the seat. He nodded formally to Colonel Eberhart and set his black satchel down beside the awakened dog. A faint odor of medicines emanated from the man and his bag.

"If someone asked me, sir," the colonel said bluntly, "I'd say you were a physician who favors herbs."

"Not far from the mark," the man replied. "Julian Aylott, M.D., Harvard University. Manufacturer and dealer in remedies for most of humanity's ills. Compounded from secret formulae of the aboriginal tribes of North America." He offered the colonel an oversized business card imprinted with a list of patent medicines.

"Colonel Lucius Eberhart of the British Army, sir. I see you are from the city of Chicago, Dr. Aylott."

"Yes. I travel occasionally out into the towns to stock the pharmacies. Do you have business in Chicago, colonel?"

Eberhart shook his head. "No, I'm on extended leave. After seeing your city I shall proceed southward with my dog and gun for some hunting. Prairie chickens, they tell me."

"I don't think of Chicago as my city," Dr. Aylott replied, his tone somewhat bitter. "Although my business has prospered, I was driven there, so to speak, from Louisville in Kentucky."

The colonel gave the doctor a puzzled look. "From your speech, sir, I would not have classed you as a Southern American. More of the southern England, or your New England, to my ear."

< **Let the Wide World Wag As It Will** >

Dr. Aylott's long nose and chin separated in a wide smile. "You are a perceptive man, Colonel Eberhart. My father was an Englishman who emigrated to Boston. I spent my youth there and inherited his modest drug business. To enlarge the business after his death I transferred it to Louisville." He sighed audibly. "Probably you know nothing or care nothing for American politics?"

"Nothing, absolutely nothing," the colonel assured him.

"In a nutshell, sir, I share the philosophy of the good old Jacksonians, the Democrats. After this infernal war began, I was too vocal in opposition to Lincoln and his Unionist Republicans. I was accused of sedition, of being a Copperhead, and my business was destroyed. There was nothing for it but to move to Chicago, where I've kept my mouth shut and prospered well."

"Do you still oppose the war, sir?"

"As I said, colonel, I keep my mouth shut about such matters. I should warn you, however, that you are visiting Chicago in a time of turmoil. My Democratic party is convening there later this week to nominate a candidate for president to oppose Lincoln. An historic event that to put it mildly is raising the old Ned among the lower strata of our society."

"High spirits among the commonality, eh?"

"Worse than high spirits," Dr. Aylott responded. He paused to take a pill from the silver box in his waistcoat pocket, and slipped it inside his lower lip.

"Only last week, the holy day of Sunday was described by our police commissioners as a day of horrors. Affrays in which two men were mortally wounded and another severely. But most inconceivable, the riots in a little village a few miles west of Chicago. Between city Irish and rural Germans. Nothing to do with politics or the war. Fifteen carloads of Irishmen and their wives and doxies rode a Rock Island excursion train out to the village of Mokena and invaded a saloon owned by Germans. I wholesale my medicines out there. A nice town. My dear mother was half Irish, but can you imagine fifteen carloads of full-blooded Irish with mighty thirsts descending in one fell swoop upon a single saloon, demanding immediate service from only four Germans? When the steins ran out, the invaders began smashing everything in sight."

Dr. Aylott made a clucking sound with his tongue, and con-

< CONSPIRACY OF KNAVES >

tinued: "The proprietor rushes upstairs, returns with his pistols, orders the mob outside, and locks the door. But the excursionists soon return with stones from the railroad ballast, hurling them at the building, their women urging them on, collecting stones in their aprons and bringing them to the men. Then they storm the building, batter down the door, and start breaking up the counters and cases, the mirrors and partitions. The barkeep raises his pistol again only to be swarmed over, the weapon taken from him, and used to beat him senseless.

"Outside some members of the mob bring up wood shavings to start a fire to burn the place down. A small boy, a child of the proprietor, rushes to stop them, but the women knock him down by casting stones at him. At the same time other little bands of excursionists are robbing the adjoining Mokena stores of groceries, clothing, and money.

"By this time three or four Germans have managed to get into the upstairs room with rifles, and their simultaneous firing drives the attackers back toward the track. The railroad engineer, aware that something more than a jolly Irish fight is in progress, sounds his whistle to announce that the excursion train is preparing for its return run into Chicago." Dr. Aylott paused to wipe his eyes with a handkerchief. "That, colonel, is the mood of the lawless city that you can now begin to see through your window."

"Ah, yes, but what a lovely uneven, unfair fight," the colonel cried. "Just the sort I rejoice to risk my neck in."

Dr. Aylott gave the colonel a searching look, his bushy eyebrows rising sharply, but he made no comment as he reached for his satchel and transferred into it some of the papers he carried in his pockets. When the train rocked to a steaming halt in the bustling overcrowded station, the doctor nodded a hasty farewell to Colonel Eberhart and hurried off the car.

With his dog leading the way, the colonel descended leisurely to the platform and went in search of the baggage room to retrieve his trunk and cased hunting gun.

The day was late by the time a horse cab brought him through crawling lines of vehicles and packed crowds of humanity to the Richmond House at Lake Street and Michigan Avenue. Weariness unsteadied his legs, but he lifted his chin and walked like a parade-

< **Let the Wide World Wag As It Will** >

ground soldier to the registry desk and signed his name: Col. L. Eberhart, England, G.B.

"We have no facilities here for dogs," the clerk said.

"My dog, sir, will sleep with me," the colonel replied sternly, and fixing steely eyes for a moment on the baffled clerk, turned abruptly away and almost collided with Major Charles Heywood.

"Pleasant journey, Sir Lucius?" Charley asked, and without waiting for a response added: "A game of billiards before supper? They have splendid new tables in the gentlemen's room."

"First things first," the colonel replied. "Come up to my room, major, and share from the bottle of Canadian whiskey I smuggled across the river Detroit."

Next morning, feeling considerably refreshed after a quiet night, Colonel Eberhart boarded a streetcar and rode out to Camp Douglas. He was dressed in his military blouse, hunting trousers, and boots. His sole companion was his dog, but he carried a cane instead of a gun. During the previous evening, Major Heywood had shown him a rough map of the prison camp, and both had agreed that a personal reconnaissance by the leader of the proposed assault was very much in order.

In the manner of an English gentleman out for a constitutional, the colonel with his hound, which ran ahead in eager search for game among the grassy sand hillocks, made a complete circuit of the sixty acres enclosed by the fourteen-foot plank walls. He took care not to approach too close to the parapets, but his practiced eye told him the sentinel boxes were about 120 paces apart, each soldier walking approximately sixty paces before making an about-face to return to his station. Whenever he saw a guard looking in his direction, Eberhart would raise his cane and shout a merry greeting.

Major Heywood had informed him that the east side of the camp appeared to be the most vulnerable, and it looked so to the colonel, with its double gate of warped pine boards hanging fairly loose on its undersized hinges. A good gate for storming, he thought, with a pole ram and two hundred sturdy bodies slamming into it. The Confederate prisoners of war, however, were housed on the west side, away from the lake, and in Eberhart's opinion that was

< CONSPIRACY OF KNAVES >

where the first ingress should be made, the first boards torn down to form an opening wide enough so that hundreds of prisoners could pour through to be armed immediately from waiting wagons loaded with carbines and rifles.

Two hundred men should do it, Eberhart estimated, provided the assault was launched without warning, with complete surprise to the guards. The thousand men promised by Major Heywood would surely attract too much attention while assembling even in a busy city. Yet there was an advantage in numbers, he thought, in bringing small platoons to the remaining three sides and using them to distract and confuse the defenders. Additional diversions inside, created by the prisoners themselves, if carefully timed with the main assault, should ensure complete success.

After circling the outside wall, Eberhart boldly approached the main entrance and showed his official British papers to the guard, who immediately summoned a captain with muttonchop whiskers and heavy spectacles. He was Captain Spooner, of course, Johnny Truscott's *bête noire*, a man easily impressed by Eberhart's crisp military manner and British speech. He swallowed the colonel's story that he was an official representative of Queen Victoria's empire sent to study the latest methods used by the United States in its treatment of prisoners of war.

"My commander, Colonel Wright, is inspecting a regiment of troops in the city," Captain Spooner said, "but if you wish, sir, I will take you on a round of the camp while we await his return."

Colonel Eberhart fairly purred his acceptance, and after being persuaded to leave his sad-faced hound fastened to the side of the guards' weather shelter, he was rewarded by a tour of the parade ground, the hospital, and then the enormous rectangle of barracks where the prisoners were confined. Although he guessed the reason why the buildings appeared to have recently been elevated four feet above the ground, he put on his guileless air and asked Captain Spooner if the barracks had been upraised to prevent dampness entering from the ground.

"To stop tunneling," the captain replied brusquely.

"Do you have many escape attempts?"

"Not since we put jack screws under the barracks."

Captain Spooner seemed determined to show the entire prisoner compound to his distinguished foreign guest. They marched up

< **Let the Wide World Wag As It Will** >

and down the rows of buildings, Spooner pointing out modern hydrants recently installed to bring piped water from Lake Michigan.

"Most of the Rebs are quite happy here," the captain declared. "See them playing ball over there? On cooler days they would be running and jumping. The older men play checkers to pass the time. More than a thousand have taken an oath of loyalty and will be sent into the Western territories to fight Indians."

Around a corner of one of the barracks they came abruptly upon a dozen men suspended by their roped thumbs to a railing, their feet dangling a few inches above the ground. One of them had fainted after vomiting down the front of his shirt. On the sandy earth between them and the fence several other prisoners, balled and chained, were working with shovels to fill in a long ditch.

"Escape tunnel caved in," Spooner explained gleefully. "Ordinarily we throw the culprits into the dungeon, but the dungeon is full."

Eberhart was suddenly aware that his presence was attracting attention from one of the barracks; the prisoners there were forming little groups on the entrance steps and on the grounds between the buildings. Down one lane he saw a man mounted and tied to a wooden horse, his feet lifted above the earth. Obviously he was suffering considerable pain. Another was walking in a slow shuffle, his ankles chained, carrying a heavy board sign on his back, ESCAPED PRISONER RECAPTURED.

Captain Spooner tried to turn his guest in another direction, but the colonel held his position. He had recognized some of the faces on the steps of that particular barracks; he had last seen them during John Morgan's raid on Hartsville in Tennessee, where they had captured two thousand Yankees and hundreds of cavalry horses. One of the young men, an officer, he had last seen at General Morgan's wedding in Murfreesboro.

Captain Spooner was explaining the reasons why the suffering man had been placed on the wooden horse.

"These men are the worst offenders among our prisoners. Followers of the Rebel bushwhacker Morgan. No manner of good treatment pleases such fellows. They'll even try to climb the lighted fence to escape."

The young Confederate officer that Eberhart remembered from

< CONSPIRACY OF KNAVES >

Morgan's wedding arose from the barracks step on which he was sitting and started walking slowly toward Spooner and the colonel. His face was older than Eberhart remembered, the eyes a bit hollow, his clothing like a scarecrow's. John Truscott, yes, the man whom Major Heywood was counting upon to lead the breakout from the inside!

To communicate directly with Truscott would be a boon, the colonel knew, but if Captain Spooner noticed any glimmer of recognition between them now, the result could be dangerous for both of them. Eberhart looked straight at Truscott and shook his head, almost imperceptibly, and was relieved to see Truscott catch the signal and turn aside.

Eberhart was shocked by the appearance of Truscott and the others, their once young faces growing old from boredom and frustration, their skins yellowing from untreated sicknesses and bad food, their eyes deadening in the demeaning atmosphere. Prisons were the dark side of war, the aging Briton admitted to himself, in some ways worse than death on the field of battle.

He recalled a mild quarrel with young Truscott during John Morgan's Christmas raid into Kentucky. They had argued about knighthood, the meaning of chivalry. The lad was too idealistic, his head full of old legends, Eberhart thought at the time (the regiment was bivouacked in a freezing rain) and he'd tried to disillusion the young man, make him see that knighthood bore its weight of evil as do all man's endeavors. At this moment, a year and a half later, in the prison yard the older man regretted his refutation of chivalry. "You are the embodiment of Brian de Bois Guilbert!" Truscott had shouted at him, and Eberhart had laughed at the boy and his saber. Now the Briton was suddenly aware that the romantic dream was essential to Truscott's being; it held him to a center, kept him from drowning in a slough of despair.

"Admirable, admirable," Colonel Eberhart said to Spooner. "Clean and airy quarters, captain, most sanitary conditions. I shall make note of these in my official report to the British Army."

Captain Spooner smiled with smug satisfaction. "They're better off here than in their own army, Colonel Eberhart."

When they returned to the camp's area of sutlers' stores near the entrance, Captain Spooner asked the colonel if he would mind waiting there while he went to see if Colonel Wright had returned

< **Let the Wide World Wag As It Will** >

to headquarters and was willing to receive a visitor from England.

"Certainly, captain," Eberhart said. "I shall step over there and buy a newspaper. Scan the heads while waiting."

He asked for a copy of the Chicago *Times*, a newspaper that the exiles in Canada had favored. The peddler at the canvas-covered stand snorted derisively. "Come along, sir, you're wasting my time. You know we can't sell that Copperhead sheet in here."

"No, sir, I did not know. I'm a simple Englishman unused to American partisanisms. Pray, what is a Copperhead?"

"Some call 'em Democrats, some Copperheads. To me they're all the same," the newspaper peddler declared with an air of self-importance. "And the city's full of 'em this week. Big convention of Democrats."

Eberhart chose another paper. THE WAR IN GEORGIA. SHERMAN VICTORY! AN ENTIRE CIRCUIT OF ATLANTA ACCOMPLISHED. He folded the sheet, glanced toward the gate, and was not surprised to find his dog observing him with the saddest of eyes. As the colonel turned slightly, he was startled to see coming from the entrance to the headquarters grounds, the familiar figure of Belle Rutledge, dressed in that coxcombical male apparel she had used for a stage costume at the Hirons House in Windsor.

Had he not seen her performances, he would not have penetrated the disguise at the distance of several yards, but there was no mistaking the fancy waistcoat, the spoony hat, and showy boots. The fop was truly Belle Rutledge as Calvin Blacklock, and walking beside the disguised actress, gesticulating impatiently, was a Union colonel, his profile as flat as a dish, his uniform very new and fresh, his manner imperious.

(If I had glanced in his direction, Colonel Eberhart told me later, he would have come forward to greet me, not to give away my true identity, but rather to meet Colonel Bartholomew Wright so that he might gain some understanding of his adversary on the night of the planned assault upon Camp Douglas. On that day, however, I was an inept spy. I had come to see Colonel Wright for two reasons—first, to learn if the commandant knew what had happened to my professional associate and old friend, Kendrich, and second, to seek the colonel's advice concerning the moneys due me from the U.S. Secret Service.

< CONSPIRACY OF KNAVES >

Colonel Wright apparently accepted my story that I had been working with Kendrich in Canada until his recent disappearance in the vicinity of Niagara Falls, but all he would tell me was that a female associate of Kendrich's also was believed to be missing. He suggested that I write to Mr. Allan Pinkerton, the head of the Secret Service in Washington about my overdue pay, and offered to endorse my letter.

Whether Kendrich's missing female associate was believed to be me, Belle Rutledge, or the unnamed young woman accompanying the "gray-bearded but energetic gentleman" who had hired a buggy at St. Catharines to drive off in the direction of Niagara Falls, I had no way of ascertaining. As I noted at the time, Kendrich could have played either character.

For me to write a letter to the Secret Service and sign it Calvin Blacklock was useless, because that organization had no knowledge of such a person. And the realization that Mr. Pinkerton's government detectives might be searching for Belle Rutledge gave me a decidedly uneasy feeling. And Lord! Had I known Colonel Lucius Eberhart recognized me with Commandant Wright, what a fidget I would have gone into. Yes, so inept was I that day, I passed only a few feet from Eberhart's yellow-spotted dog, and thought to myself how remarkably like Sir Lucius's sorrowful hound, but I dismissed the possibility of the Englishman being there, and so did not even pause to examine the dog's side for the telltale bullet scar that would have warned me of the colonel's presence and danger to me.)

Colonel Eberhart watched Belle Rutledge (as Calvin Blacklock) turn toward the camp's exit gate. He was puzzled as to her apparent close acquaintance with the Union officer. Commandant Wright, joined now by several other Union officers in resplendent new uniforms, started back toward his headquarters building. In the manner of a king dismissing a minor courtier, he shook off Captain Spooner with a wave of his open palm.

A moment later Spooner crossed the sunlit area to apologize to his patiently waiting British visitor.

"Commandant Wright can't welcome you until later in the day," he said hesitantly, a defeated expression clouding his face.

"No matter, captain," Eberhart replied in his richest British

< Let the Wide World Wag As It Will >

accent. "You have been a most courteous host. I have learned much that will be useful—to my queen's army."

"Perhaps you'll understand, sir," Spooner continued, "being an officer yourself. Military matters are coming to a boil here, with the Democratic convention and all sorts of rumors of desperadoes attacking us. Commandant Wright is making the most of his opportunity, bringing in troops from Wisconsin and elsewhere, beseeching headquarters for as many hundred-day men as can be spared."

Spooner forced a wry laugh, one eye winking behind the thick lenses of his spectacles. "Another regiment under his command, and they'll be forced to promote Bartholomew Wright to brigadier general." He nudged the Englishman familiarly with his elbow.

"That's why he's so busy today with detectives and brass-buttoned visitors, don't you see?"

"Indeed I do, captain, indeed I do. It's the old army game all around this pendent world."

He offered his hand to Spooner. "Please present your prospective brigadier with my sincerest regards, and inform him that I shall return very soon."

Saluting his obsequious host, Colonel Eberhart went to relieve the anxiety of his waiting dog by unfastening its tie and allowing it to lead him outside the gate to await a streetcar in the heat of the August noon. He saw no trace of Belle Rutledge in her male costume.

He wondered if Major Heywood knew what his mistress was pursuing at Camp Douglas. Or was she playing a double game? In most wars, large and small, in which he had participated, women such as she played at all sorts of games in the rear. He had last seen them in the cities of the Confederacy, smiling and conniving in ballrooms, dancing and feasting and flirting while they laid their little plots with no more loyalty to a cause, place, or person than wandering cats. They were like Mr. Thackeray's Becky Sharp at Brussels before Waterloo.

In his opinion, Miss Rutledge had all the magnetism of those black-eyed nymphs of paradise he'd last seen in Damascus, and she'd been letting it play upon him back there in Windsor, dropping *je ne sais pas*'s and other French phrases to catch his ear, and caressing him with her glances when she caught his eyes. A crook

< CONSPIRACY OF KNAVES >

of his finger and she would follow him to Devon and Cornwall, he was certain, but little good that would do her, with his flagging body and straitened pension. Besides, there was a wife some-where—Switzerland, France; after all the years, God knows where.

Early in the evening Major Heywood insisted that Colonel Eberhart accompany him to the courthouse square, for an outdoor rally of the Peace Democrats during which Clement Vallandigham was to speak. As it was impossible to obtain a vehicle of any kind, they walked through the masses of human beings, horses, carriages, and dray carts that clogged streets and sidewalks. Not even in London had the colonel ever seen such crowd madness; he was reminded of an Italian town in Carnival time.

What may once have been a parade swirled and halted, sections breaking loose and turning down side streets to escape the jam. From hotel balconies above the sidewalks, brass bands played at full volume, one march tune overlapping another as Colonel Eberhart and Major Heywood pushed their way toward the courthouse square.

At last they reached the outer limits of the oratory, where the speakers' words were lost in echoes. The crowd of thousands swayed back and forth, some of those caught inside crying out from the crush. A woman fainted, and two policemen fought their way out with her limp body lifted above their heads. Those on the fringes, eager to move closer to the speakers' stand, swarmed into the vortex created by the exiting policemen and were quickly drawn within the crowd. Colonel Eberhart suddenly realized that Major Heywood had vanished into the maw.

Although McClellan flags and banners of the War Democrats were flying from the courthouse, this was a Peace Democrat crowd, eager to shout for Vallandigham, who was reciting the sins of Abraham Lincoln and declaiming the phrases they wanted to hear. Breezes from the lake caught some of the words, lifting voice sounds and scattering them capriciously: ". . . masses are weary of blood and carnage . . . usurpation of the people's rights by Lincoln's minions . . . reign of terror threatened . . ."

Colonel Eberhart had heard it all before, too many times, in Canada. This was a gathering of Copperheads. Some were bold enough to wear Butternut clothing to show sympathy for the Con-

< **Let the Wide World Wag As It Will** >

federacy. He studied the faces of those nearest him. Most were straining to hear every syllable, their expressions intense, enraptured, changing quickly to anger or hatred at the sound of an emotion-laden utterance. From this mob, he guessed, would come the army that was to seize Camp Douglas and Chicago. Only three more days.

The orator's voice was rising to a climax. In minutes the inflamed crowd might be released to sweep like a prairie fire along the streets. Using his cane, the colonel forced his way through the ranks of those who had collected behind him, and started back toward the hotel district. On Lake Street he again ran into parts of a disorganized parade—a brass band, a glee club. Forced off the sidewalk by a party of blustering drunkards, he came very near being run over by a barouche drawn by four white horses with tall plumes nodding on their heads. "McClellan! McClellan!" a hoarse voice yelled at him from the shadows of the elegant carriage.

Drums beat, horns blared, fifes screamed. He was drawn into another lost section of the parade—a collection of Chinese lanterns borne by boys wearing gay-colored sashes. He escaped in time to watch a squad of McClellan supporters pass in perfect order, torchlights and transparencies held aloft.

Just before he reached Michigan Avenue and the safety of the Richmond House, a dozen young women, rosy-cheeked and full-breasted, walking with arms interlocked, a McClellan banner strung across their middles, overtook him. He tried to escape them by veering off the sidewalk, but they followed, taunting, giggling, catcalling. One Amazon snatched his cane, holding it aloft to lead the others in a chant:

> *McClellan the soldier*
> *McClellan the brave*
> *McClellan the statesman*
> *Our country will save!*

From somewhere behind them a masculine chorus echoed a Vallandigham salute, ending with: "We'll hang Abe Lincoln from a sour apple tree." Distracted for the moment, the young women relaxed their pursuit long enough for Colonel Eberhart to plunge

< CONSPIRACY OF KNAVES >

into the open entrance of the Richmond House and flee upstairs to his room.

God in Heaven, he thought as he collapsed upon the bed, why were American women, who could not vote, so warlike in their attitudes? And what evil spirit from Hades provoked the American colonists to cast away the serenity of king and parliament in exchange for such political madness?

Sometime later in the night, the telegrapher Ellsworth, who shared his room and bed, entered and awakened Eberhart and his dog. The colonel had scarcely found sleep again when Major Heywood began pounding on his door to remind him in the early dawn that they were meeting with the Sons of Liberty. The colonel responded eagerly, believing that at last he was going to encounter some of the militant Copperheads dedicated to freeing the prisoners at Camp Douglas and seizing the city of Chicago.

Almost as soon as he and Heywood entered the large meeting room in a building on Dearborn Street, disillusionment struck him. Half the seats were empty, and the men who occupied the remainder bore a collective air of gray tedium about them. From their dress and unweathered faces, the colonel judged them to be clerks and tradesmen, failed lawyers, preachers, and political hangers-on. He saw only three or four ruddy Irish and Germans, one of them a priest, who looked as if they might have the audacity to storm the walls of Camp Douglas and seize the city of Chicago. An orator, a small man with a brush of pale reddish hair, who hopped about the rostrum like an angry bird, wound up his speech by promising to give the abolitionists hell under their shirttails. He was replaced by a solemn-faced panjandrum wearing an enormous winged collar who announced that members of the Sons of Liberty action committee would assemble in room number 3.

Major Heywood tapped Colonel Eberhart on the shoulder, and led the way across a hall to a room almost too small to hold the dozen or so men who quickly assembled there. Eberhart observed that they were all wearing Butternut badges in their left lapels and McClellan badges on the right side of their breasts. Arguments began as soon as the meeting was called to order by the solemn-faced man with the spreading collar, and it became evident that about half the members wanted to delay the seizure of Chicago

< **Let the Wide World Wag As It Will** >

until after the Democrats nominated their candidate. Major Heywood angrily pointed out that action had been delayed three times in July, that he had paid out thousands of dollars for purchase of weapons and horses and other expenses, and that the entire Northwest was prepared for a rising as soon as a signal came from Chicago. He then introduced Colonel Eberhart as the man who had volunteered to lead the assault upon Camp Douglas. The committee members applauded with enthusiasm, and then the Copperhead Joseph Milligan arose to declare that he was in favor of the attack on the twenty-ninth, that he had a store of arms cached in various secret places, and that an army of twenty thousand was in or near the city, ready to take to the streets on signal. "It is my understanding, however," Milligan went on, "that the honorable Clement Vallandigham favors a delay until we have a candidate for president."

"Vallandigham has no chance to be nominated, unless we do seize Chicago," cried the little man with the brush of reddish hair, and leaping to his feet, he began an oration that was stopped only by the forceful banging of the chairman's fist against the table.

By voice vote the committee members finally decided that Milligan and Major Heywood should hasten around to the Sherman House for a meeting with Clement Vallandigham to determine what course was favored by the leaders of the Peace Democrats.

During this short adjournment, Colonel Eberhart arose to stretch himself. As he turned, he was surprised to see the gargoyle face of the patent-medicine manufacturer who had boarded his train at Kalamazoo.

"So we meet again, colonel," Dr. Aylott said, offering his hand. "When we exchanged travelers' greetings the other day, I did not dream you were an associate of Major Heywood."

"Nor I that you were a member of the Sons of Liberty."

Dr. Aylott's bushy eyebrows moved up and down. "Many good Democrats are members," he said. "The organization is necessary to counteract bullying by the Union League clubs of the Republicans."

"American politics is a puzzle to me," the colonel replied. "But even at home in England, we military men distrust the politicians."

"One must always be on guard against those in power," Dr.

Aylott agreed as he unfolded a copy of the Chicago *Times*, which lay on his lap. "I see that President Lincoln has cashiered Burnside at last."

"The general who fizzled the Petersburg mine?"

"Yes, Ambrose Burnside lost four thousand men in that crater in a single day. And at Fredericksburg he came near to losing his entire army. President Lincoln sent him out here to the Northwest to keep him from mischief only to have him do more damage to the Constitution and civil rights than any man since the nation was founded."

"What did the general do?"

"Arrested the Honorable Congressman Clement Vallandigham, that's what he did, on a charge of disloyal speech. Court-martialed and exiled him off to Canada. Then for his next iniquity, he banned publication of the *Times*, this Democrat newspaper I hold in my hand. Sent troops from Camp Douglas, surrounded the *Times* building, stopped the presses, and shredded all the papers on the premises."

"I've been told that was President Lincoln's doing."

"Oh, he may have seconded it, wanted Vallandigham out of the country and the *Times* off the streets. But the people protested with such vehemence he had to let the newspaper publish again, and sent Burnside back to field duty. Next time we may not be so fortunate." Dr. Aylott dropped a pill into his cavernous mouth. "To suppress thought is to murder the soul, eh, Colonel Eberhart?"

Before the Englishman could reply, the doctor moved close enough to whisper into his ear: "How many men will you use—in the attack upon Camp Douglas?"

"As many as Major Heywood assigns me."

"You must have a minimum in mind."

"I would attempt it with two hundred, but would prefer three hundred."

Dr. Aylott drew away smiling. "Joseph Milligan can find you that many easily—the sort I told you about—the excursionists who pillaged the village of Mokena. Do you propose to attack after dark next Monday? The twenty-ninth?"

Colonel Eberhart grew suddenly cautious. This gargoyle of a doctor was asking too many questions. Reminded him of that inquisitive Spaniard in Tangier who turned out to be what the French

< **Let the Wide World Wag As It Will** >

called an *agent provocateur*, came near getting him beheaded by the Berbers.

"To my knowledge, sir, no day or hour has been set," he replied flatly.

A moment later he was relieved to see Major Heywood and Joseph Milligan entering the door of the little room. Milligan looked pleased with himself, but Heywood appeared to be in a dark mood. As soon as the chairman called the committee back to order, Milligan reported that Vallandigham and the other leaders of the Peace Democrats wanted the Sons of Liberty to postpone a decision for action for twenty-four hours. The chairman pounded the table with his fist and the meeting was adjourned.

On the way back to the Richmond House, Charley Heywood tried to relieve his bitter mood by cursing the ineptitude of his Copperhead associates. "I have no interest in politics," he said to Eberhart, "other than to despise those involved in the filthy enterprise." He caught the Englishman by the arm and held him stock-still on the sidewalk.

"Do you know what the bastards did with the money I gave them to buy weapons and Greek fire? Funneled most of it right into the coffers of the Democrats! The bosses over there at the Sherman House had the gall to thank me and the Confederate government for our contributions. And Vallandigham, a man I've admired from afar—up to this day, that is—the scoundrel looked me right in the eyes and declared he'd never supported any plan to release our prisoners at Camp Douglas and seize Chicago. A Northwest Confederacy, yes, he's all for that, but it's a political matter, he says, must be voted on by the state legislatures."

Major Heywood released his grip on Eberhart's arm, and they continued toward the hotel.

"Then the rising is not to be?" the Englishman asked quietly.

"We have our seventy-four tried and true men in the Richmond House, Sir Lucius. And Joe Milligan swears he'll bring two or three hundred Copperheads to the meeting hall tomorrow morning. No matter what the Peace Democrats decide, we'll strike Camp Douglas Monday night and free our soldiers. They've waited too long in that prison."

Next morning was Sunday. Colonel Eberhart had not thought of that until a medley of musical church bells awakened him. He

< CONSPIRACY OF KNAVES >

dressed hurriedly, left his dog and the telegrapher Ellsworth still sleeping, and went down to the Richmond's dining room, where he found Major Heywood drinking coffee with a tall black-haired man. Heywood introduced him as Frank Jarrell.

"Frank was in Colonel Cluke's Eighth Kentucky. Got himself wounded and left behind on the big raid in Indiana, but was never captured. He's been working for us around Rock Island Prison. Believes five hundred good men can take it."

"The guards are careless," Jarrell said with a grin. "They think they're safe on that island in the river."

"Any locals to help you?" the colonel asked.

"There's an O.A.K., Order of American Knights, but they're too poorly armed and don't seem to have the stomachs for a fight."

"This is the plan," Major Heywood said in a low voice. "Joe Milligan can send five hundred of his men over there on the Rock Island Railroad. Billed as an excursion. The rifles can go by express in boxes marked tools, shovels, hoes, axes. If Frank can attack Rock Island Prison tomorrow night, colonel, about the same time we strike Camp Douglas—one hour after sundown—we'll send such a convulsion through the North, the convention is bound to swing toward the Peace Democrats."

Half an hour later, when the three men entered the meeting hall on Dearborn Street, they found only ten Sons of Liberty there. Six of them were members of the previous day's action committee. The committee members were seated together, as were the remaining four men, although the latter were perched nervously on a backless bench in the rear of the hall. This quartet was composed of laborers in Sunday dress. Their weathered faces bore the expressions of men who wished profoundly that they were somewhere else.

"The goddamned Copperheads," Major Heywood muttered. "They never start anything at the announced hour." He strode down the aisle, and in a loud voice asked the wing-collared chairman if he knew where Joseph Milligan was.

The chairman did not know, but it was his opinion that the day being Sunday, Joseph must have gone to mass with his family. "Be patient, Major Heywood, he'll be along in good time."

More than an hour later Milligan appeared, with seven men

in tow, he smiling and pleased with himself, they obviously nervous and of the same reluctant presence as the four men on the rear bench, whom they recognized and immediately joined.

"You have eleven men here, *Brother* Milligan," Heywood said sarcastically, accenting the Sons of Liberty salutation. "Yesterday you promised two or three hundred would be in this hall."

Milligan was wearing his gold sash of rank, and he kept his coat open so that no one would fail to see it. "Begging your leave, major," he replied briskly, the ends of his mustache quivering. "But I was summoned very early this morning to the Sherman House. The Peace Democrats want the city to be as quiet as possible until the convention nominates."

Milligan sat down in one of the row seats. "It's my opinion a deal has been fashioned with General McClellan's War Democrats."

"What kind of deal?" interrupted the wing-collared chairman, springing from his seat.

"Some say the Peace Democrat leaders will go with McClellan in exchange for the privilege of writing the platform."

"Betrayal!" cried the chairman. He glared down at the other members of the committee. "What say we get over to the Sherman House and beard the skulkers in their dens?"

When the others rose to follow the chairman, Major Heywood stepped into the aisle, spreading his arms to stop them.

"Sit down," he shouted. "I need a vote before you go. Some of you know Frank Jarrell." He motioned toward the tall black-haired man. "Frank is certain he can break out our prisoners of war at Rock Island with five hundred men. If we can put five hundred Sons of Liberty on an excursion train tonight, with boxed arms in the express car, the attack at Rock Island can be timed with Colonel Eberhart's assault on Camp Douglas tomorrow night. The two strokes combined will set a storm raging and stampede the convention in favor of the Peace Democrats. But I need your support to summon several hundred men to join us."

One or two of the committee members nodded approvingly; others appeared to be uncertain. Joined by Joseph Milligan, they withdrew a few yards down the aisle. After several minutes of whispering together, they stood silent while the chairman gravely

< CONSPIRACY OF KNAVES >

informed Major Heywood that they would cross the hall to room number 3 to vote by secret ballot on motions to be introduced in secret.

For several minutes Heywood, Eberhart, and Jarrell waited impatiently in the front of the auditorium. Behind them on the uncomfortable bench, the eleven proletarian Sons of Liberty shuffled and sighed and cursed in hoarse whispers. At last the solemn-faced chairman and a beaming Joseph Milligan returned. After an introductory peroration that included numerous repetitive references to "the Lincoln tyranny" and "an Empire of Northwestern States," the chairman informed Major Heywood that the Sons of Liberty could not give official sanction to attacks upon either Rock Island or Camp Douglas until after the Democratic convention adjourned. The Sons of Liberty, however, would not oppose such attacks. If Major Heywood and his Confederate forces in Chicago could recruit *volunteers* from among the twenty thousand Sons of Liberty in Chicago, they were free to do so.

"Where are these twenty thousand men?" Colonel Eberhart abruptly asked the chairman, a skeptical note in his voice.

The chairman glanced at Milligan, who smiled brightly and replied: "They'll show when the Rebels show."

Heywood's face darkened with anger. "You know we have almost a hundred good men camped over at the Richmond House," he declared. "Every man of them is ready and eager for action, with some help from you people."

"Bring us a thousand armed Confederates," Milligan said, "and twenty thousand of us will join them."

"Damn you! There's no time left to bring our Kentucky army into Chicago. But I promise you that on the day Colonel Ferree gets a signal of action here, he will lead two thousand men across the Ohio River, and thousands more will follow him through Indiana and Illinois."

Joseph Milligan struck the pose of a man in deep thought. He was enjoying his sudden ascendancy. Previously in dealings with Major Heywood and other Confederate agents, he had been the beseecher. Now he suddenly found himself the superior rather than the inferior he had always been before.

"Can't you find me just five hundred men?" Frank Jarrell begged.

< **Let the Wide World Wag As It Will** >

"Everything is ready to fall into our hands at Rock Island. Just a show of force is all that's needed."

"And give me two hundred," Colonel Eberhart demanded. "Bring them to me—right here in this hall—tonight."

Milligan hooked his thumbs in his gold sash. "I'll talk to the boys back there," he said, indicating the eleven restless men on the rear bench.

While Milligan was holding his informal conference in the rear of the hall, Charley Heywood remembered with a sudden sinking feeling that he had seen every one of those eleven earnest faces somewhere in recent weeks. Yes, together they had formed that ludicrous platoon of amateurish Copperhead militia assembled by Milligan in that wheat field outside Chicago. They were draymen, Milligan's employees.

Charley was not surprised, therefore, to see Milligan suddenly raise his arm in a gesture of dismissal, which was followed by a hurried scurrying as the eleven men departed through the nearest exit. Milligan strolled back down the aisle, with that confident air he had so recently acquired.

"I've sent the boys out through the city," he announced, "to seek volunteers for raids on Rock Island and Camp Douglas."

"How much did you tell them?" Heywood asked quickly.

"Nothing, except I advised them to enlist unmarried men first. They think we want volunteers to help guard the Democratic convention from Union Leaguers."

Although Heywood grasped for this last straw held out by Milligan, Colonel Eberhart was still dubious. During the afternoon, while Heywood occupied himself at engaging a special excursion train to Rock Island and at pressing Milligan to deliver several boxed cases of weapons for shipment on the same train, the Englishman spent the time strolling along the lakeshore with his dog.

Let the wide world wag as it will, he told himself, and avoided as much as possible the burgeoning throngs of convention delegates, journalists, souvenir peddlers, pickpockets, and other offscourings of society who were still pouring into Chicago to attend the nomination of Democratic candidates for president and vicepresident.

< CONSPIRACY OF KNAVES >

Early that evening he returned to the Richmond House, where he joined Major Heywood and Frank Jarrell in the bar. Heywood was on edge, and was drinking heavily to cover his uneasiness. Eberhart tried to calm him by suggesting that they go into the billiards room for a quiet game, but the major refused, explaining that a messenger from Joseph Milligan was overdue with a report of the number of Copperhead volunteers. Perhaps there would be more than the seven hundred they must have, he told the Englishman.

As twilight was darkening the busy street outside a window of the barroom, the messenger arrived. He was a furtive little man, slightly hunchbacked, exposing broken yellow teeth in a grimace when he handed Major Heywood a brown envelope and turned away toward the exit in a motion that reminded Colonel Eberhart of a scuttling cockroach.

"Wait a minute!" Heywood shouted, rising from his chair. His voice was thick with alcoholic rage. The messenger spun around on one leg, fear showing on his rogue's face. "I may have a reply to send," Heywood added.

He ripped the envelope open and unfolded the letter. He held the sheet so that light from the window fell upon it, read the short message quickly, and stabbed a finger at the waiting messenger.

"You. Go tell your Brigadier Joseph Milligan to roast his worthless hide in hell."

Colonel Eberhart never saw the message that Heywood tore into tiny pieces and scattered on the floor of the barroom, but some days later the major told him the number of Copperheads who had volunteered for duty. Twenty-four. And some, or all, of the twenty-four might have withdrawn when they learned that instead of guarding Democratic convention headquarters they were expected to attack Camp Douglas or Rock Island. Oh, yes, Joseph Milligan had excuses for the low number. Too short notice, family obligations, Sunday a holy day of rest, duties already assigned at the Democratic convention, and on and on.

Early Monday morning, Major Heywood called a succession of small meetings in his room at the Richmond House to inform his loyal followers, the Morgan men, that a cowardly betrayal by the Copperheads had forced another delay in their plans to free prisoners at Camp Douglas and seize Chicago. Heywood placed much of the blame upon leaders of the Peace Democrats, who appeared to be yielding to the power of the War Democrats.

"We must wait until all this brawling is ended, and the Copperheads get their minds off General George McClellan, whom they detest as much as we do. Meanwhile, Sir Lucius and I will be leaving in a day or so for southern Illinois, he to spend several days at hunting prairie chickens, I to begin rebuilding our plans and forces. The Copperheads in that region are of a much more determined persuasion than the cowardly laggards of Chicago. I've chosen ten men to go with us, and the remainder of you are free to return to Canada, or make your way down to Kentucky to join Colonel Ferree's secret army."

That afternoon, out of a burning curiosity to understand American politics in relation to the Civil War, Colonel Eberhart visited the Democratic convention, using one of the tickets that Joseph Milligan previously had presented to him. The day was bright and cool, with a hint of autumn on the rush of wind that kept flags snapping sharply along the approaches to a building that had been hastily erected on the shore of Lake Michigan. A waggish journalist had dubbed this pine-board structure "the Wigwam" but it reminded Eberhart of a huge cheesebox.

Surrounding the Wigwam was a mob as large as the one the colonel had fled on the evening of Vallandigham's speech in Courthouse Square, and if the day had not been so sunny and sparkling, he would have turned back to the Richmond House. But the long wait in line was not unpleasant.

As he entered the building at last, spirited band music greeted him and ushers directed him to a section of board seats off to the right of the main platform. Flags, streamers, oriflammes, gonfalons, pennons, and festoons curled and looped and hung from every post and rafter, virtually concealing the unpainted pine boards still fragrant with rosin. A banner heralding Gilmore's Brass Band of Boston was almost lost in the patriotic show of red, white, and blue.

Colonel Eberhart found himself in an amphitheater, well lighted and ventilated, and he had just settled himself on a board seat when the platform section swayed slowly to one side, and then, with a creaking of nails against wood, it sank to the floor beneath

< CONSPIRACY OF KNAVES >

him. Although the descent was a dozen feet or more, the speed was not precipitate, and the only casualty appeared to be a man of forty or so who was vomiting from the shock. He was being slapped on the face so vigorously by his stout wife that blood was beginning to ooze from the skin.

Ushers quickly surrounded the dispossessed seat holders of the collapsed section, and herded Colonel Eberhart among the others into an area assigned to standees. At the same time a squad of carpenters appeared for the purpose of resurrecting the fallen platform. For several minutes the sound of their hammers clashed with the beat of the band.

Colonel Eberhart was on the point of forcing his way to an exit when cries of "Vallandigham!" sounded through the amphitheater. An official rushed over to the noisy carpenters, ordering them to desist and depart. The band struck up a gay march, and suddenly there was the Copperhead leader, Vallandigham, striding to the speakers' platform, an imposing man in a frock coat, clean-shaven except for a short dark beard beneath his jawbone. Cheers and catcalls mingled, followed by shouts for other arrivals, "Seymour, Seymour!" and "Belmont, Belmont!"

By this time Colonel Eberhart was pressed against a heavy rope by a surge of bodies behind him, and someone on the rostrum was introducing the Honorable August Belmont of New York.

Belmont spoke in a rough accent that reminded the colonel of Kendrich, the Windsor gold thief: "In your hands rests, under the ruling of an all-wise providence, the future of this republic. Four years of misrule by a sectional, fanatical, and corrupt party have brought our country to the very verge of ruin. The past and the present are sufficient warning of disastrous consequences which would befall if Mr. Lincoln's reelection should be made possible by our want of patriotism and unity.

"We are here not as War Democrats nor as Peace Democrats but as citizens of this vast republic which we will strive and labor to the last to bring back to its former greatness and prosperity without one single star taken from the brilliant constellation that once encircled its youthful brow."

While Colonel Eberhart struggled to free himself from the crush, searching desperately for an exit, he heard the speaker pleading for moderation and fairness and for support of the Constitution

< **Let the Wide World Wag As It Will** >

and law over fanaticism and treason. In one final lunge, the Englishman reached an outgate and was propelled into the welcome sunshine of the late August afternoon.

Next day he was back in the Wigwam again, armed with a ticket to a more exclusive section of seats, still determined to gain some understanding of the American political process. He listened patiently to harangues against President Lincoln and General Grant, followed by even more virulent attacks against members of the Democratic party themselves, especially those whose names had been put forward for nomination to be president.

"One nominated here today is a tyrant," shouted a fiery-voiced speaker. His next words were drowned in hisses and cheers, and then he resumed: "He it was who first initiated the policy by which our rights and liberties were stricken down. That man is George B. McClellan!" Again the amphitheater became a bedlam of hoots and shouts of approval, subsiding gradually but resuming again when a hoarse voice bellowed: "Vote for Jeff Davis!"

During the confusion, the colonel noticed among a line of new arrivals Major Heywood and Belle Rutledge. They were being shown to a pair of reserved seats quite near the speakers' rostrum. Both were dressed to the nth degree, Belle in a tight-waisted maroon dress that showed off her fine figure much more sensually than would have a voluminous hoopskirt. Every man within whose view she came as she followed her escort along the aisles was mesmerized by her presence, and continued gaping until she sat down. (At least, that is what Colonel Eberhart told me afterward!)

She would indeed be a fine one to take home to England, he thought. She was as splendid a conniver as she was a beauty. Yes, what *had* she been doing at Camp Douglas prison in that masculine stage costume, speaking so intimately with the Union commandant? Had Major Heywood sent her in that male guise for some purpose, or was she a double-dealer with a sharp eye to the main chance? As many hours as the colonel had spent with Heywood in recent days, it seemed likely the major would have made some mention to him of Miss Rutledge's visit to Camp Douglas. He resolved that at first chance he would remark casually to Major Heywood that he had seen her in the prison camp with the commandant.

If the Union of States tolerated an aristocracy, the colonel

< CONSPIRACY OF KNAVES >

reflected, then Major Heywood and Belle Rutledge would belong to that class not by noble birth but because they possessed the audacity to step into the roles. And who were their Puritan enemies, the Oliver Cromwells of the Great Rebellion bent upon beheading kings and cavaliers? The Yankee Puritans of New England? Oh, but these mad tribes of Americans had turned history upside down. In Britain's civil war, Oliver Cromwell forced a republic upon the people, but at first opportunity they rejected it and returned to the rationality of king and parliament. Who could rule this tortured lost colony of the New World?

Great events certainly were afoot, but were the Northwestern states truly ripe for revolt? Where indeed were the thousands of Copperheads that Major Heywood claimed? If Lincoln's government interfered with the elections of November, would the Copperheads rise? If Abe Lincoln does not make peace, will he make himself a military dictator, a Cromwell, and then will the Northwest revolt and separate, become a Scotland? Three nations on this bleeding land would require a king to bring them together again, he told himself, yet what Englishman could ever comprehend the politics of these state-proud Americans?

A fiery orator was rampaging again: "Maryland, which has suffered so much at the hands of that man, will not submit to his nomination in silence. His offenses shall be made known. This convention is a jury appointed by the people to pass upon the merits of the public men whose names may be presented for the support of the great Democratic party. General McClellan, I repeat, is a tyrant. All the charges of usurpation and tyranny that can be brought against Lincoln I can make and substantiate against McClellan. I stand here to indict him!"

Next day the convention of Democrats nominated George B. McClellan for President of the United States of America by a vote of 202½ to 28½ for Horatio Seymour. Clement Vallandigham announced that he would support the candidate. McClellan then repudiated the peace plank that Vallandigham had been permitted to write for the party's platform. And so McClellan prepared to run for president on virtually the same "preservation of the Union" platform as his opponent, Abraham Lincoln. The American political process would remain forever an enigma to Colonel Lucius Eberhart of Great Britain.

< **Let the Wide World Wag As It Will** >

Following the close of the Democratic convention, the colonel, with his dog and gun, boarded a southbound Illinois Central train for the town of Tamaroa. In one of the cars of the same train were Major Heywood and Belle Rutledge, and scattered through other cars were several Morgan men who had been selected to journey to the little Illinois town that lay as far south as the capital of the Confederacy, and was reported to be in the heart of Copperhead country.

When the train reached the junction town of Effingham late in the afternoon and stopped there for half an hour, the colonel and his dog went for a short walk along the tracks. Nearby the depot, a loyal Democrat had already erected a sign:

GEORGE B. McCLELLAN
the
PEOPLE'S CHOICE

As man and dog were returning to the cars, a newsboy pressed the colonel to buy a paper. Not until he was back in his seat, with the dog at his feet and the train in motion, did he open the newspaper and read the startling headlines above the first column:

DEATH OF JOHN MORGAN
—
A VICTORY IN TENNESSEE
—
Surprise and Rout of Morgan's
Forces at Greeneville

The news dispatch contained only scanty details, merely a brief official report of a surprise attack, the death of Morgan, the capture of his staff and some pieces of artillery.

How this bitter woe would affect the plans of Charles Heywood and his fading remnant of reckless Morgan men Colonel Eberhart did not attempt to gauge. His first thought—that he should go through the cars to find Heywood and tell him of the tragedy—he quickly rejected. *The first bringer of unwelcome news hath but a losing office* . . . Let the wide world wag as it will.

King Arthur was dead, the days of the Round Table were closing, the castle at Tintagel would crumble to ruins. Thinking

< CONSPIRACY OF KNAVES >

of Tintagel brought visions of that craggy coast of Cornwall, where England faces the New World across three thousand miles of ocean sea, and he was suddenly sick with nostalgia. He had no further business here among these mad and alien knights. As soon as he could take his dog on one more hunt into the Illinois prairie for game birds, he would pack his gear for the last time and go home to die.

Above the rumble of the car wheels the conductor was calling Tamaroa.

16

CHEER UP, COMRADES, THEY WILL COME

AUGUST TWENTY-FOURTH was a visitors' day at Camp Douglas, and Captain John Truscott was among the group of prisoners assembled in the compound when the gates opened to admit a company of women and men bringing small offerings of sundries and solace from the outer world. What Truscott wanted more than goods or kind words was reassurance that the secret day of liberation, August twenty-ninth, was still of real substance and had not been transformed into an illusion like all the others.

This time, Truscott had been very careful to keep the date secret from members of his squad and other Morgan prisoners who had come to look upon him as their leader. Yet somehow the Kentucky boys learned enough to connect the Democratic convention with a probable act of deliverance. More than once Otis Jordan questioned Truscott about the role the prisoners were to play in the assault, and what date and hour had been chosen, but Truscott was determined to keep Jordan completely in the dark.

Back in July, before the last shattering postponement, each barracks had been assigned definite actions to be carried out simultaneously or in sequence at the time of an outside attack, and in recent days Jordan twice had asked if his barracks was still expected to join Truscott's in an onslaught designed to breach the board fence with the momentum and force of their bodies. Because he had come to suspect that Jordan was an informer, bought by

< CONSPIRACY OF KNAVES >

the camp commandant, Truscott pretended he knew nothing about any forthcoming attack, and he had warned the sergeants in each barracks to reveal nothing to Jordan.

On the afternoon of the twenty-fourth, as the visitors entered the triangular compound, Truscott assumed an air of indifference toward them, concealing the relief he felt when the parrot-shaped figure of Mrs. Evelyn Ward, with her decorative basket, appeared in the entrance gate. While Mrs. Ward attracted her usual circle of acquisitive sergeants, Truscott casually examined a list of desiderata given him by Joe Stiles, his barracks mess sergeant. First he approached some of the other visitors, obtaining a few of the items on his list, and suggesting other needs to be brought on some future visiting day.

Truscott was well aware that Captain Spooner was usually somewhere in the compound on these occasions, observing any visitor who might communicate for any length of time with a single prisoner. Spooner watched Mrs. Ward and her attendants with special diligence. Sometimes Colonel Wright, the commandant himself, was there, and Otis Jordan was always strolling about, approaching any group that formed, listening rather than joining in the talk.

With studied unconcern Truscott made his way to the circle about Evelyn Ward, waiting his turn to hold up his list to her. "Ah, you need gloves, yes," she cried, although no gloves were listed, and she handed him a pair made from thick deerskin. She rubbed her plump fingers across her nose, covering the movements of her lips as she said: "Marianna Heywood sent the gloves from Kentucky. Her letter is behind the inside lining of the palm."

"I've written to Marianna several times," Truscott said, dropping the gloves into his gunnysack, "but no letters have come from her."

"She made the mistake of enclosing greenbacks and noting so in her letters," Evelyn Ward replied. She pretended to be addressing one of the sergeants standing to one side of Truscott. "Letters enclosing greenbacks now get no farther than the camp post office."

Truscott asked her if she had any large-sized socks. "Size the twenty-ninth," he whispered. She nodded and smiled, and began leading him toward the nearer sutler's store. "The sutler has ex-

< **Cheer Up, Comrades, They Will Come** >

cellent shoe blacking," she said loudly. "I will buy some for the boys on your list."

For a few seconds they were out of earshot of anyone else. "Major Heywood and Miss Belle Rutledge came to see me last night," she said, suppressing a childish giggle. "You are to be ready at nine o'clock Monday night, the twenty-ninth." While she continued talking rapidly, he tried to conceal his relief that the suspense was ended. "I was surprised that Major Heywood would risk a visit," she went on. "A government detective watches the front of our house night and day, but the major used Judge Ward's secret rear entrance, the carriage house and snow shed." She laughed softly. "Miss Belle said it was as exciting as a melodrama. She is an actress, you know."

"An actress? What else do you know about her?" Truscott asked quickly.

"She says she is a Kentuckian. She traveled from Richmond with Major Heywood." Evelyn Ward's tone was roguish, her bright eyes giving Truscott the impression that she was flirting with him.

"When you see her again," he said, "ask her if she has a brother. A dandified young man comes here to see the commandant. He could be her twin."

Evelyn Ward frowned, but her expression of alarm changed to delight. "I shall make discreet inquiries," she said in the exaggerated whisper of a conspirator. As she turned toward a small display of waxes and soaps on the sutler's counter, Otis Jordan appeared in the doorway, his oblique gaze shifting back and forth from Truscott to Mrs. Ward.

"What devilish scheme is being hatched here?" he demanded in the menacing tone of a bad stage actor. Evelyn Ward joined in his forced laughter, but Truscott was certain that there was a trace of uneasiness in the attitude of the buxom secret sharer. Perhaps for the first time she was beginning to realize that she had ventured beyond the limits of playacting and her puerile imagination.

As soon as the visitors were ordered out of the compound, Truscott returned to his barracks with the gunnysack of gifts, which, with the exception of the deerskin gloves, he turned over to Sergeant Stiles. From the inside palm of one of the gloves he removed the letter from Marianna Heywood.

< CONSPIRACY OF KNAVES >

The words were almost too small to read, penned upon both sides of paper so thin the ink had seeped through it, yet he was surprised by the warmth of her regard for him, her sympathy for his plight, expressions that came even before her announcement of the death of her mother, not entirely unexpected, but a blow that left her alone at Little Hundred. Perhaps she might now be inclined to travel to Chicago, she wrote. She knew from the letters of other Morgan prisoners that on certain days visitors to Camp Douglas were permitted. Although she had received Truscott's letters, she could tell from his recent complaints that he had received none of hers, and therefore she was attempting to reach him through a true-hearted Kentucky lady, Mrs. Evelyn Ward of Chicago.

Truscott immediately began writing a reply, beginning with condolences for the loss of her mother. He did not dare give any hints that he might no longer be a prisoner in Camp Douglas when she reached Chicago, but he urged her to read the newspapers to make certain the city was tranquil before traveling there. "I am not meant to be imprisoned in this pit of hell like a black knight in a castle keep," he wrote, "yet in a way I may have been put here for some divine purpose, if one can manage to think of dear Charley as being divine." He added no more about her cousin, hoping that she would grasp his meaning and know of his dark suspicions that Charley may have had a hand in the events at Tamaroa that led to his imprisonment in Camp Douglas.

On the following Sunday afternoon, Truscott was summoned from his barracks by Sergeant Beadle, the brawny Union noncommissioned officer who frequently brought orders and messages from Captain Spooner.

"Your cousin has permission to see you," the sergeant said without further explanation.

Although Truscott was aware of certain distant cousins in Kentucky, he had seen none of them since childhood, and he could not believe that any of them would come to visit him in prison. The visit must be a deception, he thought, and so it turned out to be. The "cousin" awaiting him in the headquarters visitors' room was George Stubblefield, no relation, but a former lieutenant of Truscott's battalion who had been captured during the Ohio raid and

< **Cheer Up, Comrades, They Will Come** >

later managed to escape to Canada. He had been sent by Major Heywood to bring a message to Truscott.

Nearby in the meeting room, Captain Spooner sat with his recently acquired mastiff, a fat smooth-coated dog with ugly lips and notched ears. The mastiff was an ill-tempered beast, especially in its attitude toward the prisoners.

For the benefit of Captain Spooner, who was closely observing them, they talked loudly about mythical relatives in Kentucky, of how Stubblefield had been sent to Chicago by the pro-Union Louisville *Journal* to expose the perfidy of the Democrats during their Copperhead convention, and whether or not Truscott should take an oath of loyalty and thus escape the ignominy of continued captivity in Camp Douglas.

During this false show, Stubblefield was able to let Truscott know through signs and double entendres and discreetly intermingled whispers of the message he brought from Charley Heywood. The message was devastating to Truscott. The uprising was delayed again. No assault against Camp Douglas was to come on the twenty-ninth. Stubblefield could give no reason for the delay other than it was somehow involved with the Democratic convention. As far as he knew, no later date of rescue had yet been chosen.

After the first moments of dismay, Truscott's emotions turned to anger. He did not have to pretend hostility toward Stubblefield in berating him for even suggesting that Truscott lead the Morgan prisoners into taking an oath of loyalty to their former enemies. Although Stubblefield was only playing a false role, and quite convincingly, to Truscott he represented a failed chivalry, another abandonment of brother knights by irresolute cavaliers led by Charles Heywood. Heywood and Stubblefield and the others might be free men, but they were vacillators who could not summon enough courage to storm the Castle of Darkness where truehearted knights awaited liberation.

As soon as he returned to his barracks—after angrily parting from George Stubblefield—he called his most trusted men together and informed them that rumors of rescue during the Democratic convention were false, and that any hope of deliverance from Camp Douglas lay entirely in their own hands. Previous efforts to escape by tunneling had been unsuccessful, he said, because of bad planning, or perhaps because of informers among fellow prisoners.

< CONSPIRACY OF KNAVES >

Their Union captors believed that by raising the barracks flooring they had made escape by tunneling impossible. Now the Kentucky boys must prove them wrong. A tunnel would be dug, but
until it was completed no one outside their barracks must know
of its existence. During his exhortation, Truscott was able to communicate some of his inner rage to his listeners, replacing their
dashed hopes with wills to action.

The main problem was finding a point of entry that would be
out of view of guards and inspecting officers at all times. Someone
suggested the dungeon—a bricked and barred series of small cells
installed halfway into the ground and used for punishment of offenses that included attempts to escape. Those few members of
Truscott's original squad who had spent any time in the dungeon
dissuaded the others from considering it as a tunnel entry. The
cells were cramped, usually contained only one prisoner at a time,
the distance to the parapet fence was too great, and there was no
place to conceal excavated earth.

A remark by Sam Baird, one of the men captured at Tamaroa,
was what set Truscott to thinking about the barracks chimney.
Early that summer their barracks had been supplied a Farmer's
Boiler, a patented cooking stove so designed that one or two men
could prepare meals for fifty or more. The boiler had been installed
partially within the hearth of the old fireplace so that its coal smoke
would vent through the chimney. Later in the summer, when the
barracks was raised with jackscrews, workmen cut away the fram-
ing around the chimney, and were so careless in replacing it that
they left cracks wide enough to admit rodents, insects, and drafts
of cold air.

When Sam Baird called the crevices to Truscott's attention,
the captain recognized that the hearth beneath the cooking device
might be large enough for a tunnel entry. That night, after sliding
the heavy boiler off the hearth, Truscott and Joe Stiles used a long-
blade knife that the cooks were allowed to keep among their utensils
and cut the mortar between the blackened bricks. They easily
removed about a dozen of them. Beneath these bricks was a foot-
deep layer of gravel and sand supported by rough slabs laid across
two walls of the hollow chimney base.

Dropping into the square below the slabs, Truscott found that
there was just enough space for him to kneel. Candlelight revealed

< **Cheer Up, Comrades, They Will Come** >

that the lower bricks had been mortared in such slapdash fashion that a tunnel could easily be started there.

Because measurements of depth and length were needed before digging could begin, they put everything back in place to await the following day. Truscott and the others realized that the nightly routine of moving and replacing the boiler would consume a considerable amount of time. The gravel between the layer of bricks and the slab had to be carefully set aside for reuse each time, and the seams between the bricks had to be refilled with soot and sand. Yet the men's morale had never been higher; their hopes were restored after another bitter disappointment.

Next morning Truscott made estimates of the distance between the chimney and the board fence, and the depth necessary to avoid the cave-ins that had defeated several efforts of prisoners in other barracks. He also asked Sergeant Stiles and two additional men to make their own independent estimates. They all knew that the eighteen-inch-high deadline railing was ten feet inside the parapet wall. By covertly walking off the distance from the deadline to their barracks, by counting the layers of bricks visible in the chimney base beneath the building, and by careful directional conjecture, the four men reached a fairly close consensus of distances and depths.

That night they began digging what they estimated would be a forty-foot-long burrow that would bring them out four or five paces beyond the parapet. Because the soil was of a soft sandy loam, the work went rapidly, yet for the same reason the need for wooden supports quickly became evident. Barrels proved to be the best source of wood, and were not difficult to obtain. Flour, vinegar, and other rations were issued in these containers to the mess sergeants of each barracks by the U.S. Army's subsistence department. The barracks garbage details were responsible for removing empty barrels to a collection yard, where wagons came regularly to carry them away. Truscott and his resourceful Morgan men quietly began appropriating barrels from all the barracks in their area. They also filched a few boards left in and under the buildings by roofers and the jackscrew workmen.

Using buckets and spittoons for digging tools, the teams of diggers brought out so much earth every night that they were hard put to find places to distribute or conceal it. Handfuls were scat-

< CONSPIRACY OF KNAVES >

tered beneath the barracks, some was mixed with discarded kitchen wastes, and considerable quantities were carried to the toilet sinks every time the men went to relieve themselves. As the tunnel lengthened, they fashioned ropes from worn clothing and blankets, using them to pull baking pans filled with excavated dirt from the diggers to the base of the chimney.

Another problem was an insufficiency of air. At first, Truscott gave the men assigned to the chimney base a wide-brimmed hat to fan air into the tunnel, but this did not provide enough oxygen. Diggers fainted or fell suddenly ill with cramps, and so they began using candles to give them early warnings of failure of air supply. When the candles stopped burning, the men inside emerged as quickly as possible.

These delays were extremely frustrating, however, and eventually the ingenious Sergeant Stiles sacrificed his highly prized India rubber blanket—a gift from Mrs. Evelyn Ward—by stretching it over a wooden frame and using it like a Hindu punkah to keep large quantities of air moving into the tunnel.

By the end of the first week everything was going so well that the men began figuring rates of progress and counting days to freedom. When they reached a point about halfway between the deadline railing and the main wall, however, trouble abruptly beset them. Sam Baird had just crawled forward to replace Frank Barfield when a clump of sandy earth fell on his back, almost burying him, and extinguished the candle behind him. Baird pulled himself free and jerked on the rope to signal for help. Sergeant Stiles immediately crawled to his aid, bringing a fresh candle. As soon as the fallen earth was leveled away, the candlelight revealed a water pipe running across the cave-in. Above the pipe, the roots of grass sod were plainly visible.

Digging was stopped immediately and barrel staves were brought forward to shore up the cavity. After taking a close look at the near disaster, Truscott decided they had better wait until the ground surface above the tunnel could be examined by daylight. Their best hope, he told the men, was probably to change the direction of the tunnel.

Walking along the edge of the deadline railing next morning, Truscott was dismayed by what he saw. Earlier in the summer a pipe had been laid into Camp Douglas to bring water from Lake

< **Cheer Up, Comrades, They Will Come** >

Michigan to a faucet for drinking and to a wooden trough for washing clothes and bathing. The ditch for the pipe had been refilled with earth dug from it and then covered with clumps of sod. Gravity and summer rains had left a slight depression above the pipe all the way across the prison yard, but there was now a deeper hollow two or three feet long just about where the tunnel ended. Truscott was hopeful that none of the guards or inspecting officers would notice the concavity during the day, and apparently none did.

That night he sent alternate teams into the tunnel with all the wood scraps they could collect, and they worked at shoring up the sagging earth until almost time for the reveille bugle. Soon after dawn, however, their luck abandoned them. Rain began as small showers, mild precursors of a line of violent thunderstorms that swept down the edge of Lake Michigan to flood Camp Douglas with wind-driven sheets of water. All the prisoners took cover in their barracks, and the guards were permitted to stand in their small shelters on the parapets. Yet even while the storm was passing, with scattered raindrops still falling, the Morgan men in their barracks became aware of some excitement outside, of shouts coming from the parapet.

Through the nearest rain-streaked window, Truscott saw Captain Spooner, accompanied by his fat mastiff, striding across the muddy yard toward the deadline railing. He was pointing toward a large hole in the ground between him and the parapet wall. Truscott immediately guessed what had happened, and when he looked at the faces of his men, he knew that they too perceived the calamity. Water from the storm had flowed along the depression where the buried pipe lay, collapsing the thin layer of earth left above the end of the tunnel and flooding the entire excavation.

Captain Spooner, his ugly dog, and his retinue of sergeants and guards had little difficulty in tracing the tunnel to the Morgan men's barracks. Nor did Spooner waste any time before marching them out into the slackening rain across the prison yard and through the gate to the camp's parade ground.

"Any Rebel who falls out of formation will be fired upon," Spooner curtly announced in a loud voice, and then he turned his back on them and strolled casually away toward the headquarters building. Surrounded by successive platoons of Union soldiers, the

< CONSPIRACY OF KNAVES >

prisoners were held at attention under the clearing sky for what Truscott later estimated to be more than three hours.

Late in the afternoon the first prisoner collapsed, and at a crisp order from a lieutenant the guards fired randomly into the formation, wounding three men in their legs. They fell upon the ground, one of them moaning in pain. The sound of firing brought Captain Spooner and Commandant Wright out of the headquarters building. They appeared to be unhurried, indifferent to what had just taken place on the parade ground. Colonel Wright climbed upon the review platform and in his thin voice called upon the leaders of the escape attempt to step forward from the ranks. No one moved. The commandant then ordered the guard lieutenant to choose six prisoners at random. These men were brought to the reviewing stand, where their thumbs were tied with rawhide laces; they were then suspended by their thumbs from a railing, their feet dangling several inches above the ground.

By this time an ambulance wagon had arrived on the scene to remove the wounded men to the hospital. Colonel Wright now struck a self-important pose and addressed the prisoners.

"Captivity is one of the incidents of war," he declared, "and a prisoner has the right to escape if he can, taking the risks and consequences. Although it is your right to escape, it is my duty to keep you. Prisoners making an attempt to escape will be punished either by being shot by the guards in the act or by a subsequent order of mine."

Truscott, who was standing at one end of the first rank, was aware throughout Colonel Wright's brief speech that the commandant was staring directly at him, and was in this fashion blaming him for the afflictions that were being brought down upon every prisoner in the barracks. Truscott was also aware that not one of the Morgan men would bear any rancor toward him for the pains of punishment that they must now face—long days in the dungeon, reduction of food allowances, bans against talking, riding the wooden horse—whatever petty or monstrous torments that Colonel Wright and Captain Spooner might devise.

Truscott's punishment was to be balled and chained and put to work with some of the enlisted men of his old command. For several days they were kept busy at loading carts with dirt that was used

< **Cheer Up, Comrades, They Will Come** >

to fill the collapsed tunnel. The iron balls that slowed their movements weighed about fifty pounds and were fastened by five-foot chains to one ankle. Although ignominious, this punishment was not as painful as some of the others. Even so, it was not pain that most distressed the Morgan men; it was the frustration of failure.

And then, added to Captain Spooner's cruelties, came an even greater blow from outside Camp Douglas.

In a pro-Union newspaper that someone in an adjoining barracks had purchased from a sutler was a brief report of the death of General John Morgan. The paper was passed around among the Morgan prisoners, but not one of them accepted the news as being factual. To most of them John Morgan was immortal. They had heard reports of his death many times before, even read them in Southern newspapers, and they knew that some Northern editors delighted in publishing accounts of the death of the feared and hated Morgan the raider, yet never bothered to deny them when events proved the rumors false.

A few days later, however, a clipping from the Chicago *Times* was smuggled into Camp Douglas. It stated that General John Hunt Morgan was killed at Greeneville, Tennessee, in a surprise attack. Because the *Times* was a Democratic paper, dubbed by its enemies a Copperhead sheet, the Morgan men feared the worst.

This ominous report, combined with the failure of the tunnel, spread desolation among the Kentuckians. For Truscott, all purpose seemed to drain into nothingness.

Jesu mercy, said the king, where are all my noble knights become? Alas that ever I should see this doleful day, for now, said Arthur, I am come to mine end.

That night Truscott dreamed of the dying king, whose face was the face of John Morgan, of the sword Excalibur tossed into the waters where an arm and a hand caught and three times brandished the weapon, of black-hooded ladies weeping upon a barge that took the king away.

For days the bereft captives moved about the yard and barracks like drugged beings, performing the numbing tasks of punishment, swallowing the sparse and tasteless food issued them by Captain Spooner, hating the slow passage of time by day that kept them from the oblivion of sleep by night. Truscott suffered anguish each time he looked into their ashen faces, their eyes staring blankly

< CONSPIRACY OF KNAVES >

back at him. He was reminded of an attestation he had read in a book by Mr. Nathaniel Hawthorne, and he kept searching his mind for the words, something about the black flower of civilized society being a prison.

Just at daybreak one morning a young Tennessean of Morgan's Fourth Cavalry (he had been captured at Cynthiana) sprang naked from his bunk and began pacing up and down the barracks, chanting: "I see Jesus, I see Jesus!" Suddenly he pushed a door open and ran into the empty yard. A bright calcium light was still burning on the wall facing the deadline railing. "There's Jesus!" he cried. "I see his light." He leaped over the forbidden deadline, grabbed at the lamp and its reflector, tearing them loose, and then, holding them in his arms, turned triumphantly to race back toward his barracks. "Glory! glory! I have Jesus!" he shouted as a guard on the parapet fired down upon him. The bullet smashed into the light and the young Tennessean's hand; he sat weeping while his barracks mates gathered around, waiting for the guards to come and take him to the dungeon.

In those dark days, physical illnesses also began striking the hardiest of the Morgan men. Until now, few of them had suffered even a bad cold. Chills and fevers, dysentery, and then that most dreaded of all afflictions—smallpox—carried them off to the hospital by the dozens.

Jesu mercy, where are all my noble knights become, Truscott asked himself when he was informed of deaths by smallpox of two of the nine men who had been captured with him at Tamaroa. He felt a sense of guilt because he had lost the ability to feel grief for them individually; instead, he felt numb in the presence of constantly recurring death. Were the alligator horses all doomed to dust in that dismal castle keep beside Lake Michigan?

Weeks later, looking back on that dreadful time, Truscott decided that two small incidents brought a change, a slow uplifting of spirits that gradually pulled them back from the depths of despair.

One day a rumor spread that General Basil Duke had been exchanged from a prison camp somewhere in the East and had rejoined Morgan's cavalry in Virginia to take command. Duke was the Launcelot of Morgan's Table Round, and when the rumor was confirmed as fact by letters and finally by newspapers, the prisoners

< **Cheer Up, Comrades, They Will Come** >

began to hope again. (Could they have known that Morgan's once mighty force was now reduced to less than three hundred poorly mounted and scantily supplied horsemen, their expectations would surely have been dashed.)

The second small incident occurred on the first visitors' day that Truscott was permitted to attend—after the gradual fading away of Captain Spooner's period of punishment. A mild-mannered clergyman unexpectedly presented Truscott with a leather football.

"You have a puny pale gosling look," the cleric said with a smile. "I prescribe hard play with this ball." And then he added *sotto voce*: "You must all be ready on election eve."

From other sources came rumors of a rescue attempt planned for the hours preceding the presidential election, the night of November seventh. Truscott silently resolved to put no credence in the rumor, but he did not discourage the hopes of the others. He also persuaded most of them to join in rough play with the football, and in other outdoor games. Within a few days illnesses slowly began to decline; the men resumed washing their clothing and bathed more frequently; they voluntarily visited the barber in a neighboring barracks to have their frowzy hair shorn.

This communal determination to survive did not go unnoticed by their captors. Fearing another attempt at a breakout by the regenerated Morgan men, Colonel Wright decided to clothe these prisoners so that if any did succeed in escaping, they could easily be recognized outside the walls.

At roll call one frosty morning, they were ordered to remove all their outer clothing. To replace these variegated garments they were given trousers made of a coarse pepper-and-salt cottonade, and black coats cut with long spade tails and tight waists and made of the same cheap material. Not only did the wearers appear ridiculous in this uniform garb, and conspicuous even to the most casual of observers, but the porous cloth seemed meant to discourage anyone from venturing outside into the cold autumn winds of Chicago.

About this same time the first reports of ill treatment of captured Union soldiers in Confederate prison camps began to appear in Northern newspapers. After an exchange of disabled prisoners, three Union soldiers who had been confined at Andersonville, Georgia, arrived in Washington and immediately went to see President

< CONSPIRACY OF KNAVES >

Lincoln to tell him of their sufferings. Some parts of their story, according to the newspaper that circulated in Camp Douglas, were "too revolting for publication."

In the same way in which combat soldiers view the courage of their enemy counterparts, the prisoners of Camp Douglas sympathized with the unfortunate captives of Andersonville—their lack of shelter of any kind, their starvation rations, scanty clothing, shortages of medicines, the mind-killing boredom and physical torment that led some to seek death by leaping across the deadline railing into a fusillade of fire from their brutal guards.

Those words of Hawthorne's kept coming back to Johnny Truscott, the aphorism about a prison being the black flower of civilized society. Conditions were far worse in Andersonville, he acknowledged, but imprisonment anywhere was but a matter of degree. He remembered the Tennessean whose endurance had snapped from forced confinement and who in order to escape its unbearable burden convinced himself that he saw Jesus. At Camp Douglas, preservation of minds and bodies was not easy, but he had come to believe again that survival was possible.

He reckoned without the growing spitefulness of Captain Spooner and Commandant Wright, however. Neither man had known combat or suffered imprisonment, but their insular imaginations were so inflamed by what they heard and read of Andersonville that they decided the Confederate prisoners must suffer correspondingly with their Union counterparts in the South. Consequently rations were reduced to match those at Andersonville—eight ounces of corn bread and two ounces of pork per day, supplemented by two tablespoonsful of beans and two tablespoonsful of molasses twice a week. Most of the cooking and dining utensils were removed from each barracks. Prisoners were allowed to write only one letter per week on a single small sheet of paper. Incoming letters were released to addressees only after payment of ten cents in coin or sutlers' checks. Visitors' day was abolished, ending the prisoners' personal contact with the outside world and any possibility of receiving additional rations and clothing.

At roll call one morning, Commandant Wright made one of his rare visits to the prisoners' quarters. He came to announce a forthcoming inspection by General Joseph Hooker. At the sound of Hooker's name, a subdued chorus of jeers came from the prisoners' ranks, so infuriating Colonel Wright that he threatened to send an entire platoon to the dungeon if the noise was repeated.

A thorough cleanup of barracks and yards must be completed in twenty-four hours, Wright declared. All recreation activities, outdoors and indoors, were forbidden until after Hooker's visit.

Most of the prisoners were aware that Joseph Hooker had been a failure as a Union battlefield commander, and were mystified as to how he obtained his sobriquet of "Fighting Joe," especially after General Lee so soundly defeated him at Chancellorsville with an army that was outnumbered two to one. Nevertheless, Hooker was at least a veteran of combat, and Johnny Truscott and some of the others saw in his inspection tour an opportunity to expose to higher authority the unnecessarily harsh treatment that was being meted out to them by Commandant Bartholomew Wright.

Using the grapevine system by which the mess sergeants of each barracks communicated with each other, the prisoners quickly devised a plan to inform General Hooker of their grievances. If Hooker followed the procedure of previous inspecting officers, he would visit at least one or two barracks at random. Each barracks therefore was prepared with a spokesman and a list of injustices in writing that was to be handed to Fighting Joe. At the top of the list was the daily ration, so wretched that the number of hospital cases was beginning to rise again.

On the day of inspection, General Hooker was late in arriving at Camp Douglas, and the first notice the prisoners had of his presence was a thirteen-gun salute about three o'clock in the afternoon. This was followed by band music and the rhythmic sounds of marching troops on the parade ground, followed by distant echoes of oratory.

While these routines were proceeding, Captain Spooner, accompanied by his grim-visaged mastiff and several Union sergeants, entered the prisoners' yard. The sergeants ordered the prisoners out of their barracks and formed them into two continuous lines facing each other across the long yard. Captain Spooner took a position at one end of the parallel ranks, his dog squatting at his feet.

With a roll of drums, the arched gate into the prisoners' compound opened to admit a procession of vehicles. The first three coaches, with their tops down, were filled with armed soldiers;

< CONSPIRACY OF KNAVES >

these were followed by several carriages occupied by Hooker's high-ranking staff, and then at the end came a barouche drawn by two white horses. Commandant Wright and Fighting Joe occupied facing seats, both men smartly uniformed and affecting expressions almost as grim as Captain Spooner's mastiff. Hooker wore a kepi instead of a hat over his curly sandy hair, and his eyes were those of a burned-out man.

Truscott watched the procession turn into the farthest lane between the rows of barracks. He hoped that when Hooker ordered a halt he would ask for a prisoner spokesman. The carriages continued their winding course up and down the narrow passageways that separated the barracks. When this rapid convolution was completed, the vehicles formed again into a straight cavalcade between the facing ranks of prisoners, and then at a command from Captain Spooner they began rolling toward the exit gate. As soon as it became evident that General Hooker was not going to give them an opportunity to declare their grievances, several protesting shouts came from the ranks of prisoners. These were followed by loud hoots all along the lines.

"Bread and meat!" someone cried, and this was repeated in a unison of voices: "Give us bread and meat! Bread and meat!" In spite of angry commands from Captain Spooner to desist, the chanting continued until Hooker's barouche vanished through the exit gate.

For half an hour more, Captain Spooner kept the prisoners standing stiffly at attention, waiting for Commandant Wright to return and mete out a proper punishment to the incorrigible Rebels.

As soon as the formalities of General Hooker's departure from Camp Douglas were concluded, Colonel Wright returned, this time on horseback. Although Kentucky-born, Bartholomew Wright was an inept horseman. When he raised his arms to shake them in rage at these captives he believed had all but shattered his hopes of becoming a brigadier, the reins in his hands jerked at the bit in his mount's mouth, causing the animal to jump and almost unseat its overwrought rider. The commandant's face turned from pink to crimson in his wrath. The prisoners—weary from standing so long at attention and from listening to the commandant's tirade—resumed their chanting: "More bread! More meat! More bread!"

< **Cheer Up, Comrades, They Will Come** >

This was almost too much for Colonel Wright to bear. He jerked hard on the reins; the horse reared and would surely have thrown him from the saddle had not an alert Union sergeant leaped forward to grasp the halter and calm the animal.

"Captain!" the commandant shouted at Spooner. "You will stop all rations to the prisoners until further notice!" His mustache quivering, his flat nose twitching, the colonel glared at the sergeant who had saved him from a fall.

"Release my mount, sergeant," he cried in his high voice, "and step out of my way."

He turned the horse and with what remained of his dignity of rank trotted away through the wide gate.

Captain Spooner may have feared for his safety, with only a dozen sergeants and his pudgy mastiff to protect him from the hundreds of angry prisoners muttering threats. He hurriedly ordered the sergeants to dismiss them, and in the confusion of commands and movements, Spooner became separated from his dog. Evidently believing the mastiff had preceded him through the gate, Spooner waited until the last of the sergeants passed him and then ordered it closed and locked.

Less than an hour later, as autumn twilight fell over Camp Douglas, Captain Spooner returned with two platoons of heavily armed guards and made a thorough search of the yard and barracks for his missing dog. No trace could be found of the mastiff.

Next morning the camp's carpenters brought in several pieces of lumber, and by noon had erected a bulletin board beneath the eaves of the center barracks. Shortly afterward Sergeant Beadle posted two notices upon the board. One was a lined foolscap sheet with a brief statement at the top announcing that prisoners willing to take an oath of allegiance to the United States should place their names on the paper. All who did so would be transferred from the prisoner compound to barracks in White Oak Square, where they would receive full rations of the U.S. Army. The notice was signed "Bartholomew Wright, Colonel Commanding."

The second notice on the board, written with a wide-flowing pen in very black ink, described Captain Spooner's missing mastiff, and offered a reward of ten dollars for the dog's safe return.

Later that day, in the quietness of a waning afternoon, messages went out over the grapevine inviting all prisoners to partake of a delicious stew that had been secretly prepared in a certain barracks.

Just after sundown of that same day, moments before the tattoo drum signaled everyone inside, an anonymous prisoner scrawled a couplet on the bulletin board beneath Captain Spooner's notice of his missing mastiff:

> For want of meat
> That dog was eat.

Not long before midnight the men in the barracks where the dog had been stewed began digging a tunnel beneath the coal box beside their kitchen steps. Truscott became aware of this activity from Otis Jordan, who had somehow learned about the venture. Five days later, when the tunnel entry was "accidentally" discovered by Captain Spooner, Truscott was not surprised. And when Spooner commenced his ruthless punishments for the men in that barracks, Truscott was not surprised to learn that the prisoner Otis Jordan was being transferred to White Oak Square for duty as a hospital orderly.

17

BELLE RUTLEDGE

WHEN I WAS A very young girl in Louisville, one of my mother's brothers drove us in a buggy to a place on the Rolling Fork that they called a "country seat." It was owned, as I recall, by a friend of my uncle's. What impressed me was the immensity of the building, which was constructed of huge logs and wide ax-hewn planking. The main room was enormous, with a massive dining table beneath a high vaulted ceiling, and a fireplace large enough to hold a freight wagon.

Upon first entering Alonzo Colquett's house at Barton Farm outside Tamaroa in Illinois, I was reminded of that long-forgotten country seat of my childhood. Everything about the horse trader's place was larger than ordinary, and if you recall John Truscott's description of Colquett in an earlier chapter, he himself was considerably overfleshed.

Colonel Eberhart remarked that Barton Farm reminded him of a hunting lodge he had known in Scotland, and in keeping with the memory he took a Scottish shawl from his trunk to cover his shoulders, and sat with his hound beside the fireplace warming his old war wounds.

Our host, Mr. Colquett, assured us that the evening was unseasonably chilly for late summer but that the next day was bound to be a fine mild one for hunting prairie chickens.

On that first evening, the big commons room was fairly well

< CONSPIRACY OF KNAVES >

filled with men—Charley and his ten devoted Kentuckians, Colonel Eberhart, Brigadier Colquett, and four or five Missourians who dealt in livestock. Some were lounging at the roughhewn table, where we had enjoyed a supper of venison; some were in chairs; some were standing or kneeling, or stretched prone before the fireplace. Except for a Dutch woman, who with her husband served the supper, I was the only female in that spacious house. Feeling quite unnecessary, I chose a shadowy little niche near the fireplace where neither firelight nor candlelight would illuminate my presence, and I resigned myself to a frizzle-frazzle of coarse masculine talk until bedtime.

The Dutch woman brought in an earthenware demijohn of whiskey with a tray of glasses, and drinking and smoking soon began. Charley gave me a tumbler of the liquor, warning me in a whisper of its fiery potency. I managed to lap a few drops with my tongue—the way a young kitten tentatively tests cold milk—but to me that Missouri pinetop whiskey was abominable.

"A toast to our lost leader, General John Morgan!" someone called out, and Charley promptly leaped upon the big table and eulogized his dead commander in that mixture of lightheartedness and whole-soul devotion that is so characteristic of him, that stamps him as being Charley Heywood. Most of the other Morgan men followed with pale imitations of Charley's testimony, some of the younger ones closing their little speeches with broken voices and teary eyes. At the end, Colonel Eberhart saluted General Morgan with a very British tribute filled with poetic references. When he tipped his head back to swallow the Missouri whiskey, he involuntarily choked, turned and spewed the liquor into the fireplace, and then tossed his half-filled glass against the andirons, smashing it to bits and creating a momentary flare as the flames enveloped the liquid fire.

Colquett whirled around from his standing position at the other end of the mantelpiece, his bulging eyes filled with alarm and unconcealed anger.

"My apologies, brigadier," Eberhart said with a jerking, almost mocking, bow of his head. "I was quite carried away. Custom of my lancers regiment, don't you know. The glass in the fire."

Colquett said nothing, and Charley seized the moment of awkward silence to bring up the subject of Copperheads, their numbers

in southern Illinois, and their availability for service in an attempt
to seize Chicago on the eve of the presidential elections in November. I had heard variations of that discussion dozens of times before. This one began with an assertion from Colquett that an army
of fifty thousand men could be assembled in southern Illinois on
twenty-four hours' notice provided the leaders were supplied with
so many thousands of dollars to purchase arms. Transporting them
into Chicago was another problem that would require many more
thousands of dollars—preferably in gold, Colquett suggested. From
there the argument moved inevitably into a dispute between Charley and most of the others over the question of whether greater
efforts should be aimed at creating a Northwestern Confederacy,
or at freeing the prisoners in Camp Douglas. I had heard this
argument at least a hundred times.

"If the prisoners are freed and armed, they can capture Chicago," Charley said. "If the Sons of Liberty in the states around
us act in concert, we can end the war in one stroke."

Only once did Colonel Eberhart enter into the debate. "First
on the program should be the deliverance of those poor devils in
Camp Douglas," he said. "They are expiring in soul and body, and
are in no condition to do battle. I have seen the prisoners quite
recently, and aside from Miss Rutledge here, I daresay that no one
else in this room has had that unhappy experience."

Brigadier Colquett turned to search me out in my shadowy
corner. He pulled his long graying beard away from his lips, kneeled
slightly, and spat a mouthful of tobacco juice into the fireplace.

"And what does Miss Rutledge have to say about the condition
of the prisoners?" he asked, with a trace of a sneer in his voice.

"As the colonel says," I replied, "they're used up."

I regretted that Eberhart had drawn me into the limelight. I
was only a very minor performer in this drama of Charley Heywood's, and I could feel his displeasure that I had crossed him
downstage.

"The freed prisoners must be brought out of Chicago and headed
south as quickly as possible," Eberhart said. "They need time for
restitution."

"We're not driving two thousand horses into the countryside
around Chicago," Charley retorted. "As mad as Joseph Milligan
is, I must agree with him that such a plan is impractical."

"Not driven to the Chicago countryside, Major Heywood," Eberhart said soothingly, "but staggered in pens disguised as horse auction yards all the way from Chicago to the Ohio River. A sort of underground railroad in reverse, don't you see?"

This argument I also had heard scores of times before. I was growing weary of the talk, talk, talk, and quite dizzy from whiskey fumes and tobacco smoke in the room. I was pleased, therefore, to hear Colonel Eberhart announce bluntly that he must have some rest before tomorrow's hunt. I added my voice to his, and three of the Missourians joined us. Charley and the other Morgan men, however, appeared to be eager to talk, drink, and smoke well into the midnight hours.

Colquett summoned the Dutch woman, and she showed us to our separate quarters. "We're pleased to have a handsome young woman such as yourself, miss," she said to me in a very broken accent, pronouncing her *w*'s like *v*'s. "Women so seldom come to Barton Farm. We hope you will tarry with us, miss."

Evidently I was not to share a bed with Charley. My room was quite ample, although sparsely furnished. A pair of narrow haircloth couches faced each other from opposite walls, and there was only one chair, a handmade hickory rocker.

I was awakened, just before dawn I think, by a frantic rustling. Every time I would drift almost to sleep again, the rustling would resume, until at last I lighted my candle and was startled to see several field mice dancing across the rough flooring. I started to toss my shoes at them, but then, realizing they had come in through a floor crack to escape the chilly night and had no intention of harming me, I left them alone.

A mauve light from my window and the sound of horses snorting and stamping awakened me the second time. Through the dusty panes I looked out upon a purely masculine scene, a score of sobering huntsmen checking their saddles and their guns, coughing and spitting, and muttering in subdued monosyllables. I dressed hurriedly and went out on the porch to bid them good-bye.

Just as I stepped into the lovely autumnlike morning, with thin mists drifting away toward the woods across the road, Colonel Eberhart, clad in his regimental uniform and leading a horse and his hound, appeared from the stables. He looked twenty years

< **Belle Rutledge** >

younger, his dark eyes sparkling, cheeks rosy above his white side-whiskers. He saluted me with a hearty good morning and his English nobleman's twirling wave of greeting, and then Charley strode over to the porch to clasp my hands in his.

"You won't be lonely, Belle?" he asked anxiously. His eyes were bloodshot, but the old magic was still in them. "I missed you last night," he whispered.

"Yes," I said.

"We'll come back by sundown," he assured me and then turned to rejoin the others.

In a few minutes the hunting party was mounted, and at a forward command from Alonzo Colquett they formed into a file and started off. Colonel Eberhart turned in his saddle to face me, his teeth showing in a glorious smile of expectation. "The huntsman winds his horn," he shouted, "and a-hunting we will go!"

Good Lord, I suppose that's the male substitute for war, hunting, but to me it's a war on the defenseless, and besides on that day there was more serious hunting to be found in Virginia and Georgia, if any of them had an inclination to go to the killing grounds.

By noontime a warm breeze, very strong and boisterous from the south, was driving away the late summer chill, and I sat quite comfortably on the north porch reading a copy of *Blackwood's Magazine* that Colonel Eberhart had purchased in Chicago and kindly lent to me. I was deep into a story of romantic adventure when a horse and buggy appeared on the road from Tamaroa. The vehicle stopped at the gate, and I could see the driver motioning toward the house and then turning to speak to a young woman beside him.

A moment later she stepped down from the buggy and started toward the closed gate. She was dressed like a picture in *Godey's Lady's Book,* wearing as wide a hoopskirt as I'd ever seen, and a stylish green bonnet with a large black feather atop her flaxen curls. To keep the bonnet from flying away on the blustery Illinois wind, she paused at the gate long enough to tie its laces tightly beneath her chin.

Scarcely had she shut the gate behind her and started along the sandy pathway toward the house when a violent gust spun dust devils across the open enclosure. A whirl of wind tugged at her skirt and swept beneath it to balloon and lift cloth and hoops to the height of her raised arms, which she flailed like wings until the skirt was forced back down to a level of modesty. She did possess beautiful underclothing—pantalets with a multitude of ruffles—but she knew that the ruddy-faced man on the buggy seat had got an eyeful of her bottom, and there was I on the porch pressing both hands against my mouth to smother an uncontrollable burst of laughter.

She came marching on up the pathway, blushing like a proper Southern belle, until we could see the whites of each other's eyes.

"Is Major Charles Heywood here?" she asked boldly.

"Not at present," I replied.

"He *is* a guest here? This *is* Barton Farm, is it not?"

The wind kept flapping the black feather on her bonnet down over her beautiful eyes. In her wide hoopskirt, which concealed her feet, she appeared to be gliding as she walked to the bottom of the porch steps.

"Yes," I said, "this is Barton Farm and Major Heywood is staying here. He is with a hunting party."

She smiled, forced I'm sure. Southern belles use artificial smiles as a part of their arsenals.

Lifting her skirt daintily, she managed to ascend the steps, so that I could now clearly see the lineaments of her face, her translucent skin with its faint showering of faded freckles, the shape of her forehead—a feminine version of a man's face I had come to know as well as my own—so that there was no surprise for me when she told me her name. "I'm Major Heywood's cousin. Marianna Heywood."

"I'm Belle Rutledge," I replied, and her violet eyes opened wide in mild astonishment. A brief interval of silence followed while she studied me somewhat in the manner of a cat that comes unexpectedly upon a member of its own species and is not quite sure what reaction may ensue. She turned around then to wave and call to the man in the buggy, ordering him to bring her baggage on to the house.

The sounds of Marianna Heywood's arrival brought the Dutch woman out upon the porch, and it soon became evident that there had been no forewarning of the Southern belle's coming to the

< **Belle Rutledge** >

Barton Farm. "My brother sent me," was all that she had to say about it to the Dutch woman or me.

After mumbling a few words to herself in her native language, the Dutch woman put Marianna into my room, to share one of the haircloth couches. Every other bedroom in the big house was occupied.

We spent most of the afternoon together on the front porch, talking at first about the weather, both of us agreeing that it had turned out to be a delicious day, and then we parried a bit while she tried to discover why I was at Barton Farm and how close my relationship was with Charley. I was in no mood to talk or listen to talk, but Marianna—like most people who have traveled alone for several hours with no one to converse with—was as garrulous as a prowling raven, running through a range of recent experiences, describing her grief over the death of her mother, and then confessing to a guilty feeling because of the release that gradually had come over her, leaving her with a sensation of freedom for the first time since irresponsible childhood.

"I feel as if I know you, Miss Belle," she said, and then babbled on about a long wait she was forced to endure in the Louisville railroad station because a train of cars was being loaded with young Union soldiers going south. She then circled around to repeat that she was quite aware of my existence, explaining that her lifelong friend, Captain Truscott, and her newfound friend, Mrs. Evelyn Ward, both had mentioned my name in letters to her.

"It's odd that Cousin Charley has never put a word about you in his letters," she said, staring at me with her violet eyes and then slowly lowering her long lashes. I suspected that those dark lashes, contrasting with her golden hair, might drive a susceptible male into quite a passion.

She added: "But then Cousin Charley does not write me as often as he should."

"Major Heywood and I are colleagues," I said. "He must have told you of his duties."

"No," she replied firmly. "Charley is most mysterious about his comings and goings."

"That is because of the nature of what he must do," I offered.

She gave me one of her spurious smiles. "How long have you known him?" she asked.

I could have told her the exact date of my first meeting with Charley Heywood, but I feigned indifference, and murmured something about late spring or early summer. Richmond headquarters, I explained, had given the major and me correlated duties that required us to meet occasionally and compare information. At the moment, I told her, I was awaiting further orders, and did not expect to remain for long at Barton Farm. (As spies and secret lovers must, I was inventing as I went along, and did not dream how close I had come to the mark with that last fabrication.)

"You have visited my dear friend, John Truscott, in that terrible prison," she continued. "Is he in good health?"

"None of the prisoners are hale and hearty," I replied sarcastically, "but Captain Truscott appeared to be well when I saw him earlier in the summer."

Marianna looked across toward the green wood, where a few leaves were turning various shades of russet. "When you saw Johnny, did he speak of Cousin Charley—Major Heywood?"

"Yes, he asked me to urge Major Heywood to hasten liberation of the prisoners. 'Tell Charley to quit dallying' is the way he said it."

"He put no blame on Charley for his being in prison?"

"Not to me."

The day was growing late and the wind had shifted to the west, chilling the air.

"Johnny implied such in one of his letters," Marianna said. She shivered slightly. "Mrs. Ward also wrote me that he had spoken to her about the reasons for his imprisonment. He believes he was captured because of a betrayal by someone." She forced an artificial laugh.

"I'm freezing," she said through clenched teeth. "I must get a wrap."

When the hunting party returned, we were both waiting on the porch in an amber twilight. I was wearing my comfortable old gray shawl; Marianna's shoulders were covered with what appeared to be a spanking-new blue cape, hooded and tasseled and expensively lined with silk.

Charley saw us from the road, and instead of riding on to the stable with the others, he brought his horse right up to the porch, and was in the act of dismounting when he recognized Marianna. Until that last moment his eyes had been on me.

"My God! Marianna!" he cried, almost stumbling from the stirrup. He bounded up the steps, brought himself as close to his cousin as her hoops would permit, and kissed her full upon her rosebud mouth. It was as luscious a kiss as any he had ever given me in the fullness of mutual passions, and I could tell from the quiver of her throat that she relished it as much as he.

"What brings you here?" Charley demanded. He was still holding her shoulders, and I could see a Heywood madness burning in the eyes of both cousins. "And all this finery you're wearing. You wrote me that if I didn't get the war ended, you would be reduced to wearing rags. You look as if you'd found a bandbox of riches."

"Fiddlesticks!" she said, and leaned forward to give him a quick kiss. "When Wesley told me I had to come up here to Illinois in his place, I simply let him know I could not come naked in rags. So he found the greenbacks for me to buy a few things in Louisville."

Her voice softened as she spoke to Charley, never taking her eyes from him; the sound was almost like the cooing of a dove. His hands caressed her shoulders and I recalled how during those lonely times in Windsor, Colonel Eberhart had done much the same for me, telling me to think of myself as a ruffled dove and that he was smoothing down my feathers.

"Why did Wesley not come?" Charley asked with sudden severity.

She pulled some papers from the inside of her cape, handing them to him. "Wesley's message is in the sealed envelope. The broadside explains why he did not come. They're posted all over Kentucky. He's frightened to death, Charley. He was afraid to go into Louisville with me."

The heavy paper of the poster crackled as Charley unfolded it. " 'Two thousand dollars reward for the capture of any of these men,' " he read aloud. "Good God, Wesley's listed as a murderer! At Mayfield?"

He stared at her, stern-faced, and she turned to glance at me.

"Oh," he said, "Miss Rutledge—is one of us." This was the first notice he had taken of me since seeing Marianna. "Go on," he urged her. "What happened at Mayfield?"

< CONSPIRACY OF KNAVES >

"It was done months ago. A band of Quantrill's guerrillas crossed from Missouri into Kentucky. Led by a man named Anderson—"

"Bloody Bill Anderson," Charley interrupted. "Wesley should not have associated with such marauders. Confederate and Union soldiers both have tried to track down Bloody Bill and rid the world of him."

"They raided a house where the Union commander of the district kept his headquarters and lived with his family. They hanged the Union officer in the presence of his family, women and children. Wesley swore to me that he took no part in the killing, that it was a blood feud between Anderson and the Union officer."

"Damn! Now we'll have to get Wesley out of Kentucky, and I was counting on him to act as courier between us and Colonel Ferree." He shook his head slowly in exasperation.

"You should have refused to take his place, Marianna. This dangerous business is not for you."

As though on cue from a prompter, her violet eyes filled with tears, and Charley immediately began soothing her hurt feelings.

Charley forgave her, but our host did not. Before supper, Alonzo Colquett gathered his guests into the common room and conducted a veritable inquisition, after first boasting of how cleverly he had led the Tamaroa community into believing that he was entertaining a hunting party of livestock dealers from Chicago.

Since he had acquired Barton Farm, he went on, he had used the utmost care in establishing a livestock station that would appear to be a source of horses for the Union Cavalry, operated by men loyal to the Union. Earlier in the summer his carefully designed contrivance had been jeopardized by the unexpected appearance of a Captain Truscott, who foolishly brought several Confederate soldiers into the premises. Unfortunately for Truscott and his horsemen, they were captured by home guards, but fortunately Barton Farm had not been compromised. The Union authorities believed that the Confederates had come there to steal horses from Colquett.

He was quite disturbed, he continued, by the manner in which Major Heywood's female cousin, Miss Marianna Heywood, had ventured upon Barton Farm. With rude exactness, he questioned her about what she had said and done upon arriving at Tamaroa.

"Who did you speak to first?" he asked.

"The stationmaster."

"And what did you say to him?"

"I asked how far it was to Barton Farm. When he told me the distance, I inquired if it might be possible to hire a hackney to drive me and my trunk out here."

"Go on, Miss Marianna."

"The stationmaster showed me the livery stable, which is quite close by the station, and I went over there and engaged a carriage and driver."

"What was the driver's name?"

"A Mr. Berryman."

Colquett muttered something, and began nervously rubbing his balding forehead. "Berryman's a Union home-guard officer," he said to Charley. "Very suspicious of strangers. Especially anybody from the South."

"He was quite courteous to me," Marianna said.

"Yes, but he asked you a good lot of questions, didn't he?"

"In a respectful way, yes. He wanted to know where I was from and why I was visiting Barton Farm. I told him that I had come to see my cousin."

"And you named him?"

"Yes, I saw no reason not to."

Colquett pursed his lips and exhaled in a soft whistle. A pained expression appeared on Charley's face. "Lord, protect us from the innocent," Colquett said, a note of disgust in his voice.

Marianna looked as if she might begin weeping at any moment. After she said she had told the stableman that her cousin was a business partner of Mr. Colquett, the questioning ended.

Supper that evening was a subdued, almost somber affair. The hunters, being weary, went off to bed soon afterward. Colquett and Charley withdrew to a far corner of the big room, taking a jug of the horse dealer's foul whiskey with them. They began talking in undertones. For the first time I felt an ounce of sympathy for Marianna Heywood, and I suggested to her that we retreat gracefully to our bedroom.

An hour or so later, Charley knocked on our door. His manner was more restrained than I'd ever witnessed in him, and he was almost apologetic in explaining what we must do to safeguard the

< CONSPIRACY OF KNAVES >

façade of Barton Farm. Before next daylight half of Charley's Kentuckians, accompanied by the Missouri horse traders, would ride westward to the Mississippi River for a ferry crossing at Sainte Genevieve. They would spend the next several weeks contracting for horses in Missouri.

Later in the day, the other half of the Kentuckians would ride to the Tamaroa railroad station with Alonzo Colquett, who would give them a merry send-off on the Illinois Central. They were to make certain that every casual observer in the little town became aware that a considerable number of busy livestock buyers who had come to Barton Farm to hunt prairie chickens were returning home to Chicago.

None of them was actually returning to Chicago, however. They would leave the train individually at different towns along the railroad to visit Copperhead leaders in preparation for the eve of election day in November.

Charley and Marianna were to remain as guests at Barton Farm for several more days. Through the Unionist stableman at Tamaroa, Marianna had broadcast to the community that she had traveled from Kentucky to visit her cousin. After some discussion Colquett and Charley agreed that no change in this picture should be made. To recruit among the southern Illinois Copperheads, Charley needed to sustain his identity as a livestock buyer from Chicago, and Barton Farm offered an ideal strategic and secluded base for his operation.

Colonel Eberhart's presence as an exotic visitor, a huntsman from afar, might divert attention from the others, perhaps allay any suspicions arising among the rural folk in the Tamaroa community. The colonel, therefore, would remain as a guest for a while, being encouraged to spend a considerable amount of his time at following his hunting hound.

While Charley was relating this intricate scheme to Marianna and me, I wondered how much of it was his, how much was Colquett's. I had come to know Charley as a bold, sometimes reckless soul, quick to recognize danger and escape from it, but unlikely to waste time devising so many cautionary measures. At first I suspected that Alonzo Colquett was sole contriver of this fribbling program, but I was wrong—at least in that part of the melodramatic playlet in which I was to have a role.

< **Belle Rutledge** >

"As for you, Miss Rutledge," Charley said with uncharacteristic formality, "you are to travel to Kentucky. To deliver funds to Colonel Amos Ferree, and to observe the numbers and condition of his secret regiment. I believe the risks of this mission would be lessened for you if you traveled in your guise of Calvin Blacklock."

That last instructive remark should have warned me that things were not what they appeared to be on the surface, but Charley kept talking in that plausible manner of his, reproaching himself because he had not a man he could spare for the journey to Kentucky, but that he had the utmost confidence in my ability to perform a man's duty.

Good Lord, did he imagine I had forgotten that night in bed in Windsor when he begged me to rid myself of Calvin Blacklock? He knew I had held on to the fop's costume against the day when I might return to the stage, and I knew that he despised the dandified character. But events were moving too fast for me to think clearly.

Afflicted with a bad case of the jingling fits, I don't think I slept a wink before Charley was knocking on our door again, ordering me to dress for a long buggy ride. At four o'clock in the morning, the darkness was intense, but as soon as I lighted a candle, my little belle of the ball, Miss Marianna, crawled out of her blankets and dressed quickly in a modish riding habit of wool plaid. She certainly had not stinted herself at buying new clothes with the greenbacks her brother Wesley had "found" for her.

Just before bedtime the previous evening, Marianna had assisted me in clipping my hair back to a masculine length, and she seemed unduly interested in my Calvin Blacklock costume of trousers, waistcoat, and jacket, which I unpacked from my portmanteau to hang up until morning.

Now that morning had come, she insisted upon helping me with the muslin strips that I used to flatten my breasts. She tightened and fastened the bands, and prattled on about how daring I was to dress in such a manner. After I was fully clothed, with my dandy's hat aslant over my short hair, she stepped back to view me with an earnest expression on her early morning face.

"Do you have a brother?" she asked. "Who fancies such fine clothes? Might these be his?"

< CONSPIRACY OF KNAVES >

"I have no brother," I said, and a warning bell rang in my sleepy brain. What was she driving at?

"If you had a brother," she continued in that innocent tone of hers, "I would hope he'd be no namby-pamby. Like my brother, alas. Do you know my brother? Wesley Heywood?"

"I met him briefly in Canada," I said, and to change the subject added: "I see you are dressed for riding. Are you going hunting with Colonel Eberhart?"

"No," she answered sharply. "I'm going with you and Cousin Charley in the buggy."

She had said nothing to Charley about this, but of course he had not the grit to refuse her. When he came for us, he gave me a folded message and a thick pack of greenbacks wrapped in oil paper that I was to deliver to Colonel Ferree, and a wad of bills for my traveling expenses. I rolled the thick pack into underclothing in my portmanteau and stored the wad into my gentleman's pocket purse.

Instead of taking the road to Tamaroa, Charley drove us northward for seven or eight miles to a flag-stop station called Dubois. This detour was another one of his cautionary measures. The two-hour ride was fairly pleasant along mist-filled country lanes, although Marianna chose to sit next to Charley, leaving me on the chilly outer edge of the buggy seat. Whenever Charley wanted to instruct me in the duties of my journey, or review information he had already given me, he had to lean forward on the buggy reins and peer at me around his cousin's well-formed bosom. He recounted the passwords and ritual colloquies, the grips and body signs of the Knights of the Golden Circle and Sons of Liberty that had always seemed so silly to me, and made me recite and demonstrate them several times. He repeated the names and addresses of Copperheads I was to meet in Kentucky, and the railroad routes I was to take.

Not until we were nearing the village of Dubois did he inform me that I was not to return to Barton Farm. Upon completing my journey in Kentucky I was to travel to Chicago and lodge at Dr. Julian Aylott's house instead of at a hotel. He would be in communication with Dr. Aylott, and I was to report on what I observed of Colonel Ferree's regiment through the doctor, who knew how to telegraph in code.

During the buggy ride, Marianna entered only once into our conversations. When Captain Truscott's name happened to be mentioned, she immediately spoke up, demanding to know if Johnny Truscott had been betrayed into capture at Tamaroa. "He's written twice to me about that, Charley. I believe he thinks you had something to do with it."

Charley laughed, quite loudly, as though such a charge was too preposterous to deserve a reply, but he made no denial.

"Then do you think Mr. Colquett might have betrayed him?" she continued. "Something Mr. Colquett said last night made me wonder if he might have informed on Johnny—to protect himself or to ingratiate himself with the Unionists."

Oddly enough the same suspicion had occurred to me when Colquett was talking about how the presence of Captain Truscott and his party of Morgan cavalrymen had jeopardized Barton Farm until they were "unfortunately" captured. My opinion of Miss Marianna's capacity for perception rose a fraction of an inch.

Charley, however, scoffed at such an idea. "It was pure bad luck," he said positively. "Johnny Truscott and his boys happened to be in the wrong place at the wrong time. The fortunes of war. But what was bad for Johnny turned out to be good for our cause. We could not have a better man than John Truscott in Camp Douglas to lead the prisoners when the time comes for the uprising."

I could see that Marianna was not entirely satisfied with Charley's explanation. And neither was I. As for Johnny Truscott, he has not been convinced of Charley's guiltlessness down to this day.

At Dubois there was no real depot, just a brown-stained shelter where a young boy served as flagman for anyone who wanted to stop a passenger train. When the locomotive came hissing in with its rattling cars, Charley caught my arm and shouted cheerfully: "Good luck! This time we will succeed!" Marianna's gloved fingers touched my hand. "You do make a handsome man, Belle," she shouted above the clangor of the car wheels. "Are you certain you don't have a brother who resembles you?"

They waited until I was safely aboard, and the train was in motion again. From my seat window I waved to them, but Charley was already turning the buggy and they did not see me. She was

< CONSPIRACY OF KNAVES >

still nestled close by his side, and their beaming faces told me they had already dismissed Belle Rutledge from their minds.

At that moment, I suppose, I truly knew for the first time why I was being sent to Kentucky and from there to Chicago. Charley Heywood could have spared one of those men traveling to Missouri, or those going up the railroad to confer with Copperheads. George Stubblefield or any of the others would have served as a far better emissary to Colonel Amos Ferree than the coxcomb Calvin Blacklock that I had invented. No, Charley wanted me away from Barton Farm while his beloved cousin was there, Marianna, flaunting her newly found sweet sense of freedom, the two of them skylarking while Belle Rutledge was sent off in trousers to do a man's work. If I had been a locomotive at that moment, I could have vented steam from every pore.

When the conductor came by, I paid the fare to Odin, just as Charley had told me to do. At Odin, instead of buying a ticket through to Louisville, I asked for one to Seymour, Indiana, on the Ohio and Mississippi Railroad, just as I had been told to do. Cautionary measures.

On that long jostling journey across Indiana I did a lot of hard thinking about what had happened to Belle Rutledge since that rainy day I arrived in Richmond to report to Colonel Fennell. I had betrayed a trust put in me, I had betrayed my country, if I had a country, and now I was being betrayed by the man who had stolen my heart, my honor, and probably my soul, if I had a soul.

Long before the train reached Seymour I thought about that thick pack of greenbacks wrapped in oil paper in my portmanteau. I had not been told the amount in dollars, but even in small bills there was enough to take me far away to some place where I could begin life anew—as I had done more than once before. Leaving Belle Rutledge behind me would be more difficult than leaving Jennie Gray, schoolgirl of Louisville, but with that pack of greenbacks to sustain me, I knew I could do it. I yearned for a sweet sense of freedom of my own.

As soon as I left the train at Seymour, all I needed to do was buy a ticket to New York. I could stop in Cincinnati and rescue little Winslow Barber from that wretched orphanage. Perhaps we could travel together to Washington, where I would seek out the agent named Baker in the Treasury Department, the man that Kendrich had told me about. I could tell Mr. Baker everything I knew about Charles Heywood and the Copperheads, and start afresh, right where I had begun on the day Kendrich talked me into leaving the theater and walking with him down F Street, past the Treasury, and on to the White House.

Yet what did this poor lovesick mooncalf actually do when she left the train at Seymour? She did exactly what Charley Heywood had told her to do. She bought a ticket on the Jeffersonville railroad to Louisville, deluding herself with warmed-over notions that she was so essential to Charley, so faithful, that he could entrust no one else for this urgent journey. As for Marianna, was she not merely a link to his wild youth, blood kin, an orphaned young woman more to be protected than adored? Ah, what fools mortals can be.

Almost an hour past midnight, the ferry from Jeffersonville and an express coach brought me across the broad Ohio and to the familiar Louisville depot where so long ago I had begun my first journey into the world with a company of actors. Except for the usual militia guards, the place was almost deserted, stinking of the same sulphur smoke that permeated my Calvin Blacklock costume. Only one carriage was waiting. It was driven by a foul-mouthed jehu who was either so dense or so drunk that I had to use my memory of Louisville's streets to direct him to the address I sought.

Fearing the wrath of my prospective Copperhead host upon being awakened at so late an hour, I knocked gently upon his door at first, then increased the force of my blows until the door was finally flung open by a tousle-haired man in a nightshirt. He lifted his candle and snarled at sight of me.

In my richest tenor voice I gave him the first words of a Sons of Liberty greeting, and passed my right hand across my face as though stroking a mustache. I then offered him the thumb grip, at the same time reaching with my left hand for his elbow.

"Oh, come on in," he growled sourly.

That was only the beginning of my wearisome pilgrimage to the hidden headquarters of Colonel Amos Ferree. At first daylight my surly host summoned me from my bed, fed me a greasy breakfast, and loaded me into a buggy that took us eastward for ten

< CONSPIRACY OF KNAVES >

miles or more to a farmhouse. The farmer was at home, and although Colonel Ferree had spent the previous night there, he had departed that morning for his camp somewhere in the Kentucky River bottoms. After conferring for almost an hour, my escort and the farmer decided to send me to a Copperhead in Frankfort who could guide me to Ferree's camp. And so without further delay I was driven to a railroad stop called Hobbs, and after waiting there until late in the day I boarded a Louisville and Lexington train that brought me into Frankfort about sundown.

My Copperhead host in Frankfort turned out to be a far more convivial gentleman than the first two. He practiced the art of phrenology, and during the evening persuaded me to allow him to chart my head. Bringing out calipers, tape measure, and an outline drawing of a head in profile, he began methodically measuring my head and feeling for protuberances on my skull. Murmuring to himself, he jotted down on the drawing whatever it was he was discovering.

"A splendid head, Brother Blacklock," he declared at the end of perhaps two hours. "Your organ of Sagacity is well formed, and the Veneration is more extensive than I've ever seen in a male client." He rubbed a finger across the very top of my skull. "Right there it is, a considerable protuberance. You have no beard, I see, and the large Veneration may account for that, though you still appear to be quite young."

I was about to say something that might turn him off a track I did not wish him to pursue, but he changed the subject himself. Tapping a spot just above my ear, he continued: "The only fault I find in your chart is this Bump of Secretiveness. If not corrected, Brother Blacklock, it could lead to a defect in your character as you grow older. If the rising is reduced, you will become more open and honest in your dealings with others. Leeches will reduce it, sir, and if you can remain in Frankfort for a few days, I would be pleased to accommodate you—and as you are a brother of our order, the charge would be most reasonable."

I assured him that but for the urgency of my journey I would accept his offer immediately, and said that whenever I was at leisure to do so I would undertake his treatment by leeches—but of course I had no intention of ever doing so.

Early next morning he had two horses saddled and waiting,

and we were soon riding northward along the Kentucky River road to Monterey, reaching there about midafternoon to stop at the house of a physician named Dobbins. The doctor told us that Colonel Ferree had spent the night at his house, but started that morning for the mouth of Drennon Creek, where his recruits were camped. When I asked my phrenologist guide and the doctor if they could give me some estimate of the size of Colonel Ferree's command, both men were evasive in their replies, one saying that the muster rolls had to be kept secret, and that the hundreds of recruits necessarily were dispersed to avoid discovery by Union patrols.

The remainder of my journey to find Colonel Amos Ferree was excruciating, to say the least. Insisting he must return to Frankfort with both horses, the phrenologist left me in the hands of Dr. Dobbins, who most unwillingly lent me an aged mare and accompanied me along a rough trail through creek bottoms and wild forests to a cabin owned by an old recluse named McDowell. There we spent the night, three in a musty floor bed, and next morning McDowell strapped my portmanteau to a mule and off we went on foot along the winding river.

Calvin Blacklock's shoes were not meant for wilderness walking, but the mule would not take a rider. My heels were well blistered by the time we reached the riverbank opposite the mouth of the Drennon.

There we found one of Colonel Ferree's pickets seated on the bank beside a rowboat. After he and McDowell exchanged a few foul words of greeting, the picket agreed to row me across to the camp. My fine clothes were beginning to show effects of rough travel, and the poorly dressed picket obviously was contemptuous of the wearer. He did tell me that Colonel Ferree had crossed earlier in the day, and that I could find him in camp about half a mile up the creek.

Burdened with my heavy portmanteau, I had walked about a hundred paces when another picket stopped me, his rifle at the ready. None of my Copperhead signs or passwords brought any response from him, and he rudely escorted me to a little clearing where a dozen or more lean-tos stood in broken military order. In front of one of them a man in a gray coat was lying on a blanket staring up at the blue autumn sky.

< CONSPIRACY OF KNAVES >

The picket addressed him: "Look what's come to our camp, Major Heywood."

Major Heywood, I thought. My God, have I gone mad?

But it was Wesley Heywood who sat up rubbing his eyes, his slack mouth moving without sound, and then finally getting out a questioning "Yes?"

"I'm looking for Colonel Ferree," I said in my deepest tones.

"Who are you?" he asked as he stood erect.

"I am Calvin Blacklock, with a message from Major Charles Heywood. A relative of yours, perhaps?"

He nodded. "You look familiar. Did we meet in Canada?"

I shook my head. "Perhaps in Chicago, but I do not recall so. Is Colonel Ferree in camp?"

Wesley Heywood turned and squinted through the trees at a lean-to larger than most of the others. "Resting, I expect. But he's been anxious to hear from Charley—Major Heywood." He turned back to face me, his eyes narrowing again as he looked at the portmanteau I had set down.

"Did you bring us any boodle in that case? We're running short of everything out here."

"I have a packet for Colonel Ferree," I said.

Colonel Ferree was snoring under the lean-to, and when Wesley Heywood shook him awake he protested with loud oaths. As soon as he learned the reason for his being disturbed, however, he crawled out quickly, brushing leaves off his clothing as he arose to frown suspiciously at me.

He certainly was not the guerrilla chieftain I had pictured in my imagination, nothing bold or fierce about him at all. Instead he reminded me of a clergyman, a schoolmaster, or a merchant— a colorless sort of indoor man—except there was a madness in his deep-set eyes, the same desperate fury that seemed embedded in most of Charley Heywood's devil-may-care friends and associates.

"How do we know you're not a Federal spy?" he demanded.

He was jeering at me, putting on an act to demoralize the seedy-looking fop that I appeared to be. When I gave him Charley's message and the thick package of greenbacks, he warmed up immediately. He went into his lean-to and brought out a bottle of genuine bourbon to celebrate my happy arrival.

Wesley drank more than his share of the liquor, but he was

quite steady on his feet and exceedingly polite to me. Yet there was something about his attitude, his sidelong glances, that made me uneasy. He had left Canada before I performed in Calvin Blacklock's costume, but I wondered if he suspected who I truly was.

I was not especially gratified, therefore, when he invited me to sleep in his lean-to for the night. The officer who usually shared the shelter had gone off to Lexington, leaving a pair of new blankets and a deep layer of leaves and cedar twigs within a rectangle of poles on the ground.

Thus far on my frantic expedition I had occupied a succession of good and bad sleeping places, but the one in the lean-to proved to be the most pleasing to my senses. The night was calm, and the wind-cleansed wool blankets, the faint cedar scent arising from the natural cushion beneath me, the blue moonlight slanting through the lean-to entry, all combined to lull me into a state of drowsiness, even though Wesley Heywood snuffled and whistled in boozy slumber not two yards away.

I felt secure enough to unwrap the tight muslin bands from around my breasts, and with my body completely free under the blankets I must have fallen into a sleep so deep that only a nightmare could have brought me to wakefulness. And it was a dreadful dream of snakes, dozens of them, crawling from some dank cavern, their bellies like ice, coiling and twisting down my naked belly and then winding around my breasts so that I was shocked awake by the horror of it. And there in the blue light was Wesley Heywood bent above me, his breath rancid from whiskey, dots of reflected moonlight in his eyes, his hands under the blanket, squeezing my breasts.

"You're Belle Rutledge," he accused hoarsely. "I had to know."

"Now you know," I said, "get away from me."

I caught his wrist and pulled his arm from under the blanket. Somewhere out in the woods an owl hooted, and was answered by another.

Wesley Heywood's teeth were chattering from the night chill.

"Could you warm me, Belle?" His pleading tone was like that of a small boy begging for a sweetmeat.

"Go back to your bed," I said. "I'm not the harlot you take me to be."

< CONSPIRACY OF KNAVES >

"You're Charley's mistress," he said.

"That does not make me a strumpet," I retorted.

Wesley wanted to talk. With a blanket around his shoulders, he crouched in the middle of his leafy bed. His silhouette reminded me of a drawing of an old chieftain that was in Mr. George Catlin's book about North American Indians, the only book that my grandfather left in his bedroom when he died.

"My sister Marianna," Wesley began. "She went to see Charley."

"Yes, she said you sent her."

"I could not go," he replied haughtily. "I'm a wanted man. The Federals are looking for me."

"Charley thinks you should leave Kentucky," I said.

He sniffed. "That's not easy, with your name and drawings of your face everywhere in public places. If I knew where Quantrill was, I'd try to go to him. Some of Ferree's best recruits went to join Basil Duke in Virginia. I might go there."

"These remote woods seem safe enough. Could you not stay with Colonel Ferree until he's ready to invade Indiana?"

His reply was a dry scornful laugh, with no mirth in it whatsoever. "Invade with ghosts? Names on a muster roll? What you've seen here, Belle Rutledge, is Colonel Ferree's regiment."

"Charley believes he has two thousand guerrillas ready to strike in November."

He forced another laugh. "Look, Ferree made me his adjutant. I keep the muster rolls. He started with one man to a squadron, each supposed to go out and recruit. Half the names they put down are dead men, ghosts. The largest number we've ever had out here to drill was thirty men. Do you know how many are in this camp right now? Five men, since Ferree and Sergeant Rennie went off tonight with the greenbacks you brought from Charley."

"When will the colonel return?" I asked. "I need answers to some questions."

"God knows. After whatever it is he does with the money." I could see the pinpoints of his eyes again in the blue light.

"You sound bitter," I said. "You know I must tell Charley something about Colonel Ferree's command. What shall I tell him?"

"Tell him the truth."

"He'll refuse to believe it—if what you've told me is the truth."

He laughed that feverish laugh again. "I exaggerated our sufficiency," he said. "Are you going back to Barton Farm to see Charley?"

"We'll meet in Chicago," I said.

He sighed. "I was hoping you'd see Marianna—to warn her, from me, to come back home. Not to get mixed up with Cousin Charley."

I wanted to ask him how close they were, Charley and Marianna, and why a warning was necessary. But I said nothing, perhaps because I was afraid of what he might tell me.

Soon after daylight, Wesley Heywood saddled two horses from the dozen or so mounts in a pen beside the creek, and offered to guide me out of the woods. The horses evidently were castoffs or culls from carriage and dray stables; the one I was riding suffered from a slight limp that kept me rocking in my saddle. Within an hour I had a blister on my bottom that was as painful as the ones on my feet.

The autumn day was extraordinarily lovely, however, sunlight augmenting the changing colors of the leaves of oaks, hickories, and sweet gums—russets, golds, and purples, with the bright scarlets of black gums scattered here and there like exclamation points. Away from the pestilence of war, Kentucky was indeed a beautiful land.

After we left the woods and entered farming country, Wesley grew more and more cautious, leading me along obscure trails to avoid houses and settlements. Sometime after noon, he halted and told me he could go no farther. After I dismounted he unfastened my portmanteau, and used the rope for a tie to the horse I'd been riding.

"Through those trees ahead is a railroad and a little town," he said. "Pleasureville, they call it." For the first time he smiled a genuine smile with that crooked mouth of his, and then he mounted and rode away.

Unfortunately I missed the last train into Louisville and had to spend the night in a scruffy little inn. But the delay gave me an opportunity to take a washtub bath and clean the travel stains from Calvin Blacklock's costume. Next morning I rode into Louisville, where for a full five minutes I pondered the thought of changing into the dress and wig I had packed in my portmanteau, and going in search of my girlhood past. No relatives lived there any longer, however, and I knew the war had scattered most of my old friends.

And so instead I went to Wood's Theater to see Madeline Henriques in *Camille*. What the others in the crowded audience thought, seeing me as a young dandy weeping openly, I do not know or care. I shed a quart of tears, as I always do when watching that play, and felt much the better for it. In fact, I felt so good that instead of obeying Charley Heywood's dictum to proceed directly to Chicago, I took passage on a U.S. Mail Line steamer bound up the Ohio River to Cincinnati. I needed time to think of something to say to Charley about Colonel Ferree's phantom guerrillas. I wanted a boat's deck for walking off the jimjams, a leisurely dinner, and freedom from the smoke, cinders, dust, and noise of a railway car. And perhaps a good night's rest. If fate should put aboard my boat a handsome young man who cared not a fig for war or spies or conspirators, I would make a quick change in my stateroom to the dress and wig in my portmanteau and see if Belle Rutledge still possessed her old magic. Then I could forget the good night's rest.

Lord, what a dreamer! Yet perhaps I could expunge my sins in Cincinnati by rescuing little Winslow Barber from that dreadful orphans' home. Was not that the real reason for my buying a ticket on the U.S. Mail Line steamer to Cincinnati? As it was, I left the boat wearing my modish traveling dress, with Calvin Blacklock packed away in my portmanteau.

18

WE'LL RALLY 'ROUND
THE FLAG, BOYS

In Camp Douglas during October, only the weather was congenial. Commandant Wright and his officers continued their capricious and heavy-handed punishments of the prisoners of war. Deprivation of rations was the most common infliction, and from time to time the men felt the wrath of Captain Spooner, who seemed to take genuine pleasure in issuing rations of bones from which the meat had been removed, or potato peelings hauled in wheelbarrows from the Union soldiers' mess shed. Visitors' days were also canceled erratically, or switched suddenly from one day of the week to another. Colonel Wright did not stop the visitors entirely, because they sometimes gave him and his growing squad of U.S. detectives leads to what they pretended to be hotbeds of Copperheads in Chicago. Gifts of foodstuffs were forbidden, however, because they interfered with Captain Spooner's withheld-rations punishments.

New prisoners arrived almost every day, some from General Price's army, which had invaded Missouri, and they told depressing stories of how they had waited south of St. Louis for a Copperhead army to arise within the city and march out to join the Confederates in its capture. But no Copperheads whatsoever showed themselves, only a large force of Federals that encircled and captured several advance cavalry units and then drove Price's army westward away from St. Louis.

< CONSPIRACY OF KNAVES >

Few of these new prisoners were clothed for cold weather or possessed blankets. Colonel Wright's response to their petitions was to order issuance of the same thin pepper-and-salt cottonade trousers and spade-tailed coats in which he had uniformed the Morgan men. As for blankets, each prisoner was permitted only one, and it had to be obtained from the "kindly Christian ladies and gentlemen of Chicago."

Consequently, whenever one of the irregular visitors' days was announced, John Truscott was always at hand to encourage the dwindling number of sympathizers to bring blankets and warm underclothing against the approaching winter. He also was eager for any scrap of information about the rumored assault upon Camp Douglas on election eve in November.

One bright blue October afternoon, when he entered the visitors' compound a few minutes late, he was astonished to see Marianna Heywood in company with Mrs. Evelyn Ward. Marianna was dressed in a subdued black, but wore no veil, and the smile she gave Johnny Truscott jolted his heart. (Good Lord, was not she the Lady of Shalott?)

He could not wait to cross the crowded compound to grasp her hands, barely restraining a kiss, forgetting entirely that he might be compromising her with the observant Captain Spooner and the listening hospital orderly, Otis Jordan.

"I can't believe my own eyes, Marianna, that you are here," he said. How delicate is her fair skin, he thought, and how long it has been since I touched the flesh of a woman.

"I promised I would come to see you, Johnny. Thanks to my good friend, Mrs. Ward, I'm here." When she lowered and raised her dark lashes, he almost kneeled to kiss her hand. *She hath no loyal knight and true, the Lady of Shalott.*

"Cousin Charley doesn't know I'm here in Chicago. He forbade me to come. He thinks I'm back in Kentucky, at Little Hundred."

Her merry laughter was like an echo of her prankish youth when she would play tricks on him and Charley, maneuvering one of them against the other. Yet there was some subtle change in her. She was more assured than when he had last seen her at Little Hundred, more worldly and free-spirited. She was no longer the contented weaver looking down on Camelot; she had fled the safety of her castle tower for the shadows of the world.

< **We'll Rally 'Round the Flag, Boys** >

"Where is Charley?" he asked, keeping his voice low because of the crowd gathering around them.

"Oh, he's still down there at Barton Farm—"

"Not so loud, Marianna," he cautioned.

She pouted like a scolded child. "He's coming to Chicago soon," she whispered. "And won't he be surprised when he finds me here!"

Mrs. Ward was enjoying the romantic exchange between them, but she had the presence of mind to move away, guiding Marianna along with her through the crowd. Although Truscott stole glances as often as he dared at his Princess of Love and Beauty, he did not risk another conversation with her before a drum beating at the gate signaled for the visitors to leave the compound.

On the morning following Marianna Heywood's visit to Camp Douglas, Otis Jordan appeared at John Truscott's barracks, carrying his belongings in a canvas bag and relating a tale of how he had been unjustly relieved of his duties as hospital orderly and reassigned to Truscott's company of prisoners. Furthermore, he wailed, the commandant had turned against him and withdrawn a promised commission with the volunteer regiment of galvanized Yankees that was being recruited from Camp Douglas prisoners for duty in the West.

(Had I, Belle Rutledge, been present I surely would have recognized Otis Jordan's performance as a very bad piece of acting, but Johnny Truscott was so provoked by the Texan's intrusion into his tight little brotherhood of Kentucky alligator horses that he paid little attention at first to the poorly contrived charade that Jordan was performing.)

After establishing himself as comfortably as possible in the barracks, Jordan began questioning Truscott about Marianna Heywood.

"Who was that beauteous little filly I saw you talking with on visitors' day?" he asked.

"She is a friend of Mrs. Ward," Truscott replied coldly.

Jordan sniffed. "She was warming to you like a dear sweetheart."

"She knows some of my acquaintances," Truscott said, deliberately walking away from Jordan.

< CONSPIRACY OF KNAVES >

A day or so later, while Truscott was washing his shirt and socks outside at the water trough, Jordan approached him again, and slyly introduced a possibility of escape.

"There's nothing for me in this prison camp," he said. "What good did it do me to take old Bartholomew Wright's oath of loyalty? The way I've been treated, I deserve some luck in getting out of here."

He waited for a reply, but Truscott silently continued with his laundering.

"I know a way for one or two of us to escape," Jordan continued. "Without a tunnel. It's surefire, Truscott."

"Nothing's surefire in Camp Douglas," Truscott said.

"You're wrong, captain, dead wrong. You've seen the slop wagon that comes into our yard every morning. Through that arched gate over there."

Truscott knew the wagon and its routine visits to carry off the leavings of the prisoners. "We rejected that possibility long ago," he said. "The guards at the main gate inspect every load going out."

"The guards are getting careless," Jordan replied. "Especially since Colonel Wright decided to collect fifteen cents a head from citizens who want to mount the parapet and look down on us prisoners. They pay one of the guards at the gate and climb the steps there, and I've noticed the guards are always eyeing the pretty females up there showing the ruffles of their petticoats."

Truscott hated the civilians on the parapet, staring and pointing and laughing at the prisoners as though they were captive specimens in a zoological garden. But he had noticed no slackness in the guards since the practice was started by Colonel Wright. The harder that Jordan tried to persuade him to join in trying to escape in the wagon, the more resolute were Truscott's refusals. He did not trust the shifty-eyed Texan.

After a day or two of attempting to wheedle Truscott into joining him, Jordan asked if he would at least assist in an escape attempt. "If you would stroll down to the deadline at the main gate, just at the time the slop wagon is leaving, and engage the guards in conversation—just a few words to draw off their close attention from what might be hidden in the trash—I'll be forever bounden to you, captain."

< **We'll Rally 'Round the Flag, Boys** >

To be rid of Jordan and his plaintive voice, Truscott agreed to act as a distracter at the gate.

Next morning, soon after the slop wagon arrived to collect its load of waste, Truscott, from a distance, watched Jordan crawl like a swiftly slithering snake into its rear. Apparently none of the guards on the parapet saw the bold action. Truscott immediately walked to the arched gate, showed his pass to the guard there, and strode on to the sutlers' compound. In a few minutes the wagon, rolling slowly behind a pair of draft horses, passed him. He turned to follow the vehicle, but stopped still when he saw Commandant Wright appear suddenly beside the guards at the gate.

Suspecting that Colonel Wright had somehow learned of Jordan's escape attempt, Truscott waited for the denouement. When one of the guards stepped out to halt the wagon, however, the commandant beckoned the soldier back to his post and motioned the driver to pass on.

Truscott was so surprised by what he saw that he almost had to force himself to turn and walk back to the prisoners' enclosure. He knew that Colonel Wright had come through a private door that led to the main gate from his headquarters building on the parade ground, and his being there at exactly the time the slop wagon approached the gate was surely more than coincidence. The commandant must have known that Otis Jordan was on the wagon, and wanted to make certain that his escape was successful. In preparation for the escape, Colonel Wright must have assigned Jordan to Truscott's barracks, undoubtedly with instructions to convince the prisoners that he had lost his preferred standing in Camp Douglas, and his resentment now made him willing to risk everything for freedom.

Truscott was so troubled by these suppositions that he sought out Sergeant Joe Stiles as soon as he returned to the barracks. After listening to his captain's account, the sergeant became as concerned about the incident as was Truscott. "If Jordan 'escaped' the way you think he did, captain, he can be mighty dangerous. 'Specially if a new plan is afoot to break us out of here."

"We must send a warning out quick," Truscott said.

"I'd like to track down that crooked-eyed Texan," Stiles declared. "Maybe I'll just use that wagon myself tomorrow."

"And get yourself caught and thrown into the dungeon. Mrs.

< CONSPIRACY OF KNAVES >

Ward could reach Major Heywood, but we don't have time to wait for next visitors' day."

All afternoon Truscott tried desperately to think of a way to stop Otis Jordan from whatever mission Colonel Wright might have sent him on. None of the Morgan men outside the prison knew Jordan as other than an occasionally disgruntled Confederate officer, and none of their Copperhead associates knew him at all. With his ingratiating Texas manner and drawl, he could breeze his way into any group and soon be off with their plans to pass on to Colonel Wright.

Late in the afternoon, while Truscott and his men were raking dead grass and weeds from the yard, he was suddenly struck with a possible means of escape. Old barrels were being used as containers for the trash; as soon as one was filled, it was rolled over beside the small tool shed where the slop wagon stopped to pick up its loads. These same discarded barrels also were sometimes used by the barracks cooks and mess sergeants for offal and other refuse. As Truscott and his men were finishing their task, he arranged for a barrel, still filled with dead grass and other trash, to be carried over beside the barracks steps.

Before daybreak, with the help of Joe Stiles and two other trusted men, Truscott managed to squeeze his wiry frame down into the barrel, which was then refilled with its light load. Soon after sunrise, the barrel was carried out to the trash dump to await arrival of the wagon.

Except for a surprised grunt from the wagon driver when he lifted the unexpectedly heavier barrel in which Truscott was concealed, nothing adverse occurred at the loading place. As the wagon jolted along toward the prison gate, however, Truscott's crouching position in the barrel, with his knees under his chin, grew steadily more uncomfortable. He was surprised to discover two or three very thin cracks between the staves. By turning his head slightly and pushing aside grass and leaves, he could see the driver's wide hat and shoulders beneath the canvas stretched above the seat. Beyond was the high frame of the exit gate.

He wondered if Bartholomew Wright would be there waiting for him. Had Otis Jordan's escape been some kind of cunning plot devised by the commandant to lure Truscott into trying the same route to freedom?

< **We'll Rally 'Round the Flag, Boys** >

Truscott remembered that Jordan had begged him to be present at the gate deadline to divert the guards' attention. Had Colonel Wright known of this, and expected him to come there, but at the last minute decided to ensure Jordan's escape by being there himself? Had Colonel Wright seen him waiting beside the first sutler's store? And most unsettling of all, had Colonel Wright asked Jordan to urge Truscott to join in the escape? If so, the commandant must have intended using Truscott as an unwitting pilot to Charles Heywood and other plotters.

A guard's challenge brought the slow-moving wagon to a stop. Truscott heard one of the guards clambering over the wagon siding and prayed he would not thrust his bayonet into the barrels of trash. Through the stave cracks he saw a flash of dark blue uniform trousers approaching, and then almost obscuring the light. Something pressed against the trash above his head. A heavy breathing sound followed, and then boots scraped against a wagon hub.

"Drive it out!" a voice shouted from below, and the wagon jerked into forward motion again.

Truscott blew breath out and sucked in air so heavy with dust that he almost sneezed. He raised himself an inch or two to relieve the cramp in his legs.

The wagon turned left toward Lake Michigan. He guessed that its contents would be unloaded into an inlet or possibly into the lake itself. He had read in the Chicago newspapers of how the city dumped so much refuse into Lake Michigan from its sinks and slaughter pens and distilleries that a tunnel was being dug a mile long from the shoreline to pump in water pure enough to drink.

He felt an upward slant in the wagon bed, followed by rough bouncing, and then a creaking of harness and metal as the bed sloped downward. Through the barrel cracks he saw a double railroad track, and off in the distance the wooden fence of Camp Douglas. Then the wheels began running almost without sound in ruts of sand. Truscott could hear the splash of wind-driven waves against the lakeshore.

When he raised his head out of the barrel, he smelled freshness from the lake mingling with decay from a trash heap where a flock of gray-and-white birds rose with a flapping of wings and wheeled across the light blue sky.

Because of the undulating sand dunes, the driver's attention

< CONSPIRACY OF KNAVES >

was fully occupied with his horses and the jouncing wagon. Truscott slipped easily out of the barrel. When he looked to the left he saw a thicket of small trees and brush, surrounded by ridges of hard-packed sand. On hands and knees he crept to the tailgate, lifted himself over it, and dropped to the ground. Although his leg muscles were still cramped, he forced himself to run toward the coppice as fast as he could through the sand.

To his dismay the wagon turned almost parallel with him. The driver saw him instantly, pulling his team to a halt.

"Hullo!" the man yelled. "You escape, yes, like yesterday?" His voice bore a foreign accent, but seemed more Swedish than German.

Truscott stopped running, wondering if the driver was armed; if not, what harm could the man do? He turned as though to continue toward the thicket.

"Man yesterday went to same woods," the driver called in a louder voice. "They catch him there."

Truscott stopped again. "They caught him?"

"Yes, was like they waited for him there. They rode away together in a carriage, two seats."

Truscott did not know what to make of that. If Jordan had been captured yesterday morning, he should have been returned to Camp Douglas by afternoon to be paraded and punished before his fellow prisoners. Unless Colonel Wright, or someone above him, wanted to make certain that Jordan reached the right sanctuary in Chicago.

"That thicket is the only cover around here," he said, partially to himself.

"No. You go up dry streambed there. You soon find some woods by railroad track." He was pointing to the north.

Truscott walked closer to the wagon.

"Look here," he said. "You won't report my escape, will you?"

"No skin off my hunkers," the driver replied. He spat tobacco juice over the wheel below him, and slapped his lines sharply.

As soon as the wagon passed, Truscott started northward, following the sand-ribbed bed of a dry stream that evidently flowed only after rainstorms.

He found patches of woods near the railroad, but instead of concealing himself and his prison garb among fallen leaves and

< **We'll Rally 'Round the Flag, Boys** >

briers, he entered an unpainted shack that was partially filled with railroad ties. Surrounded by a pleasant scent of drying oak wood, he let the afternoon drift by. At last, after four months in that black flower of civilized society, he was free. But was he?

Now I know how a runaway slave feels, he thought. The world sheds its boundaries and is freighted with more fear than a prison or slave quarters. My salt-and-pepper cottonades and the spade-tail coat are like the black skin of a fugitive slave. I can shed the clothing, and I shall, but a black slave cannot shed his skin. He knew that never again could he look with equanimity upon slaves, whom as a youth he had accepted as a part of society. Never again could he look upon them without a shudder of horror. He was grateful that his family had never owned slaves, and that most Kentuckians he knew had freed theirs long before the war.

His head whirled at the thought of freedom. Now his own actions were all that counted. His perceptions, dulled by the months of imprisonment, already seemed sharper.

He watched the passing cars on the railroad until dusk fell. When complete darkness enveloped the land, he left the shack and followed the tracks almost to the Chicago depot, leaving the railroad there until he found a street marker that told him he was on Michigan Avenue. Avoiding gas lamps, walking whenever he could in shadow, he felt himself becoming a part of the city, the rattling carriages and wagons and carts, the people old and young, walking so briskly in the sweet crisp air of freedom. Once again he was a part of humankind.

He knew the number of Mrs. Ward's house on Randolph Street. She had given it to her favorite young men in the prison camp against the day when they might escape and need assistance. But he did not know how to find his way to Randolph Street.

Ahead of him in the dim light was an old woman, a bag slung over her back, rags pushing out the top. When he came alongside, he quietly asked her the direction to Randolph Street. She gave him a look filled with suspicion, and muttered three or four unintelligible words. Beneath a dirty kerchief tied round her head, strands of unkempt gray hair hung over her wrinkled forehead.

"Randolph Street," he repeated. "Randolph."

Her eyes lighted suddenly, and she pointed a finger ahead, and smiled, revealing almost toothless gums.. Truscott thought there

< CONSPIRACY OF KNAVES >

was something crafty in her smile, as though she knew more than she was willing to tell. He thanked her and hurried on ahead.

Soon the street pressed closer to the lakeshore, and he came to a wharf busy with steam and sail ships loading and unloading cargoes in the dark. Lanterns flickered along the embankment, and the lake breeze was filled with the sounds of shouts and curses and the clatter of lumber being relayed from ships to dray wagons.

Four sailors in navy uniforms swung out of the murk into a circle of light beneath a gas lamp. They were laughing and talking, boys younger than Truscott. He wondered if he dared call to them from the shadows, asking if they knew Chicago streets. He saw the marker then, faded lettering on a board, twisted askew so that it barely caught light beams from the lamp: Randolph Street.

Most houses were numbered, and he soon reached the block he sought. Before he read the number on the gatepost, he knew it was the Ward house. Across the street from it a man was pacing back and forth, weary and bored from the duty assigned by Colonel Wright. Truscott did not break his stride. Looking straight ahead, he continued to the next corner and turned right. When he came to an alleyway, he glanced back to make certain the detective had not followed, and then sidestepped into the darker shadows.

In a minute or so he found the carriage house, the one that Evelyn Ward had told him Charley Heywood and the actress Belle Rutledge used to pay her a visit. The wide double door was latched but not locked, and as soon as he opened it he smelled horses and old leather in the blackness.

Stumbling against the shafts of a carriage, he felt his way along the vehicle until he found a narrow door that opened upon Judge Ward's snow shed, a roofed and walled passageway along a brick sidewalk that brought him to the kitchen door of the house.

Before he knocked, he heard feminine voices and laughter, but after his knock there was complete silence inside. Worried by the long stillness, he rapped at the door again, and then at last Evelyn Ward's girlish voice sounded behind the door. "Is that you, Judge Ward?"

"John Truscott," he replied.

When she opened the door, she was holding a candle high to light his face. Her childish delight upon recognizing him was almost cloying to Truscott. She squeezed one of his cheeks with her plump

< **We'll Rally 'Round the Flag, Boys** >

fingers, burbling excitedly about his courage and manliness, and then led the way into the sitting room, where Marianna greeted him even more effusively than had Evelyn Ward. She kept repeating his name and hugging him as though he were the last male on earth, while at the same time Mrs. Ward was asking him over and over: "How, how, how, did you escape, Captain Truscott?"

As soon as they calmed down, he told them that Otis Jordan's arranged escape had forced him to take a chance on the same wagon. While he was explaining why he believed Jordan was acting as an agent for the Camp Douglas commandant, he noticed that Evelyn Ward's cherubic face had suddenly turned pale.

"Mr. Jordan was here last night," she said. "I gave him clothes and greenbacks."

"Did he know of the carriage-house entrance?" Truscott asked quickly.

"No, I think not. He came right to the front door and knocked."

"That proves his falseness. With detectives watching your house day and night, he would have been stopped and questioned, perhaps recognized and arrested."

"Had I known his treachery," she said angrily, "I would have refused him aid."

Truscott shook his head. "He was sent here to compromise you, Mrs. Ward. You may be forced to flee Chicago."

"Oh, dear no," she replied, her eyes moistening with sudden tears. "Judge Ward would never permit them to harm me."

"Where is your husband?"

"I believe he is attending a special meeting of the Sons of Liberty. He may be home soon."

"Let's hope that Otis Jordan did not find his way into that meeting. Do either of you know where Major Heywood is? I must warn him about Jordan."

"Judge Ward heard that Cousin Charley was coming to Chicago today," Marianna said brightly. "But we have heard nothing yet." She sighed. "Of course Charley doesn't know I'm here. He'll be mad as hops when he finds me out."

With some hesitancy, Truscott asked Mrs. Ward if she might have clothing that would fit him, and was surprised to learn that she kept a collection of men's garments in a special closet adjoining her bedroom. Most of the clothes were workingmen's jeans, brown

< CONSPIRACY OF KNAVES >

and dark blue, with shirts of rough osnaburg. Trial and error, Evelyn Ward told him, had proved that fugitives traveling in ordinary work clothes were less likely to be noticed than if they were clad in fancy broadcloth.

The act of shedding the hated prison garb lifted Truscott's spirits considerably, and this bracer, combined with being in the presence of his Lady of Shalott, who seemed to reciprocate his adoration, made him feel as if an oppressive burden had been lifted from his fortunes. Nothing could daunt him now, neither dragons nor a host of black knights.

From the adjoining hallway came a slight rapping noise, and Evelyn Ward almost jumped from the painted chair in which she sat, crying out: "That's the judge's knock!" She scampered like a schoolgirl to open the front door, and Truscott heard her ask her husband if the detective was on duty.

"Two of them tonight," he replied in a fretful voice. "I spoke to them and they looked like scairt rabbits. But happily, my dear Evie, I have news that should please Miss Marianna."

By this time they had reached the door of the sitting room, and Truscott was surprised to see a man some inches shorter than himself, wizened almost, with brush-stiff graying red hair that appeared to be pink in the candlelight. Yet he was imbued with a madcap energy that was evident in the way he moved and spoke.

"What news do you have for me, Judge Ward?" Marianna asked eagerly. She arose from her chair, moving toward him.

"Hold on to yourself, girl," he said, peering hard at Truscott. "Is this another one of your beau sabreurs?"

"The gentleman is Captain Truscott," Mrs. Ward said. "You've heard me speak of him, judge."

"Another escaped prisoner, eh? Did them watchdogs out there see you come in here, son?"

Truscott said that he believed they had not, and then the judge surprised both him and Marianna by announcing that Major Heywood had arrived in Chicago.

"Where is he?" Truscott and Marianna asked almost at the same instant.

Judge Ward twisted his thin lips as if trying to find words to answer. "Where is he now?" he echoed. "Likely at Joseph Milligan's place out on Cottage Grove. Fact, I heard him say the new brigadier who come up with him from southern Illinois, and himself, would stay the night at Milligan's." He touched a finger to his nose and rolled his pale blue eyes upward. "Arms, you know. Milligan wants to be back in the scheme real bad. Soon as he heard about all the Sons of Liberty coming up from Fayette and Coles counties. But maybe I'm talking out of turn."

"I must see Charley Heywood tonight," Truscott said, and went on to explain the threat of danger from Otis Jordan.

The judge did not know whether or not Jordan had been present at the Copperhead meeting. Several strangers were there, he said, but he had met none of them nor heard their names. Then he suggested that Truscott travel by horsecar if he felt compelled to go to Cottage Grove before morning, but when Evelyn Ward pointed out that the streetcars stopped running at ten o'clock, the judge offered to hitch up his carriage and drive Truscott to the Milligan house.

Upon hearing this, Marianna immediately insisted that she must accompany the two men. They opposed her going, but because she was the Lady of Shalott her words were not put as a plea but as a demand. When the carriage rolled quietly out of the alleyway behind the Ward house, Marianna Heywood was seated like a queen between Judge Ward and Johnny Truscott.

In the intoxicating excitement of freedom and of being with his adored Marianna, Truscott had forgotten that Cottage Grove ran directly in front of Camp Douglas. When Judge Ward turned the carriage out of the darkness of Thirty-first Street and Truscott saw the gas lamps of the Cottage Grove Hotel facing the walls of the hated prison from which he had escaped only a few hours past, he was struck with an involuntary spasm of betrayal. Who was doing this to him? The scrawny little judge holding the horse to a slow walk? Surely not Marianna, his beloved? Was it all a comic jape devised by the fleshly pixie, Evie Ward? The wide-haunched mare pulling the carriage clop-clopped over the paving in front of the main portal of Camp Douglas until hooves and wheels were silenced suddenly when they reached the sandy surface of the street running parallel with the lake, where houses were few and widely separated.

The late October night was cold, but the heavy lap robe provided by Judge Ward kept them warm. They talked of inconse-

< CONSPIRACY OF KNAVES >

quential matters—the city and its people, its noises and aromas, of how bright the stars were over the lake. Then suddenly Marianna asked: "Judge Ward, was that woman with Charley?"

"What woman?" the judge asked. "There were no women at the meeting."

"The actress. Belle Rutledge."

"Oh, Miss Belle? The major said nothing of her."

"She went to Kentucky dressed as a man," Marianna said. "I hope she stayed there."

"Dressed as a man?" Truscott asked quickly. "You said she dressed as a man?"

"Cousin Charley wanted her to go that way."

"She fooled me," Truscott said. "I thought she was a young fop who resembled Belle Rutledge, perhaps a brother."

Marianna turned to face him in the darkness. "You saw her dressed as a man in Camp Douglas?"

"She was visiting the commandant," Truscott said. "Now there are two betrayers I must warn Charley to beware of."

Joseph Milligan's house was less than a quarter mile from Camp Douglas. It was built of sturdy planks, nothing fancy, but roomy with two floors and an attic. Behind the house Truscott could see the shape of a barn, twice as large as the dwelling, with pens and outhouses surrounding it.

Judge Ward hitched the mare at the gate and led the way to the porch. He knocked on the door with the imperious air that small-sized human beings sometimes affect when forced into unwelcome situations. Truscott noticed that a light was extinguished in one of the side rooms almost immediately after the judge banged his knuckles against the wood. Three or four minutes passed before the door opened a crack to expose a lighted candle and a peering eye.

"God almighty," Joseph Milligan cried. "It's Judge Ward! What brings you way out here so late, judge?" The door opened wider. "Come on in." Milligan looked from Truscott to Marianna and then back again to Truscott. "I've seen you before, young fellow. Never forget a face, but don't recollect the name."

"We met at Barton Farm," Truscott said, and added his name. He did not try to conceal the bitterness in his voice. For all he knew, Milligan may have been part of the scheme that led to his capture at the abandoned Tamaroa chapel.

"I'm looking for Major Charles Heywood," he said then. "Is he here?"

Milligan gave Judge Ward a look that was a silent inquiry. Truscott saw the judge's quick nod, and then Milligan crossed the hall to a closed door and opened it. His candlelight revealed the silhouettes of two men seated at opposite ends of a sofa in Milligan's parlor. One of the men sitting in the dark was Charley Heywood. He turned and lighted a candle on a stand between him and a piano.

"My God!" he cried. "John Truscott." His mouth opened slightly when he recognized Marianna, and for a moment he obviously found it difficult to speak. "You! With him! I am confounded. No one is where they are supposed to be."

In front of him on the floor, on a table, and atop the closed piano were hand weapons of various shapes and sizes—old pistols, new revolvers—two or three hundred of them.

The man with Heywood was introduced as Jeremiah Grundy from Christian County, a Sons of Liberty brigadier in command of volunteer forces that Heywood said would be coming to Chicago before election day in November. Grundy was a young man, in his middle twenties, but he looked as if he had lived hard and violently. One of his ears was partially mangled and his short Vandyke beard had been carelessly scissored. In his coat lapels he wore several stickpins, and on his fingers were four or five rings, all of which sparkled in the light from the candle.

After the formalities of introduction were concluded, Heywood guided Truscott and Marianna into a small sewing room that adjoined the parlor. As soon as he closed the door, all three began talking at once until Heywood pushed Truscott and Marianna down upon a settee and stood towering over them in a threatening manner.

"It was most unwise of both of you," he said in a parental tone of chastisement, "to do what you have done. Marianna, you have put yourself in great danger, and you Johnny, you should not have escaped, old friend. You should not have done it. We need you in Camp Douglas to lead our boys on the night of the uprising."

< CONSPIRACY OF KNAVES >

"Somebody had to warn you about Otis Jordan, and also I think, of your actress friend, Belle Rutledge."

Heywood sat down in a wicker chair facing them, and fingered a small cheroot from a waistcoat pocket. He bit the end off the cigar but did not light it.

"Ah, Johnny, you've been a foolish gosling," he said with a chuckle. "I've known Jordan was a rotten apple since the big raid, and so do all my boys. We'll use him to pass misdirected information to his lords and masters. As for Miss Rutledge, she's a Kentuckian, one of us at heart, whatever she may seem to you. She's quite clever at playing the male, eh? My dear boy, I know everything about the lady, far more than you could know caged in that prison camp. . . ."

It's like the old days, Truscott thought, the three of us together again, with Charley flaunting his superiority, trying to show me up as a silly fool to Marianna. Truscott's anger, long suppressed, boiled over in a rush of accusations.

"I think it was you who arranged the trap at that Tamaroa chapel, Charley. You may not have been there, but you wanted me and my boys captured and brought to Camp Douglas. And all your schemes to rescue us. All failures. Three times we prepared ourselves for freedom and three times you lacked the courage to deliver us from that hell."

"Johnny, Johnny, you don't understand, boy. It was not we who lacked the will to try, it was the Copperheads who failed us. Every time. Cowards all. But election night will be different." Charley smiled, yet for the first time in Truscott's memory he saw pain in those arrogant blue eyes he had known from childhood.

"Now that you've discomposed us by breaking out," he continued, "you can help us in another way, little John." He rose from the wicker chair and turned to open the door.

"Let's go back into the parlor. Jeremiah Grundy will back up what I tell you about our new plan for election night. While I'm off to Canada to scrape up some gold, I want you to go down to Barton Farm and ride herd on Alonzo Colquett. I don't trust the bastard to deliver our horses."

To this proposal, Truscott objected with a resounding refusal, and was surprised that Charley did not press him. But it was only a delay—until Marianna was no longer present.

With his usual artfulness Charley arranged matters so that Truscott stayed the night at Milligan's, while Marianna returned in the carriage to Judge Ward's house. This was managed when Joseph Milligan's mother-in-law came down from upstairs with two of her rosy-cheeked granddaughters and informed her son-in-law that she was ready to be driven home to Clark Street. After Milligan's daughters and their grandmother—Grandma Berna-dine—were introduced to the visitors, Charley suggested that the merry Irishwoman could be driven home in Judge Ward's carriage, provided that Truscott gave up his seat to her and spent the night at Milligan's.

"Johnny and I have many matters to discuss," Charley added, "before I leave for Canada tomorrow."

Grandma Bernadine, a smiling talkative woman, supported the suggestion and went off with Judge Ward and Marianna, twitting the judge for being out at such a late hour with two ravishing coquettes while his poor wife waited lonely at home.

As soon as they departed, Charley returned to the subject of Barton Farm, reinforcing his demand upon Truscott by bringing Marianna into the venture. "You must take her with you as far as Odin on the Illinois Central, and see that she boards the train for Kentucky there. Then you go on to a flag stop called Dubois. I'll give you the name of a good Copperhead who will drive you to Barton Farm. Colonel Eberhart is still there, but he has been unwell, and we need a determined man like you, John, to keep a whip hand over Colquett until he provides us with two thousand horses to put between Confederate knees."

Truscott again resisted firmly, reminding Charley that the last time he visited Colquett at Barton Farm, he had been captured and imprisoned. "I would sooner go to hell than return to Camp Douglas," he said.

"That won't happen again, Johnny. Barton Farm is now a virtual Copperhead fort. Colquett may be a knave, but he knows there's a fortune down the road for him if our enterprise succeeds. And this time it will succeed." He turned toward Jeremiah Grundy, who had sat silent through most of the evening, reacting with thick-lipped grins to whatever was being said. He had a habit of closing and unclosing his long fingers so that the gems in the rings he wore were constantly twinkling.

< CONSPIRACY OF KNAVES >

"It's true, Captain Truscott," Grundy declared, rolling his words out in a slow-pitched voice. "We can't fail. Two thousand men will begin arriving in Chicago during the next few days to carry out Major Heywood's plan."

"I can double that number," Joseph Milligan interrupted eagerly.

Charley laughed, almost derisively. "You failed us last time, Joseph. But we can use all the men you can raise for us. You could learn something about recruiting from Jeremiah." He winked at Truscott. "I found Jeremiah in the dark ways of the sons of folly. That was in a billiard room in East St. Louis. An Ancient Brother in a little Copperhead outfit—what was it called, Jeremiah?"

"Order of the Mighty Host," Grundy replied with a grin.

"I recruited him into the Sons of Liberty, and he was off like a shot. The county temples in southern Illinois elected him brigadier for the Chicago operation."

Milligan rose from his chair and began pacing back and forth. "We could've done better here in Chicago if Vallandigham had not spoke out against armed action."

"Vallandigham is all talk," Charley said. "He spouts off like a steam engine. 'Resistance to Tyrants Is Obedience to God' may be his motto, but his kind of resistance is all bombast."

Truscott wondered if there was not a considerable amount of bombast in Charley Heywood. Or would the conspirators really bring it off this time, and break the prisoners out of Camp Douglas on election eve? Would two thousand men summon their courage and come to Chicago to risk their lives to rescue prisoners few of them knew or had ever seen?

"Are you certain they will come?" he asked Grundy.

Grundy looked surprised. "Who? Certain that *who* will come?"

"Your two thousand men. Why will they come?"

"Oh. The boodle, of course," Grundy said, with one of his foxy grins. "The greenbacks."

Milligan, who had gone to the other end of the parlor to stir coals in a small fireplace, turned quickly to ask: "How much are you paying them, Major Heywood?"

"We've promised a thousand dollars a man," Heywood replied. "If they do their duty—free the prisoners and seize Chicago—they get a thousand dollars and a railway ticket home. That's why we

< **We'll Rally 'Round the Flag, Boys** >

can't fail. A thousand greenbacks is more money than most of these southern Illinois bumpkins have seen in a lifetime."

"You give me half a thousand a man," Milligan said, "and I'll collect twice as many good scrappers right here in Chicago. You won't have to buy passage home for 'em, either."

Heywood shrugged. "As I told you, Joseph, the men you've shown me before did not hearten my hopes. But if you think money will bring out their fighting spirits, make your promises to them. I'm told our treasury in Canada has been refilled with a fortune that Mosby's Rangers captured from a paymaster on a B. & O. train. I'll be bringing the pelf back from Canada in a few days."

"I could use some more to buy guns with," Milligan said impulsively.

"Forget the guns. With all the pistols in this room, the shotguns in your cellar, and the rifles in your hay barn, we'll have all we can use after we capture the armories."

Truscott listened to this exchange with growing disillusionment. That Copperheads were mercenaries was no more than he had expected of them, yet from the beginning of the mission that had brought him into the conspiracy, he had viewed his role as that of a knight. Inside Camp Douglas he had dreamed of brother knights charging the castle keep to rescue him and his young chevaliers from the evil forces that kept them in confinement. Now the vision had been cheapened. Charley and his ignoble associate, Grundy, were buying rogues to accomplish what true knights should do for God and country and honor. Was this what he had risked his life for, in escaping from the prison camp?

Poor Truscott! He remembered the men he had left behind, however, survivors of the squad he had led into misery, and the hundreds of other Morgan men imprisoned by those high board fences.

Next morning, wearing a false beard and a pair of spectacles supplied by Charley Heywood, he was waiting in the Illinois Central depot for Marianna to join him. More than anything else about this perilous journey to Barton Farm, he looked forward to the several hours on the cars that he would share with his Lady of Shalott.

The locomotive bell was ringing its ten-minute departure alert when Judge Ward, almost swallowed up in a greatcoat too large for him, and wearing his hat brim pulled down, materialized beside Truscott. The judge slipped a small envelope into Truscott's hand and murmured something about being watched and followed.

"How did you recognize me?" Truscott asked in an alarmed whisper.

"You're wearing Major Heywood's stage whiskers and one of my old hats," the judge replied, and without further explanation scurried off in the direction of Michigan Avenue.

Inside the envelope was a note from Marianna:

Johnny dear,
I'm not ready to leave Chicago yet. My good friend, Mrs. Ward, has promised to introduce me to her favorite milliners where I hope to spend some of the money Cousin Charley gave me to buy a railroad ticket to Kentucky. I hope you will not think of me, dear Johnny, as a wild young filly kicking over the buggy traces. Please try to understand how a taste of freedom feels to someone who has never known it before. I pray that Providence will guard you on your journey. Forgive me, Johnny, and have faith that you and Charley and I will all be together again quite soon.

Your dearly beloved,
Marianna

Truscott folded the letter back into its envelope and wondered what he should do next. If he went to the Wards' house to try to convince Marianna to change her mind, the good luck that had blessed him since he escaped from Camp Douglas might turn sour. Yet he had heard Charley warn Marianna not to remain in Chicago. "Should the lid blow off the pot," Charley told her, "you could get yourself arrested and brought before a military court."

On the other hand, Charley had convinced Truscott that his immediate presence at Barton Farm was vital to the second phase of the grand plan. To ensure the freed prisoners' passage out of Illinois, horses and saddles must be waiting for them at the sham auction yards the Copperheads supposedly had established from Mattoon southward. Truscott's duty was to press Alonzo Colquett into filling the yards with the best available animals before the first week in November. Colonel Eberhart was doing his best, Charley repeated, but recurrent fevers and rheumatism hindered the En-

< **We'll Rally 'Round the Flag, Boys** >

glishman's efforts. Early that morning Charley had sent a coded telegram to a man at Dubois, and the Copperheads there would be expecting Truscott's arrival on the train which at that moment was preparing to depart from Chicago.

After reading Marianna's letter once again, Truscott decided that he no longer possessed the power to change the obstinate will of this metamorphosed Lady of Shalott. He was shaken by the realization that even in a hostile world of black knights and dragons and other barbaric evils, his Southern belle might be capable of defending herself.

And so when the Illinois Central train rolled out of the depot and was chuffling along the shoreline of Lake Michigan, John Truscott was aboard a passenger car, staring through his false spectacles at the same landscape that he had first seen while locked in a livestock car four months earlier. As the high fences of Camp Douglas receded into the distance, he swore to himself that he would return in November like young Lochinvar, his avenging sword unsheathed, to free his noble chevaliers. Only when this deed was done could he turn his heart and soul to the wooing and winning of the fair Marianna.

19

BELLE RUTLEDGE

WHEN I ARRIVED in Chicago after my visit to Cincinnati, a cold wind-driven rain was falling. At the station entrance I waited several minutes in the smoke-gray late afternoon for a vehicle to transport me through the dismal weather to Dr. Julian Aylott's house on State Street. During this time I had a strange feeling that I was being watched, but I saw no one doing so. At the last moment, however, as three or four empty cabriolets pulled up for passengers, I was aware of a furtive figure scuttling to a vehicle drawn by a large gray horse immediately behind the cab I was entering. Just for a moment, the man's eyes were turned in my direction, giving me a most uneasy feeling that I had known him from some unpleasant meeting in the past.

By the time I reached Dr. Aylott's house, the incident was almost forgotten, but when I paid the driver and stepped down to the sidewalk, my disquietude was revived by what I saw halfway down the block behind me. Halted there was a cab drawn by a gray horse—one of those Shire coach horses—with bunches of muddy white hair covering its pasterns to the hooves like soiled gaiters. While I walked on to the entrance of the Aylott house and pulled the bell cord, the other cab held its position down the street, but no one left it. The horse was still blowing vapor from its recent exertions.

Ilena Aylott answered my ring. Her eyes brightened a bit at

< **Belle Rutledge** >

the sight of me, but her dark face showed little more emotion than simple recognition.

"Major Heywood asked me to come here," I explained. "I hope he gave you some notice."

"Maybe to Dr. Aylott," she answered flatly, and started to lead the way toward his study.

"Could you wait a minute?" I asked. "While I glance out your street windows. I might have been followed here."

She opened the door to the austerely furnished front room, where Dr. Aylott's few patients were usually kept waiting.

"Snuff the candle," I said, and went to one of the windows and opened the curtains a crack. The gray horse with the feathered pasterns now stood directly in front of the house. A man stepped from the cab into the slackening rain and came close enough to the entrance to read Dr. Aylott's name and house number on the copper plate. In the dying light his features were clear enough for me to recognize him. He was the arrogant black-haired man with the badly focused eyes who had literally forced me to pose for a tintype with him in Camp Douglas. Captain Truscott disliked him, and as I recalled, also distrusted him. Jordan. Otis Jordan, that was his name. What was he doing outside Camp Douglas? Obviously following me. But for what reason?

"Ilena," I said. "Would you take a look at—"

She had already gone to the other window to part the curtains carefully. "I know that man," I told her. "If he comes to the door and asks for—"

"What's the matter?" Dr. Aylott's voice startled me. He had entered in his soft carpet slippers, holding a candle above his head.

My explanation of what was happening obviously disturbed him, and he said he had long feared the authorities would resort to surveillance of his house because of the nature of some of his visitors. When I told him that Otis Jordan was a Camp Douglas prisoner whom I had met while visiting Captain Truscott there, Dr. Aylott seemed even more perturbed.

"The man is back in the cab," Ilena said from the window. "It's leaving."

We all breathed sighs of relief, but I should have known that Otis Jordan was not finished with whatever it was he wanted of me.

< CONSPIRACY OF KNAVES >

Next morning, soon after breakfast, the bell rang in the study, and Ilena went to the front door to answer it. She returned straightaway, her usually calm voice and manner somewhat apprehensive. "It's that man we saw last night," she said. "He's asking for you, Miss Belle. I told him I would inquire of the doctor."

Dr. Aylott dropped his newspaper and glared across the room at me. "What shall I tell him?" he cried.

"Tell him simply that no one by that name is in the house," I said. "If he persists in his demands, say that a woman was admitted last evening for medical consultation, but that she gave no such name as Belle Rutledge."

Ilena turned a forlorn expression upon the doctor, and he arose reluctantly from his chair. "I suppose I must confront the rascal," he murmured, and he went off grudgingly to do so.

When he returned he was chewing on one of the brown medicinal tablets he favored, his long nose and narrow pointed chin working agitatedly.

"He was a most offensive rogue," he said. "Claims to be a U.S. detective." He then looked straight at me. "I must ask you, Miss Rutledge, to find quarters elsewhere as soon as possible. Your presence here creates dangers for Ilena and me."

I reminded him politely that I was under strict instructions to communicate with Major Heywood through him, and that I would likely attract more attention by making frequent visits to his house than if I simply remained there until Major Heywood arrived. When Dr. Aylott still expressed reluctance, I told him of my Calvin Blacklock costume, of how well I had used it in Kentucky, and that there was no reason why I could not become a young male patient of his and thus throw the prying Otis Jordan off the track. Not until I had clipped my hair short again and donned the costume did Dr. Aylott consent to the ruse, doing so almost with enthusiasm and a passionate gleam I had never seen in his eyes before.

In my tight breeches, he said, my thighs and calves would delight the soul of a painter or sculptor. I replied flippantly that my legs were much better molded in my stage tights, a remark that appeared to shock Ilena, but pleasured the doctor.

I remained in the Aylott house for another day before going outside, and would not have done so then had there been any message from Charley Heywood. A coded telegram sent a few days earlier by the doctor to Charley at Barton Farm had been reported as being undeliverable, and he hesitated to send others for fear that Charley was in some sort of trouble. Under such circumstances the message would be tracked back to the sender.

Dr. Aylott and I were both aware that the Morgan men and other associates of Charley usually stopped at the Richmond House when in Chicago, and he agreed that it would be less risky for me as Calvin Blacklock, than for him, to go there in search of information concerning Charley's whereabouts.

Consequently, on a brisk October morning, in my most resplendent masculine togs, I walked down State to Lake Street and fought a gale wind to Michigan, where I found refuge in the warm foyer of the Richmond House. Early though the day was, the barroom was already filled with cigar smoke and the aromas of malt and whiskey. I strolled about the foyer, took a quick glance at the registry book, purchased a newspaper, and entered the dining room. While drinking a cup of coffee, I read about General Price's disastrous cavalry battle with a Union force at Westport, Missouri, and the continued heavy fighting between Grant and Lee at Petersburg, Virginia. By this time it was evident to me that unless the Morgan men were sleeping until noon, none of them that I knew was tarrying at the Richmond House.

Quite disappointed, I decided to return to Dr. Aylott's, but as I was nearing the exit door of the Richmond, a stranger surprised me with a sharp tap on my arm. Forgetting for a moment that I was a man instead of a woman, I almost slapped the supposed libertine for his familiarity with my person, but recovered my wits before my open palm reached his face.

"Please come with me, sir," the man purred into my ear. "Any resistance you offer will cause you much more trouble than any you can inflict upon me."

"What do you want?" I asked in my deepest register.

"Colonel Wright wants to see you," he said as he propelled me quite forcefully out upon the sidewalk and into one of the cabs at the hotel's stand.

The vehicle wheeled along Michigan Avenue, but instead of continuing southward it turned into Washington Street.

< CONSPIRACY OF KNAVES >

"Why aren't we going to Camp Douglas?" I asked.

The man merely shrugged. Admittedly my anxiety was rapidly turning to fear, but Calvin Blacklock was determined not to reveal Belle Rutledge's unmanliness.

We soon stopped in front of a wooden structure that bore no street number. The entrance door was of heavy weathered boards; the street windows were shuttered. My unbidden guide knocked on the door and it was opened by a soldier armed with a bayoneted rifle. Inside, three or four men seated on facing benches appeared to be waiting for something. I avoided any direct meeting of the eyes with them, but they had the marks of U.S. detectives all over them. When I recognized Otis Jordan at the end of one of the benches, my heart skipped a beat, and Calvin Blacklock silently called upon Belle Rutledge's ability as a dramatic performer. Jordan's eyelids were heavy from lack of sleep, however, and he showed no interest in my presence.

A minute or so later I was inside a comfortable little room that bore some resemblance to a Southern kitchen—with its fireplace, rafters, and calico curtains over the lower halves of the window. In the middle of the room was a round table covered with writing materials, a potted plant, and a stack of posters announcing rewards for the capture of escaped prisoners of war. Three or four cushioned rocking chairs were scattered around the table. Colonel Bartholomew Wright occupied one of them. The only other person in the room was a soldier standing beside the doors with his arms folded. The soldier's large eyes gave me a quick sidewise glance, then returned to staring into infinity.

For several moments, Colonel Wright ignored my presence by pretending to be studying the dancing flames in the fireplace. Then he turned suddenly, an accusing expression in his deep-set eyes.

"Where have you been, Mr. Blacklock?" he demanded. "My detectives have searched the city over for you."

At the sound of his querulous voice, my stage-trained mind immediately began creating a sketch for him. "After our last meeting," I lied, as spies must, "I traveled to Washington for consultation with my superiors. The unexpected death of Kendrich left me without direction—unsupported, you might say, sir."

With thumb and forefinger he caressed his drooping mustache.

"When my men were unable to find you," he said, "I tele-

< **Belle Rutledge** >

graphed Pinkerton's Secret Service in Washington. They reported they had no record of a Calvin Blacklock."

Lord, I thought, the fat is in the fire. Colonel Wright had tossed me a line that was not in my promptbook, but I determined to brazen it out.

"Yes, I recall your advising me at our last meeting to write to the Pinkertons. I could not tell you then, being sworn to secrecy in the White House, that Kendrich and I were on special duty."

He nodded and I waited for another blow to fall.

"So they informed me," he said. "It seems that Mr. Kendrich shared some information with the Pinkertons, but he told them nothing about his assistants. They advised me to communicate with a man named Baker in the Treasury Department. I telegraphed this Baker, but have received no reply or acknowledgment."

My fluttering heart resumed its normal beating.

"Only President Lincoln's closest aides could reveal full details of my assignment," I lied again, and he was clearly impressed by my fabrication.

"I seek your help again," he said, almost apologetically. "Perhaps you recall the report you posted to me late in the summer—regarding the woman Mrs. Evelyn Ward, whom we suspected of close connections with the Copperhead conspirators. As I recall, your judgment was that Mrs. Ward is a foolish lightheaded female, misguided but incapable of causing any harm because of her scatterbrained nature. I have had my detectives keep a close watch upon her and her husband—who regularly attends Copperhead meetings—and I believe the two of them are a threat to our government."

"Possibly, sir," I said, maintaining the judicious tone I had got into my voice.

"In your meetings with Mrs. Ward last summer," he continued, "did you gain her confidence? Or was she suspicious—"

"Oh, no, sir," I interrupted. "She accepted me as a fellow Kentuckian sympathetic with McClellan instead of Lincoln."

"I see. Then you could visit her in her home, perhaps learn something about her intimates. I am especially interested in her relations with a prisoner who escaped recently, a Captain Truscott, a very dangerous young man. I believe Mrs. Ward may have

< CONSPIRACY OF KNAVES >

assisted him, perhaps knows of his present whereabouts. You could not only be of great help to me, Mr. Blacklock, but you might gain plaudits from Pinkerton's Secret Service."

"I will do what I can, colonel," I assured him, "in the limited time I have left to me in Chicago."

A burning log in the fireplace collapsed upon the coals, sending out an explosion of sparks that sounded like small arms fire. Startled by the noise, Colonel Wright jerked his head back. Then he turned to peer in a confidential manner at me, his voice lowering almost to a whisper.

"As you may know, the Pinkertons were concerned with that incident at Niagara Falls," he said. "A woman was seen with Kendrich there, and the Pinkertons believed at first that she might have died with him. From some of his papers recently discovered, however, they identified her as a scandalous actress using the name Belle Rutledge." His small round nose twitched as he paused for breath. He never took his eyes from me, and I wondered if my sudden breathlessness would bring me to a faint, and a possible revelation of my true sex if an attempt was made to revive me. I said nothing in reply because I knew that at the moment I could not keep my voice anywhere near a masculine timbre.

"Some time ago," he continued in his confidential whisper, "one of my inside informers reported that a woman using the name Belle Rutledge entered the prison compound on a visitors' day. She came there in company with Mrs. Evelyn Ward. Does not that strike you as being quite . . . ah . . . quite—"

"Extraordinary," I said.

"Yes. When I received the Pinkerton report naming one of Kendrich's associates as Belle Rutledge, my memory told me to go through my file record. I found her name there." He paused a moment to slip a tintype from one of the folders on the table. "And here is something else that was passed to me by one of my inside informers. A likeness of Belle Rutledge."

He handed me the tintype, and Lord, there I was, no more than six feet from Colonel Wright in my fop's clothing, staring at an image of my own true feminine face fully revealed in those seconds after Otis Jordan took the open fan from my hand in that canvas-walled ferrotype studio at Camp Douglas. Yes, there was my likeness in a prim matron's wig and wearing the dowdy gray

< **Belle Rutledge** >

dress of a gentlewoman missionary. How could they ever describe me as a scandalous actress?

"We must find this young woman," the colonel said. "We don't know if she's a spy or counterspy. Whatever she is we must find her. Mrs. Ward, I believe, can lead us to her, but so far none of my detectives has been able to gain her confidence. I need a young man such as you, Mr. Blacklock, who already has the trust of Mrs. Ward, to find this mysterious Belle Rutledge."

My feeling at the moment was that I desperately needed a folding fan to hide my facial lineaments, which certainly resembled those in the tintype before me.

"She could be a murderess, you know," the colonel said. "Your friend Kendrich's assassin."

"Possibly," I replied, "but my first duty, sir, is to hasten to Washington and report what I have learned about the Northwestern Conspiracy."

An expression of alarm spread quickly across his face.

"You must do this before election day? Could you give me some inkling of the nature of your findings?"

I knew why Colonel Wright was uneasy about my imaginary report, and I decided to torment him further.

"In the main," I said, "I shall inform my superiors that we have found no real Copperhead threat here. The Northwestern Copperheads are windbags, sir, all air and no substance."

His face was now a perfect caricature of dismay. "But . . . are you certain? How thorough has been your investigation? Where—"

"I can't tell you the full extent, colonel. Others have been working with me. Let me say in addition to a penetration of the organization here in Chicago, we've tested southern Illinois, Indiana, Kentucky, and the Canadian connections."

The commandant's chin quivered, but he soon steadied himself.

"I see I must confide in you, Mr. Blacklock." He licked his lips nervously. "All is not as it seems. Yes, you are quite right. There is no real *Copperhead* threat. The threat is from McClellan and the Democrats." He laughed but without humor. "Don't you see, we need the Copperheads to frighten the people into voting for Lincoln. I don't know who your superiors are, Mr. Blacklock, but from what you say, they are very close to the President himself

< CONSPIRACY OF KNAVES >

If word goes out before election day that the Copperheads are mostly phantoms—created by a few dissidents and traitors—but cultivated by we Unionists—the damage could be disastrous."

He sighed, as though beset by intolerable burdens. "I have convinced my superiors that the Copperhead threat is so great here that they are giving me command of two more regiments to ensure safety on election day. Coming with those regiments will be my promotion to brigadier general. That rank means a great deal to me, young man. I beg you to delay your report to Washington— for only a few days more."

I rested my chin in one hand and tried to look thoughtful and understanding.

"What you say, colonel, is most convincing. Perhaps I should delay at least long enough for me to track down your mysterious Belle Rutledge—who may threaten all our plans."

He gave me a beatific smile. When I stood up as though to leave him, I believe that if I had so commanded, he would have come forward and kissed my boots.

"Shall I call upon you here, colonel?" I asked. "Say in three days or earlier?"

"By all means, Mr. Blacklock. Through election day this building will be headquarters for the provost marshal, and I shall spend much of my time here with him instead of at the prison camp."

Lord, but isn't it wonderful to have the upper hand! Especially over a man like Colonel Bartholomew Wright. Even if only for a few hours.

Charley Heywood arrived in Chicago during the week, but business with the Copperheads kept him at Joseph Milligan's house through the first night. With his usual boldness, he was at Dr. Aylott's front door the next morning, accompanied by a hard-faced bejeweled man he introduced as Brigadier Jeremiah Grundy, commander of the Copperhead army coming to Chicago on election eve.

Charley was in quite a temper because none of his vassals was behaving properly. His Southern belle cousin had journeyed to Chicago against his advice and without his permission. Johnny Truscott had escaped from Camp Douglas just at the time he was needed there. And I had failed to transmit with sufficient promptness a report of the size and capability of Colonel Amos Ferree's guerrilla army in Kentucky.

With Dr. Aylott's aid I managed to convince Charley that a coded telegram reporting on my visit to Colonel Ferree had been sent him immediately after I arrived in Chicago. The telegraph company, however, had declared the message undeliverable.

"A pity," Charley said. "I needed exact numbers and other information before I left southern Illinois." He then asked me to tell him briefly what I had learned.

"Colonel Ferree has no army," I said.

My blunt statement only served to increase Charley's testiness. I should have known better than to say what I did within earshot of the Copperhead leader, Brigadier Grundy, who no doubt had been promised an invasion by a large force of Rebels to coincide with the planned attack upon Chicago.

"This is no time for joking," Charley growled, his voice heavy with disgust. "You know very well that Colonel Ferree has more than two thousand armed men ready to cross the Ohio and strike into the heart of the Northwest."

"I'm sorry for the levity, Major Heywood," I replied. "I shall give you a proper report later, sir."

There was so much I had to tell Charley, intimate trifles that I longed to share privately with him. I wanted to tell him how after our days apart, the first sight of his stalwart figure, the first sound of his vibrant voice, expunged all doubts I might have had about the bond that had sealed my heart to his since the day I first saw him in the Richmond railroad depot.

He must have held the same fancy. At any rate, within an hour of his arrival he adroitly arranged for us to be alone in one of those airy rooms beyond the long hallway where Dr. Aylott stored his medicines. A little business, he explained to the doctor, of a confidential nature. After our intimacies, I told him of my journey by way of Cincinnati, and of how I had visited the orphanage to see Winslow Barber.

"How was the little devil?" Charley asked eagerly.

"He did not see me," I said. "I watched him playing with the other children—through a window."

"You didn't talk to him?"

"No. I feared a short meeting would be painful for both of us.

< CONSPIRACY OF KNAVES >

If he had begged me to take him away with me, I could not have refused."

Charley sighed, and began fastening the loops on his shirt. "One of these days—when this business is finished—Winslow will be with us again. I promise you, Belle."

"There was a sadness in the child's face," I continued. "Resignation, I suppose. You remember how Winslow was always laughing. Angry at times, but never sad, the way he is now."

Although Charley refused to listen to my disillusioning truths about Colonel Ferree's phantasmal army (he actually accused me of impertinence for discrediting it!), he wanted to know all about Otis Jordan, the details of how he followed me from the railroad station to Dr. Aylott's. He was very indignant when I told him I'd later seen Jordan in company with Colonel Bartholomew Wright's detectives, but his mood changed to spirited laughter when I described my meeting with the colonel while I was in the guise of Calvin Blacklock.

"So the Union colonel wants Calvin Blacklock to find Belle Rutledge. How very rich, indeed. How was it he described her?"

"A scandalous actress," I said, and we both laughed together.

"The only fault in it," I said soberly, "I dare not go out on the streets of Chicago again—except as Calvin Blacklock."

"No matter," Charley replied. "You're traveling with me to Canada tonight. But as soon as we leave Chicago, I shall drown Mr. Blacklock in Lake Michigan."

By that last remark, he meant that we would be leaving Chicago on a boat instead of a railroad car. U.S. detectives were watching all the stations in Chicago, Charley explained, and a swarm of them frequented the Windsor ferry wharf in Detroit.

Soon after darkness fell, we boarded a small fishing vessel at a landing on the Chicago River and were quickly out into Lake Michigan. The pilot was beetle-browed and thick-necked, and his left hand had been mangled, so that only a stub of a thumb remained. There was a sinister air about him that made my skin crawl when I first saw him. His boat looked unkempt and smelled of fish, but the cabin that Charley and I shared was neat and clean, the walls being paneled in cherry wood, and the bed was a delightful place to spend the night in the arms of my heart's desire.

< **Belle Rutledge** >

With the morning came a chilly swirling mist, and when Charley and I climbed to the narrow deck, I was on the point of turning back down the steps, but the pilot, seeing me shivering, kindly offered to provide me with a waterproof. I pulled the cowl over my head, and the coat kept me quite snug from wind and damp. By daylight the pilot proved not to be sinister at all, but a polite well-informed lake sailor who spoke with a charming Scottish burr. As I should have known, one can't judge a pie by its crust.

Sometime late in the day we put in at Grand Haven, and after a short wait boarded a train that took us across the state of Michigan. The cars were frightfully cold and uncomfortable, but at Port Sarnia we transferred to the familiar Grand Trunk and rode straight through to Toronto.

There in the luxurious Queen's Hotel, we found a small group of Morgan men in the midst of a grand celebration. News had just come from eastern Canada that Bennett Young and his little band of brigands had recently invaded Vermont, robbed the banks at St. Albans, and escaped across the border with thousands of dollars. Some of the men were under arrest by Canadian authorities, but all the celebrators in the Queen's were confident their comrades would soon be freed and the captured booty forwarded to Toronto.

While we were in Toronto, I became aware of two other daring plots being hatched by that wild gang in Canada. John Headley and Rob Kennedy were the ring leaders in a scheme to burn the city of New York. The Vermont raiders, to cover their escape flight, successfully used Greek fire to set blazes in St. Albans, and Headley and Kennedy were certain that with hundreds of bottles of that fiendish substance they could burn all the hotels in the city, as well as such popular places as Barnum's Museum, Niblo's, the Winter Garden, and Wallack's Theater. With his usual élan, Charley was champing at the bit to become a member of this band of Rebel incendiaries, and he persuaded the leaders to delay the raid until after the elections so that he would be free to join them from Chicago.

When I learned that theaters were on the arson list, I told Charley I would never forgive him if he set fire to a single one of them, and he solemnly promised to spare all theaters during the burning of New York City. For reasons that I will later make clear, Charley was unable to join the New York saboteurs. Because that

< CONSPIRACY OF KNAVES >

absurd fiasco has been so much written up in the newspapers and weeklies, and had little to do with what happened in Chicago, I will omit the details from my narrative.

The other plot being devised in Toronto involved both Charley and me. Many of its aspects were never revealed to me, but I'm certain the scheme was very dangerous to all concerned. My first knowledge of it began with what appeared to be a casual inquiry from Charley.

"Belle, would it be possible," he asked, "for you to apply stage makeup to both of us, so that I would appear to be an elderly gentleman and you his aging wife?"

"Certainly," I replied. "I have played old ladies, hags, and witches on several occasions. But I would need a few supplies. Possibly I can obtain them from one of the Toronto theaters."

"Please do try," he said. "We must be very careful in returning to the States."

By pretending to be involved in amateur playacting and *tableaux vivants,* I persuaded the manager of a theater to sell me a small supply of stage powders, putty, and pencils. That night in our hotel room, I transformed Charley and me into a pair of ancients. He was as delighted as a small boy with a new rocking horse, and proved to be an apt pupil while I showed him how to hold his body and walk in a manner that matched his appearance. The next morning we tested our disguises by wearing them into the Queen's dining hall and not one of our friends recognized us.

With an abruptness to which I was growing accustomed in my life with Charley Heywood, we left Toronto the following day, journeyed to Port Stanley, and there took passage on a lake steamer. Every stateroom on the small vessel was filled, however, and we were assigned cots in the salon, along with a dozen other passengers. This was an unforeseen botheration that challenged my ingenuity. Stage makeup is short-lived, and we had been counting on repairing our disguises in the privacy of a stateroom. I managed, however, to pass the necessary materials to Charley, instructing him how to apply them in a toilet stall. No one apparently noticed any changes in our appearance during the evening; in fact, two or three travelers commiserated with us for having to sleep on open cots at our advanced ages.

< **Belle Rutledge** >

The night turned out to be quite stormy. Frequent gusts kept the cots sliding about on the salon flooring, and the tremors of the steamer caused the glass pendants on the old chandelier above us to jingle continuously through the night. The tinkling glass, the creaking of the boat, the contented suspirations of Charley on the adjoining cot—combined with the rolling and pitching—recalled for me that dreadful water journey from City Point to Baltimore. I was greatly relieved at last to hear the ringing of the steamer's landing bells, the sound of its hoarse whistle, and the voice of a boat's officer calling "Sandusky!"

During the few days we spent in Sandusky, Ohio, Charley was very close-mouthed about his activities. From what hints he gave me, from what I heard others say and what I have learned since, he was evidently laying the groundwork for a plot to free the Rebel prisoners at nearby Watson's Bluff, a rescue designed to take place simultaneously with the planned election-eve attacks upon Camp Douglas and Chicago. At the boardinghouse where we stayed in Sandusky, he posed as a Cleveland businessman who in his old age was liquidating land properties in northern Ohio. The only strangers that he brought to our rooms were two men that he later told me were officers of the Order of the Star, a local Copperhead organization.

One morning Charley arose before daylight, waked me to tell me he would be gone for two days, and shambled out of the bedroom, chuckling as he exaggerated his old man's manner of walking. When he failed to return on the third day, I grew very anxious. He had left me with only a few greenbacks, and with absolutely nothing to do but limp around like a failing old lady. After supper that evening, I actually felt like a penniless gray-haired widow as I sat watching darkness fall over the wintry-appearing Ohio town.

Lighting a candle, I picked up a copy of *Harper's Weekly* to read an account of General Sherman's triumphs in Georgia. A moment later voices sounded on the staircase outside the closed door. Two men were conversing in muffled tones, interrupted by a child's query. A knock sounded and I invited them to enter.

Charley's head appeared from behind the partially opened door, his wide-brimmed hat at a jaunty angle. His "old man" disguise

< C O N S P I R A C Y   O F   K N A V E S >

had been abandoned. His dark beard was freshly trimmed, and his blue eyes were shining with that mischievous joy that for me had become his hallmark.

"Surprise!" he shouted, and thrust his cousin Wesley Heywood ahead of him into the room.

Well, it was a surprise, but not a particularly pleasant one for me, especially with the contrast between the two Heywoods being so vivid, the two of them side by side, one representing male determination and vigor, the other male irresolution and hollowness.

"Second surprise!" Charley cried, flinging the door all the way open, and glancing proudly down at his side. I could not believe what I saw, his hand holding little Winslow Barber's. The youngster, dressed like a princeling by Charley, evidently did not recognize me in my old lady's clothing and lined face, and so I pulled off my wig and with a handkerchief removed the stage cosmetics.

As I leaned down to lift the boy in my arms, he recognized me suddenly, his eyes widening in terror. He quickly drew away, trying to hide behind Charley's legs, shaking his mop of yellow hair from side to side, his wide mouth crying "No, no, no!" so pitiably I wanted to weep. He was like a mistreated puppy shrilly barking defiance.

I was the being who had imprisoned him in that orphanage in Cincinnati; therefore, I was the ogress. Charley had rescued him, and therefore Charley was the redeemer. Charley did not comprehend this at first; he had brought Winslow to me as a gift, but the gift was turning the tables and rejecting its intended receiver.

With his warped sentiments, Wesley Heywood saw the situation clearly. "I told you, Charley, you should've left the brat there," he said. "Now you're stuck with him."

"Damned if I am," Charley growled.

"Damn, damn, damn!" Winslow shouted in his high treble.

"I'll wash your mouth," Charley threatened, and the boy broke into uncontrollable sobbing.

"Don't tell him that," I said. "He's had to live with such bullying all these months now."

Winslow stopped sobbing and peered at me from between Charley's legs, an animal wariness in his face and stance.

"All right, you hellion!" Charley cried, and without warning turned and lifted the boy high above his head. "At least you've found your tongue."

"The little monkey didn't speak ten words all the way from Cincinnati," Wesley Heywood said.

One morning, a few days later, I used the remainder of our theatrical materials to prepare Charley and me for a journey on the cars from Sandusky to Chicago. We would be traveling as grandparents escorting a grandchild, a simple pretension that we were certain would mislead the most astute of Colonel Bartholomew Wright's U.S. detectives.

Winslow was fascinated by the applications of our disguises, but his face remained solemn, sometimes sad, and he kept a considerable distance between himself and me, as though fearful that I might reach out and make a captive of him.

From Charley's conversations with Wesley Heywood, I gathered that he was leaving his cousin in Sandusky to continue whatever scheme was afoot there. Apparently the Fielding brothers had turned up somewhere and were en route to join Wesley in the undertaking.

Not until we were bound for Chicago on the Lake Shore and Michigan Southern Railroad did Charley give me some inkling of the Sandusky plot. The smooth swaying of the car on the level track soon put Winslow to sleep, and Charley laid the little boy upon an empty seat and joined me for the first time. His revelations came out in a teasing way as he outlined the role he had planned for me in Sandusky.

"You were going to be Madam Rose," he said. "In charge of a high-class troupe of daughters of joy I recruited down in Cincinnati. Finest-looking courtesans you'll ever set eyes on anywhere. Cost us far more than we're paying the Copperheads coming up from southern Illinois. Anyway, you remember the two gentlemen from the Order of the Star? They've rented a fancy house down near the ferry landing, and they've been cultivating close friendships with the prison commandant and his officers. You as Madam Rose, and your charming jezebels, would be entertaining those Yankee watchdogs tomorrow night had I not needed you with me in Chicago."

< CONSPIRACY OF KNAVES >

I gave him my oft-practiced stage expression of outraged propriety.

"Sir, do you have so small a regard for me, you would make of me a procuress?"

He took me seriously. "You're an actress, Belle. Merely a character for you to play—in a good cause."

(Whether I would have taken that part, I cannot say. I think not, but in those days Charley Heywood held my heart and soul in bondage, and it would have been difficult for me to refuse him. As for the outcome of the plot, everyone who reads the newspapers knows what a fiasco that turned out to be.)

"Now that I'm not available to play Madam Rose," I asked, "who will take my place?"

"Oh, the oldest of the doves from Cincinnati, I suppose. They're Cousin Wesley's responsibility now. What a pity you and I can't be there to enjoy the fun." He shook his head in disappointment. "Wesley's likely to throw everything off the track, but with the Fielding brothers to help him, something's bound to happen at Watson's Bluff while we're seizing Chicago and Camp Douglas."

When little Winslow awakened an hour or so later, Charley had to join him in the seat across the aisle. The boy simply refused, with physical stubbornness, to share a seat with me.

At Toledo, everyone left the cars for a noon meal in one of those barnlike sheds where passengers must bolt badly prepared food in great haste before being herded like sheep back aboard the cars. Poor little Winslow had swallowed only a few bites of his porridge before the train porters began bellowing at us to return to our car seats or be left behind. With the locomotive bell ringing a frantic summons, I slipped out of the line and hurriedly purchased a ripe pear and a packet of taffy from a peddler, and almost split my old lady's skirt rushing aboard the train before it jerked into motion.

Although I could tell from Winslow's eyes that he was starving for the pear I'd brought him, he refused to take it until I gave it to Charley, from whose hand the dear little demon literally seized the fruit and bit into it until juice ran down his chin.

< **Belle Rutledge** >

I resolved, however, that there would be no middle man for the glossy rolls of taffy that I displayed in my lap. I broke a piece from one of these sweetmeats, popped it into my mouth, and offered the other half to Winslow. He turned his head away, then slyly glanced back at me, not directly, but cautiously, like a dog awaiting a blow from a cruel mistress.

"Jehoshaphat!" I cried angrily. "I bought these sweets for you, you little brat!"

His pouting lips parted slightly. "Jehoshaphat!" he shouted back at me, and ardently repeated the word: "Jehoshaphat!" He slid off the plush seat, reached across the aisle, seized one of the larger pieces of taffy from my lap, crammed it into his mouth crosswise, and began shaking with laughter. He could not stop laughing, and seconds later the candy flew out of his mouth to land upon the dirty car floor.

For a moment he looked as if he were going to burst into tears, but I quickly gave him another piece. When he turned his eyes away, I motioned to Charley to bring him over to my seat. The little tadpole offered no objections whatsoever, settling down between Charley and me, and glancing up at my face from time to time, shouting "Jehoshaphat!" and then wiping his sticky hands and mouth on my old lady's dress. Lord, I would not have cared a whit if he had covered me with tackiness. I had won back the bratling elf's trust in Belle Rutledge, and God helping me, I meant for him to keep it to eternity.

After Winslow fell asleep again, in my lap this time, Charley offered his opinion that what the boy needed was a new stock of swear words. "He's afraid to use the old ones he knew, the ones that embarrassed you, Belle, because that wretched orphanage beat them out of him. You saw how pleased he was with 'Jehoshaphat.' We'll have to think up a new set of oaths for him."

For a while Charley repeated a few mythological and Biblical names, trying them out in a voice meant to be imitative of an old man reviling the world and everybody in it, but to my trained ear they sounded more like the bleats of a tired old goat. Charley's locutions attracted some attention from the passengers, who were trying to nod off to sleep, and he soon quieted down. He slid a sailcloth bag from under the seat, opened its draw cord, and withdrew a roll of paper that was covered with columns of numbers written in purple ink. For several minutes he studied the columns carefully.

"What we have here, Belle," he said in a husky whisper, "is the last of the Canadian hoard. When the greenbacks and gold pieces in this bag are gone, there'll be no more for Northwestern Copperheads. If 'fickle chance' is kind to us next Monday we shan't need any more boodle from Canada or England; we'll have the wealth of Chicago and the state of Illinois in our hands."

"Then what, Charley? Emperor Vallandigham? Or maybe King Charles Heywood?"

He grimaced. "You have a shrew's tongue, Belle Rutledge. Are you growing weary of the game, my love?" He laughed. "First thing I want us to do when Abe Lincoln turns wise and lets the Confederacy go free is to pack our bags and sail for Europe to see the elephant."

"You said something like that to me once before," I replied. "While we were traveling to Niagara Falls. Remember?"

The smile left his face instantly. I should have known by then that he preferred not to remember Niagara Falls. He continued, but without his previous heartiness.

"I have enough salted away in the Bank of Upper Canada to keep us for quite a while. And I'm saddled with no obligations— except to my naïve female cousin Marianna—can't let her lose Little Hundred, don't you know. . . ." His voice faded, his head lolled against the back of the plush seat, he sighed, and then fell asleep. The rhythmic clacking of the car wheels set words to sounding in my head, a refrain from a sad old song so popular in those last months of the war:

> *Backward, turn backward, O Time in your flight!*
> *Make me a child again just for tonight.*

That Charley's last thought before falling asleep was of his cousin Marianna should have been a warning to me. But good Lord, what an adoring ninny was I whenever that audacious man was at my side!

When we arrived in Chicago—grandfather, grandmother, and little grandson Winslow—we left our bags (except for the sailcloth

< **Belle Rutledge** >

one) in the care of the depot's baggage master and rode in a battered old hackney right up to the front of Dr. Aylott's house on State Street. Almost in the same instant, Charley and I recognized the U.S. detective in an overcoat crouched on the shadowy steps of a house directly opposite.

From sheer weariness and the lateness of the hour, Winslow had fallen into deep sleep, his body limp as a rope, and Charley carried him in both arms up to the entrance. I pulled the bell cord, and after a rather long delay Ilena came with a candle and opened the door. She stared with some animosity at what appeared to her to be three strangers.

"Doctor does not receive patients so late at night," she said firmly.

"But madame, this child is very ill," Charley shouted for the benefit of the detective across the street, and so loudly that Winslow began squirming to wakefulness.

"Ilena," I whispered. "I'm Belle. And Major Heywood."

Her eyes opened wide in astonishment, but she let us step inside, and a few minutes later we were confronted by a worried-looking Dr. Aylott, who scolded us for coming to his house even though we were disguised. He appeared to be much disturbed by the presence of Winslow, who was suddenly wide awake and running about the doctor's study like a wild colt and shrieking words from the new Vulgar Tongue that Charley had taught him on the train.

Charley soothed the doctor by showing him the contents of his sailcloth bag and informing him that one hundred thousand dollars would be placed in his keeping for disbursement to Copperheads as they arrived in the city. After we quieted Winslow with warm milk provided by Ilena, we spent a comfortable night in one of the good doctor's rear bedrooms.

The following day dragged very slowly for me. Although our theatrical materials were now exhausted, I believed it might be safe enough to go out in my old lady's wig and dress, especially with Winslow accompanying me. The boy, however, refused to leave the house, setting up such a banshee wailing when I led him to the front door that I did not dare to force him outside. He may have believed that Chicago was Cincinnati, and that I intended returning him to the dreaded orphanage. Therefore, I was obliged

< CONSPIRACY OF KNAVES >

to pass the day a virtual prisoner, a captive nursemaid to that dear little brat.

After informing Ilena and me that they would be spending the day arranging an important meeting for that evening, Dr. Aylott in his professional frock coat and Charley costumed as a workman departed together on a dray cart that delivered some boxes of medicinal roots and herbs to the rear of the house.

"Several gentlemen will be arriving here during the day, most of them by way of the adjoining rooftop and through the first bedroom window," Charley told me at the last minute. "So leave the window unlocked. Treat them hospitably until we return."

Before the day was over I was beginning to learn a few things about the maternal trials of an adoptive mother. For his playground, Winslow chose the long hardwood-floored hallway between the shelves of Dr. Aylott's medicines. First off, I learned that children of his age prefer running to walking. Up and down he ran for hours, stamping the heels and soles of the fancy boots Charley had bought him, and shouting "Beelzebub" and "Taradiddle," two of his newest oaths.

From time to time in the afternoon, we greeted one or more of the Copperheads and escaped prisoners of war that Charley had warned us would appear through the window of the bedroom. Either Ilena or I would escort them to the study, where we gave them coffee or tea. As I recall, there were nine of them, including two Rebels I had seen in Windsor, as well as the obnoxious Joseph Milligan heavily scented with apple pomade, and the southern Illinois brigadier, Jeremiah Grundy, flourishing his sparkling rings and stickpins. Some of the men smoked cigars of such rank tobacco they fouled the air, and some expressed resentment because of the absence of strong drink with which to beguile the afternoon.

Eventually Charley and the doctor returned to the alleyway entrance, riding in the dray cart in which they had left. They had retrieved our baggage from the railway station, and it was quickly brought into the lower level of the house and carried upstairs to our bedroom.

The evening began with a late dinner at which neither Ilena nor I was present. We dined in the adjoining small kitchen with Winslow, and I could hear Charley talking and laughing with more

< **Belle Rutledge** >

than the usual gusto that flowed from him when he was in full command of a group of conspirators of any stripe.

Soon after the plotters had removed themselves to the doctor's study, Charley sought me out to join them for what was to be the last meeting of Copperheads that I would ever attend. For the occasion I dressed in a seductive outfit of soft mull muslin, fluffy and fluted and covered with Valenciennes lace, bought in Toronto. But precious little good the dress did me. Somewhat as he had done in the Packet House at Cincinnati, Charley placed me away from the main scene, in the angular library alcove, where, as I have mentioned before, the flaking leather-bound volumes seemed permeated with the odors of the drug formulas they contained.

My duty was to keep a notebook record of what was discussed and decided upon by Charley, his Confederates, and the Copperheads. This meeting was quite similar to others I have previously described; therefore I shall forbear burdening my readers with too many details. Suffice it to say that there was much coarse talk about Greek fire, quantities of weapons and ammunition supposedly concealed in barns and livery stables around Chicago, the thousands of Sons of Liberty who would magically appear at the appointed time on the streets of the city, and the multitudes of Confederate guerrillas ready to cross the Ohio River and gallop through cheering crowds welcoming deliverance of the Northwestern states.

Seated in a high-backed chair that almost concealed my presence, I had only to turn my head slightly to look out from my shadowy recess at the faces and forms of the conspirators. They sat in a semicircle in front of Charley, who strode back and forth, haranguing, emboldening, or admonishing them as the mood struck him.

For some reason—possibly the flickering candles and lamps casting overlaying shadows, the constantly clashing voices, or the utter absurdity of the entire scene—the group gradually assumed the shapes of different animals of the wild. I was reminded abruptly of a long-forgotten fairy tale, a bedtime story, that my grandfather told me, often at my repeated urgings even after I had heard it countless times. A fox was spellbinding animals of the forest, hoodwinking the bear while the bear was deceiving the fox. Charley

< CONSPIRACY OF KNAVES >

was the fox, so enwrapped in deceiving the bear that he was not beyond being duped himself by the bear, or by the weasel, the cougar or the wolf, the ferret, the skunk, the possum, the squirrel, or the panther. I saw no lion, not even a tiger among that gathering of deceivers, beguilers, tricksters, and liars.

Truthfully there was not even that much solidity in the gathering. Only I, Belle Rutledge, possessed any substance. Only I among all of them, including some not present who were colonels and brigadiers of the Union Army, only I knew for certain that they were nothing more than cardboard figures, no more corporeal than the paper dolls that in my childhood I cut from *Godey's Lady's Book of Fashion*. Three sets of knaves had built a house of cards, too insubstantial to withstand the slightest breath of wind. The Union colonels had frightened their superiors, including their own president, who feared what he termed "a fire in the rear." The audacious Rebels in their turn had deceived the Copperheads into believing a mighty host would be sweeping northward to help them seize the power of Chicago. And the Copperheads had bamboozled the Rebels into believing that a multitude would rise to shatter the Union. All sides of the flimsy triumvirate had alarmed the Northern population, split the Democrats into war and peace antagonists, and forwarded the reelection of Mr. Lincoln.

On that Friday evening before the Tuesday elections, I saw it all with great clarity there in Dr. Aylott's smoke-filled study, while the Fox and his listening animals of the wild planned an assault upon Camp Douglas.

They had a map of the prison, drawn fittingly upon cardboard to match their own brittleness. Eight hundred mythical fighting men armed with mythical pistols, rifles, and shotguns would assail the walls, two hundred men to each side of the rough square. Major Heywood would lead the strike against the west wall, crashing through the wooden boards into the prisoners' compound. From the north, Sir Lucius Eberhart would lead the mounted charge, a flank attack as it were, relieving any pressure upon Heywood and his men, and also assisting Captain John Truscott attacking from the lake side. Truscott's force would storm through the main entrance gate into the garrison headquarters grounds and capture by surprise the artillery pieces stationed there. On the south side, Jeremiah Grundy and his two hundred would create a noisy di-

< **Belle Rutledge** >

version to draw off as many of the Union defenders as possible.

They discussed every detail with great seriousness as if they all truly supposed the attack would be carried out. Possibly the Copperheads still envisioned a city filling up with Confederate soldiers in mufti, and possibly Charley Heywood and his Rebel companions still believed that swarms of armed Copperheads were at last going to materialize on the streets of Chicago. More likely each group was laughing in their sleeves at the other.

And yet I noted down the essentials as if I also believed that the capture of Chicago was predestined. I swear, however, that deep in my heart I did not believe so. If I had regarded the conspiracy as more than an illusion, I would have acted to stop it. Not by going to the Union Army imbeciles in command at Chicago, but by sending a telegram to Washington. Truly I thought of doing that, but saw no point in it at all. Meanwhile . . .

The Fox said to the Ferret: You and your men are responsible for cutting all telegraph wires leaving the city.

The Ferret asked the Fox: And burning the railroad depots?

The Fox replied: If necessary, to stop railroad cars leaving the city.

The Fox then said to the Weasel: We shall need tools to destroy the wooden fence. Heavy tools for smashing and prying. The fence boards are one inch thick.

They argued over the thickness of the boards for several minutes.

And yes, I noted it all down in Pitman shorthand, just as if it were an official government record. Men assigned to the attack upon Camp Douglas would report in staggered shifts to the corner of Randolph and State streets beginning at 4:00 P.M. on Monday, and travel by streetcar and cabs to designated stops near the prison camp.

Throughout the evening, Dr. Aylott seldom spoke. When Charley turned to him and announced that Aylott would be responsible for meeting Copperheads coming from the south, providing them with funds, and finding rooms for them, the doctor looked terrified for an instant, his hands trembling violently until he interlaced his fingers.

The Fox said to the doctor: They will be arriving tomorrow and Sunday. Take them first to the house at 113 Michigan, then

< CONSPIRACY OF KNAVES >

find them more permanent rooms elsewhere as quickly as possible.

The doctor replied: Violence must be controlled, limited. I am in this because I am against the war. The country cannot be united by war.

The Fox ignored the doctor's remark, and said to the Possum: Clothing will be needed for the freed prisoners. Warm coats especially. Clothes must be included with the arms and ammunition in the wagons waiting near the lakeshore.

The Fox then said to the Panther: Time of attack is seven o'clock P.M. Monday night. Skyrockets, dependable dry powder rockets, must be fired off at the same time from several sections of Chicago to signal the attacks. Seventy-two hours from now our brothers in Camp Douglas will be free, and Chicago and the Northwest will be ours.

The Cougar said to the Fox: We'll send the abolitionists to hell in a hand basket.

The Squirrel joined in: We'll give 'em hell under their shirttails.

Yes, I noted it all down, even when the dunderheads turned away from the subject and talked about capturing Mexico and Cuba and annexing them to the Confederate States of America. Good Lord, had they not read the newspapers recently? SHERMAN VICTORIOUS. GRANT ADVANCING ON RICHMOND. PRICE'S REBELS FLEE UNION CAVALRY IN MISSOURI.

Near the end of the palavering, Ilena knocked on the door and announced the arrival of a telegram. Dr. Aylott arose from his chair, his sweated wing collar hanging like gills beneath his sickly yellow face; he resembled a fish too long out of water. Ilena handed the flimsy paper to the Fox, who read the code words aloud, and then deciphered: Eight men leaving Bloomington for Chicago in farm wagon.

The Fox laughed and said to his audience: An error of the telegraph dispatcher. We recruited *eighty* men in Bloomington, not eight.

Delivery of the telegram evidently made Dr. Aylott very uneasy. He dropped a pill into his mouth and crushed it with his nutcracker jaw.

20

TRAITORS IN OUR
MIDST WE'VE FOUND

This chapter is derived almost entirely from the proceedings of the U.S. Military Commission that convened at Indianapolis, Indiana, for the trial of Dr. Julian Aylott and other prisoners brought before it. The proceedings, recorded by a stenographic clerk, were published in the daily newspapers, copies of which came to my hand. As I was not present, nor were any of my trusted informers present, when Dr. Aylott visited the provost marshal in Chicago to reveal his recent history, I cannot vouch for the exactness of what was said. Nor can I be certain of the truthfulness of Dr. Aylott, who to my knowledge told one falsehood and may have told others, yet he was judged not guilty by the courts. The rigid unadorned words of a courtroom transcription do not always reveal the emotions of the speakers, and I have tried to show such feelings when my perceptions of these persons made it possible to do so.

B.R.

EARLY ON THE MORNING of November 5, the Saturday preceding national election day, Dr. Julian Aylott left his house on State Street in Chicago and walked to a nondescript building on Washington Street. He was carrying a sailcloth bag, bulging and heavy with gold coins and greenbacks. A soldier guarded the entrance door, which bore a newly painted sign: U.S. PROVOST MARSHAL. The guard refused to admit Aylott until the doctor wrote a short note on the back of one of his large business cards, which was then handed inside. After a wait of several minutes, Aylott

< CONSPIRACY OF KNAVES >

was permitted to enter, and was immediately led into the inner office by a lieutenant who introduced him to a Colonel Miles Sommers, recently arrived in Chicago to replace a transferred provost marshal.

What was said during this first meeting was not completely disclosed in the military trial, but evidently Colonel Sommers asked Dr. Aylott to wait in the reception room while a messenger was sent to Camp Douglas.

The time was about midmorning when Commandant Bartholomew Wright entered through the street door. He was wearing a splendid new double-breasted dark blue uniform frock coat with a star on each shoulder strap. Without waiting to be announced, he entered the inner office, and a few moments later, Dr. Aylott was summoned to join him and Colonel Sommers. Aylott had seen the commandant only once before—at the last Independence Day celebration at Camp Douglas, when Wright was a colonel. The doctor was mildly surprised that he was now a general; he had not read the morning papers, which contained brief announcements of the promotion in rank.

"You say that you are Dr. Julian Aylott, and that you have vital information concerning the Sons of Liberty and their plans for election day," General Wright began. "How did you come by this information?"

"Through my association with members of the Sons of Liberty," Aylott replied. "But before I go further with my statement, I beg permission to furnish some personal reasons for becoming a member of that organization."

"Permission is granted," the general replied sharply.

"First I must tell you that I am a partisan Democrat. I believe sincerely in the principles of Jefferson and Jackson."

Disregarding General Wright's obvious irritation, Aylott continued by relating how he had moved his drug business from Boston to Louisville to establish it in a central location and with expectations that the political climate there would be more congenial to his beliefs. The outbreak of the war, however, had brought so much trouble because of his activities as a Democrat that he had literally been forced to remove to Chicago.

"You sided with the Rebel cause?" Wright interrupted.

"I believed the war to be unnecessary."

"I am a Kentuckian myself, Dr. Aylott," Wright continued, "and I have personal knowledge of what was occurring in Louisville early in the war. I submit that the Democrats laid schemes to force Kentucky from the Union and into the Confederacy."

"The party was divided, sir. I never supported leaving the Union, nor did many other Democrats. I advocated a policy of neutrality."

"Which was an impossibility."

"So I discovered. My only reason for mentioning the matter now is to explain why I left Kentucky to come to Chicago. Constant turmoil and uncertainty are bad for business. In Chicago I know where I stand and the atmosphere around me has remained stable so that my business prospers."

Colonel Sommers nodded as though in agreement with Aylott's statement. He was a wiry gray-haired man with a mustache like a wisp of smoke over a cruel thin-lipped mouth. (I was to see Sommers later at the time I was awaiting trial.) He would have looked down at the tabletop and then responded to Dr. Aylott in a high accusing whisper: "Yet you joined a traitorous organization, the Sons of Liberty, whose objective is to create turmoil through revolution, by overthrowing the government."

Dr. Aylott shook his head. "I first joined a local society of Democrats, the Sons of Illini, most members of which later allied themselves with a national organization known as the Knights of the Golden Circle. Because of my ardent partisanship I was made an Ancient Brother, and I soon became a high officer of the Knights. It was during this later time that I first became aware of links with the Confederate government."

"What led you to this awareness?" General Wright asked.

"A visit by an officer in the Confederate Army. He came through the lines from Richmond and journeyed here to Chicago. At first he was very circumspect, posing as a national leader of the Knights of the Golden Circle from the state of Maryland. He evidently heard about me in Louisville, and for some reason believed me to be loyal to the Confederacy. He, and no doubt some of his spies— for he was in command of Confederate intelligence—made an investigation of my activities in Kentucky and Chicago, and mistook my allegiance to the Democrats for allegiance to the Confederacy."

< CONSPIRACY OF KNAVES >

Colonel Sommers's thin mouth would have shaped into a sneer as he said: "In my opinion those allegiances are one and the same."

"I must differ with you, sir," Dr. Aylott said. "There are generals in the Union Army who are Democrats."

"But not members of a Copperhead organization, as you are," Sommers retorted. "An organization that you yourself just said was linked with the Confederacy."

General Wright interrupted impatiently: "What was the Confederate officer's name?"

"Fennell. Richard Fennell. A colonel, I believe. He became so convinced of my loyalty to his cause that before he left Chicago he gave me a code book with instructions for transmitting telegraph messages by a secret route to his very headquarters in Richmond."

Both Union officers expressed consternation and disbelief at Dr. Aylott's statement.

"Are you certain of this?" Colonel Sommers asked.

"I have sent messages and received replies within forty-eight hours," the doctor replied. "But usually three or four days are required."

"Your action was treasonable," Sommers said accusingly, his voice no doubt like acid. "Providing information to the enemy."

"I assure you, sir, that nothing harmful to the Union ever went over the telegraph from me. It was mostly bombast, about the Knights and later the Sons of Liberty. Fennell received from me what I thought he wanted to hear. Vastly exaggerated figures of membership. Sometimes a report on the arrival or departure of one or the other of his spies."

"We will want that code book," Wright declared. "And names of spies."

Dr. Aylott slipped a narrow gray-backed tablet from an inside pocket and laid it on the table in front of the commandant.

"Can you tell us how the messages travel? Over which wires, through which cities?" Wright asked.

"I was told to send the telegrams to a man in Louisville. Probably a false name. What the next destination was I do not know."

Colonel Sommers then asked: "If you are as loyal to the Union as you say, why did you not report this to military authorities here in Chicago?"

"I did so. At once," Dr. Aylott replied. "My first report was made months ago—to your predecessor, sir."

"To the provost marshal?"

"Yes. To General Grider. Andrew Grider."

Sommers glanced at General Wright, his sly expression indicating skepticism of the doctor's statement.

"You must know that General Grider is out of the States. Somewhere in Dakota Territory."

"Yes. When I first read that he had been suddenly posted from Chicago, I wrote him a letter, inquiring what I should do. So far I have heard nothing."

"You must also know that weeks are required for mail to go up and come down the Missouri River. Why did you not report this to me earlier?"

Dr. Aylott hesitated a moment before replying.

"I was hoping to hear first from General Grider. So that I would possess written proof that I served covertly for him. And was not myself a traitor. From the very first, he asked me to be extremely cautious so as not to arouse suspicions among the Sons of Liberty. I was to keep nothing in writing. I was never to visit the provost marshal's headquarters. General Grider was also distrustful of the post office, believing it to be infested with Copperheads, and he asked me not to send reports by mail. When I had information to impart, I sent him a handbill advertising my herbal remedies. This was a signal for him to send Captain Fairchild around to my office for 'medical treatment.' The captain never came in his uniform. I gave him either an oral or written report to take to General Grider."

"Is Captain Fairchild still in Chicago?" Sommers asked.

"I believe he went west with General Grider."

Wright interrupted: "Yes, he was the general's adjutant. I knew him casually. Dr. Aylott, what sort of information did you furnish General Grider?"

"Names of the leaders. Places and dates mainly, for attacks upon Camp Douglas and Chicago. Attacks that as yet have never come off."

Sommers again cast a doubting glance at General Wright, who said brusquely: "Yes. General Grider passed some information to me, especially during the Democrats' convention last August."

< C O N S P I R A C Y   O F   K N A V E S >

Wright then turned back to Aylott. "That brings us to your reason for being here, doctor. The information you say you have of Copperhead plans for election day."

Aylott corrected him. "Election eve. Monday night. Large numbers of Copperheads from downstate are said to be coming to join the Chicago Sons of Liberty for attacks upon Camp Douglas and important buildings in the city." He reached down and lifted the heavy sailcloth bag he had brought with him and set it upon the round table.

"I was given this money to supply Copperheads coming into Chicago. You will find about fifty thousand dollars in this bag, gentlemen."

(That, of course, was the one falsehood told by Dr. Aylott that I was aware of. I was present when Charley Heywood presented the doctor with the entire contents of one hundred thousand dollars, which was brought from Canada by way of Sandusky, Ohio. What happened to the other fifty thousand is as much a mystery as what happened to the treasure of the fleeing Confederate government after it reached the piney woods of Georgia.)

The general and the colonel must have eyed that bag of gold and greenbacks with considerable affection. And certainly nothing could have been more fitting than for them to sing a duet chorus from Mr. Charles Boynton's stirring ballad denouncing the Copperheads. "What's the Matter?" it was called, a ditty that was very popular that year in the theaters of the North:

> Traitors in our midst we've found,
> That's what's the matter,
> Peddling here their treason round,
> That's what's the matter.
>
> That's what's the matter now,
> That's what's the matter,
> Treason here we won't allow
> That's what's the matter!

But of course the general and the colonel did nothing of the kind. I don't know why such a theatrical conceit came to my mind when I read the courtroom proceedings. As I observed before, however, the lackluster dialogue recorded during the examination of witnesses needed stage directions to give it flair, to make it histrionic.

No, instead of performing, both men immediately demanded to know how much money the Confederates had given Aylott and other Copperheads, and what it had been used for.

"The money came in spurts," Dr. Aylott replied. "Sometimes they had none to give us, but we had only to be patient and they'd bring us what we asked for. We convinced them that the Sons of Liberty were raising an army that needed to be armed. The army was a myth. Most of the money they gave us to buy arms with went to the Democratic party—for the convention, the Wigwam, for watchers to guarantee the freedom of the ballot box next Tuesday."

"Who brought this money to you?" Colonel Sommers asked.

"Major Charles Heywood either brought it or sent it," Aylott replied.

Bartholomew Wright declared that the name was known to him. A most elusive character, that Major Heywood. None of the Camp Douglas detectives had been able to obtain even a good description of the slippery rascal. Heywood was one of the bushwhacker Morgan's officers, was he not?

He was indeed, the doctor said, as were most of his associates who came and went with impunity from Canada to Chicago and southern Illinois.

General Wright evidently was not pleased with that last remark.

"I have an insufficient number of detectives to track enemies within," he said. "I need all the help I can get in locating and trapping those who may now be in Chicago. I intend to capture Major Heywood and see that he is tried for espionage and conspiracy." He paused a moment to consult a memorandum book. "Have you any knowledge of a Confederate captain, John Truscott, recently escaped from Camp Douglas?"

"I don't know where Captain Truscott is," the doctor replied,

< CONSPIRACY OF KNAVES >

"but I can tell you he has been assigned command of one of the attacking parties against Camp Douglas."

"I should've hanged that incorrigible hotspur when he first came under my restraint," Wright said. "He and Heywood may be clever young men, but I'll warrant you that both will receive their due. Both are a disgrace to their native Bluegrass."

In the published proceedings of the U.S. Military Commission that convened in Indianapolis for examination of witnesses, one may find the names first revealed by Dr. Julian Aylott that morning in the provost marshal's office in Chicago. Many of Charley Heywood's associates whom I had met in Canada and Chicago are there, as well as Copperheads such as Joseph Milligan and Jeremiah Grundy, and that whimsical couple, Judge Ward and his wife Evelyn. When Colonel Lucius Eberhart was named and identified as a British officer, alas, General Wright attacked him as a foreign trespasser, an agent of an enemy power who most certainly should be hanged when captured.

In addition to Mrs. Evelyn Ward, only one other female is on Dr. Aylott's roll call of conspirators. I, Belle Rutledge. When the original questioning of Aylott in Chicago was repeated for benefit of the court in Indianapolis, General Wright was prepared for the introduction of my name and the disclosure that followed. In Chicago, however, he was not prepared.

This is the bare record of testimony:

GENERAL WRIGHT: Could you tell us, Dr. Aylott, more about the woman known as Belle Rutledge? Did she aid the Confederate bushwhacker, Major Heywood, in the conspiracy to attack Camp Douglas and seize the city of Chicago?

DR. AYLOTT: Yes, sir. Belle Rutledge was Major Heywood's confidante. She traveled on missions for him. She assisted him in plans for the conspiracy.

GENERAL WRIGHT: Would you say the two were intimate?

DR. AYLOTT: She was his mistress, if that is what you mean, sir.

GENERAL WRIGHT: Did she ever speak of a man named Kendrich?

DR. AYLOTT: I vaguely remember her mentioning that name. Sometimes she spoke of Kendrich when she was reminiscing about her career as an actress.

GENERAL WRIGHT: She said Kendrich was an actor?

DR. AYLOTT: Yes, as I recall, she said they had acted together in Washington theaters.

GENERAL WRIGHT: Did she say anything about Kendrich being a detective for the Union?

DR. AYLOTT: No, sir.

GENERAL WRIGHT: She never said anything about serving with Kendrich as a detective.

DR. AYLOTT: No, sir.

GENERAL WRIGHT: Did Miss Rutledge ever mention being at Niagara Falls? With the Confederate Major Heywood?

DR. AYLOTT: Yes. While Major Heywood and Miss Rutledge were visiting at my house, she made some mention of Niagara Falls.

GENERAL WRIGHT: Can you recall what she said?

DR. AYLOTT: Not exactly. I recall that Major Heywood appeared to be nettled by her remark. He changed the subject.

GENERAL WRIGHT: Do you know anything else about Belle Rutledge that should be added to the record?

DR. AYLOTT: I assume you are aware, sir, that she sometimes disguised herself as a man—to obtain information for Major Heywood.

At this point, the bare printed words give no hint of Bartholomew Wright's facial expression, the dismay that must have shaken him when Dr. Aylott replied to the next question.

GENERAL WRIGHT: You say she dressed as a man?

DR. AYLOTT: Yes, she did. I believe she may have visited you, sir, in the guise of a jack-a-dandy. As you know, Miss Rutledge was an actress.

There must have been a long silence in the provost marshal's office before Wright could bring himself to ask the next question.

GENERAL WRIGHT: Do you know if Belle Rutledge used a masculine name while so disguised?

DR. AYLOTT: Yes, sir. She called herself Calvin Blacklock.

Lord in Heaven, would not I have given my eyeteeth, my finest pearls, all my chances for theatrical glory, merely to have been close enough to observe Bartholomew Wright's response to the sound of the name Calvin Blacklock. Did his deep-set hound-dog eyes leap from their sockets? did his button nose wrinkle out of control? did he chew the ends of his drooping mustache?—what did he say, how did he look, when Dr. Aylott dropped the name of Calvin Blacklock upon him, leaving him with the dreadful realization that he had been royally hoodwinked by a female in breeches?

GENERAL WRIGHT: For lack of proof of your innocence in this affair, Dr. Aylott, I must recommend to the provost marshal that you be held in arrest.

COLONEL SOMMERS: I concur with General Wright's recommendation. You are under arrest, Dr. Aylott.

21

BELLE RUTLEDGE

AFTER DR. AYLOTT left his house that Saturday morning, I tried to convince Winslow that we should go for a walk outside, but the little monster would not be persuaded to leave either by the front or back door. A detective was slouching across the street from the front entrance, and a man who might have been a detective was either asleep or pretending to be asleep in an empty coal wagon near the rear entrance. Perhaps it was just as well that we did not risk affronting either of them.

Along toward noontime I was beginning to get the blue willies from being kept prisoner in that umber-scented house of dried oots and herbs. Suddenly it occurred to me that Winslow might be tricked into leaving by way of the bedroom window and the roof. I went about this subterfuge with great care, first asking him to help me unhook the window so that we could look out at the roofs and their smoking chimneys under the dull gray November sky. I had not noticed before how completely shielded this window was from view of the cobbled alley at the rear of the house. Also there were no vehicles to remind Winslow of the bustling streets of Cincinnati through which I had taken him to the orphanage.

On the previous day the boy had seen some of the Copperheads arriving by the window, and when I crawled over the sill to the slate gutter outside, his curiosity got the better of him and he scrambled fearlessly after me. I led the way down the gently sloping

< CONSPIRACY OF KNAVES >

trough beneath the eaves until it ended at a drop-off just broad enough for a long stride to an adjoining roof. There a wide board had been laid alongside a railing where some laundered bedclothing was hung to dry. At the end of the board walk we found a closed door, and just beyond the door was a perpendicular ladder that took us down to a sidewalk that led into a street.

By this time Winslow was so enjoying the adventure that he showed but little anxiety when we entered the busy thoroughfare. I would not have dared signal a cab, however, lest it remind him of that last ride we'd had together in Cincinnati. He clung tightly to my hand until we entered a dry-goods store, where I offered him a choice of a cap or hat or some sort of head covering against the autumn chill. He chose almost immediately a replica for children of one of those shiny flat-billed forage caps with dark blue cord around the crown that Union soldiers were wearing everywhere.

He had no sooner put the cap on his head than he spied a rag doll with buttons for eyes and nose, and a strip of red felt for its mouth. I might have denied him the plaything had its face not resembled his own, even to the overwide mouth.

Outside again, we were enveloped by a cutting wind from the lake, and I could feel Winslow shivering against me when I paused to read a wall poster. Laura Keene was at the McVickers! A Saturday matinee. I had a sudden craving to see my idol of the stage— Miss Keene. Only those who have lived in the world of the theater can know how strong is the magnetic attraction of a great actor or actress to struggling performers who aspire to similar glory.

And so off we went at a fast pace to Madison Street, where I bought tickets for us in the parquet of the McVickers. Any qualms I may have had about Winslow's behavior in the theater soon vanished. He was as entranced by the melodrama as I was entranced by Laura Keene's glorious and inimitable performance. Only twice did my little gaboon break his silence, each time to make perfectly sensible but full-voiced inquiries concerning the meaning of certain actions upon the stage. Laura Keene herself heard Winslow's second piping query, and it so amused her that she turned her face toward the footlights for a moment and sounded one of her gentle forgiving chuckles that only she can use with such grandioso virtu. Oh, but I would have adored to call upon

Miss Keene in her dressing room after the matinee, but such a long line of gentlemen carrying bouquets and baskets of fruit were ahead of us that I desisted. Besides, a November night was closing over the city, the wind was icy, and Winslow was hungry and sleepy. We hurried back to our secret entranceway behind State Street, climbed the ladder, crossed the roofs, and entered the bedroom window to find Ilena Aylott in a condition of near hysteria.

Her father had left early that morning and had not come home. Never before had he parted from her without leaving a note or telling her when he would be returning. She feared that some calamity might have befallen Dr. Aylott. Around noon, when she discovered that Winslow and I had also vanished, her anxiety was increased.

"We went to the theater," I explained, "on the spur of the moment. I wanted to see—"

"Do you suppose the doctor has been injured—struck by a runaway wagon?—fallen on the street?" She clutched at my arms, her eyes growing wilder with each word. Ilena was not a pretty girl, and her agitation made her appear even less attractive.

I reminded her that Dr. Aylott bore the responsibility of meeting Copperheads coming into Chicago and providing them with lodgings and money. He was no doubt very busy with these unusual duties.

She looked slightly relieved. "It is so. The moneybag was not under his desk after he left."

At last, bedtime came, but there was still no sign or word from Dr. Aylott. Ilena insisted on walking to the police station to report him as missing. I would have accompanied her, but I did not wish to leave Winslow alone in that big house. He had already been put into bed, but as usual he was fighting sleep, jabbering about the play we had seen that afternoon. I lay down beside him, hoping that my presence would induce him to drowse off.

As it was, I fell asleep before Winslow did, becoming enmeshed in a mad dream, with Laura Keene on one side of me and Dr. Aylott on the other. They were tugging fiercely at my arms as though to pull me apart.

I awoke to find Winslow shaking my elbow and crying "Charley, Charley!" The single candle on the bedstand had guttered to a flicker, but I could see that the boy was pointing to the dark

< CONSPIRACY OF KNAVES >

window from which came a sharp tapping sound. Wide awake now, I recognized Charley's silhouette through the glass panes and went quickly to unlock the frame and let him inside.

"My God," Charley said, "you sleep like a swill pot. I feared I'd waken the guards, and believe me there are plenty out there watching both doors of this house."

I lighted a fresh candle. "Ilena went to the police to report the doctor missing," I said. "I don't know if she's returned yet."

Charley shook himself out of his heavy coat. For the first time in weeks he was wearing his long-barreled pistol on his right hip. His face above his dark beard was flushed, and the gleam in his blue eyes warned me of danger before he spoke the words.

"Pack your smallest valise," he said. "Take only what you and the boy most need. The provost marshal will soon force entry to this house."

"What's happened?" I asked.

He opened the closet door and took out two small bags, sliding one across the floor to me.

"Pack now," he said flatly. "We may have an hour, we may have only minutes."

"I'll need the big portmanteau," I said, "for Winslow and me."

"You can't run with it," he said impatiently.

"What's happened?" I asked again.

"Dr. Aylott has been arrested. He told some tales. I just got wind of it over at the Tremont. We slipped out minutes before they came to our meeting room." Charley was getting that edgy look I'd seen before when he was in danger.

"Pack your things, Belle, let's go." He folded a pair of trousers into his valise and closed it.

His urgency made me angry, but I followed his example and hastily crammed clothes into the bag. He began dressing Winslow, and to amuse the sleepy boy he pretended to be in awe of the Union forage cap.

"Shouldn't we call Ilena?" I asked.

"If she went to the police they would not have let her return. Come on." He slipped on his coat and extinguished the candle. Then he opened the window carefully, listened for a long moment, and helped Winslow and me outside.

"Walk quietly," he whispered, and led us along the slate gutter.

< **Belle Rutledge** >

Crossing the roofs in the darkness—while at the same time balancing a valise and making certain that Winslow did not fall—was not easy, but minutes later we were safely down in the alleyway. Charley told us to stand still while he walked silently to the street; then he beckoned us to follow him. A cab was waiting there. In a matter of seconds we were moving, the horse's hooves clopping loudly against the stone pavement of the deserted street.

Winslow was wide awake now, struggling in my arms, alternately sobbing and shouting words from his new Vulgar Tongue.

Charley started to clap a hand over the boy's mouth.

"No," I said, pulling Winslow away from him. "Tell the child where we're going."

"We're going for a boat ride," Charley said.

Winslow stopped crying, but I could still feel the tension in his body. Whenever we passed a gas lamp, his eyes warily studied the buildings on both sides of the street.

The cab halted at the same landing on the Chicago River where some weeks earlier Charley and I had boarded a fishing boat to cross Lake Michigan. As soon as we left the cab I recognized the shabby old boat moored there.

"Wait here," Charley told the driver.

We went aboard, but the Scots pilot was not on deck or in either of the tiny cabins.

"He must be in a saloon somewhere nearby," Charley said. He lighted a lamp in the paneled cabin we had shared before, and placed our bags against a wall.

Winslow was crowing with relief that he was not back in the orphanage. He leaped upon the bed and bounced up and down, still giggling.

"You had an escape planned," I said.

"Wise rats and wise men know where an exit waits." He smiled for the first time.

"So do actors on a stage," I said.

He sighed. "You're a good actress, Belle. A creator of illusions, Sir Lucius described you. But as somebody has said, you can't fool all of the people all of the time."

He was still smiling, almost like the old Charley Heywood, but I guessed he was playing a part for me. He had suffered too many failures to find anything to beam about now.

< CONSPIRACY OF KNAVES >

"You were in it for both sides," he said, almost amiably.

"I am in it for myself," I retorted. "For Belle Rutledge."

"Sir Lucius saw right through you. So did Johnny Truscott, and my naïve cousin Marianna."

"What about you, Major Heywood?"

He laughed—that old familiar cascade of laughter. "I had a whiff of doubt about you in Richmond, an intimation. Something's too perfect about this lady, too apropos, my instincts told me, but I paid little heed to the alarm bell until Canada. At Niagara Falls I knew for certain."

"Did you kill Kendrich?"

"Kendrich killed himself, or rather greed killed him by drowning. And he took someone with him. A woman, I think."

I sat on the bed beside Winslow, who was lying quite still. I removed the soldier's cap from his head and smoothed his sweated hair. "I never did anything to endanger you, Charley. But why did you let me stay on with you, pretend to trust me?"

"Because you're a Kentucky girl and a Rebel at heart," he replied lightly.

Why could he not have told me what I would have told him had our roles been reversed? I thought.

Because I could not bear going on without you, I would have said.

"What do we do now?" I asked. "Wait for the ugly Scotsman and run for Canada?"

"There's always a place in this world for adventurers like you and me, Belle. We have many qualities in common, we two."

He buttoned the collar of his coat and turned toward the cabin door, then hesitated, unbuttoning, and withdrew a silk packet thick with greenbacks. He handed a large portion of the bills to me. "Keep them safe. I'm not afraid of Bartholomew Wright's blockheaded detectives, but too many cutthroat bandits prowl Chicago after dark."

I folded the money into my pocket purse. "Are you going to look for the Scotsman?"

"No. He'll come back soon enough. I must find Johnny Truscott and the boys from Canada—to warn them to skedaddle."

"Do you know where they are?"

"Yes." Again he turned toward the door. "You'll be safe enough here. When the pilot returns, drunk or sober, tell him to fire up the boiler."

He was gone then, and I had a cold gray metallic foreboding that I would never see Charley Heywood again.

A speech from an old play I had seen long ago chattered in my head: "death hath ten thousand several doors for men to take their exit." I lay on the bed beside the sleeping boy and wept for the first time since I had gotten myself trapped in the nasty deceitful business of spying and betrayal.

22

AVENGE THE
PATRIOTIC GORE

WHEN JOHN TRUSCOTT was returning to Chicago on the Illinois Central Railroad, he noticed half a dozen men seated together near one end of the passenger car. They were dressed somewhat as he was—black slouch hats, black jeans trousers, long-tailed black kersey coats, checked vests, and black Wellington boots—in what had become a uniform of sorts for wartime live-stock traders. Truscott also wore the false spectacles supplied by Charles Heywood when he had left Chicago in October, but he had let his beard grow during the month he was in southern Illinois, and so did not wear the artificial whiskers. He was disappointed in his beard, which he considered too downy and too blond, being much lighter in color than the hair on his head.

He was fairly certain that the stockmen on the car were Copperheads journeying to Chicago to join in Monday night's assault upon Camp Douglas and the city. As passengers came and went at various stops during the morning, he moved closer to the group of stockmen, hoping to overhear some scrap of conversation that might confirm his supposition, but nothing was said by any of them to indicate the purpose of their journey. When the train reached the Illinois Central depot, he followed them out to the cabstand, and then joined two of them in a hackney that took them to the Stockman's House. They told him they were from Effingham and were seeking buyers for beef cattle and draft horses; he told them

< **Avenge the Patriotic Gore** >

he was from Tamaroa and was hoping to dispose of a quantity of Missouri mules. Because they seemed to be suspicious of him, Truscott was rather certain the two men, if not the entire party on the train, were Copperheads.

Although he had meant to stay at the Richmond House, he decided to remain for a day in his trader's guise by taking a room at the Stockman's. He had scarcely unpacked his bag when a soft knock sounded on the door. He opened it to a smiling young man who made two Sons of Liberty signs, then offered his hand in the secret grip. Well schooled by this time in Copperhead gestures and watchwords, Truscott met the test. The young man drew a yellow envelope from his pocket, presented it to Truscott, and told him to await further instructions.

"Welcome to the city," he said, and departed still smiling.

The envelope contained five hundred dollars in greenbacks. Folded around the money was a printed circular listing the churches of Chicago.

On the margin was a scrawled note suggesting that the recipient worship Sunday morning at the church of his faith, but Sunday afternoon should be reserved for a secular meeting that would disclose what action was necessary to receive the second half of the promised thousand dollars.

Truscott was disgusted that the conspirators had resorted to mercenary enticements to raise an army of knights to liberate the captives in Camp Douglas. Nevertheless he placed the five hundred dollars in an inside pocket of his frock coat, and set out to find the Richmond House.

He had come to Chicago a day earlier than Charley Heywood specified in his letter of instructions because he wanted Charley to know as early as possible the true state of affairs in the chain of "underground" horse corrals that were supposed to be used in mounting the freed prisoners when they fled southward from the city.

With but slight difficulty he found the Richmond House, and as soon as he entered the foyer he began searching for the faces of any Morgan men who might have arrived there a day or two early. Seeing no one that he recognized, he followed the aromas of food coming from one of the short hallways and discovered a barroom, where, for twenty cents, he obtained a large bowl of bean soup,

< CONSPIRACY OF KNAVES >

slices of dark German bread, some cheese, and a large stein of beer.

From the small table where he sat, he faced a wall mirror in which he watched the reversed figures of men going and coming behind him. Occasionally one would stop at a tobacco stand, and he suddenly realized there was something familiar about the shape and gestures of a well-dressed man who purchased a plug of tobacco and took a bite from it before dropping the plug into his pocket. When the man turned so that his front was reflected in the mirror, Truscott found himself looking into the face of a prosperous appearing Otis Jordan.

At first he thought Jordan had greeted him with a furtive gesture, but when a man sitting to one side of Truscott rose to meet Jordan at the adjoining bar, Truscott remembered the obliqueness of Jordan's natural gaze. Also, Jordan had never seen him bearded, wearing eyeglasses, or dressed in decent clothing. Jordan had in fact signaled to a man in a neat broadcloth suit and a rounded-crown felt hat—a detective almost certainly.

At the bar, which was only a yard or two from Truscott's table, Jordan ordered two drinks, and said quietly to his partner: "The Englishman is here. Signed his real name on the register, bold as you please."

"You want me to go to the provost marshal?"

"Not yet. I sent my card up. If the old son of a bitch invites me to see him, I may learn a good lot more. You wait here in the Richmond."

Truscott guessed that the "Englishman" must be Colonel Lucius Eberhart. He knew that Eberhart was coming to Chicago from Tamaroa to lead one wing of the assault against Camp Douglas, but he was not aware that the colonel had also arrived early.

With a glance at Jordan and the detective, each of whom was starting a second glass of whiskey, Truscott left his table and returned to the hotel's foyer. The desk clerk willingly turned the guest registry so that he could read it. Among the day's fresh signatures was that of Col. L. Eberhart, England, G.B., room 205.

As Truscott scanned the roster, another name written on the ruled page in a girlish hand almost startled him into an involuntary cry of surprise. Marianna Heywood had arrived at the Richmond sometime that very morning!

< **Avenge the Patriotic Gore** >

Memorizing the number of her room, he turned to the stairway and climbed hurriedly to the next floor. He followed the hallway to the right until he came to room 205. He wanted to give Colonel Eberhart an immediate warning about Otis Jordan; then he would seek out Marianna to learn her reasons for being at the hotel alone rather than at the house of Judge Ward. The Richmond, with its intrigues and swarms of conspirators and spies, was no safe refuge for the Lady of Shalott.

Truscott knocked on the door. It opened at the first pressure of his hand to reveal Colonel Eberhart seated in a red velvet chair, one boot propped upon a small brass-bound trunk, the other partially concealed by the colonel's sad-eyed spotted hound, which was resting its yellow chin against the boot's toe.

Truscott removed his false spectacles and made a mock salute of greeting to the Britisher. "I see we both came early to the city."

"Yes, Captain Truscott. Are you ready to open the ball come Monday night?"

Truscott nodded. "You also, sir?"

"Never felt better. We'll ride the whirlwind and direct the storm, eh? Sit down, captain, sit down."

Truscott took one of a pair of cane-seated chairs and placed it so he would face Eberhart. Three other men were in the room, two lounging on the bed; one with his shirt off was pouring water from a pitcher into a bowl on the washstand. With broad gestures Eberhart named them.

"You young fellows must know Captain Truscott," he added.

Truscott had never seen the two on the bed, but he remembered the lean one at the washbowl.

"Alex Cantey," he said. "You were in Dick Morgan's regiment."

"Yes, Fourteenth Kentucky. Captured somewhere between Pomeroy and the Buffington crossing, but got away in the fog. Stole a farmer's jeans off a clothesline and made my way to Canada."

"How long have you been here?"

"Crossed over yesterday," Cantey replied as he washed his hands.

"How many came with you?"

"Two of us left Toronto last Wednesday, traveling alone and by different routes. I've seen none of the others yet."

Truscott turned to Colonel Eberhart.

"Sir, I came here to warn you about Otis Jordan. I believe he just now sent up his card."

Eberhart bent forward and picked up a small card from the top of the brass-bound trunk.

"Otis Jordan. Who is this Jordan? Am I supposed to know him?"

"I recall that you once accused him of stealing horses from you—the winter we camped at Murfreesboro."

"Ah, yes! The low-born Texan. Captain Jordan, he called himself. He was going to sell my horses to General Johnson's Q.M. How absentminded I am becoming."

"I remember that cock-eyed bastard," Alex Cantey said. "Biggest damned scoundrel in the world. Always asking for handouts. Tobacco, socks, whiskey, anything he could scrounge. He never repaid anything."

Colonel Eberhart shifted his haunches in the velvet chair, slightly disturbing the spotted hound.

"Why in God's name would Otis Jordan wish to see me?"

"He's a spy for the Camp Douglas commandant," Truscott said. "This time he'll be wanting to steal information instead of horses from you."

"Then by all means let us invite him up. Fill the bugger's head with a lot of clamjamfry. Will one of you boys take this card down to the desk and ask the clerk to notify Mr. Jordan that I will be delighted to receive him?"

One of the young men on the bed, a freckle-faced redhead, offered to serve as messenger. As soon as he was out of the door, Cantey asked: "Who is that red-haired fellow? Is he a Morgan man?"

"He's a Copperhead," Colonel Eberhart replied. "As wild and reckless a horseman as you'll ever see, Mr. Cantey. The devil wouldn't have him in hell. Came up with me from southern Illinois. Major Heywood thinks so highly of the boy he gave him his full thousand in advance. You know what the chap said to me?" The Britisher laughed before continuing. "Said he'd use the money to buy a substitute. He's been drafted to the Union Army, don't you know."

Cantey pulled a fresh shirt over his head. He whistled softly

< **Avenge the Patriotic Gore** >

for a minute, trying to find the tune he was seeking, and then sang to himself: "Oh, what shall we do when this war breaks up?"

Eberhart smiled at him. "Major Heywood says you will all be kings of the Northwest," he said. "As for me, if I survive Monday night, I'll be shipping back to merry old England."

"How many Morgan men can we count on for Monday night?" Truscott asked.

"Not as many as we had here last August," Cantey replied. "Some of the best went off to Virginia to help Basil Duke put the Second Kentucky Cavalry back together again."

"Major Heywood tells me five hundred men are coming from Canada," Eberhart said. "Fifteen hundred from Chicago and Illinois."

"We'll be lucky to get fifty from Canada. I don't know about—"

The freckle-faced young man, returning from downstairs, interrupted what Cantey was saying by banging the door open.

"I reckon your man Jordan will be right up," he said to Colonel Eberhart.

"Leave the door open," Eberhart told him. "The air's a bit close in here. Also, I want a good look at the scoundrel as he comes in."

Jordan arrived a few minutes later, halting uncertainly in the open doorway, awkwardly holding a bottle of brandy, obviously surprised to find five men in the room instead of one.

"Good afternoon to you, Colonel Eberhart," he said, advancing nervously a few steps to present the liquor.

"Ah, my favorite spirits, Mr. Jordan," Eberhart said, taking the bottle but not bothering to rise or offer his hand. As he examined the gift, he added with barely concealed contempt: "This is not the Emperor Napoleon's preferred stamp, however."

"The best the house could supply me," Jordan mumbled obsequiously.

"What brings you to my quarters, Mr. Jordan?"

"I came to offer my services, colonel, hoping our past misunderstanding has been laid to rest. Let bygones be bygones, I always say."

Eberhart remained silent, as though awaiting further explanation.

< CONSPIRACY OF KNAVES >

"I just recently escaped from Camp Douglas," Jordan said, "and I offer my services in whatever enterprise may be afoot."

He glanced uneasily at the others in the room for the first time, his head jerking back when he recognized Truscott.

"Goddamn, it's you, Captain Truscott. I heard you escaped soon after I did, but I had no idea you were still in Chicago." His eyes seemed unable to fix their gaze anywhere in the room, shifting from the floor to the bed, to the hound and back to Truscott.

"You can vouch for me, captain, how I was under a parole of honor not to attempt escape. I forfeited that parole so I could—"

"So you could what?" Alex Cantey interrupted coldly. He was leaning casually against one of the bedposts.

"Jordan, you're a goddamned thieving abolitionist son of a bitch." Cantey's perfectly controlled voice was barely audible within the room.

The remark struck a raw nerve in Jordan's senses. His teeth bared in anger, he shouted back at Cantey: "You're a damned stinking liar!"

Colonel Eberhart scolded him. "Talk more softly."

Fright suddenly filled Jordan's face. Eberhart, Cantey, Truscott, and the two other men sitting on the bed all rose to their feet. For a few seconds the anxious Jordan feared they were threatening his person. Then he became aware that they were looking past him to the open door, and when he turned he saw a fair young woman in a dark maroon hoopskirt of such circumference that it almost filled the entryway.

"Colonel Eberhart," she was saying, "I hope you do not think me too forward. But when I learned you were in the hotel, I was sure you would help me find my cousin." She saw Truscott then.

"Dear Johnny, dear, dear Johnny, how glad I am to find you here! Do any of you gentlemen know where Major Heywood can be found?"

The colonel was bowing and inviting Marianna to be seated in the velvet chair, but she refused.

"You must help me find Cousin Charley and warn him of his danger," she persisted. "Have you seen the evening newspaper?"

None of them had read a paper since early morning. Marianna, with the earnestness of a monitor, told them of how she had gone to the stores to shop in the afternoon and on returning to Judge

< **Avenge the Patriotic Gore** >

Ward's house found it surrounded by a guard of detectives and policemen. They refused to allow her to enter, the officer in charge rudely informing her that the Wards were under house arrest and if she wanted to know the reasons why, then she should read the evening newspaper. She had taken a cab to the Richmond House, expecting to find Major Heywood registered there.

"His name is not on the registry," she said. "But it is in the newspaper, along with Judge Ward's and my dear friend Evelyn Ward's, and several other people accused of plotting to set fire to the city and attack Camp Douglas."

"Good God," Colonel Eberhart cried. His face turned brick-red. "Do you have this newspaper, Miss Marianna?"

She shook her head, her own fears heightened when she recognized the consternation she had brought to her listeners. "No, sir, the desk clerk of the Richmond House kindly permitted me to read his copy."

"Humbug, it could be humbug," Otis Jordan said, with a forced conviction in his voice. "They're just guessing. Picked up a few wild rumors and printed base humbug. What can newspaper scribblers know?"

Cantey stepped closer to Jordan and said quietly: "What can they know? Maybe what you told 'em, Jordan."

Jordan rose from his chair, adjusted his hat, and looked at Colonel Eberhart.

"If you gentlemen don't want my services, I shall take my leave, sir."

Cantey, however, was already between him and the open door.

"No, I think not, Jordan. And if you have a weapon, I suggest you—"

Marianna suppressed a gasping outcry that brought Truscott quickly to her side. Taking her arm, he led her through the door and into the hall.

"Come along," he said. "I believe I know where we may find Charley."

In the lead-gray light of the dying November day, they boarded a Cottage Grove streetcar. Not quite an hour later they passed the front entrance of Camp Douglas, with its gas lamps burning brightly, the car halting briefly to discharge a few soldiers. Truscott was

< CONSPIRACY OF KNAVES >

relieved when the car moved on, rolling at a faster pace, as though horse and driver were eager to reach their goal so they might turn back from the dark vault of the countryside and return to the lighted streets of the city. He and Marianna were the last passengers aboard when the driver announced the end of the line.

Having seen Joseph Milligan's house only during the October night's visit in Judge Ward's carriage, neither Truscott nor Marianna knew what the distance was from the end of the streetcar tracks to the dwelling. As their eyes grew accustomed to the blackness, they could see a vague shape of a house against the sky. When Truscott found a gate, a dog barked savagely at the first rattle. He then discerned the low roof line of the house and knew it was not Milligan's.

Arms linked, they walked slowly ahead, with the sound of waves slapping at the lakeshore on their right. Since leaving the hotel they had exchanged only a few words. To Truscott the hours since his return to Chicago possessed a dreamlike quality, an illusion culminating in the sudden appearance of Marianna, his Lady of Shalott . . . *She hath no loyal knight and true . . .*

At last he was alone with her. He was a knight-errant escorting her out of the shadows of the world. He was Ivanhoe shielding Rowena. He was a Scottish chief delivering the Lady Helen.

A small fire was burning across the sandy street from Joseph Milligan's high-gabled house. Four men were standing or squatting around the flickering light, warming their hands, hawking and spitting, stamping their boots, grumbling about the chill wind from the lake. Truscott assumed they were guards assigned to watch Milligan's house; he guided Marianna away from them.

Off to the left he recognized the large barn where the Morgan men were to gather by Sunday in preparation for the Monday night assault upon the nearby prison camp. Dismissing a sudden notion of taking Marianna to the safety of the barn, he boldly opened the yard gate and led her along the pathway to the house.

Milligan answered his knock. The Copperhead was so agitated that he almost denied entry to both of them. Not until he summoned Heywood was the door opened wide enough for Marianna to bring her hoopskirt inside.

Charley had shaved his beard, and he looked strangely vulnerable without it. He evidently was more shocked to see Truscott

< **Avenge the Patriotic Gore** >

and his cousin than when they had arrived at Milligan's unexpectedly on the night in October.

"Unwise, Johnny, most ill-considered of you to come here. Your action has placed Marianna in great jeopardy."

"She was in greater danger at the Richmond House," Truscott said.

Charley clucked his tongue at his cousin as though shaming a child.

"You promised me you would go home to Kentucky."

"I went out this afternoon to buy clothes for the journey," Marianna said. "When I came back to the Wards' house, the guards would not let me in."

"So you jumped from the frying pan into the heat of the Richmond House?"

"I wanted to find you, Charley. Even more urgently when I saw your name in the newspaper with the Wards'."

Charley smiled, then reached out and lifted her chin gently with his hand. "Heywood blood will always tell, won't it?"

"Yes," she agreed, and then frowned at him. "Why have you shaved your beard, Cousin Charley?"

Jeremiah Grundy, the Copperhead from southern Illinois, appeared at the top of the stairs that led down to the entrance hall. He was carrying an armful of shotguns. Behind him was a younger version of Joseph Milligan, his son, followed by one of Milligan's daughters. Both were struggling with canvas bags of buckshot. They disappeared through an open door to the cellar.

"When I went to the Richmond House," Truscott said, "I was looking for you also, Charley. I wanted you to know how inadequate the horse corrals are between Mattoon and the Ohio River."

"Yes?"

"Alonzo Colquett sent dozens of spavined animals up from Barton Farm. Any Q.M. would reject the lot of them. Not enough quality horses at Mattoon to mount a corporal's guard."

A flash of anger crossed Heywood's face. "Colquett's a liar and a cheat. When I think of all the shekels I've given—" He stopped and sighed. "But what does it matter now?"

"Was Colquett my betrayer at the Tamaroa chapel?" Truscott asked.

"What does it matter now?" Heywood repeated impatiently.

"We're going ahead with the attack plan, aren't we?" An urgency was in Truscott's voice. "Colonel Eberhart and the Morgan men are waiting a final word from you."

"Good God, Johnny, don't you know this one is finished! They know too much about our design. This house, this arsenal of Joe Milligan's is surrounded. If you leave by the front door or back door, you'll be arrested. When orders come from Camp Douglas and the city's provost marshal, they'll force entry and arrest whom they please."

A gentle, almost timid knock sounded at the front door. Joseph Milligan, who had been standing in an attitude of dejection at the entrance to the parlor, started with fear.

"That must be your daughter with Grandma Bernadine," Charley said.

He opened the door and the two women entered almost gaily, the daughter's cheeks rosy from the air of the November night, the grandmother's eyes sparkling with Irish mischief.

"Now Major Heywood," she greeted him. "We'll just trade clothes in a twinkle and off you can be on whatever devilment you'll be flying to."

"How many did you see out there?" Heywood asked her.

"Four rowdies hunkered around a fire," the grandmother replied.

Jeremiah Grundy spoke up from the end of the hallway. "I just now counted the same out back, between the house and the barn."

Heywood led the grandmother and her granddaughter to the foot of the stairs.

"The program has changed, Grandma Bernadine," he said. "Instead of I, Captain Truscott will be wearing your clothes. And your granddaughter will exchange with Marianna instead of Mr. Grundy. So upstairs, the three of you ladies."

"For God's sake, why?" Marianna demanded. She stared at the plain cape and flounced dress the Milligan daughter was wearing and then looked down at the expensive maroon hoopskirt she had acquired only that afternoon.

"To save your skin, dear cousin," Charley answered bluntly, and then turned to Truscott. "You never could sprout proper whiskers, could you, Johnny? Yet it's too much of a beard for a grand-

< **Avenge the Patriotic Gore** >

mother. So follow me back to a washstand and I'll whack it off with Joe Milligan's razor."

"No," Truscott said. "This is your way out, Charley. Take it, with Marianna."

"They know you, little John. They don't know me from Adam. This time they'll hang you for sedition. An escaped prisoner caught in a nest of Copperheads armed to the teeth."

He waved the three hesitant women up the stairs, seized Truscott's arm in a tight grip, and propelled him toward the rear of the house.

"Besides, I owe you, Johnny, and payment's overdue."

A few minutes later, a tearful Marianna in the Milligan girl's cape and dress, and a protesting Truscott in the grandmother's shawl, bonnet, and flowing skirt, almost literally were forced out the front door. Once outside, however, they quickly assumed the roles Heywood had ordered them to play.

As Truscott expected, the men at the fire ordered them to halt, demanding to know where they were going.

"You didn't stay long," one of the guards said suspiciously.

Marianna explained that they had brought medicine for her ailing mother and that she was accompanying her grandmother back to her home. The men appeared to be satisfied, and let them pass.

At the end of the streetcar track, an empty car waited in the darkness. By the light of a lantern, the driver was adjusting his horse's harness. He seemed pleased to see two passengers appear out of the night. "Last car this evening," he said. "Five minutes later, you ladies would've walked to wherever you're going."

They were going to the first stand of cabs on State Street, and there they left the streetcar. Marianna asked the nearest coachman to take them to a boat landing on the Chicago River, reciting the directions that Heywood had given them.

The vehicle was old, with no cover against the weather. The passenger seat was a hard board close behind the driver, who appeared to be as ancient and dilapidated as his hackney. He mumbled to himself as they approached the descent to the river.

Truscott hated the silent part he was performing, the ignominy of the costume he wore. Because his voice would reveal his sex, he was no longer the knight-errant. Marianna had become *his* protector, *his* communicator with the denizens of the dark world.

Soon after the vehicle started down the earthern slope, the driver pulled hard on his lines. "Are you ladies certain this is the place?"

"Down there," Marianna said, pointing to the shadowy shapes of the boats.

Lofty winds were clearing the overcast, and starlight was reflected on the water. Odors of pine tar and fish floated in the air.

"That there is a fishing boat," the driver said, and turned the hackney in a half circle so the horse faced back toward the street they had just left. "I can't go no further down."

The fishing boat was twenty yards away, a dim light flickering near its stern.

"I'll go and make certain," Truscott whispered hoarsely to Marianna.

He stepped down awkwardly, almost tripping over the hem of the unfamiliar skirt.

As he neared the boat, a woman holding a small boy by the hand appeared at the end of the boarding plank.

"Is this MacPherson's boat?" Truscott asked her.

"Yes," she replied, and he noted the anxiety in her voice.

"I have a message for him."

A man carrying a lantern appeared then from the engine house. "I'm MacPherson."

Truscott turned and called to Marianna: "This is the boat."

Instead of stepping down from the hackney, however, Marianna reached past the coachman, jerked his whip from its boot, and lashed the startled horse into a sudden bound forward. The driver almost fell from his seat, and for several moments lost control of his lines. Before Truscott grasped what was happening, the vehicle was halfway up to the street.

"What is the message, ma'am?" MacPherson asked.

Truscott stood sideways on the boarding plank. He was angry at his sudden irresolution, his inability to act before the hackney vanished into the gloom of the city. Marianna had fled his brittle shield of chivalry, leaving him as helpless as the old woman he impersonated.

"Come aboard, madam," MacPherson said, lifting his lantern with a gesture of impatience.

Again Truscott's boot caught in the hem of the long dress. He stumbled, and had the boatman not stepped forward quickly and seized his arm, he might have fallen into the water between boat and landing.

From the pocket of Grandmother Bernadine's dress, Truscott withdrew the coarse paper envelope that Heywood had given him at the last moment, an envelope containing several greenbacks and a hastily scrawled note.

Still holding Truscott steady, the boatman passed his lantern to the woman and clasped the envelope between thumb and palm of his mutilated left hand.

"You'd best take the old lady below, miss," he said, "and give her a brandy. She's under some uncommon stress, I daresay."

The woman led the way down the short steps to the cabin, the little boy close at her side. While she lighted a whale-oil lamp in the darkness, Truscott removed the bonnet and shawl, and when she turned she recognized him with a quick intake of breath.

"Captain Truscott," she said.

"If this was meant to be a trap for Major Heywood," he said, "you've failed. Whoever you may be, Belle Rutledge or Blacklock, we know you are an agent for the Union." He saw a kind of panic come into her eyes, but he misunderstood the reason for it.

"Where is Major Heywood?" she demanded.

"He sent me in his place."

"Why?"

"Most likely to save himself. He knows what you are."

A chugging sound and a vibration that shook the whole structure of the boat were followed by a sudden wrench that set the small vessel into motion.

"We're moving," Truscott cried. "And I don't intend to go."

"MacPherson won't go without Charley—Major Heywood. He must be changing wharfs."

She took a brandy bottle from a wall cabinet and quickly poured two small glasses, handing one of them to Truscott.

"You can sit on the bed."

He sat beside the boy, who was studying him with the intense curiosity of the very young.

< CONSPIRACY OF KNAVES >

The boat was moving much faster now. The swish of displaced water was loud against the side of the cabin.

"I'll go up and ask him where he's taking us," she said. "Perhaps to a safer rendezvous."

She took a long swallow of the brandy and vanished through the open door. He heard her unhurried footsteps on the stair.

The little boy slid off the bed so that he could stand directly in front of Truscott. "You look like a girl," he said, "in that dress."

Truscott tried to smile. "Yes."

"Will you be good to Miss Belle and me?" the boy asked. "Charley's always good to us."

She came back down the steps much faster than she had climbed them; she was obviously distraught. "Where is Charley Heywood? Was he in trouble when you left him?"

Truscott explained the circumstances of his leaving Joseph Milligan's house with Marianna. "I didn't understand why he wanted us to do it."

"That was Marianna Heywood who came in the cab with you?"

"Yes. Charley wanted her to come with me."

"But she refused to escape without Charley, didn't she?"

"Escape?"

"Yes, Captain Truscott. We are escaping to Canada. Charley's message to MacPherson ordered him to leave immediately you were on board, promising to join us later in Toronto."

Truscott stood up, his trembling fingers almost dropping the brandy glass. "I've failed him, haven't I? He trusted me to take Marianna to safety."

He looked down, and the sight of the soiled hem of the woman's dress folded over the tops of his boots added to his feeling of utter humiliation.

"The Knight of the Woeful Figure," he groaned. "A Don Quixote of the Kentucky cavalry."

She reached for the half-empty brandy bottle.

"Don't fret yourself, captain," she said wryly. "The Heywoods know how to survive."

"Yes," he said. "They always do, don't they?"

She lifted her glass. "And so does Belle Rutledge."

23

EXCERPTS FROM A CHICAGO SCRAPBOOK

AUGUST–DECEMBER 1864

WANTED

SUBSTITUTES!   SUBSTITUTES!   SUBSTITUTES!

Do You Want One?

We can furnish you more than any other office in Chicago, and for less money. Wm. H. Murphy & Co., Corner Randolph and Lexington Sts.—In the Basement.

COPPERHEAD GATHERING

A Mis-called Mass Meeting of Working Men— A Convention of Soreheads—Harangue by the Banshee Tamer and Others—Speakers on the Rampage

Bryan Hall was closely packed with workingmen in response to a call published in the daily newspapers.

From Richmond

A TERRIFIC REBEL THREAT
Some Large Northern City To Be Laid in Ashes

STARTLING NEWS FROM
NORTHERN VERMONT

—

Rebel Raid into St. Albans
$150,000 Stolen

—

Five Citizens Shot

—

Burlington, Vt.—Wed. Oct. 19—
A party of 25 armed men rode into St. Albans this P.M. and robbed the
three banks there of $150,000. It is supposed they were Southerners from
the border of Canada. Five citizens were shot; one, it is thought, fatally.
Having accomplished their object, the band left immediately for Canada.
Later: the man Morrison, who was shot, has since died.

Remarks:—St. Albans, the county seat of Franklin County, Vt., is a
thriving town of about 4,000 inhabitants, situated on the Vermont Central
Railroad, about twenty-five miles from Rouse's Point, at the head of Lake
Champlain, the Canada border. The nearest Canadian town of any importance is St. Armand.

MAGIC LANTERNS!

The best children's entertainment on winter evenings are to be had at all prices
and of all sizes at the optical establishment of

JAMES FORESTER, JR. & CO.
46 Clark St. near Sherman House

Brighton Course

TWO DAYS GREAT RACING

First Day Tuesday
PURSE $500

For the accommodation of the public a special train will leave Chicago, Alton &
St. Louis Depot at three o'clock for the course, and return as soon as the race is
over.

< **Chicago Scrapbook, August–December 1864** >

McVicker's Theatre

Madison Street Between State and Dearborn

Revival of the Gorgeous Spectacular Engagement
of the celebrated actress

MISS LAURA KEENE

Drama entitled:

The Sea of Ice

Saturday Afternoon Matinee
Dress Circle and Parquette. Sixty Cents
Second Circle. Twenty-five Cents
Private Boxes. $6.00 and $4.00

FOR LAKE SUPERIOR

The Fast Sailing Sidewheel Steamer

S E A B I R D

Capt. S. W. Morgan
Will leave for Ontonagon, Sunday Evening
Oct. 17

THE REBEL PLOT

—

Attempt to Burn New York

—

All the Principal Hotels Simultaneously
Set on Fire

—

The Fires Promptly Extinguished

SHERMAN'S MARCH

—

His Rapid Progress Through Georgia

—

Certain to Crash Through to the Seaboard

< CONSPIRACY OF KNAVES >

LOST—Sunday Oct. 9—In going from Richmond House to Trinity Church, Jackson St., a jet sleeve button with a pearly cross on it. The finder will be rewarded by leaving it at the Richmond House.

STEAM TO EUROPE

Persons about to visit Europe would do well to call and see the general agent of the Liverpool, New York & Philadelphia Steamship Co., in Chicago before leaving for the East, as he is issuing return tickets to Liverpool and Queenstown at reduced rates of passage.
Steamers leave N.Y. as follows:

City of Baltimore —Sat. Aug. 27
Etna —Sat. Sept. 3
Edinburg —Sat. Sept. 10

F. A. Emory, Corner of Clark and Lake Streets.

SPIRITUAL CONVENTION

Chicago has been highly honored. The first national convention of the Spiritualists commenced its session in this city on Tuesday last and is still in operation. Five or six hundred delegates are present from all parts of the country, about one half of whom are women. The men are distinguished by the number of bald heads and large abdomens, and the women by sharp noses and vinegary aspect. There are, however, exceptions, and the spirits have occasionally shown the good taste to take up their abode with a pretty face and a graceful form.

The proceedings have been interesting—decidedly so. Women's rights, free love, marital relations, etc.

STRAWS:

A vote of the soldiers in the general hospital at Philadelphia was taken a couple of days ago with the following results:

Lincoln— 1,069
McClellan— 163

Majority— 906

< **Chicago Scrapbook, August—December 1864** >

GRAND DEMONSTRATION
FOR THE UNION

Patience, Perseverance and Pluck
"First Subjugate, then Educate"

BRYAN HALL

Clark, Lake, Dearborn and LaSalle Streets
Packed Full of Men, Women and Children

GRAND PARADE

A GUERILLA RAID ON CHICAGO
—

Arrival of Sixty Butternuts via the
Chicago, Alton & St. Louis Railroad
—

WHAT ARE THEY HERE FOR?
—

Our military authorities were notified by telegraph yesterday of the presence of sixty mysterious passengers in butternut uniforms on the Chicago, Alton & St. Louis Railroad, holding tickets for Chicago. These individuals were said to be armed, but the utmost efforts of their fellow passengers failed to get any information regarding their movements or purposes, except that they were under the leadership of one Dr. Berrett, or Bossett, of Vandalia, Illinois. They had no baggage, and they kept their mouths shut with a vigilance quite uncommon among persons of their persuasion. The presumption created by their presence at Bloomington where they transferred themselves from the Illinois Central to the Alton road was that they were rebel spies or raiders en route for Chicago to make an attack on Camp Douglas, or to fire the city on election day, in accordance with the plan concocted in Canada the other day.

Have they come to give us a St. Albans raid? Or are they here for the purpose of making a hole in the wall of Camp Douglas, or have they come merely to take possession of the polls, and stuff the ballot boxes, next Tuesday?

THE REBEL PLOT

—

Details of the Plan—The Polls to Be Invaded—
The Prisoners at Camp Douglas to Be Set Free

—

A GENERAL SACK OF THE CITY INTENDED

—

PLUNDER—RAPINE—FIRE—
BLOODSHED IN THE STREETS
OF CHICAGO

A VICTORY OF GIGANTIC PROPORTIONS

—

RE-ELECTION OF ABRAHAM LINCOLN

—

The People for the War Into the End

—

The Peace Sneak Utterly Defeated

—

OUR BOYS IN BLUE SUSTAINED

THE INDIANAPOLIS MILITARY TRIALS

—

New and Startling Phase of the Exposure

—

NONE BUT DEMOCRATS ADMITTED
TO THE ORDER

SAVANNAH OURS!

—

Sherman's Christmas Present

24

BELLE RUTLEDGE

WAR BRINGS OUT the worst in those caught up in its furious entangling web. I have heard politicians orating and ministers preachifying and old men philosophizing on the glories of war. The urgencies of war, they tell us, bring out our finest instincts. War is a crucible of fire that burns the dross from ordinary humankind and makes saints and demigods of us all. Humbug and bull pizzle! Nothing could be further from the truth. Almost every one I know who was enveloped by the war was impaired by it. Some are dead, bravely or not bravely. Many were mutilated in body or mind or spirit.

More of us lied and cheated because of the war than performed brave deeds, I can assure you. It turned honest men into thieves, good women into bad. It turned thousands of young men under the sod, severing half a century from their prospects of life, or left thousands more of them armless, legless, or eyeless.

Preening about the land nowadays are small armies of former military leaders who never risked their hides in any crucible of fire. Most men of their ilk kept miles away from the bloody fray, yet they go about now in search of ballots and high office, prating of "our brave boys in blue, our noble sons in gray."

Who can say what the brave boys and noble sons might have become had war not discomposed their lives—Charley Heywood and Johnny Truscott, even to Joseph Milligan and Dr. Aylott, and

< CONSPIRACY OF KNAVES >

all those foolhardy Morgan men in search of their Holy Grail? And what of the women such as Marianna Heywood and I, Belle Rutledge, dreamer of glory upon the stages of the world—actress, diva, danseuse, chanteuse—corrupted by Mammon and a false Goddess of Love? When war comes, God deserts us all; it is every soul for itself.

Johnny Truscott continues to blame the Copperheads for our personal descent into misery, but to me they were only an absurd collection of straw men. Sometimes he dwells at length on how they failed Morgan's cavalry invasion of Indiana and Ohio after guaranteeing a great uprising of Rebel sympathizers at the instant the hooves of the Kentuckians' horses touched the soil of the Union. He blames them for the failure to liberate his comrades in Camp Douglas, and he also believes that Copperheads may have been responsible for his own capture and imprisonment.

I admit the Copperheads beguiled me during my first association with them at Cincinnati, when their alleged leaders were boasting to Charley Heywood of thousands upon thousands of members in each Northwestern state. Yet as time passed I came to the realization that they were little more than cardboard shapes, although clever enough to invent plausible reasons for massive heaps of greenbacks and gold required from Major Heywood and the Confederacy's constantly replenishing hoard in Canada.

Because of my peculiar position as an alternate spy for the Union and Confederacy, I was offered opportunities to view the seamy sides of both the conspirators and their exposers. From what I observed, it is my opinion that the boasted thousands of Knights of the Golden Circle and Sons of Liberty were merely members of the Democratic party in the North, most of whom were as loyal to the Union as their Republican rivals. They surely scoffed at the very idea of a Northwestern Confederacy, and would not have supported any violent effort to free the Rebel prisoners at Camp Douglas. Yet in the end they were victims of a clever plot, expedited by a conniving press, to create an ogre where none existed except in the minds of a handful of fanatical conspirators, puffballs eager to be Somebodys. What they accomplished was to frighten themselves into reelecting Mr. Lincoln—only a few hours after I fled to Canada.

<   **Belle Rutledge**   >

Upon our arrival in Canada, Johnny Truscott, little Winslow, and I began an eager but anxious wait for news of Charley Heywood, and his cousin Marianna, whom we had last seen dashing away in the Chicago night to rescue him. We possessed greenbacks in plenty (stolen no doubt from the thrifty folk of St. Albans, Vermont, before being transferred to Charley and then to us), and we saw no reason to preserve them. We three lived like royalty in Toronto's Queen's Hotel, hopeful at the end of each day that Charley would join us on the next.

We began to fear that U.S. detectives might have caught him at Joseph Milligan's house soon after Johnny and Marianna escaped in the disguises that Charley had originally arranged for himself and the Copperhead Jeremiah Grundy. Eventually, however— thanks to a few compatriots in Toronto—we obtained clippings from Chicago newspapers that told us of the arrests of Colonel Eberhart, Otis Jordan, Alex Cantey, and a few other Morgan men at the Richmond House, and also Dr. Aylott and Judge Ward and his wife Evelyn, Joseph Milligan, and Jeremiah Grundy. They all had been placed in confinement at Camp Douglas, awaiting an early trial at Indianapolis.

Attached to a rather lengthy account of the conspiracy as described by General Bartholomew Wright was a brief paragraph that afforded me some release combined with considerable apprehension. At least Charley was still safe, but for how much longer? The news account stated that detectives employed by military authorities in Chicago were confident of a speedy capture of "the notorious bushwhacker Major Heywood and his paramour Belle Rutledge, who sometimes conceals her sex by wearing men's clothing."

After a few weeks our funds began to dwindle, and we left the Queen's Hotel and moved to a cheap boardinghouse. As time passed we lived a bit more penuriously day by day, until at last we had so little left that Johnny and I realized we must turn to honest toil. The best he could find was a laborer's drudgery in a livery stable that paid so poorly I had to begin working as a cook in the boardinghouse in order to earn our meals. Lord, how I do hate to cook, but even so, I endured those dreadful days with far better fortitude than did Mr. John Truscott, former gentleman of the Bluegrass.

< C O N S P I R A C Y   O F   K N A V E S >

Manual labor was a shocking experience to that young cavalier. He had no previous acquaintance with peacetime deprivation, a condition I had survived numerous times in my checkered past and was confident I could survive again.

In the afternoons I began visiting theaters, not to attend the plays—which I could no longer afford—but to see the managers and attempt to convince them that I could dance and act with the best of their performers. At first I deliberately avoided showing off my Washington repertoire—the naughty skits I had played with Kendrich—but desperation drove me to it, and I was immediately employed in a shady little house down near the harbor.

The money I earned was just about enough to pay for our boardinghouse meals, but at least I was no longer entertaining a kitchen stove. The sailors who made up most of my audiences loved me, and when I tantalized them with high kicks, they would shower the stage with coins, which I squirreled away in anticipation of a better day.

From time to time, Johnny and I would see one of our old acquaintances—who were either too poor to leave Canada, or were fearful of arrest if they went home. In most instances everybody brought a little bad news, but one day a young man came up from Windsor with some very recent information about Charley Heywood that he had heard secondhand. Charley had escaped from Chicago, made his way to Kentucky and then to Virginia, where he joined his old regiment, the Second Kentucky Cavalry under General Basil Duke. As the young man from Windsor told it, Charley escaped capture at Joseph Milligan's house by hiding under a feather bed upon which Grandma Bernadine lay moaning in the agonies of death, quite convincingly, according to Charley. After a platoon of soldiers and several U.S. detectives searched the house and carried off Joseph Milligan and Jeremiah Grundy, Charley slipped away toward Lake Michigan and was soon out of the city.

When I asked our informant from Windsor if Charley had made any mention of his cousin Marianna, the young man could not say. He had not seen Charley's letter, but had only heard of its contents from the receiver. I was quite relieved to learn that Charley was free, and still in the land of the living, but I wasted little time in puzzling over what might have happened to Marianna. Johnny,

< **Belle Rutledge** >

on the other hand, was terribly concerned about his Lady of Shalott, and seldom mentioned Charley.

Because of our different hours of work, Johnny and I saw very
little of each other outside our bedroom. He usually came home
late in the day, weary and dispirited, smelling of draft horses and
manure, and he would take over the care of Winslow while I rushed
off for the theater. Once in a while Johnny would raise the question
of why Charley had ordered him to wear the old woman's disguise
and escape with Marianna. Was it merely a flaunting gesture, or
was it a true act of sacrifice, an atonement for the capture at
Tamaroa and all the months of imprisonment he had endured in
Camp Douglas? Or was there something devious in Charley's mo-
tive? I could tell that Johnny was dubious of his old comrade's
good intentions, and in these discussions I would always take Charley's part, praising him for unselfishly risking his life by sending
Johnny off with Marianna instead of escaping with her himself.

Late in the winter we saw a Chicago newspaper that reported
the opening of the trials of the conspirators. In the same paper the
news made it clear that the war itself was coming to a dismal
ending. Federal soldiers captured Richmond, and I was saddened
to read of the burning of many buildings in the city. Among them
was the Spotswood Hotel, where I spent so many pleasant hours
trying to be a spy. In its sitting room I had first looked deep into
the magnetic blue eyes of Major Charles Heywood.

About this time, late March as I recall, I decided to write to
President Lincoln at the White House, relating how I had met him
briefly in company with another actor, Kendrich, in preparation
for my departure to Richmond. I asked for his forgiveness and a
pardon for my transgressions, assuring the President that nothing
I had done or failed to do had harmed the cause of the Union, but
that I had allowed my emotions as a Kentuckian of the South and
a woman in love to sway me from the course I had sworn to pursue.

A day or so later I wrote another letter, this one to the bank
in Washington that Kendrich had told me of, the District of Columbia Bank, and asked them to transmit to me the moneys that
an official named Baker had deposited in the name of Belle
Rutledge.

I never received a reply from President Lincoln. Only a few

days after I posted my letter, the Toronto newspapers were printing the first bulletins of the hideous assassination. I felt disgraced because the deed was committed in Mr. John T. Ford's theater (with Laura Keene on stage) by a member of my profession, albeit a wretched sort of actor whom I had occasionally seen hanging about theaters in Washington where Kendrich and I performed. Like most of my countrymen and countrywomen, I was deeply grieved by the death of Mr. Lincoln.

Except for the man named Baker, whom I had never met, no one was now living who could offer testimony that I had done good work in Richmond for the Union. The arrival of a letter replying to my request to the District of Columbia Bank virtually ended all hopes I had of restoring my good name and returning as a free citizen to my native land.

"Our records show," an officer of the bank curtly replied, "that funds deposited in the name of Belle Rutledge have been returned to the government official who deposited them. Furthermore, papers attached to the closed account offer sworn proof of the death of said Belle Rutledge by drowning at Niagara Falls in the month of August 1864."

About the same time that I received this letter, newsboys were crying extras in the Toronto streets reporting the ending of the Civil War. Most of the Rebel refugees in Toronto quickly sought each other out to discuss the hazards of returning home. Hopes were dashed a few days later by the assassination of President Lincoln; almost everyone feared that returning Rebels would now be targets for revenge.

Letters and newspapers from the States gradually reassured us. Johnny, who was terribly homesick, was one of the first to cross into Detroit. He was so short of money, I had to dig into my precious collection of coins to help him buy his railroad ticket and provide him with a stake for board and room.

A week after his departure from Toronto, he sent a very cheerful letter from Detroit. He had reported to the local provost marshal and identified himself as an escaped Confederate prisoner of war, fully expecting to be confined or punished in some way. Instead, all he was asked to do was sign a parole and swear never to bear arms against the United States. In addition to this good news, he had found employment driving a coach for Andrews' Rail

Road Hotel, with quarters provided in that hostelry for his "family."
He wanted us to come at once.

My heart truly pounded like a drum when I stepped off the old
ferry from Windsor and set foot upon the Detroit dock. I felt like
bending down and kissing the oily planking.

Being aware that certain authorities in Washington knew who
Belle Rutledge was, yet believed her dead, I decided to call myself
Jennie Truscott upon arrival in Detroit. Johnny and I discussed
marriage occasionally, mainly for Winslow's future, but neither of
us was in love with the other, and neither summoned the courage
to carry out the act. Besides, I'm convinced that he has always
regarded me as Queen Guinevere, although Charley certainly was
not his King Arthur. His lost leader of the Round Table was John
Morgan, while Charley, to his mind, was one of the untrustworthy
knights.

We had not been long in Detroit before the lure of the footlights
drew me back to a theater there. I gave my stage name to the
manager as Jennie Gray, my true birth name, and tried to alter
my style of performing. It simply did not signify. If you think
names do not matter, try changing yours sometime. Belle Rutledge
was a creature of spirited joy, with a pure sensual vitality that
radiated to her audiences. Poor Jennie Gray, she was but a pale
imitation. Nevertheless, the sympathetic manager, perhaps per-
ceiving some hidden talent beneath Jennie's lackluster performance, kept me on as an entr'acte dancer.

One evening, after I had just slipped into my pink tights and
fringed tunic, a loud knock sounded on my dressing-room door.
Without waiting for an acknowledgment, one of those beefy waxed-
mustached males whose very demeanors identify them as odious
U.S. detectives, swung open the door and stood spraddle-legged
in front of me. He held a small photograph that I recognized as
the portrait a Washington theater once used for advertising and
for sale to my admirers among the boys in blue.

He glanced back and forth from photograph to me, and finally
cried out: "You are Belle Rutledge, and I arrest you by order of
General Joseph Hooker, commanding the Department of the Lakes."

Nothing I could say would dissuade him. Both of the letters I
had sent to Washington were in the hands of Mr. Allan Pinkerton's

< CONSPIRACY OF KNAVES >

Secret Service, and they had traced me from Toronto to Detroit. I was given only enough time to pack a portmanteau, and to say good-bye to Winslow and Johnny. My heart was warmed by the solicitude, indeed tearful anxiety, that both of my young men showed for me. A few days later, after I had been incarcerated in a dingy old jail in Indianapolis, I was even more surprised when my little "family" came for a visit. Johnny had given up his post with the Rail Road Hotel, and moved Winslow and himself to Indianapolis to be near me.

To make a long story short, the Northwest Conspiracy trials that had been in progress through the winter were coming to an end. The lawyers, the judges, and the military courts were weary of the endless testimony, and with the closing of the war, the revengeful mood of the victors began to ebb. Also, too much of the testimony was beginning to hint at the hollowness of the military's charges. What I had recognized earlier than most, now gradually became evident to all—the Republican party and Union Army officers were as guilty as the Democrats and their Southern sympathizers in creating Copperheads and the great myth of the Northwestern Conspiracy and the plot to seize Chicago. Anyhow, after I spent a month in that wretched prison, accusations against me were withdrawn for lack of any sound evidence that I had conspired to overthrow the government of the United States.

Some were not so lucky as I, however. Because he was a foreigner, I suppose, and a Briton to boot, poor old Colonel Lucius Eberhart was sentenced to die by hanging. President Andrew Johnson commuted the sentence to imprisonment for life. Joseph Milligan, Jeremiah Grundy, and several of the Morgan men arrested at the Richmond House were sentenced to five years. Dr. Julian Aylott and Otis Jordan were both pardoned for cooperating and giving evidence. My friend Evelyn Ward, who had done so much to alleviate the discomforts of prisoners in Camp Douglas, was never brought to trial. Her husband, the judge, was sentenced to one year, but because of his age and his obvious muddleheadedness, he was quickly pardoned.

On the morning that I was released from the Indianapolis jail, Johnny and Winslow were waiting for me. Without revealing his plans, Johnny had spent almost every penny he possessed to buy tickets to Louisville on the Jeffersonville and Indianapolis Railway.

< **Belle Rutledge** >

Before that day ended, we were home in Kentucky! Oh, happy day!

Poor though we were, we found almost everyone else in the same brier patch. An old friend of my mother's allowed us to share a part of her run-down house, and Johnny was soon training horses for a rich Yankee who had come to Kentucky to restore the sport of kings. All our friends and relatives assumed we were man and wife, and to this date we have seen no reason to disillusion them.

Some good comes from the worst of experiences, say the wise philosophers, and I accept that maxim as a partial truth at the least. My unpleasant stay in the Indianapolis jail, which led to withdrawal of all charges against Belle Rutledge, enabled me to regain that name. And so for the second time in my life I packed poor colorless Jennie Gray away. Within a few days I was rehearsing with a small troupe of locals, but when I discovered the impresario was planning to take the company on a long tour across America, I changed my mind and withdrew. I had been too long away from my native heath to desert it so soon; I was part of a "family" that I had no desire to leave; I was weary of the constant roaming and rambling that had been so much a part of my life since the day I met Charley Heywood in Richmond. Let the wide world wag as it will, I said to myself, I will be gay and happy still.

Colonel Lucius Eberhart, poor devil, he was much in the newspapers for a few days. Although the colonel was saved from a hanging, he was carried off to an island somewhere between Florida and Cuba to live out the remainder of his life. He begged for the return of his spotted hound, his truest friend, he declared, to accompany him upon this prison exile. But the provost marshal sold the dog to a greedy showman, who soon made a small fortune in Chicago by exhibiting the animal for a twenty-five-cents admission charge, and was planning to take it on a tour of the nation before the populace forgot the quixotic British officer.

From the first days of our return to Kentucky, Johnny Truscott fretted about the fate of his Lady of Shalott. None of his acquaintances in Louisville could tell him very much about the Heywoods, either Marianna or her brother Wesley. I was not surprised, therefore, when Johnny announced one Saturday morning that he was traveling down to Little Hundred. He said I was welcome to accompany him, but I knew I was not, truly, and so I declined.

< CONSPIRACY OF KNAVES >

He returned Monday evening, looking very much like a dog that has hunted too hard. Barely able to talk, unable to eat a bite of food, he gradually managed to unload a full budget of news. Marianna and Charley, he moaned, were husband and wife. A few days before Charley departed for Virginia, the cousins had been married quietly at Little Hundred. Johnny believed this story, but I could not. To my mind, it was one of those Southern belle fantasies, a grown-up's fairy tale concocted by the Lady of Shalott.

"What proof did she offer?" I asked.

"I did not ask to see the papers," Johnny replied coldly. "But she evidently is with child."

I held my tongue, but I counted my fingers.

Johnny was certain that Charley had wed Marianna so that he would have Little Hundred when he returned from the war. Old Edmund, Charley's father, had died debt-ridden in the last months of the war. With him went Heywood Hundred, all its acres, its stables, and decaying mansion. A meat packer from Cincinnati bought the lien; he had profited mightily from the war by supplying wormy bacon, so they say, to the Union troops.

According to Johnny, the fields at Little Hundred were under cultivation with Lijah in charge of the farmhands, and Marianna was confident that Charley would soon return from Mexico, where he had journeyed with a few diehard Confederate officers to join Maximilian's French army. She expected no assistance from her brother Wesley, who had left Kentucky to join a band of Missourians dedicated to keeping the peace in that turbulent postwar border country. These protectors of the common folks, Marianna said, were led by a young man named Jesse James.

Much to my surprise, Johnny also brought back from Little Hundred a box about a cubic foot in size, made of some exotic tropical wood, the joints tightly fitted and bradded with horseshoe nails. My name was scrawled in charcoal on one side in Charley's unmistakable slanted handwriting. The box had been brought to Little Hundred, along with some presents for Marianna, by a Mercer County man returning from Mexico. In Charley's accompanying letter to Marianna he instructed her to forward the package to me at the earliest opportunity.

We had a difficult time opening the box, but the effort was certainly more than worth it. Inside was a scarlet Mexican dress, tight-waisted, wide-hemmed. Around the voluminous hem was a double row of conchas coated with some sort of opaque waxlike substance. At first I thought the covering was meant to conceal the cheapness of the conchas, that they were not silver, but when I scratched the wax away from one of them, I saw that the concha was a Mexican silver dollar. I counted more than fifty. Charley had coated them against the possibility that someone might recognize their value and remove them from the dancing dress before I received it. Thanks to him I possessed more wealth than I had owned since returning to the States.

On the very next day, I used a small amount of that wealth to rent a hard-floored loft and to place a notice in the Louisville *Journal* announcing that Belle Rutledge was opening a dramatic school in which acting and dancing and singing would be taught ladies and gentlemen of all ages by a *première* performer of the stage.

During the weeks that I was establishing my dramatic school, I was aware that Johnny was exchanging frequent letters with Marianna. He never offered any of them to me to read, but he usually passed on any news that he thought might be of interest. One day he told me that Charley had written to Marianna from Cuba. Soon after that, the newspapers published short accounts of the escape of "the infamous British soldier of fortune, Colonel Eberhart" from his island prison during a storm. It was believed that he had drowned at sea.

Neither Johnny nor I connected the two events until a letter addressed to both of us arrived one day from France. It was from Charley.

"Sir Lucius and I," he wrote, "are en route to Egypt to soldier for the Grand Pasha." Evidently he had assisted Colonel Eberhart in his daring escape. "At last," he boasted, "I have succeeded in freeing an old comrade from a prison." The letter was quite formal in its tone, with no mention of Marianna, no tender asides to me. Nor did he append any address.

Shortly afterward a message arrived from Marianna announcing the birth of her child, a boy, and Johnny could not wait to rush down to Little Hundred. Upon his return to Louisville, he appeared to be much more tranquil in his mind than he had been after his previous visit. Apparently he had accepted the inevita-

< CONSPIRACY OF KNAVES >

ble—that insofar as he was concerned Marianna was a phantom of his mind, an airy being beyond his grasp.

"Her child," he told me dreamily, "looks for all the world like Charley."

"No baby can be that handsome," I retorted, biting my tongue too late to stop the words.

But what can you do about a grown man who regards you as Queen Guinevere and believes himself to be a Knight of the Round Table? Perhaps some of it has rubbed off on me. At times, like the Lady of Shalott looking down from her tower toward Camelot, I look down from the window of my school of dramatics at a red brick sidewalk, following it with my eyes toward the railroad depot, fancying that I can see striding toward me a well-turned man with a black slouch hat slightly tilted over one ear, his dark beard neatly trimmed, his vibrant blue eyes regarding the world with amused indifference. Cavalry boots encase his legs, a long-barreled pistol is holstered at one hip.

But then again I tell myself that until the end of his days Charley Heywood will be roaming the earth in search of a romantic war, as if there were such a phenomenon. Or perhaps he is just waiting around for somebody to rob another bank for him.

So let the wide world wag as it will! One of these days Belle Rutledge will return to the stage. When she does, Winslow will go with her. That bright little boy outshines the best of my students at jig dancing and mimicry, but as always I must constantly watch his mouth. During the time he spends with Johnny at the racetrack, he picks up words peculiar to that world of horses and wagerers, some very pungent expressions that are not acceptable in a politer society than we move in.

And so the time has come to end this homely discourse. I would like to say, as Mr. Geoffrey Chaucer did at the end of his book, that if there be anything herein that displeases those who may read it, then I pray they will blame it upon my want of ability and not my will. I would gladly have done better if I had the power. *Exeunt Omnes.*

ABOUT THE AUTHOR

Dee Brown is the bestselling author of *Bury My Heart at Wounded Knee*, *Creek Mary's Blood*, *Wondrous Times on the Frontier*, *Hear That Lonesome Whistle Blow*, *Killdeer Mountain*, and 24 other books about the American frontier. He grew up in northern Louisiana and southern Arkansas. After many rigorous years reporting in the Ozark Mountains and a long career as agriculture librarian at the University of Illinois, Mr. Brown currently makes his home in Little Rock.